The Towers OF BABYLON

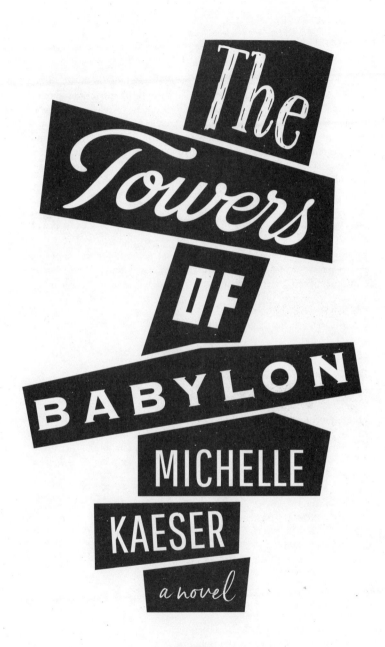

The Towers OF BABYLON

MICHELLE KAESER

a novel

Freehand Books acknowledges the financial support for its publishing program provided by the Canada Council for the Arts and the Alberta Media Fund, and by the Government of Canada through the Canada Book Fund.

Freehand Books
515 – 815 1st Street SW Calgary, Alberta T2P 1N3
www.freehand-books.com

Book orders: LitDistCo
8300 Lawson Road Milton, Ontario L9T 0A4
Telephone: 1–800–591–6250 Fax: 1–800–591–6251
orders@litdistco.ca · www.litdistco.ca

Library and Archives Canada Cataloguing in Publication
Title: The towers of Babylon : a novel / Michelle Kaeser.
Names: Kaeser, Michelle, 1982- author.
Identifiers: Canadiana (print) 20190139617
Canadiana (ebook) 20190139641
ISBN 9781988298498 (softcover)
ISBN 9781988298504 (HTML)
ISBN 9781988298511 (PDF)
Classification: LCC PS8621.A41 T69 2019
DDC C813/.6—dc23

Edited by Rosemary Nixon
Cover design by Grace Cheong
Cover photo: iStock.com/ZargonDesign
Image on page 216 © Oleg Mit/Shutterstock
Printed on FSC® recycled paper and bound in Canada by Houghton Boston

Contents

Then they said, "Come, let us build ourselves a city, and a tower with its top in the heavens, and let us make a name for ourselves; otherwise we shall be scattered abroad upon the face of the whole earth."

The Lord came down to see the city and the tower, which mortals had built.

And the Lord said, "Look, they are one people, and they have all one language; and this is only the beginning of what they will do; nothing that they propose to do now will be impossible for them.

"Come, let us go down, and confuse their language there, so that they will not understand one another's speech."

So the Lord scattered them abroad from there over the face of all the earth, and they left off building the city.

Therefore it was called Babel, because there the Lord confused the language of all the earth.

—GENESIS 11:4-9

Book one

JOLY

$\overline{1}$

"WELCOME, WELCOME, WELCOME! And thanks, gang, for coming in today!"

On a hard yellow chair—wooden, with chipping paint, one of several arranged in a small circle—Joly absorbs this spirited greeting and tries to ramp up a matching enthusiasm. This is her first job interview in months—so what if it's for a coffee shop!

"Now buckle up," continues Greg, the manager here at Nature's Grounds, "because this is going to be a job interview ride like you've never had."

It's already a much different ride than Joly expected. For one, she wasn't expecting a group interview—nobody mentioned that in the email. She thought she'd walk in, meet Greg, endure a short, simple consultation in which he would ask her a few logistical questions about her availability, gauge her attitude as upbeat and friendly, then hire her on the spot. But the barista job market seems to have developed over the last fifteen years.

"We're not a corporate place, we're not looking for corporate robots," Greg says, radiating a huge smile that reveals two rows of unusually small teeth. He is *pumped*! "We just want to get a feel for who you are. The real you! Isn't that right, Reza?"

"Right," says Reza, his second-in-command, the weekend manager, flanking him on the left.

"So no pressure, huh? Let's just relax and have fun."

Greg pauses, giving the five candidates the opportunity to register this benevolent generosity. The other candidates are all about Joly's age—thirties—and all looking remarkably self-assured, wearing easy job-interview smiles. Which un-nerves Joly, whose stomach is buckling and whose pulse has shot way up. She isn't good with public speaking—groups of more than three make her shaky. She blames this failing on her small stature, squeaking out at just over five feet, a hair over a hundred pounds.

"Why don't we start with some simple introductions," says Greg, fiddling with the fitbit on his wrist. His hair is a touch on the shaggy side and there's some patchy scruff on his face. His shirt is a light blue button-down, the top buttons left undone and the sleeves rolled up. Coffee-shop casual. But still authoritative. Joly pegs him at something over forty, though pretending not to be. "Let's go around the circle and get your names . . . oh and what the hell, maybe a fun fact about yourself."

Uh-oh. Joly didn't prepare a fun fact. She prefers those allit-erative introductions made up of your name and an adjective that best describes you. Super Sue. Daring Dave. Mysterious Mary. Jolly Joly. She's got that one nailed down.

"Fun facts are always good ice breakers, eh Reza?" Greg says.

"Mm-hmm." Reza doesn't say much, his expression never changes, he hardly moves. His purpose here seems to be to serve as symbolic support, or audience, for Greg. But he is holding a clipboard.

Greg scans the circle, settling his eyes on Joly, to whom he gives an encouraging nod, a signal to kick off the chorus of fun facts.

"Oh. Me? Yeah. Sure." Fun fact . . . fun fact . . . what's a fun fact about herself? Barista is the job she had as a teenager? Before she spent four years getting an undergrad degree in sociology and three more getting a grad degree in fine arts (creative writing)? Before she went many-thousand dollars into debt to pay for these accreditations? She thought there would be an income premium on higher education—she's sure people told her that. The same people who encouraged her to "follow your bliss"—her parents, teachers, guidance counsellors, professors, friends, neighbours, popular books, TV shows—everyone, really, except her brother Yannick, who only ever advised her to become a banker. Oh how he rolled his eyes when she applied to writing school—but he's always been smarter. Because now, sitting in an interview at a coffee shop, in a circle of smiley faces, reaching for a fun fact, it takes an almost heroic determination not to succumb to the total disheartenment of having sunk all those years and all that money into academics and artistic endeavours only to wind up exactly where she started.

But she is heroically determined! She won't be kept down. Chin up, Joly. Chin up. Here we go. A fun fact. "Hi. I'm Joly."

Greg frowns right away. He looks over at the clipboard Reza is holding and says, "Joly? I have a Jolanda-Lydia." He pronounces the J like a Y.

"Yeah, that's me. But it's Joly," she says, returning the J to its affricate sound. "I go by Joly."

The frown on Greg's face persists—she hasn't sufficiently accounted for the nickname. "It's kind of a long story," she says by way of apology.

No problem for Greg. He's nodding ferociously, leaning way forward in his chair, his hands on his knees, elbows splayed wide. He wants the long story. And since Joly has nothing else with which to fill the silence, she starts to tell it. "Well, my mom wanted to name me Jolanda—she's Swiss, so she spelled it with a J."

"Okay, we're with you," says Greg, his whole face lit up with a beatific smile. He nods around the circle. "The gang's all with you."

"But my dad wanted Lydia. They fought about it, I guess, and eventually agreed to the hyphenate: Jolanda-Lydia."

"Uh-huh, uh-huh."

"But no one was happy with that in practice. Too many syllables to get through when you're screaming at someone to quiet down, right?"

A sharp hiccup of laughter sounds out from someone to her left, a shabby-chic sort of guy in flannel and a ponytail who seems to sympathize with bouts of parental shouting.

"So they abridged it to Jo-ly," she says, pronouncing it Yo-ly. But why, in a job interview, is she taking up whole minutes telling this idiotic story? Beside her, Reza is taking notes on his clipboard, maintaining an impassive expression that has her worried. She hears the quiver in her own voice as she continues: "And then—"

"And then from there, we got to *Jo*-ly," Greg breaks in. "Neat-o! Well, Joly, it looks like your name and fun fact are rolled into one, huh?"

Jolted by the interruption, Joly takes a last stab at ingratiating herself. "Uh . . . yeah. That's the kind of efficiency I aim for, Greg."

Greg keeps his gaze on her for a beat too long, like he's trying to decide on something—is Joly Nature's Grounds material, or maybe just a smartass?

The fun facts carry on around the circle, and Joly instinctively gauges her response against the others'. This is why group interviews are terrible. This being pitted against each other. And yet, she can't stop herself from savouring the realization that she's come out near the top. Greg certainly seemed more tickled by the etymology of her name than he does by Riley, with his flannel and ponytail, whose fun fact is that he plays bass in a band, or April, who has travelled to twenty-two countries (though when pressed, it's uncovered that she counts England, Wales, and Scotland as three separate notches on her post), or Jenn, who used to be a competitive sailor. But Greg does have an interest in and a few follow-up questions for Devang, who claims not to have eaten breakfast in over six years.

"Whoa now, just whoa. No breakfast at all?"

"Nothing."

"No fruit? Not even a slice of bread?"

"Just coffee," Devang says with a smile that wins Greg over.

"Ahahaha. Well of course coffee! We can't have you working here if you're not a die-hard coffee fiend, am I right, Reza?"

"Right."

The baton of fun facts, having been passed off to all five interviewees, now arrives at Greg, who sits a little taller, grins a little wider, and says, "Well, I guess it's my turn, huh? All right then, let's see here. Fun fact about Greg."

Hmm . . . this guy, well, he's not exactly what Joly was expecting in a Nature's Grounds manager. She had soaring hopes for this place, with its non-corporate ethos. To go by its website, the coffee shop is big into environmentalism. And humanitarianism. They use biodegradable cups, sell fair trade beans, compost the grounds, and use the compost in a little vegetable garden they have out back. The wall art is made by local artists, the tables by local craftspeople. So as Joly was writing up her cover letter, she got to thinking (in that way she sometimes does, where her thoughts spiral through the upper echelons of optimism until they spin off into free-wheeling delusions) that this coffee shop might be a fantastic place to work! The perfect place! The staff members probably hang out after their shifts, sipping their fair trade coffees and talking politics and philosophy. Maybe after hours the place transforms into a sort of French salon, bursting with lively discussion and debate, a Café de Flore, and she a Simone de Beauvoir, provoking and being provoked, a kind of exchange that inspires huge, sweeping changes in consciousness! This is where it all starts, isn't it? At the neighbourhood pubs and bars and coffee shops?

"All right . . . how about this for a fact," says Greg. He leans back in his chair and stretches his legs out into the centre of the circle, crossing them at the heels, letting his khaki pants ride up his shin an inch. Joly is sure she can see him flexing his calf. "I just ran my first marathon last month. Ran the whole thing. Pretty good time too, if I say so myself. About three and a half hours." Which Joly figures means something over four.

Greg scans the group's faces for signs of awe, but all he gets is polite nods. "Any runners here?"

Only Jenn, the ex-competitive sailor, raises a shaky hand.

"Oh yeah? You run?" he says.

"Yeah, sort of. Sometimes."

"It's crazy addictive, huh? Once you get into it?"

"Yeah, definitely. I'm not up to marathon level yet or any-thing," she says, really working him now. "But maybe one day. I hope!"

"Oh you can't just up and decide to run a marathon, no. You have to train. Follow a program. It's actually a fairly enormous commitment." Greg interlaces his fingers and cracks his knuckles. "It can take some people years to get in the right shape for it."

"I'd definitely like to get on a training program."

"Oh yeah, you absolutely should, absolutely. I've got a great program I can tell you about and talk you through. We'll have to do that sometime. But I don't want to bore the whole group with a running clinic. Haha." As Greg checks his fitbit watch, he forces a grimace, an exaggerated *yikes* expression at how they've all gotten carried away with this marathon talk. "And we really need to move along here anyway, don't we, Reza?"

"Yes."

"Oh, but wait, wait . . . we forgot about you. Want to give us a little intro? A fun fact about yourself?"

Reza looks up from his clipboard, but it's only his eyes that move. "My name is Reza. My fun fact is that my parents are Iranian refugees."

Greg turns solemn in the wake of this one. "You see, this is the kind of diversity we have here," he says. "That's what makes this place so interesting to work at. Iranian refugees, musicians, breakfast-abstainers, elite marathon athletes. It takes all kinds, doesn't it? Takes all kinds to build a community. And that's really what we're about here. Community."

The candidates send out dumbstruck stares, which bounce right off Greg. For the next few minutes, he describes the guiding principles of the coffee shop, a lecture that soon detours into his own personal history—including a passing mention to having made his high school honour roll—and then into his career in coffee. He sits perched on the edge of his chair throughout, his knees bouncing and his hands flying out from his body, so whipped up is he by his excitement, and finally he arrives at a place where he's ready to put some actual questions to the group.

"Every good CEO, from those Google guys to Oprah, they all like to ask curveball questions in job interviews. Now me, I don't always like to take advice from those corporate types, but I do like the idea of mixing things up. So I'm gonna throw you a bit of a curveball myself."

Greg zeroes in on Devang, who's scratching an itch on his left shoulder. "Ah . . . ah . . . aaah, you're looking a little tight there, Devang. But don't worry, buddy, this one's gonna be fun." Greg claps his hands together, agleam with excitement. "Okay, so here's what's gonna happen. Reza's gonna read you three quotes. All quotes by famous people, quotes about coffee, okay? You with me? Everybody with me?"

The coerced murmurs of assent rally forth from the interviewees.

"Okay, so Reza here will read the quotes, then I want you to tell us which is your favourite. And why. Something to get your brain thinking a little differently. So Reza? What's our first quote?"

Reza flips to a back sheet on the clipboard and begins: "Number one: 'I have measured out my life with coffee spoons.' T.S. Eliot," he reads.

"That's the poet T.S. Eliot," says Greg with a lift of the eyebrows and a strange sucking sound. "Famous poet. What's our second quote, Reza?"

"Number two: 'Ah! How sweet coffee tastes. Lovelier than a thousand kisses. Sweeter far than muscatel wine.' J.S. Bach."

"Interesting, interesting. For all you music lovers, eh Riley? And number three?"

"Number three: 'Where coffee is served, there is grace and splendour and friendship and happiness.' Sheikh Ansari Djerzeri Hanball Abd-Al-Kadir."

"Whew, there's a name, huh? A real mouthful. Say that name five times fast. He was a Sufi mystic, that one," Greg makes a weird gesture toward Reza with his chin. Reza must be a kind of mystic too? Or Reza, being an export from the Middle East, must be well educated about Sufism in general and this coffee sheikh in particular? "Of course, I don't expect anyone here to know who all these people are. I didn't know myself. I just looked up the quotes online. But they are pretty good, huh? Some real doozies there, right Reza?"

"Right."

"Okay then. So let's get to it. How 'bout we start with you, Joly?"

"Oh, me first again?"

"Would you like me to start with someone else? Give you more time to think it over?"

This seems like a trick question. "Um . . . no, no, that's fine. So you want me to pick a favourite?" Her nerves are ringing in her ears.

"Right. Which speaks to you?"

"Um . . . let me think . . ." Pick one, Joly! Hurry! "Uh . . . the second one?" Middle seems like the safest choice.

"Okay, okay, and why? What did you like about it?"

"Oh . . . well . . . I thought it was evocative. It made me want a cup of coffee, you know?"

"Hm. All right."

Next up is Jenn: "I really like the last one, the idea of happiness and friendship being wherever coffee is." Then she launches into a whole story about her childhood and her caffeine-dependent father, a man who was often away on business, but who, whenever he was around, brewed a pot of strong coffee in the morning. As she gets going on how the smell of that coffee was the smell of comfort, because it meant her beloved father was home at last, the rest of the candidates trade *oh-fuck-off* looks. She ends the story with this gem: "So that's what coffee means to me. Family. And happiness. Like the Sheikh says."

Greg is thrilled—oh boy howdy is he thrilled—sporting a smile that lands somewhere between expansive and de-ranged. Watching him open up his entire expression to Jenn—the desperate smile, the painfully ingenuous eyes—a strange sympathy sweeps through Joly. The poor guy is just lonely. Like everyone. And this strained, prolonged interview is his attempt to mitigate that loneliness for however long he can. Which explains why they have already been here for almost forty minutes.

The favourite-quotation question travels around the group, but no one's response manages to delight Greg quite as much as Jenn's childhood reminiscence. "That was fun, wasn't it? Like I said at the start, not the kind of interview you're used to, but—"

"Greg, we're getting short on time," Reza says, venturing an unprompted sentence for the first time today.

Greg steals a frightened glance at his watch and grinds his small teeth. "Oh shoot. Oh right. Okay. Let's wrap things up here. Now that you've all gotten to know each other a little, I've got one last question. Riley, let's start with you this time."

"Okay," Riley's ponytail bobs up and down.

"Excluding yourself, if you could pick one person you think should advance to the next round of interviews, who would that be? Just a name. I don't need a reason for this one."

"Wait, sorry," Joly says, the words tumbling from her mouth before she can stop them. "How many rounds of interviews are there exactly? I mean . . . I'm just curious."

"I guess it depends how far you make it in the process. Doesn't it? Haha. And now that you've taken the floor, Joly, you might as well lead us off on this last question. So tell us, who would you put through to the next round?"

"Oh, hm." The spirit of this question saddens her; it's the worst of all the bogus questions he's asked today. "I don't really want to throw anyone under the bus."

"Not so easy being the boss, huh? Making the tough decisions."

"Everyone here seems nice and competent. Good barista potential in all of us, I think. I think everyone should make it through."

"I'm looking for one name."

"I'd really rather not single anyone out."

Reza notes this response without expression. When Greg throws the same question to each of the others, they answer with a clear choice. One name. No one picks Joly.

2

THE GUEST BEDROOM in Yannick's house is wonderfully furnished, with a bouncy queen bed in a rich upholstered frame, matching white side tables and dresser, and a small antique desk, at which Joly sits and reviews the supplementary take-home form that Reza handed out to the candidates at the end of the interview: six pages of short-answer questions, front and back. *What complaints did you have about your last boss? What issues have you previously had with coworkers? What skills have helped you stand out in your previous jobs? What does 'community' mean to you? Describe what makes you extraordinary.*

Joly trills her lips, slumps low in the chair, and eventually puddles onto the floor, like a child in front of a pile of homework.

When it comes to her own writing—oh boy, her hilarious, genius short stories—she can spend hours bolted to the desk. Days, weeks, months flying by almost unnoticed! Which is why, a few months back, after emerging from a period of particularly intensive and sensational artistic creativity, she was shocked to discover that her savings had haemorrhaged from her bank account and she could no longer make her rent.

. When Joly first moved in here, she was helpful. Yannick and Karen were finishing up the last in a series of renovations on this 2.5 million dollar Danforth-area home, and someone had to be around to let in the painters and the delivery guys and sound system guys while they were both off at their Very Important Jobs. It was a blessing, really, that Joly was unemployed and available to help out. But since then, her position in the house has turned a little iffier than she'd like. She still cleans all 3.5 bathrooms once a week, loads the dishwasher, does the laundry, takes little Yvie to swimming lessons, babysits whenever they ask her to. But Yannick is getting testy. She needs an exit strategy.

Joly gropes for the Nature's Ground document up on her desk and gives it another look. Come on now, Joly. Just fill it out. Do it! But her belly turns over at the sight of this document—a literal queasiness. Or else it's residual nerves from the interview itself. Curled up on her side, she clutches her stomach, winces, and allows a moment of reflection. How did she get to this point? There must have been at least one critical juncture at which she chose the wrong path.

But then maybe everyone has a shaky decade or two. There's still time to turn it all around! She just needs her one real break.

3

"THE WORLD'S TALLEST slum is in Venezuela," says Joly, reading facts off her laptop, at the kitchen island, which is cluttered with a confusing array of household crap. The cleaning lady who's supposed to come once a month has been on vacation. And the dishwasher's broken again. Everything's so much harder when the dishwasher's broken. She's sure she just did the dishes yesterday, so how is there already another shaky pile in the sink?

"Uh-huh," says Yannick, slumped over his bowl of Cheerios across from her.

"It's a 54-storey skyscraper."

"Oh yeah."

"Did you know that? D'you know about this?"

"No. I'm not up on my slums, I guess."

Joly looks at her brother sloppily spooning his cereal. At 6:10am, it's really too early to be eating—but 6:00 is when Yannick gets up and Joly can't stand the idea of him eating alone, so she always sets her alarm to match his. It's really not so bad today; the summer morning sun is already flooding in, radiating off the pewter-glazed kitchen cabinets. "It's an abandoned skyscraper," she says. "That's interesting to think about, no? Says here they ran out of money before they could finish building it."

"Hm." Drops of milk spill onto the sports section of the newspaper he's sort of working his way through. He's not listening to her. But he rarely does. So she doesn't let his disinterest stop her from talking about what she wants to talk about.

"And the homeless just invaded it en masse. Isn't that interesting?"

"Shouldn't you be looking for a job?"

"I am looking. Always looking. And *actually*," she says with a flourish of her cereal spoon, "I had a job interview just yesterday."

"Well-a-well-a-well." Yannick glances up from the sports page spread out on the white-and-grey marble countertop. Oh, he's listening now. "Look at you."

"Look at me," she says, savouring this flicker of pride before plunging back into the laptop. "So they call it the Tower of David, this skyscraper."

"What kind of job?"

"Or *Torre David*," she says, trying it out with a Spanish accent and enjoying the way the words roll around in her mouth. She's long believed that speaking multiple languages holds a civic importance. Knowing a language other than one's own offers insight into another culture, into a people, and into that people's way of thinking. And okay, just putting on an accent, however well-articulated, doesn't technically qualify as *knowing* a language, but it does provide a window. So she says the words again, really letting the Rs roll this time. "*Torre David*."

"I heard you the first time, dummy," Yannick says. "What kind of job?"

"And they say it looks like the Tower of Babel. You know, half finished, half broken. There are no windows in most of it. Just big gaping holes. And thousands of people living there. Isn't that something?"

"Joly."

"There are no elevators. That's obvious, I guess. But they've built these ramps over some of the stairs. And there are these guys, like cabbies, who'll drive you up the tower on their motorcycles. Like, if you live on a high floor. And you've had a rough day."

"What was the job interview?"

She squints and braces herself. "Barista."

"Oh Jesus Christ." Yannick throws his spoon into his bowl; the clang echoes around the cabinetry.

"No, no, it's a cool place," she says, still trying to believe this is true. "And tips are supposed to be good. People tip baristas now."

"Who tips? I don't tip." He returns his half-assed focus to the newspaper.

"Because you only ever buy drip coffee. You don't have to tip for drip. Now check this out: it's, like, gang-controlled, this tower. These gangs run the whole operation. You have to pay them to gain entry."

"You can tell I'm not really listening to you, right?"

"But there are regular families who live there too. Just ordinary working people looking for a home. That's interesting. Don't you think that's interesting?"

Yannick looks up at her once more. "Joly, I don't know. I guess so. But I also sort of don't care."

"What?"

"Look for a real job."

"But no one ever calls me back. And you know, I'm not even sure I'd like most of these 'real jobs' I've been applying for. These dumb admin jobs at these boring companies."

"Of course you don't like the jobs." He gets up from the island, abandoning the sports section. He doesn't read as much as he used to. Not books, not articles. Not even the sports stats.

"Right. So, like, what's the point of applying, you know?"

"What? What are you talking about? Nobody likes their job. Don't you know that? You just go to work, then come home, then collect a paycheque and otherwise pretend it never happened." He deposits another pod into the coffee machine and waits with his arms firmly crossed. "Christ, I hate my job."

He says this all the time, how he hates the long hours, hates his boss, hates the dummies whose slack he has to pick up. But he also seems to revel in the imagined prestige of his work, the gross culture of finance. She's seen him out with his work buddies, swearing and laughing and racking up thousand dollar bar tabs. That's a required part of the lifestyle, he tells her. And he likes that part, she's sure of it.

"This fucking vinegar deal is gonna kill me," he says, slouching on the marble counter, watching the coffee dribble into his cup. "I'm gonna be working straight through the weekend again."

Joly looks up from her slideshow of life inside the Venezuelan slum. "Well, wait, so you're not coming to baseball then? Again?"

"What did I just say? I gotta work, dummy."

"But no one should work on Sundays."

"Thank you, Joly. You pick that up at one of your bullshit Occupy rallies?"

"Didn't have to," she says. "Sunday, day of rest."

The Sunday baseball games at Christie Pits are a tradition for them, have been since forever. Their parents used to take them to watch the games when they were kids, and although the practice fizzled some when Yannick hit his teenage years and developed weekend interests that didn't include hanging with his parents and his little sister, it was Yannick himself who resurrected the tradition a few years ago, just after his own kid was born. "Traditions are important," he told Joly then. "We can't lose ours."

For a whole season, they packed up the family every Sunday, along with a six-pack and whatever friends they could round up, and they spent the afternoon on the grassy hill overlooking right field. But now Karen spends most of her weekends up in Thornhill, parading Yvie off to her parents. And Yannick, for one reason or another, some work or family or social obligation, hasn't been making it out to the ballpark as often as he used to. Of the four games so far this season, he's only actually been to one and a half. But still, every Sunday Joly wakes up expecting the tradition to endure.

"You gotta come this week," she says.

"I don't know," he says. "I'll try."

"Oh." Her disappointment is physical. It's in her deflated chest and her sloshing belly. Though the belly thing might be something else. She's been trying to decide all through breakfast whether she's queasy or not. The Cheerios aren't sitting well. Or maybe it's the unpasteurized milk that Karen has been getting through some shady online network, ever since she read that raw milk provides a perfect cocktail of nutrients for pre-pregnancy.

"Jesus, I said I'll try," Yannick says, a little too loudly, at a volume amplified by guilt, or maybe just impatience. "Can't Lou go with you?"

"She's coming. But I like it when there are more of us."

"Can't your communist boyfriend go?"

"He's working on Sunday. Also, Ben is not technically a communist." Joly has learned, after many exhausting discussions with Ben, that the distinction is important. Ben is not a communist. Although it's an easy mistake to make. Because he does lean pretty hard to the left. In a way that's obvious from even a few minutes of conversation with him. But he's *not* a communist. He's explained to her many times about the nuanced distinctions between various branches of left-wing ideologies. "He's a social anarchist," she corrects.

"Are you kidding me?"

"No."

"What's the fucking difference?"

"I think it's mostly a branding thing."

"But both those brands suck." Yannick gives her one of those headshakes that conveys both his bafflement and disappointment with her, then throws back the rest of his coffee and plunks the empty mug down beside his empty cereal bowl. "All right, I gotta go."

Once he's gone, Joly decides to do a bit of cleaning, to make herself useful, to remind her brother that she's good for something. But halfway through the stack of dishes, the murmuring in her stomach erupts into an urgent, screeching nausea. She makes it to the bathroom just in time to puke up her morning cereal and raw milk. A few specks land on the hand-painted tiles of the bathroom floor.

She spends the next fifteen minutes lying on these tiles. It's not so bad down here—the tiles are warmed by a radiant heating system. Her stomach starts to settle, but the room smells foul. It's not just the lingering notes of puke, it's also the soaps and air fresheners and that weird cinnamon toothpaste that are blending together into a surprisingly putrid stink.

It's the third morning in a row now that she's hurled, and this time she starts to worry in earnest that she might be knocked up.

4

NO WAY! IMPOSSIBLE! Sitting on the plush carpet of her bedroom, Joly peers at her stomach and tries to imagine an actual human slow-cooking in there. Nah, can't be. It's never happened to her before, for one. No close calls, no real scares. She has a system, a good system, based on cycles and timing and instinct, and so far, this system has been flawless—so flawless that Joly has even wondered on occasion if she might be barren.

But pregnancy worries, once entertained, are hard to shake loose. So when Joly hears Karen and Yvie leave for the day, she sneaks up to the third floor, to the master bedroom and through to the ensuite, to the drawers in which Karen keeps a trove of pregnancy tests so that anytime she's even one day late or thinks her breasts have swollen or that "things just feel different," she has a test on hand to settle the question, hoping, always hoping, for baby number two. A handful of times now, Joly has sat with her, side by side on the edge of the clawfoot tub, waiting for the test to deliver its (inevitably negative) result, and for Karen to heave out a smile and say, "That's okay, next month."

Now it's Joly's turn to pee on the stick. She does. Then she waits . . . and waits . . . and waits . . . then looks.

Oh boy.

5

"WHAT AM I gonna do?!" Joly canters around Louise's wide back deck as she wails. Despite the twenty-minute sprinted bike ride to Don Mills, a boundless energy pumps through her limbs. The ride up left her drenched, sweat stains at her armpits already the size of saucers. It's unseasonably hot—again. Unless this is just what pregnancy is like? Disrupting hormones? Spiking sweat glands?

"Well to start," says Lou, splitting open an apricot. "I think you should probably talk to Ben."

"Are you crazy? I can't talk to Ben. Not without a plan. You know how he is. He'll bamboozle me!"

Ben's imposing bearing, his great height and weight, his booming bass voice, and his vast breadth of knowledge have always rendered Joly helpless. She can't squirm her way out of any debate with him.

Also . . . she and Ben did once discuss this possibility—the possibility of a system failure. It was a short conversation in which they both agreed the problem would be handled quickly, tidily, reasonably. No one would weep or shriek or lose their mind over a simple in-and-out medical procedure. But that was a few years ago, when she was still in her twenties. Now that she's stormed through the door of thirty, the abortion instinct doesn't ring out quite as loudly as it once did. Right now, marching around Lou's deck, she is surprised—and a little alarmed—that she can't hear it ringing at all.

Lou grabs her by the upper arm and steers her to the built-in bench. "Calm down. Let's think."

Lou pulls up a metal patio chair and sits directly across from her, studying her with care, but also with an almost scientific detachment, like a nurse evaluating a newly admitted patient. There has always been something remote about Lou's nurturing instinct, like she doesn't quite understand how to do it. Joly attributes this quirk to the early death of Lou's mother, who kicked it when they were kids. Twenty-five years on, it's still one of the saddest events Joly can think of.

"Do you want a Xanax?" Lou asks gently. "Clonazepam?"

"What? No!"

"Some pot maybe?"

Joly gapes at her belly, its vulnerable contents.

"One pill or joint won't make a difference," Lou assures her. "Besides, my doctor says stress is the worst thing for your health. Silent killer." Expertly, Lou rolls a joint on her lap, her hands resting on the light cotton of her peach summer dress. "So you want to keep it then? Is that what we're thinking?"

"No! How am I gonna do that? I have no money." Ben has no money either. Social anarchists rarely do. "I'm completely broke, Lou. And practically unemployable. I have no marketable skills. I had an interview at a *coffee shop* yesterday! Barista, Lou!"

"Aw Jesus."

"And I don't even know if I made it to round two!"

"Round two? How many rounds are there?"

"Who knows!" Joly stares glumly out at the huge yard that backs onto the ravine, where she and Louise used to play as kids. They grew up together, on this very street, spent hundreds of evenings and weekends and endless summer hours running up and down that ravine, picking up neighbourhood kids as they went, playing legendary games of hide-and-seek or building forts in the ravine with scraps of wood swiped from parents' garages or just sitting in the bushes telling stories until enough mothers hollered "Dinner!" and the games broke up. Joly's parents sold the house a few years ago, when they decided to return to the motherland. Shortly after that, it was Lou's father who wanted to downsize. But Lou couldn't let the house go, so she and Elliott bought it themselves.

"I've wasted my life," Joly declares. "I've got nothing to show for the last fifteen years. They've just whooshed by. While I've been churning out these stories that nobody ever reads. Whoooooosh!" Joly sweeps an arm over the entire width of the table.

"Pffff. You wanna know about a wasted life, try working in marketing." Lou is supposed to be at work at this exact moment, but when Joly called with the pregnancy news, Lou said that she was taking a sick day and instructed Joly to come here for a debrief.

"You know what I've done every day for the last five months?" Lou lights her joint with a long pull, then offers it to Joly, who waves it away. "Meetings. About audio billboards." She stretches one leg after the other up onto Joly's lap. "That and take anti-anxiety medication so I don't kill myself."

"Yeah, but you're not broke." Joly gives Lou's ankle a quick squeeze. "It's important to be not broke, I'm starting to realize."

"I don't know, Joly. Our jobs are revolting. Elliott's is worse than mine. He's down a rabbit hole with this wedding photography garbage." Lou's left eye flickers and Joly wonders, not for the first time, about the health of their marriage. "Every dollar you make with your writing is worth a hundred of ours. Besides, your stories are hilarious. They have social value."

"Yeah," Joly says pensively, "they're funny." Since grad school, she has been working on a collection of side-splitting, madcap stories that perfectly encapsulate the wacky uncertainty of modern times. But although she has managed to publish a handful of them in fringe magazines and websites, she hasn't gotten any nibbles on the collection as a whole. The dour industry gatekeepers just don't like Funny.

"Social value," Joly repeats.

"I send your stories around at work," Lou says through another deep inhale of the pot. "Every time one comes out. People fucking love them. You have *fans*. That one about the amateur detective investigating those decapitated sea lions? Solid gold."

"Yeah," says Joly, for whom praise of this sort goes down like candy, "that one is a minor masterpiece." Talk of her writing has an eclipsing effect. It sends a manic buzz through her body. She can't sit still. Her legs start to bounce on the bench, making Lou's feet bob up and down. "You should get a load of this next one I'm working on," she says. "It's about a man who—okay, get this—his back hair suddenly turns into porcupine quills! Ha! Hahaha. Which pisses his girlfriend off, because his sharp quills keep puncturing her hands when she tries to fuck him!" Almost doubled over with laughter now, Joly smacks at Lou's shins. "It's like Kafka . . . but even funnier!"

When she manages to straighten up again, her laughter subsiding, she sees Lou smiling with her head thrown back on the chair, staring up at the lazy branches of the maple trees with goofy eyes. Joly wipes at the sweat on her forehead. "Seriously, I need an actual job. Yannick is threatening to kick me out."

"He'll never kick you out."

"He might. Or Karen will."

"Yeah, well, Karen's a cunt."

"Hey now. She's all right. She's good, actually. Great, really . . . once you get to know her."

"Well . . ." Lou stubs out the joint in the pale green plastic ashtray already full of butts. "What kind of jobs are you looking at? It shouldn't be this hard for you to get hired. You're smarter than everyone at my office."

Whipping out her phone, Joly pulls up the bookmarked job postings page. "Okay . . . best I've seen lately is an opening for a technical writer at Holt Renfrew."

"Holt Renfrew!" Lou laughs hard, in big bursts. She reaches forward to grab at Joly's faded and sweaty grey T-shirt, which years ago belonged to Yannick, and her plain no-name jean shorts. "I don't think you'd do well there. You're not a high-end department store kind of person."

"I don't think I'm qualified. Listen to this, this is one of their qualifications: 'Be extraordinary.'"

"What?"

"That's what it says. Under qualifications. 'Be extraordinary.' What extraordinary person wants to be a technical writer at Holt Renfrew?" Joly chucks her phone onto the glass patio table and flings herself back on the bench, her arms above her head. She looks up at the canopy of maples. "Everywhere you go now, you have to be extraordinary. Even that stupid coffee shop wants me be to be extraordinary. It's meaningless. Where are all the ordinary people supposed to go?"

"Maybe they're all technical writers for Walmart."

Lou swoops the phone toward her and scrolls through the job postings, muttering her confident contempt for what's on offer. But it's all so much easier for Lou, this work stuff. Lou, although she hates most people, understands them much better than Joly does. Lou would never blow a job interview. She charms people. She draws attention easily. And expresses it easily. Even today, on a sick day, in her $5 summer dress from a consignment store, she looks amazing.

Joly never charms people. They don't even notice her. Not until she was twenty-two did anyone notice her long enough to kiss her. She's plain, average, a Jane Eyre. Where Lou, being of Japanese, British, and Spanish extraction, displays an ethnicity that's striking and hard to place, Joly's pallor and features suggest nothing but a deep, deep-reaching Western European ancestry. In her early teenage years, Joly used to lock herself in the bathroom and study her face in the mirror, tugging at her eyes, pulling the edges outward, convinced that she would be way more beautiful, way more desirable if she had even a hint of Asian heritage, something to offset the hundreds of years of Swiss peasantry in her blood.

"Your phone's dying," says Lou.

"What? I just charged it." Joly sits up, grabs at the device, and jams her fingers into the screen. "What a hunk of junk."

"Cobalt," says Lou, wagging her hand at the phone.

"What?"

"That's what makes the battery work. Cobalt. Mostly from the Congo. Where kids dig around for it in open pits. With their tiny little hands. Until they die from toxic fumes. Or in tunnel collapses."

"Jesus." More and more frequently, Lou has been briefing Joly on these choice bits of news from around the world. She used to send an article a week, now it's one almost every day—just yesterday, she sent her the piece about the Venezuelan slum.

With a shrug, Lou sends the phone sliding down the glass tabletop. "I need more fruit. Ooh, and some nuts."

While Lou is in the kitchen, Joly turns to face the ravine. She looks at her bike pitched on its side in the grass. Everything in this huge wooded yard is just like it was when they were kids—the stalwart army of maple trees, the few sleepy willows, the lush undergrowth of ferns and bushes, the fat black squirrels and dumb rabbits and flitting birds. An idyll.

Lou returns, carrying a wooden fruit bowl, overflowing with offerings, and a bowl of whole walnuts. But Joly can't eat.

"I should probably get rid of the baby, right? Obviously. That's the answer, right?"

"It's *an* answer." Lou cracks a walnut with enormous attention.

Joly studies her quietly. "Do you ever think about it?"

Lou's pregnancy predicament struck at sixteen. But her resolve back then was immediate and unshakeable. She didn't even discuss it with Joly, just announced that she would be needing a ride to the clinic, because she didn't want to tell the father (Joly never did know who it was), nor did she want to tell her own father. So it was Joly who, fresh off her driver's test, chauffeured Lou to the clinic. Lou endured the process well, with unwavering determination from start to finish. But Lou is so much stronger.

"Never," says Lou, though there's a stiffening in her features as she wrestles bits of the nut from its shell. Joly's not sure she believes her.

"I think I would. A lot."

"You should talk to Ben."

6

IT'S ALMOST DUSK by the time Joly steers her bike off Bloor and onto Ossington: Ben's neighbourhood. The doorbell doesn't work, it hasn't in the eight years that Ben has lived here, so she hammers at the door, which, after a few minutes, is opened by one of Ben's roommates. One of his five room-mates. The house is a sort of commune, made up of students and strays, anyone interested in cheap rent and zero amen-ities. The roommate who answers is Runkle, a guy in his forties, whose life, Ben has told her, is in free fall.

"Ben around?"

Waving her in, Runkle says, "Probably. I think they're brew-ing today, actually. Check for yourself."

She passes through the living room, on to the kitchen at the back of the house, and out onto the stoop, where the giant brew kettle sits boiling on its propane-powered burner. Ben's happiest when he's brewing; he finds religious fulfill-ment in the task. "It takes monkish discipline to make good beer," he told her the first time she watched him brew. And true enough, the operation dragged on the whole day, much longer than she'd anticipated and far past the point where she could sustain even a feigned interest.

Ben is down in the chaos of the yard, to the left of the irregularly-shaped vegetable garden patches, and to the right of the home-built cinder block fire pit, inside of which he roasted an entire pig last May Day. He's sitting in a lawn chair amid the overgrown grass with his back to her, tossing bagels at a garden gnome about twenty feet away, trying to land each around the gnome's pointy red hat. Egged on by Marko (another roommate, another ex-grad student), Ben chucks bagel after bagel, and when he finally lands one, his huge frame erupts out of the chair with a roaring cheer. The first time she ever caught sight of Ben, his big build, his full black beard, magnificent waves of dark hair, already streaked grey, Joly felt her whole body stir. *A Viking!* she whispered to herself. And his ragged clothes only added to the effect: a shipwrecked Viking. He seemed to have been dropped into this world from another time and place.

At the sight of him now, steeped in this jubilance, Joly's

composure cracks. A raw panic pumps through her, bringing a burning flush to her cheeks. She hesitates on the stoop.

Ben approaches the target zone to retrieve his cache of tossed bagels, catches sight of her, and throws up a hand with happy surprise. "Hey there, doll!" He strides up the steps to meet her and kisses the top of her head. "What are you doing here?"

"In the neighbourhood. D'you have a few minutes? I have some news."

"Oh-ho. News over the wires? How exciting." He grabs a few bottles from the outdoor beer fridge and waves her down to the backyard.

"Look, Marko, we have ourselves a guest. The woman comes bearing news."

"Bagel toss?" Marko asks, offering a sesame seed bagel on a hand covered in dark bike grease. His loose T-shirt and jeans are similarly stained.

Joly looks at the scattering of bagels around the gnome. "This seems wasteful."

"Ah, but it only *seems* so," says Ben, who routinely steals bagels from work. "These are week-olds from the pit. I thought I could try to make breadcrumbs with them, but . . . young Geoffrey broke the blender this morning. So . . . repurposed!" He sends his bagel flying, missing the gnome by feet, a failure that draws hoots from Marko. They are both plastered, clearly, as they always are on brew days.

"Grab yourself a perch," Ben says.

So she drags a plastic chair from the cluster by the fence. She picks the best of the bunch, but it still only has one armrest. The whole lot are found chairs, treasures from curbsides and alleyways, the backyard littered with scavenged street finds.

"What news now, my little dove?" asks Ben, squeezing her knee absentmindedly.

"Um. What are you brewing?" Joly asks.

"A red ale." Ben pumps a fist. "A deep, strong red. We're calling it the InternationALE."

"The working man's beer," adds Marko.

"Because it's so red, get it?" Ben and Marko chuckle delightedly. But Joly has trouble finding her way to the punchline. The pressure in her head is thick.

"What's wrong with you, woman?" Ben demands. "That's funny."

"Um . . . I'm pregnant," she says.

Marko slides out of his chair with a low whistle. "God speed," he says, slapping Ben's shoulder before he disappears into the house with a fading chuckle.

Ben grips an armrest and draws in an enormous breath, which he doesn't seem to exhale; his chest stays frozen on the strained inhalation. "No," he says, at last releasing some air. "I'm afraid that's impossible. You're not pregnant."

"Right. Except I am."

"But your system?"

"Malfunctioned."

Slowly, he rises from his chair, twirling a bagel between his fingers. "Okay," he says, pacing erratically. "Okay then." He stops in front of her. "I am at your service. What do you need from me? A ride to the clinic? I'll arrange it. I'll borrow the good Reverend's van. Whatever you need."

From his full height, he stares down at her; she manages to hold the gaze for just a few seconds before dropping her eyes to her tensed fingers.

"Joly," he says.

"Ben."

"Joly, did we not talk about this very eventuality?"

"We did. But I don't feel . . . quite as abortion-y as I expected to. So I just want us to think about it for a second. Because we're both getting older. And I mean, this is the sort of thing people do, like biologically. They have babies."

"An infant child?" Ben whips out an arm that catches the back of his flimsy lawn chair and sends it flying. "Into this decaying and brutish world?"

"Don't be so hysterical, Benny," she says.

"Hysterical?" He stalks the grass between her and the gnome. "This civilization is collapsing around us! The whole world will be warring over water in a few decades! You want to expose a child to that kind of future?"

It's all doom and dystopia with Ben. When she first met him, he still had some modest hope for the future, a hope that manifested in personal ambition. He was a Ph.D. student then, on track to becoming a professor of history. But that plan was abandoned last year when he declared academia to be morally bankrupt, a body no longer interested in challenging power or seeking truth, preferring instead to fall in step with the corporate interests that fund it. He paced around his bedroom one night saying he would have to be out of his mind, right out of his goddamned mind, to throw more time and treasure into an institutional system that had become corrupted by the capitalist machinery. But he doesn't seem much happier now, working for minimum wage at the bagel shop.

"Joly," he says, pausing his march right beside the grinning gnome, "as you may have noticed, I'm hammered. But let me try to take a look at what you're suggesting. Logically."

Oh boy, she hates when he applies *logic* to arguments. And he's all harsh edges; she doesn't do well with harsh edges. Tears appear on the horizon.

"Who will pay for this child? Where will it live? Will you and the offspring be moving into the Sanctum?"

She looks back at the lopsided house, with its sinking roof. Full of roommates. And mould on the bathroom walls, and mice in the bedrooms, and sketchy plumbing, and the old stove that has at least once caught fire. "No. Not here."

"Ah-ha." He rests a bare foot on the gnome's red hat and rocks the ornament back and forth. "With your brother perhaps? The high-powered financier bankrolling our little family forever?"

"I obviously don't think that."

"I'm not sure that's obvious." She's a few stern words away from a descent into sobs. Drawing her knees to her chest, she curls into a tight ball, her chin resting on her knees, and she stares at the high parched grass. When she next dares to look up, she finds his eyes rapidly scanning her scrunched body, his mouth agape with a concern that borders on horror.

"What?" she says.

"Can you even carry my mighty seed?" he croaks, genuinely flabbergasted by the idea. "Look at you. Look at me. Your runty frame would split right open!"

Okay, that'll do it. Here come the tears, in full streams.

But in a second, Ben is kneeling in front of her, his big hands cupped over her bony knees. "Hey, hey now." His voice gets soft, but it retains its deep register, so that it seems to surround her in a shell of protective sound. "I'm sorry."

He wipes her tears with his thumbs and holds her cheeks. His hazel eyes, with their swirls and speckles, bore into her through his glasses. She looks away from them, down an inch or two, first at the breadth of his face, then at his rough beard, which she touches with the back of her hand. In their early days together, after she told him how much she liked the sensation of his beard against her skin, he used to spend full minutes passing his bearded cheeks and chin across her back, up and down her spine, along the sides of her body and her thighs and her calves. He does it still, when he's feeling sentimental. He does it right now. He presses his bearded chin into her forehead and says, "I'm sorry, doll. Please. Don't cry."

1

LATE THAT NIGHT, on Joly's bike ride home, she passes one construction site after another, each abandoned for the night. It seems like every few blocks there's a crane looming above her, a net of scaffolding spun up from the ground, a tower half-built. Ben told her recently that this city is leading the world in condo construction, with hundreds of projects planned or already underway. Hundreds of towers of Babel all across the city.

She rides by a site along Bloor St. and tries to imagine it slowly filling with squatters, as did the tower in Caracas. There's something captivating . . . no, glorious! . . . about what those Venezuelans are getting up to. A mass takeover of a skyscraper! People uniting! Creating their own extra-legal community. One that's functioning, even with all its flaws. The slideshow she scrolled through earlier showed image after image of families inside the slum, their rooms sometimes jazzed up with a brightly painted wall or a collage of posters or makeshift curtains. Bare concrete spaces transformed into cozy little homes. The more she thinks about it, the more communal passion and momentum she imbues into the project. Squatters gaining in numbers each year. Advancing ever further upward, skyward, heavenward. What solidarity! What spirit! The same spirit that inspired Babel itself.

She's always loved the story of Babel. A group of people terrified of being alone in the big wide world. What's more relatable than that? They tackle their terror by building themselves a city. And a mighty tower—a beacon for them all, forever marking the place where they belong. A tower that says: welcome home. It's a story about *nesting*. She hadn't realized that until now.

8

JOLY MOVES HER way up the levels of the house, bathroom by bathroom. It takes almost two hours to clean them all—a half hour more than usual—because she takes breaks in each bathroom to study herself in the mirror. She's sure her breasts are already bigger. They feel bigger. And tender. She forces her stomach outward and imagines how it will swell if she lets things run their natural course. The idea of the swell pleases her. She'd like to feel heavier, curvier. Womanly.

By the time she finishes with the ensuite on the top floor, the odours from the various cleaning agents—the Lysol all-purpose cleaner, the extra astringent toilet bowl cleaner, the Windex—are making her throat hurt. She'll need to talk to Yannick about getting some natural cleaners. She can't be breathing in this toxic shit anymore. This is the kind of thing that leads to birth defects.

With her dirty rags and towels gathered into an unwieldy clump, she trudges down to the laundry room, but an obstacle on the stairs blocks her path. Three-year old Yvie is splayed out on the third step from the bottom, where she's reading a book, or pretending to.

"How's the book?" Joly asks, flicking the cover with her toe.

"It's about a whale."

"Ooh, good stuff." She drops the ball of rags onto the stairs and sinks down beside Yvie, resting her chin on the little goober's sandy hair and reading over her head.

"You're not even a practising Catholic!" shouts Yannick from the living room.

"I practise all the time!" Karen hollers.

"When was the last time you went to church?"

"That is not the point!"

"Karen! No way. We're not baptizing the kid."

This argument, which has been raging throughout the home again lately, first reared its head when Yvie was in utero. Karen mentioned a baptism, but Yannick dug in his heels, a rarity for him, and Karen agreed to leave it be. Something, though, has since tweaked inside of her and made her revive the bid, this time with vehemence. And this time, Yannick will relent, Joly knows he will. He doesn't have the stamina for prolonged fights.

"I'm going to get bap-sized," Yvie whispers. Even she knows it's inevitable that her dad will cave. But she's wary of her fate.

"It's just a ceremony!" Karen yells. "What do you care about a little ceremony? Why are you making such a big deal out of it?"

"Because! I'm not Catholic! And Yvie is not Catholic!"

"Oh yes she is!"

Yvie cuddles up against Joly's side. As Joly cradles her, she glances up at the staircase wall, decorated with dozens of framed photographs of Yannick and Karen—their engage-ment, their big white wedding, their tropical vacations. She's seen these vanity walls, or ones like them, in the homes of most of Yannick and Karen's married friends, but she's still confused by the concept. Where once a couple might have hung a painting, they now go with a mosaic of them-selves—sometimes a single blown-up photograph—elevating their love to the status of art.

"You don't just get to change your mind, Karen!"

"I was hormonal. It was coerced."

"Oh bullshit."

Abandoning the dirty rags, Joly scoops up the goober along with her whale book. "We need some fresh air, Yvie-bug," she says. "Let's go outside."

"But it's so hot outside."

"Nah, it's just right."

Joly carries her out to the backyard, into the impossibly

humid heat, and sets her down on one of the big rocks by the water feature: a wide-mouthed waterfall that cascades from a stone wall into an immaculate pond. It's the focal point of the landscaped yard. Rock gardens, in elliptical shapes, edge the perimeter and a small patch of lawn fills out the centre. It's all very pretty, but Joly prefers the wild backyard of her childhood.

"Were you bap-sized?" Yvie asks. She clambers onto Joly's lap and squishes herself into a ball.

"No." Joly crosses her hands on top of Yvie's head, securing it like a helmet.

"Was Daddy?"

"No."

"Mama was."

"Yes. She was baptized."

"And I'm going to be."

"If you say so, Yvie-bug."

"No, not bug."

"What then?"

"A tiger," she says and pounces around onto Joly's back.

With careless effort, Joly tips her over her shoulders, pinning her to the grass amid delighted squeals. "You're too little to be a tiger. You're tiny. A teeny tiny Yvie-bug."

"—don't give a shit what your mother says!" Yannick's voice flies out through the open door. "Why does your mother get a vote on the baptism?"

Joly moves to close the door, but before she is allowed to stand up, Yvie yanks at her hand. "What's bap-sized mean?"

"It means someone dunks your head in water."

"Like at swimming?"

"Pretty much. Only you'll be wearing a dress. Your mom'll probably get you a pretty white dress."

"No-oh!" The absurdity of this is too much for Yvie, who explodes into laughter. "The dress will get all wet!"

"Hi Yvie!" calls a voice from the fence. It's the neighbour boy with whom Yvie sometimes conferences, his face half-visible through the crack between the fence boards. But she's not supposed to play with him—Yannick and Karen think he's a delinquent.

Straight away, Yvie races to answer his call, leaving Joly alone on the lawn. So she checks her phone for the hundredth time today, hoping to find an email from Greg at Nature's Grounds. She finally filled in the supplementary form yesterday—with paragraphs of beautifully crafted bullshit. But so far, no response.

If she gets hired, she's looking at what . . . maybe $250 a week. Plus tips? Add in Ben's meagre earnings. They could sponge all of Yvie's hand-me-downs. How bad is it really? True, they can't afford their own place, but is it the end of the world if she and Ben and their little one squat in the basement for a few months or a year? Could be a romp! A year of screwball comedy and crazy pranks, the whole lot of them all camped out in this house together, up to their armpits in impish hijinks!

A few problems do come to mind. Yannick, for one. It would take some convincing to get him on board. But he might come to recognize the advantages of communal living—permanent babysitters, that's a plus!

At the fence, Yvie and the boy are engrossed in earnest discussion. Maybe this boy's parents are looking for a babysitter too? Loads of parents must be struggling to find suitable childcare. It's an *opportunity*. Joly could welcome *all* the neighbourhood kids to the house, open up a daycare in the backyard. She'd charge only a small fee, or ask to be paid in kind, with prepared food items or with knitted wares for the baby. It'd be the start of an old-fashioned neighbourhood exchange. A great community initiative! And once everyone gets a taste for it, for all this camaraderie and neighbourly spirit, they could go a step or two or three further and transform this lot, and the adjacent ones, into a housing co-op or something. And over time, as the co-op grows to be an indispensible anchor for the entire neighbourhood, a model for the entire city, the necessary management and organizational duties could fall to Joly, and this could become . . . well, a career! Why not? Is that so insane?

"Catholic priests are all psychopaths and pedophiles!" bellows Yannick. Hmm . . . he's trying out a new attack. He must be on the ropes.

"That is a low blow, Yannick."

"Low blow? Every week it's in the paper. Every fucking week! It doesn't stop. It's your whole organization."

"My—?!"

A minute later, her brother charges out onto the deck, whipping the sliding door shut behind him. He stands for a moment, staring at the water feature with his hands in his hips, then walks over and drops onto a rock beside Joly.

"So the baptism battle rages on," Joly says.

"You agree on things. That should be the end of it." Yannick grabs a pebble from the rock garden and flings it into the pond. Plunk! Then he seizes a whole handful of pebbles and hurls them, one after another—plunk, plunk, plunk! The noise disrupts Yvie's chatter; she swings around, follows the arc of a few thrown pebbles, then returns to her own business.

Joly watches her brother fume. How opposed he is to the idea of religion! However restrained the dose. They didn't grow up religious, no, but neither did their parents instil in them an animosity for theological exploration. And if . . . let's just say . . . she and Ben decide to have the tiny little baby-bud incubating inside of her . . . she wouldn't object if Ben, devout in his own strange way, wanted it baptized. Her. The baby girl. She's started thinking of it as a girl—that happened sometime over the last couple of days. It seems impossible that she could be mother to a son. But a daughter . . . a little girl! Joly can see the little buttercup. She's about seven, with long dark hair and thick bangs shielding her freckled face; she's sitting on the floor somewhere, leaning over her crossed legs and reading an encyclopaedia. She has Ben's weak eyes, so she reads through thick glasses. Who cares if she's baptized or not?

"Is it really such a big deal?" she asks. "You're making it too religious."

"It's a fucking baptism. How is it not religious?" Yannick stands up with a dismissive sniff. "I'm gonna get dinner. Karen says sushi tonight. Want anything particular?"

"Nah. Whatever. Oh wait, actually . . . maybe just veggie rolls."

Before he leaves, he takes a look at Yvie still deep in it with the boy at the fence. "Make sure she doesn't spend too much time with that kid, will you? He's a delinquent."

9

HUNCHED OVER HER laptop, listening only to the clickety-clack of her fingers flying across the keyboard, Joly churns out page after page depicting the misadventures of this poor guy with the porcupine quills. Ha. Hahahaha. She's busting a gut!

This story is almost as good as that one she wrote last month about a rhinoceros who becomes a bureaucrat, only nobody notices! Oh boy, that one cracks her up! This latest batch of stories is killer.

Hope swells in her as she conjures a vision of a rejiggered collection made up of a perfect combination of these new titles and some of her older work. She'll have to comb her archives carefully, pull out only the gems, spiff them up, and work out a wicked pitch for the whole shebang—but the talent is undeniable. Lou is right. There's Social Value here. This is Art.

Amid this burst of creativity, Joly hammers out more pages, pausing only to accommodate her own raucous laughter (boy oh boy, this poor guy!), and when she next looks up, she's surprised to see that it's already evening and she's way late for a date with Ben. Hours and hours have passed. As years and years have passed. Whoosh!

10

"SPOILS FROM THE pit," Ben says, pulling a plastic bag of six bagels from his smelly backpack. "There's a rosemary in there."

It's Saturday evening at St. James Park, and they've settled on a shady picnic spot far from the cathedral. Ben had business at the church earlier, a meeting to expand the community dinners he runs through his own parish.

"Dill cream cheese too." He tosses her the container plucked from his bag, but the cream cheese, which she usually likes, today looks like a sickening slop that she can't imagine ingesting.

"So good day at the office then?" she asks.

"Of course not," he says, cheerily enough.

This park is where they first met. Back then it was filled with tents and protestors, with posters and chants and a blend of ideologies. A spirit of solidarity and possibility. Of history. The park was Occupied.

It was fall and already cold when the Occupy movement rolled into the city. But Joly didn't mind the weather then, nobody did. Legions of protestors huddled together in the rain, standing shoulder to shoulder in the trenches. Oh boy, the excitement of those days! It soaked into her bones. But that energy is hard to tap into now, with the quiet heat smothering them all. Not a lot people are around tonight and those who are move slowly. Even the homeless guy collecting bottles is languid on his beat.

Ben stuffs a cream cheese-smeared bagel between his teeth and fiddles with the portable radio he found in his church's basement a few months ago. The reception isn't great, but a classical station sputters through. This is the sort of thing they do. Budget dates.

"So . . . matters stand before us," he says.

"I know."

"Did you make the appointment?"

"I'm thinking about it." She studies the rosemary flecks in her bagel.

"And what, exactly, are you thinking?"

"I think it's a girl."

"That is not what I meant."

"I don't know why. I had this, like, vision of her the other day. A little girl, she looked like you. Dark hair and glasses."

"Ah yes. And who paid for those glasses?"

Joly rips off a small piece of the bagel and tentatively places it in her mouth, where it sits. "I don't know. That wasn't in the vision."

The homeless guy has wandered their way, flashing a smile that reminds Joly that her vision also failed to account for dental care.

But this barista job will stanch the bleeding. Until her reconfigured story collection sells. And once she gets that first book deal, it will be a cinch to get a second, and a third. Each deal more lucrative than the last, as her fan base turns legion. And in five, ten years, when the financial end has finally sorted itself out, she and Ben will gaze upon their little bespectacled, encyclopaedia-reading child and think back on the stress of this time and at their waffling and they'll laugh, with a wild mirth, knowing that they dodged a bullet, because what would life be without their little buttercup? And who knows, who really knows, maybe the little one will grow up and do something amazing for the world, lead a revolution or something, and Joly will end her life soaked in the twin happinesses of having had a career of great passion and acclaim and having bred a charismatic revolutionary who ushered in an age of utopia. That kind of thing happens.

"I'm worried that you're not looking at this reasonably," Ben says.

"I definitely am."

"What stability can we offer a child? We have nothing to offer."

She tries to get back to those heady Occupy days, when she and Ben first met. She came down to check out the demonstrations, thinking she'd stay a few hours, but then she saw him—the Viking, emerging from his tent, readying himself for a raid. His old green Canadian Tire tent was on the opposite side of the park, much closer to the church. She spent several nights in that tent, inside its closed confines, buzzing with nerves each time. She was afraid to touch him, awe-struck—and love-struck. It was like petting a lion in a cage, equal elements of danger and exhilaration.

And now his Viking blood is alive in her. Already she can feel it making her stronger and bolder. How *necessary* this baby feels. If only Ben appreciated the necessity of his own propagation. They could work out a path forward, a plan. And there must be a way forward. It can't be that procreation has become a privilege allotted to only the wealthy.

She just needs a little more time to develop a reasoned defense for the surprising position she has almost settled on: keeping her.

48

"Benny, do you think we could talk about the pregnancy another time?" she says, reclining onto her elbows.

"Another time? This creature is growing." He places a giant paw on her stomach, the spread of his fingers covering the width of her torso, and he stares near-horrified at her body beneath his hand. "As we speak, it multiplies its cells."

"I know. Just not tonight."

"When then?"

"Soon."

"Tomorrow?"

"Fine. Yes. Sure. Tomorrow." Gathering a firm fistful of his beard, she tips his chin down toward her.

"But for real, Joly," he says before he kisses her.

"Okay."

THEY TAKE A long, but easy meander through the city toward Ben's place, for a double-feature of Marx Brothers movies he borrowed from the library. When she can, Joly watches their shadows, elongated in the evening light, and she chuckles softly to herself at the cartoonish size disparity between her and Ben. The sun sinks as they go, but even in the fading dusk, the heat sticks. For a few blocks at a time, they walk hand in hand, but it's too hot for contact and soon they let go. But then a short while later, one or the other of them forgets and reaches out a hand again.

About a half hour into the walk, Joly feels a blister forming on her toe, and fifteen minutes after that, on a quiet residential street, she stops to inspect the foot. She sits down on the curb and takes off her shoe.

"Whoa mama! Look at the size of this thing!" she says. It's the sandals, these cheap flip-flops. The strap's been digging hard into the side of her foot, just beneath her big toe. She's wearing the wrong shoes for a cross-city distance. She looks at Ben's feet, in his Army Surplus boots. He always wears these boots, one shoe for all seasons. He has no other pairs.

Ben takes her foot in his hands. "I might have a bandaid."

He rifles through his backpack and she through hers; her hands find her phone and reflexively check for messages. No calls, no texts, but there is one email. From Greg at Nature's Grounds.

Hi Jolanda-Lydia,

It's with a heavy heart that I write to inform you that you were, unfortunately, not selected to advance to the next round of interviews for a position here at Nature's Grounds. :(

Competition this time around was stiff. We had many extraordinary candidates, but sadly only two can advance. I know how discouraging this must be for you, but we appreciate your interest in being part of the Nature's Grounds family and always encourage applicants to apply again in the future. You never know what tomorrow will bring!

Don't forget to think of us for all your caffeine-infused needs!

Sincerely,

Greg J. Baals

Joly lets the phone fall through her fingers and clatter against the sidewalk. "I didn't get that job. That stupid barista job. Didn't even make the next round."

"There's a second round?"

"I know!"

"Well . . . fuck 'em."

Not even extraordinary enough to make coffee! With her bare foot, she punts a garbage bin, which wobbles, but doesn't fall.

"Hey, don't worry, doll." He's found a single bandaid, much

too large for this purpose. Setting her foot on his lap, he rips open the wrapper. "There are millions of coffee shops in the city. Or fast food joints."

Fast food. How can her job prospects have dwindled to fast food joints? When she was younger, people used to remark on her potential, both hers and Yannick's, like the world was just waiting for them to take hold of it and shape it. But the world, although it's been receptive enough to her brother's will, keeps rejecting her attempts to mould it.

"Maybe I should've gone to business school," she says, looking at the chipped tangerine nail polish on her toes. "Like Yannick. I should've just gotten a job in finance."

With squinty-eyed attention, Ben applies the band-aid to the inside edge of her foot. "The financial sector is where the worst of humanity go to fondle each other. Everyone knows that."

"Yannick's not smarter than me. I could do what he does!"

"You want to be like your brother? Whose job is morally bankrupt? Full of gross exploitation and theft."

"Hey," she says, jerking her foot free from his grip, "you're the one stealing bagels all the time."

Ben shakes his head, didactic in his manner, and pulls her foot back onto his lap. "It is not immoral to steal from Caesar."

She shouldn't have brought up her brother. Ben and Yannick manage to get along, for her sake, but they don't understand each other. There's no point talking with one about the other. The guy whose wardrobe consists of exactly one pair of boots, two pairs of pants bought from the Salvation Army, and T-shirts bought in packs of three will never see the world from the same perspective as the guy who chooses which of his two-hundred-dollar dress shirts to slip on in the morning.

"Your brother is soul sick, Joly."

"What does that mean?"

"He's drinking all the time . . . "

"Only on weekends."

"He looks five, maybe ten years older than he is."

"Because he's tired. He works a thousand times harder than you or I do."

"A slave to his greed."

"Greed? He plans to retire in a few years. Freedom Forty! How is that greedy?" She shoves her foot back into her flip-flop, even though the bandaid isn't sitting right.

"Wasn't this originally a Freedom Thirty plan?"

"Yeah. But that was a bit unrealistic."

"And then a Freedom Thirty-Five plan?"

"There were unforeseen expenses." She collects her phone and the bandaid wrapper, and chucks them into her bag.

"Soon it'll be a Freedom Fifty thing. Then Freedom Sixty. Those golden handcuffs will shackle him until his death." Ben stands up beside her. "And he won't even mind—because his soul is sick, Joly."

"Maybe everyone's is."

AT BEN'S PLACE, they skip the movies and drop straight into his bed, his nest—a thin foam mattress that sits directly on the floor. No sex tonight, no one's in the mood. It's too hot up here anyway. Ben, as ever, falls asleep within a minute, but the heat keeps Joly awake.

She fidgets next to Ben for about an hour, then pops right out of the bed. There's an A/C at home, and a better mattress, and no looming breakfast conversation about the state of her pregnancy. She leaves his house before the subway stops running, and Ben sleeps too deeply to notice her go.

11

THE LIGHTS ARE on in the kitchen when Joly gets home. Under their beaming glare, on the wooden floor, is Yannick, lying face down in front of the stainless steel oven. Drunk from the look and smell of him, and trying to cook a frozen pizza. But he must have passed out during the wait, because the oven is starting to smoke.

"Jesus, Yannick."

He stirs, but not into consciousness. She turns off the oven and leaves its door open to let the heat and smoke escape. He used to do this sort of thing all the time when he was first starting to drink. At seventeen, he and his buddies made their first fake IDs—they scratched out the last digit of their birth year on their driver's licences and edited in an earlier year with a marker. A crude job, but one club or another always let them in. After a night spent lighting up some dirty club, Yannick could rarely find his house key when he got home, so he'd shuffle in through a window. Or, when the degree of his intoxication precluded this feat, he'd rap-rap-rap on Joly's bedroom window until she staggered down to unlock the back door. Then came the stumbling clatter in the kitchen. This thing with the pizzas burning in the oven—it's happened at least a dozen times. But not much since their teenage years. Must have had a rough night.

"Hey Yannick," she says, more softly this time. She kneels beside him and shakes his shoulder.

"What? Eh? What is it?"

"You burned your pizza, dummy."

"Ughghgh."

His eyes squint open. As he pushes himself to sitting, Joly notices the crushed lei around his neck. That's right, it was a bachelor party tonight—Hawaiian themed. She remembers him saying something about it. About how "fucking stupid it is to have a bachelor party for a wedding still three months away." The Hawaiian wedding is in September and he, Karen, and Yvie are all making the trip. To Hawaii. Just for the weekend.

The skin on Yannick's face, around his eyes, looks discoloured, almost haggard, way beyond the ordinary flush of drunkenness.

"Well shit." He rubs his eyes, focuses them on the blackened pizza and decides to give it a go anyway, attacking it over the sink so that the charred bits don't crumble off onto the floor.

"Hey," he grunts, then stretches a fist out for a bump. "Baseball tomorrow?"

"What? Yeah!" She jumps up and bumps his hanging fist. "I thought you had to work!"

"Breakthrough with the vinegar assholes."

He looks like he'll be in bad shape tomorrow. But it's hard to tell with Yannick. He has remarkable bounce-back potential. From the pit of drunken depths, he can rise almost miraculously, clawing his way back into competence through an act of brute will. Even now, as he stands yawning over the sink, she can see some force returning to him. His eyes are still wonky, but he's shaking himself into strength.

He yawns again, a chasm opening up in his face, one big, gaping, disgusting expansion of his polluted mouth, and a story idea pops into Joly's head. About a dead hippopotamus. And an overworked businessman, who climbs inside its rotting mouth, just to get a little peace and quiet. Quickly, she grabs a notepad from the clutter on the island and jots down a few notes, a soft cackle breaking out from her throat despite her glum mood.

"What? What are doing?" asks Yannick, waving his last slice of pizza at her notepad. Apart from the scraps in the sink, he has inhaled the whole thing.

"Nothing. Just . . . some notes to myself."

"Job ideas, maybe?" He picks off a burnt pepperoni chunk and flings it into the sink.

"Heh. Sorta," she says, stifling another hearty chuckle. "A story idea."

"Oh dear god." Yannick lets his entire upper body collapse onto the marble countertop.

"What?"

He pulls himself together and points his rigid, half-eaten pizza slice straight at her. "For fuck's sake, Joly!" he bawls. "Can you please, for the love of Christ, just get a real fucking job?"

His voice comes out in such a desperate cry that her pencil drops. The backs of her eyes flood with tears.

"I'm going to bed," Yannick throws the pizza slice into the sink and lurches out of the kitchen.

"Hey!" she calls out after him, when she's sure her voice will hold. "I have *fans!*"

But he's already halfway up the stairs, headed for a crash landing into his giant king-sized bed.

12

THE DAY, AS EXPECTED, is hot, very hot, one of those Toronto-in-the-summer days where it's almost impossible to be outside, where all you can do is lie still where you are. Even the baseball players are sluggish; the game has barely any action.

Joly sits in the shade high above right field amid a small group spread over a single beach blanket. On her right is Lou, who always comes to the ball games. She used to pitch as a teenager. A real hotshot too. To Joly's left is Yannick, who rallied just fine after last night. And beside him sits Anosh, one of his work buddies, making a first-time appearance at Christie Pits. The beach blanket was Anosh's idea. He's wearing designer jeans that he doesn't want "all fucked up with grass stains." He's been complaining about one thing or another since he got here.

"What's with these slow pitchers?"

Joly watches Lou tighten with a thinly suppressed anger.

"They're not slow," says Lou.

"Slower than the Jays pitchers, that's for damn sure. And the Jays aren't even good."

"The Jays have been really good. And this isn't the majors. This is a semi-pro league. That's why it's free."

"Well these guys fucking suck."

This is the problem with Yannick and his friends. They're all cocky and belligerent, made so by their money and by the alcohol they consume. Anosh and Yannick are already on their third beers and it's only the top of the fourth.

"Gotta be hard to play in this kind of heat, though," says Joly.

"It's their fucking *job*," says Anosh, adjusting himself on the beach blanket—he's at the edge after all, and perilously close to having a partial buttock of designer denim fall into direct contact with the grass.

Out on the field, a full count adds some pressure to the no-run game. The next pitch curves to the outside, and after a checked swing, the ump calls it a strike. The call is met with lackluster cheering from the dehydrated, over-heated fans.

"What? Get the fuck outta here," Anosh says. He waves his half-empty can at the field. "That was a ball. By a mile. I guess the semi-pro umpires suck too. Good to know."

"The pitch was good," says Lou.

"You're dreaming."

"Hey, you're talking to an ex–Team Canada baseball player here," says Joly.

"Yeah, buddy," says Yannick. "Lou knows baseball."

"Oh you used to play, did you?" Anosh asks, his tone mocking. He tilts forward to better see Lou at the other end of their little group, and Joly wonders if, in this deranged, combative approach, he's trying to flirt with her. Guys often flirt with Lou. Her wedding ring seems only to encourage them.

"I did," Lou says, the words clipped with irritation.

"You mean softball? Don't girls play softball?" Anosh says.

"No. I don't mean softball, asshole. I mean baseball."

"Whoa, easy there, Lou," says Yannick calmly.

"Well they must not have taught you about good pitching in your little lady league. Because that last pitch was garbage."

Sometimes with Lou, it's like Joly can see inside her brain, and watch the tethers that restrain Lou's rage. She can see when they weaken, when they snap, and right now the tethers are mighty frayed. Lou leans across Joly's legs. "I think you don't know what the hell you're talking about, cool guy."

"Easy, Lou, easy. He's just fucking around," says Yannick. He puts a gentle hand on her shoulder and leaves it there.

"Whoa-ho, touchy, huh?" says Anosh.

It's not a comment that encourages Lou to simmer, and the situation seems poised to devolve into real unpleasantness, but a well-timed distraction usurps the group's attention. Ben. There he is, coming at them with his heavy, lumbering gait.

"Oh hey, hey, look here," Yannick says. "Hey Ben. How's it going?"

Ben shrugs. "I maintain."

"Want a beer?"

"I wouldn't say no to a beer."

Yannick nods him around to his other side, where the bag of beer and the Dixie cups are stashed. Ben pours a can of beer into a cup and heaves himself down behind Joly. His presence must trigger in Yannick thoughts of low-wage, low-skilled jobs, because it's right then that Yannick says, "Oh hey, Joly, you hear back about that shitty barista job yet?"

"I did, in fact." She takes a slow sip of water.

"Oh my god," he says, glaring at her while she hides her face behind the water bottle. "You didn't get it?"

"It's a very competitive job market."

Yannick drains his beer and burps. "Well hang in there, Joly. Soon enough I'm sure you'll manage to land yourself the exact same job you had as a teenager." He laughs. So does his buddy.

Ben sets a comforting hand on her back, rubbing gentle circles over her shoulder blades. Then he leans in close. "You vanished in the night," he whispers.

"It was hot. I couldn't sleep."

"Matters are pressing, Joly. We were supposed to talk this through today."

"Now? I'm watching a game here."

"Joly," he says, firmly enough to draw a look from Yannick.

If there's going to be a scene, it's better that it happen in private. "Okay, okay, I gotta go back to the car anyway." She's low on water, she's hungry, and there are oranges on the back seat.

So they climb the hill to the street, an arduous few minutes' journey in the pounding sun. At the car, she sits in the back seat so her head is shaded, but keeps the door wide open for air and lets her legs hang out. She peels an orange.

Ben stands on the sidewalk a few feet away. "I thought we were having breakfast."

Joly piles the orange peel onto her lap and bites into a segment, which squirts and drips. She leans forward to let the juice fall onto the pavement.

"Now look, doll, I know you don't want to talk about this, but that's not an option. This is time-sensitive."

"Mm-hmm." But she's distracted by the dribbling juice. It's

all over her hands, every finger sticky. She's never encountered an orange this juicy. Does heat cause the juice inside the fruit to expand and act up?

"Joly. Can you look at me? Can you pay attention?"

She drops the whole mess of orange onto the ground and looks at him. "You want me to abort it. I get it."

They stare at each other. It's a contest that lasts at least a minute before Ben yields to his mounting frustration.

"I don't know what I'm supposed to do," he says. "It's your decision, that's how this works. But I'm on the record as a strong, very definite no."

"Yeah, I get that. Loud and clear."

"It is irresponsible." He puts a hand on her shoulder and looks her dead in the eye. "We are not in any position to be having a kid."

"But people in far worse positions have kids all the time," Joly says, wriggling free from his grip.

"Yeah, and everywhere I see the result of people who had kids they were unable to provide for. Kids they didn't want. Those kids turn out fucked, Joly."

"But maybe I *do* want her."

Joly climbs out of the car, picks up the orange peel, and chucks it into some nearby bushes. She wipes her sticky hands on the leaves of the bush. When she turns back to him, she feels the full force of the sun. "Life can't be this difficult. We're conjuring up all kinds of difficulties."

"We're not conjuring them. They exist."

"But this is one of the richest countries in the world! I mean, just the other day . . . okay, I was reading this article about this skyscraper slum in Venezuela, this tower. And families, good honest families, with kids and stuff, are living there. And they're making it work. I'm not saying that's ideal or anything, I'm just saying—well, our perspective is a bit skewed up here. Our perspective about how much we need to get by."

"Venezuela? You mean that Tower of David? In Caracas?"

"Yeah!" she says, startled that he knows what she's talking about. "That's right."

"But they cleared out that squat. No one lives there anymore."

Joly's brain functioning slows. "What?"

"Yeah. The government went in and threw everyone out. Relocated them."

"When? To where?" The news punctures something inside of her. She can feel the deflation in her lungs. Her breathing turns shallow.

"I don't know. It was news. Some time ago. You're the one talking about it. Don't you know?"

She only read the one article about the place. A feature article, several thousand words, plus a slideshow, but just the one. And she didn't check its date. Ben reads the news every day, multiple outlets. "But how could they just evict them? There were thousands of people—they'd built up a whole community in there."

"Well. It's gone. That's how things go. Not that it matters anymore anyway. Since millions of people have fled the country in the last few years. That's what you should be concerned about."

"But Jesus." How stupid she is. Romanticizing a movement, drawing real-world inspiration from a situation that already doesn't exist anymore. How terrifically fucking stupid.

"I don't know why you'd expect anything different. This is the way of our world. This is Babylon, baby. We're all living in Babylon."

Over Ben's shoulder, Joly sees Yannick plodding toward them on what must be a beer run. She shakes her head through the heat. "But wait, hang on, this is crazy. Where did they put those people?"

"Housing projects. In towns outside the city, if I'm not

mistaken. I forget exactly where. But outside the capital. So that it was *entirely* inconvenient for them to get to work."

"They just split them all up?" She can hear her own voice hitting shrill decibels. "They scattered them?"

"Look, why are we talking about this? Can we focus here?" Ben's voice bumps up in volume as it chases hers.

This moment of raised voices coincides with Yannick's arrival at the car. "What are you two fighting about?"

"Nothing," she says.

"Let me guess: which brand of communism to shill?" He laughs at his own joke.

"Shut up," Joly says.

"Which communist dictator to worship?"

"Stop it."

"Lenin or Stalin?"

"Fuck off, Yannick."

"Maybe Mao?"

"We're fighting because I'm pregnant, you fucking asshole."

Her brother faces her, emitting residual laughter for another second. But then his face morphs in the most abrupt change of expression she's ever seen from him.

"You gotta be fucking kidding me, Joly," he says.

She keeps stone-faced, but offers a slight shake of the head.

"What the hell are you thinking?"

"I didn't do it on purpose!"

Yannick scrunches his eyes and when he opens them, he shoots them straight at Ben. "And you, Ben! For Christ's sake, what business do you have getting anyone pregnant? How the hell are you going to support a baby?"

Ben's big head drops an inch and waves of his long dark hair flop forward over his face.

Nobody wants this baby. Nowhere is there a flicker of excitement. And really, maybe she doesn't want it either. What she's feeling might be nothing more than a biological mechanism firing off, like hunger pangs or a circadian rhythm, and like these, it can be overridden for the moment. It's not like she's spent her life pining for children. She's never been sure which way she wanted to go with that. What if she has the baby, over all objections, only to discover she has no aptitude for motherhood, no interest even? Then with no money, no house, no job, no prospects, no talents, she'll come to resent the kid—a little boy after all. And the stress of having the screaming, unwanted infant will, of course, annihilate any love left between her and Ben, who will disappear into a monastery, where he can spend the rest of his life alone and atoning. The kid meanwhile, starved right from the get-go for affection and security, will grow up to become one of the world's wretched. A kid that turns out fucked. It will happen just like Ben says it will. Or it could at least. It's conceivable. And doesn't that make it too great a moral risk?

"Don't worry, Yannick," she says, unable to look at Ben. "I'm not gonna keep it."

Her brother false starts on a few sentences, but finally he goes with: "Jesus! I just came up here to get beer. I need a beer."

He takes a can from the cooler in the trunk, cracks it, and slugs half of it in a go. The few remaining cans he drops into a cloth shopping bag and without another word, disappears back toward the hill and ball game.

When Joly finally looks at Ben, his cheeks are puffed out, but slowly deflating. He exhales his enormous relief.

FIFTEEN MINUTES LATER, after Ben has left, after Joly told him to get lost, she's back on the grassy hill next to Lou—the other side of Lou this time, as far as possible from her brother. The whole configuration of the group has changed, in fact.

In her absence, Anosh seized on the opportunity to move to the very centre of the beach blanket, either to better protect his jeans or to get closer to Lou. Yannick and Joly are out on the flanks now, both on the bare grass.

Joly lies on her stomach, hiding her face in the grass to mask the tears that go unnoticed by Lou, who's busy disputing some fundamentals about women's athletics.

"No one wants to pay real money to see women's professional sports," Anosh is saying. "That's the bottom line. So there's no point to them."

"That's insane. Plenty of people like women's sports."

"Then why don't they make any money?"

"They do. Just not as much. And that doesn't mean there's no point to them."

"It does. And more than that, it means there's no point in even funding amateur programs for women. It's a waste of resources." He crushes his beer can and tosses it onto the grass. "And it gives false hope to those girls."

"Are you out of your mind?" Lou says. She looks at his discarded can and adds, "And can you not litter in a public fucking park?"

Anosh kicks the beer can her way. "Look, it's simple supply and demand."

"Sports aren't just about economics."

"Of course they are. All the good ones anyway." Anosh stands up, with a grin, like he's won this idiotic argument, and he marches down the hill to the bathrooms.

"Hey!" Lou calls out to him as he goes.

He turns back to look at her. "Mm?"

"Your jeans look really fucking stupid."

Joly wipes her wet nose and cheeks on the grass. Lou will have to take her to the clinic; Ben's presence would make it unbearable. It will be a simple inversion of their last visit. Although she and Lou are twice as old now, a baby still seems no more feasible than it did then. This time Joly will be the one called upon to display a stoic determination while she is freed of this spark of life. But she won't take it nearly as well.

13

ON THE CAR ride home from the park, Joly stares out the window at the passing city and listens to rap music she doesn't recognize while her brother drives. The satellite radio in the car is forever tuned to this channel, rap being Yannick's preferred genre since he was a preteen and blasting Young MC in his bedroom, busting out the lyrics in front of the mirror while Joly looked on in stitches. She never got the hang of rap. She and Lou grew up into grunge music and flannel shirts.

Although Yannick stopped drinking after that fourth beer, and although they stopped to grab tacos down at a place on College St., his blood alcohol level is still definitely on the illegal side of the limit. But he's in much better shape to drive than she is. So he's behind the wheel, heading south toward the Gardiner Expressway.

"Hey listen," Yannick says, "I reacted badly. It's not like it's terrible news."

"It's not good news."

"It could be, though. If you wanted it. You don't have to get rid of it."

"I think I do."

"But if it's just a money thing, we can help, you know that, don't you?" His elbow hangs out the open driver's side window, his fingers mindlessly tapping out the beat against the frame. "You should do whatever you think is right. Obviously. But if it's just about money. We have money . . ."

"You help me enough," says Joly.

"You'd help me if situations were reversed."

"But they'd never be reversed. That's the thing."

"No," he says flatly. "That's true."

They travel on southward until Joly can see the lake shimmering up ahead.

"It'd be good if Yvie had a little cousin," Yannick continues. "They could grow up together. She needs someone to beat up on anyway. It'll toughen her up."

His kindness is threatening to bring on a fresh batch of tears. Joly stares hard out the window, working to suppress the flow. She can feel Yannick sneak glances at her. "What's that shitty grunge station you like?"

"Lithium."

Yannick fiddles with the satellite radio console, adding distracted driving to impaired driving. But he is practised in these arts. Soon angsty '90s rock music pours from the speakers.

Once up on the Gardiner, they set forth through the corridor of condos that rise up alongside them. It's one after another glass and concrete tower, built so close to the expressway, within metres of it, that you can see people in their living rooms, can even make out their haircuts. Up and down these towers, people are sectioned off into little units, never having to speak with their neighbours, never being called upon to form a neighbourhood.

"I hate these condos," Joly says.

"No one likes them."

"Well some people must. There's, like, a million of them."

"Yeah, but nobody *likes* them."

"What do you mean?"

"Karen says average occupancy in these towers is like two years. So no one really takes care of them. Upkeep on them is shit. And construction isn't even good to begin with. They're built to fall apart."

"Really?"

"Makes sense though, right? Who would live here long term? Right by the highway? Fucking nightmare."

"Huh," says Joly, feeling the heavy *fuck-you* thump of a Rage Against the Machine anthem in her chest.

"Yeah, some realtors have called them slums in the making. Fifty years from now, this whole corridor will be one long, shitty, waterfront slum." Yannick is becoming talkative. Maybe it's the alcohol. But more likely it's the relief of having hit on a topic of conversation free of emotional strain.

A Honda makes an abrupt move into the lane ahead of them, forcing Yannick to tap the brakes. "Fucking dick," he mumbles, then rides his horn until the Honda veers back over to the right, chastened.

"But look at all these buildings," Joly says, gesturing with both arms to the row of condos moving past them on both sides, the walls of glass fired up by the evening sun. "That's a pretty big slum you're talking about."

"People keep flooding into this city. With no money and no-where to go. I could see it. I could see it happening."

"Just fifty years?" she asks.

"Yeah, but hey, on the bright side, in fifty years, you and I will both be dead."

Joly looks up at the buildings and imagines them trans-formed by time and circumstance from the aspirational homes of the young and (sort of) financially solvent into towers of vertical squalor. She pictures denizens leaning out of broken windows in the summer heat, because the A/Cs have long stopped working. Or standing side by side on their crumbling balconies catching the breeze off passing trucks. Fifty years doesn't seem like a long time for a booming sector of the city to turn into a slum. But maybe that's just how things go. They fall apart.

Book Two

LOUISE

—
1
—

LOUISE WATCHES THE firm pads of his fingertips run up the insides of her thighs. When he reaches her hips, he brushes his thumbs across the mouth of her cunt, before he switches directions, drawing his thumbs down along the outside of her legs, with decisive pressure, digging deep into the muscle the way she likes. She focuses on the path of his thumbs as they approach her knees. When she was younger and still playing baseball, she used to have power in her limbs, a defined musculature that could easily be traced and marvelled at. She flexes her quadriceps against his hands to feel what remains of that strength. She's still fit, she keeps in shape, but she's no athlete anymore. She's aging.

Yannick keeps with this up-and-down business on her thighs, punctuated by the teasing brush at the centre, and by the time he rises to fuck her, she is well past ready for it. As, clearly, is he.

"Oh god, yeah," he says upon entry. "That's fucking good."

Yannick's chatty during sex. He likes to update her on how it's all going, how it's all feeling for him, and he likes for her to reciprocate this running commentary, to validate his efforts. But Louise prefers sex without dialogue.

"That's good, isn't it?" he says.

"Mm," she says.

"You like that?"

"Mm."

The hotel sheets against her back are soft, very soft, high thread count. It's a small boutique hotel that serves as the location for these extramarital trysts—Yannick knows the manager. She doesn't know what Yannick's exact arrangement is, but they get this room in this pricey hotel for an hour or so whenever they want it. Nobody raises an eyebrow. The place is a huge improvement on the venues of their earliest fucks, when they were teenagers stealing moments in the backs of cars in empty lots.

YANNICK WAS ONE of Louise's first lovers. Not the very first—that distinction, unfortunately, went to a pervy baseball coach. Nor was Yannick the second or third—those were a short-term high school boyfriend who, astonishingly for a teenage boy, had erectile difficulties, and the butchy centre fielder on her baseball team who browbeat her into believing she might be a lesbian. For all those early experiences lacked, they stoked a profound curiosity. She experimented. Widely. She does well with men. They like her.

But Yannick was the first to introduce her to any real sexual satisfaction. He sought to please her. And he didn't treat her—the way many of the white guys she later fucked did—as a novelty. He didn't look at her a little too wide-eyed when it came time to undress, wasn't a little too curious about what shade her nipples would be, what her cunt would feel like, a little too expectant for some unknown but definitely extant cultural difference in the imminent sex. That sort of thing happened on the regular, but it wasn't until the second time a man playfully remarked on his "yellow fever" that she recognized this attention for what it was. After that she took precautions. She devoted hours to the effort to play down her Japanese-ness and highlight the British and Spanish heritages instead. Not that it did much good. She's inherited all of Mai's features. Her half-Japanese mother is present all over her face. And although this ancestry makes up only a quarter of her genetic code, no matter what she does, how she cuts her hair, how she dyes it, styles it, what kind of makeup she puts on, leaves off, she always skews at least a little Asian.

"Jesus Christ, you've got my dick so hard," Yannick says.

"Mm."

"You're gonna make me come, Lou."

"Mm."

"Wait, wait, slow down."

But it's not Louise who's setting pace at the moment, so he must be talking to himself. That's fine. Better to himself than to her. And he does slow down. Also fine. It's always a series of fast and slow, fast and slow, with Yannick.

They've been fucking on-and-off for over fifteen years. In their teenage days, it was simple clandestine physical explo- ration, never anything close to coupledom. And although no romantic bond ever developed, neither did the physical chemistry ever wane, and so they kept screwing each other through the years, breaking off for long stretches when one or the other of them moved out of town, or started a new re- lationship, or just got sidetracked and lost touch. She thinks of Yannick sometimes as a forgotten, but familiar food. A food that trends for a while, then falls out of favour, only to be resurrected a few years later and put back into the rotation.

Like a mango. Uncommon enough to be interesting, but not so uncommon that it ever seems wholly new. That's how it is with Yannick. He's a mango.

The clandestine nature of their relationship has endured too. Louise has never mentioned it to anyone, not even Joly. She thought it was a simple fling at the start and so saw no point in creating any weird tensions around the situation. Then too much time passed to mention it without awkward and lengthy explanations. And now that the affair is adulterous (on both sides) . . . well, she'll never tell anyone about it now.

"Hang on a second," Yannick says. "I want you up like this." He pushes himself up to a kneel and drags her hips up onto his thighs, her legs over his shoulders, for a different, deeper angle. "You like that?" he asks.

"Mm," she says.

She does like it. She likes when their positions become acrobatic, testing her flexibility and finding it intact. He has a tendency to showboat with these preliminary positions, but she doesn't mind obliging, so long as she eventually finds her way on top for the finish. That's when she becomes demanding and decisive because that's when she can best get off.

It's maybe ten minutes before she finds herself in charge and on top. She closes her eyes and focuses on the exquisite pressure building inside her. When she's this close to an orgasm, it's almost possible to forget about Yannick altogether, in a way she never quite manages with Elliott. Sex with her husband is too cluttered with emotion—or it used to be, when he still bothered to fuck her. She could never empty out her head with him. And it's empty-headedness that she likes best. The pure physicality of body against body. The freedom of abandoning the mental, succumbing to the physical: it's fundamentally athletic.

When the pressure reaches an absolute maximum, she pushes off him to allow the flood of her orgasm to expel from her cunt, carrying along with it all thoughts in her head. She's only faintly aware of things in the following minutes, of the mess she made on the towel beneath them, which they put there for this very purpose, and of him re-entering her, and pumping fast, and saying, "Oh god, here it is, here it is!"

And then there it goes. But not before he pulls out, as she's instructed him to do, because, although she's on the pill, she's adamant that coming inside of her is a strictly marital privilege, reserved only for Elliott, as though she might some day be able to point to this oh-so-faint line she's drawn in the sand and save herself from the severest of judgments.

Yannick aims for the towel, but misses and hits the sheets instead, which someone else will strip and clean, which she always feels bad about.

She lies on her stomach. He rests a hand on her ass cheek.

"That was really fucking hot," he says.

"Mm-hmm."

They relax like this on the bed for a minute or two before the alarm on his phone goes off. He always sets an alarm, which usually only sounds once they're done, but sometimes happens to go off right in the middle of things, just as they're really delving into it, and the hanging threat of that alarm gives their meetings the peculiar feel of a therapy session, like at any time, no matter what might be transpiring at that moment, what is being exposed, they're liable to be interrupted by the gentle, but conclusive *ding-ding, time's up.*

Obedient to the alarm, Yannick pops out of the bed and into the shower, grabbing soap from his bag along the way. He brings his own soap to the hotel, a familiar scent from home, so that Karen won't sniff out the affair. It's a smart idea, he's smart about things, but Louise foregoes this precaution.

No point. Elliott doesn't pay enough attention to her.

While Yannick showers, Louise lies still, reflecting on the lingering effects of her orgasm. Her limbs feel drained, but heavy. No part of her moves or shifts or even twitches, because no part of her, not a shoulder, an arm, or a finger, registers anything less than perfect comfort. Her breathing is slow. She's tired, almost exhausted. Her orgasms used to be different. Clitoral. More invigorating, but limited to the higher registers. Melody orgasms, she thinks of them. But these vaginal orgasms, these are bass orgasms, these make her feel like her body is tuned to some primal vibration, like she's in chorus with the low hum of chanting monks.

It's a development she's pleased with on the whole. Though she read once that the vaginal orgasm is a sign of maturity, which means of aging, which means of death. Her body is changing, like it's getting ready for something. For illness? For collapse? Her left leg twitches. Then her arm. And just like that, a noticeable and familiar discomfort fans out across her body. Sickness and early death have always preoccupied her, but the preoccupation has been worse lately, transformed into an obsessive dread. It's her upcoming birthday, that's what's doing it. Her thirty-third. That beacon of terror draws nearer and nearer, looking ever more horrifying the closer it gets. In a little over a week she'll be thirty-three, a bad age to be, the absolute worst age for her to be, because thirty-three was the age at which Mother Mai died. And Louise, a dead ringer for her dead mother, has always in some shadowy part of her soul believed—*known*—that she will not make it past that benchmark either.

Yannick bounds out of the bathroom, moving with hyper-efficiency. He yanks on his boxers and suit pants and breezes into his button-down shirt. "Gotta go," he says, almost apologetically, as though she has ever once complained about his abrupt departures. "It's this vinegar deal. We're trying to sell off this vinegar company. It's been one headache after another."

"I thought you were selling a windows company. A windows manufacturer."

That's what he told her last time they met. She's sure she remembers windows.

"No, we're *buying* the windows company. Or looking to. We're working out a leveraged buyout with them. Separate headache."

"Hm."

"But we're selling the vinegar company. And that's the real fucking nightmare. Because their guys are being assholes."

"Hm."

"Incompetent assholes."

Yannick leans over her and kisses her, hard, on the mouth, tugging on her lips, and then he's gone. After her own shower, she stands naked in front of the bathroom mirror, studying herself, the breasts especially. Does everything look okay? As it always has? For now, maybe. But things deteriorate quickly. Healthy one month, sick the next, dead the month after that. That's how it went with Mother Mai, so why wouldn't it be the same for her? Why wouldn't the time bomb in Mai's breast tissue have passed into Louise's genetic makeup? That bomb must be locked inside her cells right now, ticking, ticking, ticking, just waiting for the trigger—the biological age, the particular palindromic signal—that will set off the internal explosion.

2

THE ROOF OF St. Michael's Cathedral is newly hand-painted, twilight blue with 18,000 gold-leafed stars. A solicitous middle-aged woman explained about the stars (along with a thousand other details of the recent restoration) to Louise after her second appearance at the noon-hour Mass. "You can buy the stars," the woman explained upon catching Louise staring up at the ceiling, open-mouthed and dead-eyed. "Well . . . claim them. By making a donation." Then, with a finger waving into the vacuum above them: "Mm . . . that one there. No, no, wait . . . that one. That one's mine. So you can't have *that* one."

Attending these masses is another thing Louise does in secret. Because isn't it foolish, even passé, to be a true believer? Her submission, however minimal, to the Church comes with a brick-load of embarrassment. But the Catholic cathedral, located a few blocks from her office, kept popping up on her lunch hour meanders until one day, earlier in the summer, she meandered right in through the open doors, desperate for any kind of salvation from the horror of another ordinary workday.

Today's priest is young and fit, with excellent posture, and he is exuberant in his reading of the scripture, all of which makes it easier for Louise to pay attention. But it does nothing to bring clarity to the content.

"The kingdom of heaven is like treasure hidden in a field, which someone found and hid; then in his joy he goes and sells all that he has and buys that field," reads the priest with a friendly voice that bounces around the sparsely populated pews.

None of the readings ever make sense to Louise, but the parables are among the worst offenders. She has not comprehensively understood a single one of them, not even with the guidance of the priests. The parables come and go too quickly. Before she can even start to grapple with one, Jesus has already zipped on to a fresh metaphor that is similarly impossible to understand. It's shoddy communication. Louise would be fired if she ever wrote copy like this.

"Again, the kingdom of heaven is like a merchant in search of fine pearls; on finding one pearl of great value, he went and sold all that he had and bought it."

But she tries very hard to understand the readings, because there must be something to all of this. Thousands of years of theological scholarship must have turned up a few nuggets of metaphysical wisdom. And with her death just about imminent now, she has started to worry about the Big Questions, about the moral reckoning that might soon take place. Because if there *is* a grand accounting at the bitter end, some metric used to measure the worth of one's life, she's pretty sure that, as things stand, she'll come up short. Way short. And it's getting late to make up that ground.

But despite a rapt attention to the readings and ensuing sermon, Louise once again understands almost nothing. Soon she tilts her head back to study the stars on the ceiling, which remind her of the glow-in-the-dark stars in her childhood bedroom. When the mass eventually moves into quiet prayer, sitting in these pews is almost like being in a planetarium. In fact, had the city's planetarium not closed years ago, she might well have wound up there instead, finding comfort in her own complete cosmic insignificance rather than in the murky promises of the Church.

WHEN LOUISE EMERGES from the cathedral to face the brutal sensory assault of the city centre, she has to force her feet back toward the office tower. But with each step it becomes more apparent that she simply can't go back to work today. The thought of returning to the office dweebs and the passive-aggressive emails and the meetings and meetings and meetings, it all prompts an acute queasiness.

This career in marketing—billboard space in particular—is wreaking havoc on her system. She spends her days working up ways to advertise advertising space, doing her part in the mass effort to push increasingly susceptible populations into buying shit they don't need. It's a career of coercion and Louise excels at it. But it's making her nauseous.

"Hey Nicky, it's Lou," she says into her phone, speaking in her flat workplace affect. "Listen, I'm not feeling well. I just threw up in an alley." Only a mild exaggeration.

"Oh god. Well . . . are you all right?"

"I might have caught a bug." This is the most effective lie, because Pregnant Nicky is terrified of contagion.

"Okay, Lou. You just go home, all right? Don't come back in today."

"Are you sure, Nicky? I might be able to tough it out."

"No no. No, absolutely not. I'll cover for you. But if you can, Lou, at least try to finish the ABPP report? Rob doesn't want to let the grass grow long on this one."

"Mm, I mean, I'll try. But he's asking for fairly in-depth analysis. And honestly . . . is this even our department's responsibility?" Louise says, even though she finished the Audio Billboard Pilot Project report days ago.

"I'm with you, Lou. He's not being completely reasonable. But he's getting a lot of pressure from higher up. And that's cascading down. Just see what you can do, okay?"

"Sure, I'll try to crank something out."

3

ALTHOUGH IT'S ELLIOTT'S turn to cook dinner, Louise is seasoning the chicken breasts and minding the rice pot, because Elliott is "working" tonight.

"I'm not saying I *won't* do it," he told her when he got home from the framing shop he manages. "I'm just saying I'll do it later. We'll eat late. Spanish-style, my senorita. You'll love it."

"But I'm hungry *now*. I put in a long day."

"Eat a banana," he said and shrugged, then brushed his lips across her cheek—not enough effort for an actual pucker—and vanished into the study to edit his latest batch of wedding photographs, a one-time weekend hobby that has metastasized into something more like a career. He was supposed to be a photojournalist, that's who he was when she met him. He documented what was going on the world: the corruptions and injustices and arbitrary sufferings. He was passionate about that work. He told her once he didn't think he could change the world—that was a naïve expectation—but that at the very least he could bear witness to the grief of the abject. That's what he said: "the grief of the abject." But weddings, it turns out, pay more.

She smothers the chicken breasts with turmeric powder, because turmeric is a superfood. Remarkable antioxidant properties. This turmeric, though, is ancient—the tin dented, the label flaking off. There's no scent left at all. Her father's turmeric. Everything in this old kitchen belonged to her father—and to Mother Mai—every dish, utensil, spice jar, and oven mitt occupying the same spot it did thirty years ago, the entire set-up neatly ossified in place.

With the chicken in the oven and nothing else to do, nobody to talk to, a flurry of hypochondriacal thoughts zip through Louise's head. She pings into and out of the living room, dining room, foyer, kitchen. Her left eye keeps twitching, the bottom lid. And she's light-headed again, the world teetering around her.

But she skips her anti-anxiety pills tonight. She only got them after her fourth panic attack landed her in a doctor's office—easier to accept prescriptions than put up a fight. But she doesn't like the Xanax. And she doesn't like the clonazepam. Brutal side effects, especially on the libido. The pills obliterated her interest in the one activity she still wholeheartedly enjoys. Besides, there's no defect in her brain. This chronic anxiety is induced by moral failing, not mental illness. She *should* be anxious—because there's not a single thing she can point to in her little life that will commend her to a Great Beyond.

Elliott. She used to think he would serve as her something Good. For hours and hours she'd listen to him recount the horrific shit he'd seen abroad. He'd rail on and on about, say, the depths of poverty in Bangladesh, where he'd spent a lot of time before they met; he'd rant about the exploitation of that country's factory workers. And Louise thought he was a rare man doing something of actual use and importance—really wrestling with the horrors of this chaotic world. She thought loving him, supporting him would be enough to redeem her in some way. But there's no rub-off redemption from a wedding photographer.

Calm down, calm calm calm. Sweat is pouring from her body. She steps outside to catch her breath, but the night is humid. No oxygen anywhere. She reminds herself that the dread seeping outward from the centre of her chest is familiar. Normal, almost. It always happens around sundown, once the day has ended and the new one threatens to begin. It's the dread of the inevitable return to work. It'll pass. Once she's smoked her evening joint. If she can just light it. *Come on, come on, steady.* Her hands are so jittery it takes three tries before the joint catches.

In the depths of the dark yard, beyond the low fence: a shadow, moving. What? What is it? An apparition? Mother Mai used to see things and hear things—being-type things—in the weeks before she died. She kept telling Louise to "look, look right there! Do you see them, do you hear them?" Neither Louise nor her father had any idea what Mai was talking about when she implored them to look and listen. The cancer had spread to her head by the end and they took irregularities in her behaviour to be the delusions of a damaged brain.

But something is definitely lurking in the yard. The shape eludes focus, but it *is* there. Looming. Stalking. Louise is locked rigid on the top step.

Her phone erupts. In fits and jerks on the deck.

"Fuck! Jesus!"

Her hand grasps at her heart thrashing against her ribs. She inhales, wheezing.

"My boobs, Lou!" wails Joly's high, thin voice over the phone.

"What?"

"My boobs. Are huge. They've never been this big before. Not even that year I was fat. And last night . . . I felt the baby moving."

"You're eight weeks. You can't feel a baby at eight weeks."

"I *swear* I could. I felt her foot."

"*It* probably doesn't even have a proper foot yet."

Emboldened by an ally on the phone, Louise ventures toward the back of the yard, from where she can now hear a low rustle. Quiet in her approach, light on her toes, she spots the source: a deer, just a deer. She gets within a few metres of the animal before it jerks its head and disappears between the trunks of the maple trees, and Louise is left alone at the very back of the yard.

"Then her head!" screams Joly. "I felt something, Lou. What if I left it too long? It's not right to abort her when I can already feel her moving!"

"But you can't. That's impossible." Louise puts out the joint, half-finished, on the fence post. There's silence on the other end of the line. "Listen to me, Joly. That's gas. Or shit. It's definitely not the tiny collection of cells in your uterus that will be gone in a few days."

"How can you be sure?"

"Eight weeks. It's science."

"I read that it hurts. It's gonna be terrible, isn't it? I'm not good with pain."

"It'll be fine," Louise lies. "You won't even remember it."

She lingers by the fence, gazing into the dark pitch of the forest. She tries to internalize the shadowy quiet of nature, maybe find some peace in it, a calming influence, but nothing works.

LOUISE HAS PROMISED herself never to follow Elliott into his office, seeking him out like a puppy wanting a pat on the head, but it's a promise she has broken a thousand times. Tonight is no exception.

Taking a few steps into the office, she glances over his shoulder at the photograph on the monitor, a happy couple mid-kiss at the altar. Directly above them, in the stained glass windows, hangs Jesus, mid-crucifixion. Elliott has set the shot so that the sacrificed saviour's feet sit right above the couple's kissing heads, while the two thieves, bony-kneed, edge the frame. She hopes Elliott has done this on purpose, an ironic statement on wedded bliss.

"Interesting shot," she says.

"Needs tweaking," he says.

"I like Jesus's face. Real fun and festive. Good wedding stuff."

Elliott turns his pale boyish face toward her. Six years older, but not aging nearly as noticeably as she is. No misery has yet inscribed itself on his face. Only a few well-placed wrinkles around the eyes and forehead that chisel a hint of gravity into his youthful features. He's still beautiful. "It needs work."

When he turns back to his computer, she starts to sift through the piles of glossy brides and grooms on his desk, looking for any of his old journalism photographs. There was once a series on a garment factory collapse in Bangladesh. A nightmarish episode. Even after massive cracks were found in the building's foundation, workers were kept inside, forced to stitch together clothes for popular labels—Joe Fresh, Benetton, Walmart—until the place collapsed on their heads. In one particularly wrenching shot, an elderly woman stares at the rubble not with anguish or concern, but with pure exhaustion, such a distilled emptiness in her expression that looking at her made Louise feel sick for a week.

Where *is* that photograph? Where are *any* of his old photographs? They should all be here. On this desk. In these drawers. She wrenches open a drawer and out spills a stream of beaming brides, falling all over the magenta carpet.

Elliott spins around in his chair. "Hey! What's wrong with you? Why are you so squirrely?"

"I'm not." But her quaking hands make it hard to gather up the brides.

"Louie, you need a vacation. I keep telling you."

"I can't get time off work," she says. "I call in sick too much."

"Yeah, because you need a vacation." Elliott swivels back and forth in his chair, watching her clean up. "Mr. Fang was telling me about a nice place he stayed at in Costa Rica. Might be fun? I've got that destination wedding there in the fall."

Louise crawls under the desk to retrieve a last wayward bride. "Why are you always talking to Mr. Fang?" she asks.

"What?"

"Or to Mrs. Eisenberg? Or to Marguerite? Or Dennis? Or any of the neighbours?"

"I'm being friendly. What's wrong with you?

"It's suspicious! These people aren't that interesting." She sets all the photographs back on the desk and slouches against the wall, kicking her legs out in front of her. Then she pulls out her half-smoked joint, relights it, takes a deep draw, and offers it to Elliott, who considers for a moment before accepting.

"Here's something interesting from Mr. Fang," he says. "You know that little rundown grey house? That backs onto the school? Sold for 1.1 million."

"So what?"

Elliott drags a hand through his thick hair. "So it's time to sell, Lou. It's time we moved out of here."

"No. No, I don't agree." She takes back the joint. It's only been three years since they bought the house from her father, after he moved to a small condo way out in the west end, something that better complemented his new snowbird lifestyle. He offered them the house at a generous price, relieved not to have the trouble of cleaning out over thirty-years' worth of accumulated crap. Except for a few pieces of furniture that he took to the new condo, he left them the house as is, as it always was.

"Look at you." Elliott waves a hand up and down her body. "You're miserable."

"Yeah, but not because of this house."

"No? We need to get out of this . . . this . . . suburban purgatory."

"This isn't the suburbs. This is Toronto proper. Says so on our mailing address."

"Don Mills is not the city. It's not downtown. Let's go live among the people."

"Among the people? Elliott. Do you even hear yourself?"

Downtown living might kill her. Even Don Mills is experiencing a devastating population boom. New condos keep materializing, bringing with them more noise, more traffic, more commerce, more *people*. It's a disaster.

"This isn't healthy, us living here like this," Elliott says, gently kicking the sole of her foot. "It's like being in one of those ghost towns, where everything is left frozen in time. It's like Chernobyl, and you're one of those old babushkas still rattling around the place even though everyone else is long gone. Christ, it's still 1989 in this house."

Louise runs her hand over the faded pink carpet, she looks at the kaleidoscope-patterned wallpaper, peeling near the ceiling. "I'll think about it," she says, just to get out of this conversation.

"Good. Now . . . where's my chicken?"

She flips him off, but he grabs hold of her extended finger and touches it to his lips. "Hey, hey, kidding. Come here." He draws her near, and she yields, immediately, hoping that he'll continue to kiss her, touch her . . . fuck her? But as quickly as he pulls her in, he pushes her away. "Just gimme a few more minutes to finish up," he says and pats her ass out of the office.

"1986," she says at the door.

"What?"

"Chernobyl happened in '86. And you know what Chernobyl is now? An animal sanctuary. The animals have all come back, because it turns out that nuclear fallout is much less hazardous than an actual human population. Chernobyl is a haven."

DEEP INTO THE night, Louise roams the house, drifting from room to room, quiet as a ghost. She hasn't slept straight through till morning in weeks. Every night, she's awakened by some new discomfort—a pain in her left side, in her chest, her neck, her throat, her teeth. Not even the pot keeps her asleep.

On her millionth pass through the living room, her eye catches a gilded shimmer from the oak wall unit. Peering at the shelves crammed full of books, she spots the small volume with gold lettering on its spine: a pocket bible. Louise doesn't recognize it, but it must have been here for decades. Whose was it? There's Catholicism on her father's side, a splash of Protestantism on Mother Mai's, but these made only a commercial appearance in her life—Christmas presents, Easter brunches. Did a visiting relative once leave this behind? Or maybe it was gifted to one of her parents by a proselytizing street zealot. It might have arrived as part of a bulk garage sale purchase. Mai liked to hit up the street sales for books at basement prices. A quarter a piece. A dime. There are still boxes and boxes of trashy old novels in the basement. Mai liked to read fiction. So Louise likes it much less.

She pulls the small bible from the shelf and passes a palm over the hard maroon cover, which hangs limply from the frayed remains of its binding. Settling down on the leather couch, she flicks on the reading lamp and gives it a shot. Maybe it'll put her to sleep.

5

TODAY LOUISE'S ATTITUDE is on a rare upswing. Already Friday! She's able to keep herself composed for most of the morning commute. There are only a few moments when the workday dread resurfaces with a searing thrust. When she first cruises onto the highway, for example, it makes an appearance, prompting a brief daydream of being rescued from all this interminable drudgery right here, right now, by a swift, merciful collision with a telephone pole. But that passes.

On the short walk from the parking garage to the office, Louise runs the gauntlet of obtrusive commerce. The electric advertising, the video billboards, the neon storefronts, the loud panhandlers ready to sell, the tittering tourists eager to buy. And up ahead, a block from her office tower, is UpTick Media's home billboard, currently featuring a giant glass of very icy iced tea with a cartoonish bird hovering beside it. The bright bird is the mascot of Zing!® Iced Tea, one of her company's top clients, the first of their clients to venture bravely into the realm of audio billboards.

As she approaches the tower, her steps are slowed by an instinctive self-preservation mechanism. But she pushes on bravely, one foot in front of the other, and then—there it is!—a sudden bouncy voice saying:

"Hot day? How about a cool iced tea? Zing!"

"Hot day? How about a cool iced tea? Zing!"

The voice comes out of nowhere, as though it's been injected straight into her head. Despite knowing the source, despite the endless meetings about how directional sound technology works, despite this being the fourth day that the speakers are up and running, it still jolts her each time she steps through the sound beam. It stops her dead in the middle of the sidewalk.

"Hot day? How about a cool iced tea? Zing!"

She stares up at the billboard and tries to spot the speakers, but they're well disguised. So she drags herself onward and within a few steps the sound disappears. There's some minimal spillover for a foot or two . . . then nothing, like it never happened. Except that she suddenly wants an iced tea.

THE MORNING BRINGS bad news. Very bad news. It's Team Building Day. Shit.

This is much worse than another meeting about the audio billboards and the forever discussions about what hip and edgy approach to take to market them. Louise must have repressed it (reasonable), but now the shock of a day filled with chart paper and acronyms and magic markers and games and an upbeat facilitator has her clutching the edge of her desk in panic.

"You forgot about it?" says Jerry, who sits across from her, already working his way through a bag of morning candy. All day long she listens to his crunching and chewing. He hits up the vending machine three times daily, like clockwork. She's charted his trips: 9:15am, a bag of candy; 1:00pm, chips or pretzels; 3:45pm, a chocolate bar. She had to use his keyboard once. It was covered in Cheeto dusting; her fingers were orange for the rest of the day. "How could you forget about it?" he says. "It's practically a day off."

"I don't know," says Louise, digging her fingertips into her desk. "I must have been too excited."

The kitchen is a-bustle with office drones grabbing coffee and snacks before they are all condemned to Meeting Room 2. The counter and sink are littered with dirty mugs and yesterday's dishes, because these people are animals. Only one clean mug remains in the cupboard. On it, a pug with a Santa hat and the caption: *Feliz Navidog*. This was Neil's—a gag gift, because Neil had no cheery feelings toward either Christmas or dogs, a contrarian stance that Louise appreciated.

Neil was one of her favourite office mates—quiet, reasonable, *and* a little bit funny: a unicorn. But Neil is gone. He took sick leave at the start of the year (cancer, what else?), a diagnosis which came out of left field for the otherwise fit man in his early forties. The prognosis seemed hopeful at first, but reports trickling into the office turned increasingly grim, so Louise was not surprised when the final report arrived a few weeks ago, announcing that he had succumbed, leaving behind two small children and this pug mug. The office drones seemed to take it hard for a day or two, with tearful sessions and disbelieving headshakes, but they've bounced back. Louise, though, finds it hard not to interpret this as an omen: she's next.

She takes a tentative taste of the slop in the coffee pot. Bad. Really bad and bitter. She searches the fridge for milk, maybe cream, anything to mask the burnt, gas-station flavour. A carton of milk on the bottom shelf . . . smells okay. She chances it, adds a healthy splash to her mug and returns the milk to its place, next to a sad-looking ham and cheese sandwich marked *Stephanie*. The name is written on a piece of bright red paper with the Zing!® Iced Tea logo plastered across the top. These notepads are everywhere, popping up like an invasive species: one on top of the fridge, another on Louise's desk, on everyone's desk, because Zing!® Iced Tea sent over a mountain of swag to celebrate the launch of the audio campaign.

When Louise arrives at Meeting Room 2, which for some

reason always smells like decay, as though a litter of rats is forever decomposing in the drywall, she finds the laminate tables arranged into three big clusters. The room is full-up with staff, twenty-five people from across all departments. At a table near the front, Rob, her department head, is waving to the open seat beside him. He's been guarding the spot with his navy blazer, which he once confided—with revolting pride—was bespoke. No surprise he's saved the seat. Rob emails her regularly throughout the day with "goofy" (vaguely sexual) videos or listicles he is "just sure" she'll get a kick out of. He messages her outside of work, "just to chat." He likes to proclaim within earshot that "mixed-race girls are the hottest." He jumps at the chance to offer her a ride home on those rare occasions that she feels obligated to drag herself out for happy hour drinks. Then there's that one time, at the Christmas party, when he asked her how old she was when she lost her virginity. She'd ask him to cool it with this trend, but then he'd be offended, then angry, then spiteful, which would have workplace consequences. She'd ask Stephanie from HR to talk to him about it, but Stephanie from HR is an incompetent lunatic.

"Hey slow dog," he whispers, tapping at his shiny silver Tissot wristwatch. "You're cutting it close, huh?" But he's smiling, then nudging her side with his elbow. Always very liberal with the physical contact.

"Hasn't even started yet," she says.

"Gonna be a long day, huh?" He gives her a bored look, like *isn't this lame*, but Louise knows that Team Building Day is one of his favourite days of the year. A chance to show off for the office dweebs.

"Nice work on the ABPP report, by the way. I took a look at it last night. A few things we'll need to go over . . . maybe we can touch base at the break? Or over lunch?"

Louise is spared a response, because just then,

Stephanie from HR calls: "Good morning, everybody. Good morning." She claps her hands several times to rally attention. "I'm so glad we're having this session today! We really need this one, don't we, guys? I know we're all still struggling with recent . . . um . . . personnel setbacks . . . but this is just the thing we need to lift our spirits!"

In her bumbling, desperately cheerful way, Stephanie introduces the day's facilitator: the middle-aged, box-dyed blonde woman who's been trotting around the front of the room, next to the easel with the chart paper. A fist-sized gold necklace hangs at her jugular notch. Her name is Barbara Mills. And she couldn't be happier to be here with them all today.

After the merry-go-round of introductions, Barbara Mills explains the day's first exercise. "You'll like this one!" she says and starts to weave a path around the tables, carrying three fat manila envelopes. "As you may have noticed, you're already separated into three groups. Now I'm giving each group one of these envelopes. Inside you'll find a jigsaw puzzle." She deposits an envelope in front of Louise with a bizarrely encouraging smile. "First group to assemble their puzzle wins. Simple enough, right?" Barbara nods at each group, then lets her expression turn mischievous. "But you'll discover a few wrinkles as you go. Sound good?"

"Uh . . . quick question," says Keith from IT, whom Louise has long suspected is on the spectrum. He shoots his arm up exactly vertically, his fingers locked firmly together. "Do we all have the same puzzle?"

"That's one of the things you'll have to figure out," says Barbara with a coy smile.

"Follow-up question." He keeps his hand in the air. "If the puzzles are different, are they all at the same difficulty level?"

"Again, that's for you to discover."

"The reason I ask is because the group sizes are uneven. Our group and Rob's group, we're both down a member. Frank's group has an extra person. That's not fair."

"If it helps, I think I count as two people these days," says Nicky with a proud rub of her expansive belly.

Keith stares at the belly with a stern frown. "But your foetus can't help us with the jigsaw puzzle."

"I know that, Keith." Nicky sighs, forcing patience. "It was a joke—"

"And besides, it still wouldn't be fair for Rob's group."

"Why are you calling it *Rob's* group?" asks Mia. "You keep saying *Rob's* group, like he's our leader."

"I don't mind being Team Leader," interjects Rob as he turns on a politician's smile. "I'll throw my hat in the ring."

"Oh . . . were we supposed to appoint team leaders? I think I missed that."

"Piggy-backing on Keith's question," says Frank of the unfairly advantaged team, "should someone from our group sit out to make things more even?"

"No, that won't—" Barbara says, flitting nervously toward their table, her huge necklace thumping against her chest.

"I don't mind sitting out," volunteers Tracy. "I'm terrible at puzzles anyway."

"Oh, thanks Tracy. Thanks for being a team player. We don't want to win because of an unfair advantage."

"What makes you think you'll win, Frank?"

"Always do."

"I don't think anybody should sit out," says Stephanie. "This is *a team building* exercise."

"Do we know what pictures these puzzles are of? Did I miss that part too?"

"I'm not sure. I think that's part of the challenge?"

"Picking up on what the group is saying, it sounds like everyone just wants the game to be fair." Rob is up on his feet, taking full command of the room. "Barbara? Can you ensure that the most difficult puzzle goes to Frank's group? That might allay some of the concerns we've been hearing."

"It's not *Frank's* group either."

"But we haven't established that any of the puzzles are more difficult," says Keith. "That was the point of my question and she—" he flings an arm in Barbara's direction—"hasn't answered it yet."

"Okay everybody, I appreciate all this enthusiasm and engagement," says Barbara, her plastered smile showing some cracks. "Why don't we go ahead and get started and see how it goes. I can assure you the puzzles are all equally difficult."

"Oh, good, okay. I'll sit out then?" says Tracy.

"No, nobody sits out."

"So . . . to clarify . . ."

Ten minutes later, when things have been sorted to nobody's satisfaction, the task begins. It's all mumbles and whispers until Rob, leader that he is, decides to get things going with a bout of assertive hollering: "Okay, okay, I got a corner piece. Who's got edge pieces? We need edge pieces! Over here!"

Louise recognizes the colour schemes on the pieces laid out on the table: three of UpTick's current billboards. Bright red (Zing!), turquoise-and-blue (Euphoria Shampoo), and silver (Hiromi Electronics). Ah-ha, a wrinkle: the puzzle pieces are all mixed up among the groups. They'll have to negotiate with each other to complete this task. When her phone vibrates in her pocket (thank god!) and she excuses herself, Rob and Mia are so engrossed in their argument over strategy that they don't even notice her leave.

"Hey Yannick," she says in the hallway.

"Lou. That was so fucking hot yesterday."

"I'm at work."

"You can't talk for a minute?"

"No. What is it?"

"I've been thinking about it all morning. Yesterday, fucking awesome, wasn't it?"

"Hm."

"I wanna fuck you again."

"Hm."

"You want that, Lou?"

She scans her soul for the guilt she ought to be feeling over this affair. But as usual, she can't locate it. Maybe it's eclipsed by her guilt over a hundred other more severe transgressions—this career, for one. Still, each time with Yannick is supposed to be her last. But already she's craving that singular pleasure he brings about, which spreads through her limbs, uniformly, no blockages in its path, a pervasive hum of pleasure that feels almost like health. "I do."

"I got time next Friday."

Her thirty-third birthday. At least she can count on him not to remember the occasion. He's far too busy, with work and family and with what she suspects is a developing depression.

"Friday," she agrees.

Through the window of Meeting Room 2, she can see that negotiations are underway. Next to the easel, Rob and Frank are deep into a dick-swinging contest, both brandishing puzzle pieces, chests puffed way out.

"Can't wait, Lou," says Yannick.

Louise detours to the washroom, splashes cold water on her face, sits in a stall for a while and reads a news article on her phone—just one quick item before it's back to the perky pits of hell. An update to a story she's been following about suicides at a Foxconn electronics factory in China. Suicide nets had to be erected around the whole building because workers kept throwing themselves off the roof. Now when these workers try to kill themselves, they just rebound off the nets, straight back into the factory, back to work making cell phones, so that these devices can be shipped across the world without delay, directly into Louise's hand so that she can sit in a toilet stall in a billboard marketing office and read all about it. Globalism at work.

When she returns to the buzz of Meeting Room 2, the three puzzles have been assembled and the earlier expressions of consternation have been supplanted with triumph.

"So," says Barbara, flashing a very encouraging smile, "what did this exercise require of you? What qualities did you have to draw on? Let's discuss!" She's holding a blue Sharpie at the ready in front of a crisp sheet of chart paper.

"Oh I think communication was key," says Rob.

Barbara bounces on her toes. "Yes! Communication. Exactly. And we all know how important good communication is in a functioning team, don't we? So let's put that up here." She writes out the word *Communication* on the chart paper in neat block letters, underlining the C, while Stephanie furiously scribbles down notes.

This debrief of critical success factors continues for an eternity until—under Barbara's heavy-handed guidance—a list is compiled and committed to the chart paper in big blue letters.

Communication
Anticipation
Reciprocation
Engagement

"So let's look at what we've come up with here," she says, tapping her chin with the back of the Sharpie as she looks over her list. "You communicated with your teammates—that's

C. Communication." She points at the word with one of her short fingers. "You anticipated their needs—that's A. You reciprocated their energy and commitment. R. And you engaged with them, and with the exercise. E. Engagement. In a word . . ." she swivels on her heels to face them, " . . . you CARE-d." Ta-da.

It's at this point that Louise thinks seriously about throwing herself out the office window.

But! Salvation lies ahead. Because here's one more secret she's been keeping from Elliott: she's on vacation next week. She booked it off months ago, planned it for the week of her birthday, a weak attempt at offsetting the doomsday anxiety. She'd have been happy to share news of a vacation with Elliott, except he'd have made her coordinate it with one of his destination weddings. And that's just impossible.

She used to dream he'd ask her to come with him on his trips—but that was when he was travelling because there was news to report. Issues of global concern that he thought should be broadcast to wide audiences. Not that she'd have been any help to him. The destitute factory workers of Bangladesh probably don't have much use for her stellar billboard marketing skills. But maybe they had no use for Elliott and his photographs either. It's not like he actually accomplished anything with that work—his subjects remain where they've always been, their situation unchanged.

These destination weddings, though . . . a whole other shitshow. Louise can't bear to watch Elliott snap shots of bubbly brides prancing across the Instagram-worthy beaches of a developing country, with perfectly pedicured toes, oblivious or indifferent to the impoverished children begging for pennies on the roadside or coerced into working on inland plantations. She'd spend her entire vacation in feverish distress, wondering why her once-crusading husband no longer cares about these perverse realities.

No, there was no telling Elliott. And now on Monday, when the week begins, she'll simply have to pretend to go to work in the morning, then sneak home an hour later, once he's gone off to the framing shop, so that she can spend the day in peaceful solitude, sitting on the back deck or in the kitchen or lying on the living room floor.

"I know some of you may think this is a bit cheesy," Barbara is saying as she adjusts a fallen bra strap, "and I can see that. It is a little cheesy. But it's also a handy-dandy mnemonic. So let's try to apply the CARE strategy to some common problems you run into here. What are things that come to mind?"

Rob leans toward Louise, his breath on her neck as he whispers, "Bet you're wishing you took that vacation a week sooner, eh?"

But before she can reply, he tosses up a hand, keen to get in on the group discussion. "One problem we've all been banging our heads against is how to market the new audio billboards. We've got a cutting edge service, but we need a killer strategy for the expansion. I'd say that's our top-priority problem."

A small chorus of affirmation breaks out across the room.

"Okay great! Great! Let's see if we can CARE about that!"

MONDAY MORNING LOUISE wakes up with the rare spring and hop of a good mood. She cruises through her morning routine: quick shower, splash of perfume, blazer and silk blouse, solid breakfast of grapefruit, yogurt, and homemade granola. She waits for Elliott to kiss her goodbye, then zips over to the outdoor mall and sits on the patio at Aroma, the coffee shop, revelling in the start of her vacation.

She's got about half an hour to kill at this coffee shop before she can be sure that Elliott has left for work himself. Forty minutes, to be safe. No problem. She's great at killing time—a skill honed during her years of office work. In forty minutes, she'll walk home, leaving the car here for the rest of the workday, just in case Mr. Fang or Mrs. Eisenberg or any of the other neighbours notice it in the driveway and, being "friendly," remark on it to Elliott.

As Louise nurses her black coffee, she watches early shoppers criss-cross the Astroturfed "Town Square" at the centre of the outdoor mall. The coffee shop patio edges this faux-public space, which is owned and operated by corporate interests. 8:45 in the morning and already the mall is piping party anthems in through the outdoor speakers to keep people moving and shopping. No loiterers allowed. No vagrants, no drifters. Only shoppers. The square was built a few years ago when they redid the whole mall—part of the recent Don Mills boom.

Louise looks away from the garish Astroturf and into the depths of her purse, searching for the old pocket bible she packed this morning. When she cracked it open the other night, she had no idea where to start. She flipped through its pages, waiting for divine inspiration to guide her hand, but wound up reading a passage of endless genealogy, which was of no use whatsoever. Now she starts at the beginning, as she would with any book.

The first few chapters of Genesis are familiar: Adam and Eve, Cain and Abel, Noah and the Flood, the story of Babel. But she doesn't know what personal moral lessons to draw from these stories; each is more ambiguous than the last.

On first read, the Babel story seems to be a cautionary tale, a story of divine punishment. God, upset that people are building a city and a tower, punishes them by mixing up their languages. Only it seems less like a punishment, more like a pre-emptive attack, like he's frightened of them. Is God frightened of us?

At a loss, she turns to the internet for guidance, but the search results that pop up on her phone add confusion onto confusion, which causes a creeping irritability that threatens her good mood. Even the word—Babel—is unclear. Its etymology is Akkadian, meaning *Gate of God*. But then . . . in a Hebrew translation, the word Babel is identical to the word Babylon. So if she were reading the bible in Hebrew, there'd be no distinction at all between the Babel of Genesis and the historic Babylon. And in an early Greek translation . . . things are turned on their head again. The word Babel doesn't even exist in that version. Instead, it's translated as *Confusion*. The Tower of Confusion. But how can one word mean both *Gate of God* and *Confusion*? What holiness is to be found in being confused?

She reads the Babel story once more, and when she finishes this third read, she looks at her watch. It's been almost an hour and she's only on page ten.

"JESUS! IT'S LIKE a hotbox in here," says Elliott, popping his head into the bathroom, where Louise is mid-soak in the avocado green tub.

She ashes her joint in the tray on the tub's ledge and watches him push through the thick steam to take a seat on the matching green toilet. Already gone is her buoyant vacation mood. It disappeared sometime during her afternoon nap on the living room floor, which left her with a crick in the neck and aching shoulders. Her eye is still twitching intermittently and there's a ghost of discomfort under her ribcage. Which of these flickers will mark the first sign of total system collapse?

"And what is this smell?" Leaning over the tub, he sniffs at the water blanketed in soapy bubbles. "Lavender?"

"*Mountain* lavender," she says, picking up the small bottle of purple bubble bath, never before used—part of a gift set endowed to her at the office Secret Santa last year. She spotted it in the vanity drawer earlier, next to the toilet paper, and thought: why not indulge? She is, after all, on vacation.

"Why are you taking a bath?" Elliott plucks the joint from her hand and helps himself to a pull. "It's a hundred degrees outside."

"I'm all achy," she says, which is true. She stretches out in the tub, filling it out like a coffin. "My office chair is shit."

Elliott returns the joint to its perch between her fingers, and they sit in silence for a minute, listening to the erratic drip of the leaky faucet.

Drip . . .drip . . . drip, drip, driiiiiip.

"So . . . the house?" he says, watching the droplets trickle from the tap. "You thought any more about selling?"

"What? No." She shifts heavily in the tub, causing the water to slosh.

"You said you'd think about it."

"Hm." But Louise fixes her attention on the bubble bath bottle, reading the label intently. The listed ingredients reveal it to be palm oil–based. No surprise. This stuff is in everything. A few weeks ago, she read an article about how the palm oil industry is riddled with human rights abuses, full of trafficked workers who are carted off to palm plantations deep in remote jungles, where they're hidden from sight, exposed to chemicals that slowly poison them and deform their unborn children, forced into gruelling labour for which they're barely paid—but which *does* produce just the right constituent materials to create a beautiful mountain lavender bubble bath product, the crown jewel in the Serenity Spa Gift Set.

"Louie . . . ?"

"Come on, Elliott." With one long final pull, she polishes off the joint and stubs out the butt. "I had a tough day. I'm worn out."

"You're working too hard."

"Yeah. Definitely."

Elliott frowns at his fingers and picks at the nails, then he searches the medicine cabinet for the clippers. Once he's found them, hidden among god knows what shit in there, he returns to the toilet and clips his nails over the countertop.

Clip, clip. Drip, drip . . . . *drip. CLIP.*

Louise hates the sound of the nail clippers, each *clip* digs into her nervous system, like fingernails on a chalk-board—she's told him so a thousand times.

"Oh hey," he says, working on his ring finger, "were you at Aroma this morning?"

Louise jerks her head to look at him. "Me?"

"Mm."

"Uh . . ." Her stomach tightens under the blanket of lavender bubbles. The heavy steam and lingering pot vapours make it hard to think. "This morning?"

"Yeah."

"Of course not. I was at work."

"Oh. Marguerite thought she saw you on the patio."

"Marguerite's a batty old loon," says Louise, sinking low in the water, taking cover beneath the opaque foam. "Last week she confused me with Alice again." Louise has been mistaken for Alice, the half-Chinese woman who lives on the other side of the block, more times than she can count. But not recently, not by Marguerite.

"No," says Elliott. *Clip, clip.* "She was sure it was you. She said you were scowling."

"Lots of people scowl. And when did you talk to Marguerite?"

"I ran into her earlier. Watering her plants."

Louise fiddles with the ashtray, twirling it gently at first, then spinning it faster and faster. "I don't know why you want· to move, Elliott, when you're so cozy with the neighbours. Always running into them. Chatting with them all the time."

"So it wasn't you?"

She drapes her upper body over the edge of the tub and looks him in the eye, forcing confidence. "Definitely not. I was at work."

"Mm." He squints at her for a moment. "Strange." Then he shrugs and tosses the nail clippers onto the countertop. "Well . . . I got some editing to catch up on. You should hit the hay early tonight, Louie. You *really* are working too hard."

And off he goes to his study for the evening, while Louise is left alone in the tub, her pulse thick and hot in her neck.

THE BIBLE IS unreadable. Day two of her vacation and Louise has been trying to make inroads with the book, but it's impossible. In the living room, lying on the floor, working her way through a bowl of apricots, she's still stuck in the story of Babel, when a car screeches into her driveway, triggering cat-like reflexes.

Fast as lightning, Louise dives for the foyer closet, swipes a baseball bat, and bounds up to her bedroom to assess the situation from a more secure vantage point. Since that series of midday break-ins on the street, Louise has been on extra high alert whenever she's home alone. Crouched at the window, hands gripped tight around the bat, she peeks through the blinds.

Christ! Worse than an intruder! Elliott's green Jetta is parked in the driveway.

Panic sends Louise flying across the narrow hall to her childhood room, where she rips open the small window, whips off the screen, and hurls it into the backyard. Her body is draped through the frame when she hears Elliott enter the house. Then a second set of footsteps, accompanied by a voice—a woman's voice. What's this? Who's this? Louise stalls her getaway and worms back inside, slithers across the burnt-orange carpet, and hides under the twin bed.

"I'm so glad you called, Elliott," says a bird-like voice that Louise recognizes, but can't quite place. Blood pulses through her ears, making it hard to think. "I haven't been up here in *ages*."

"Lou's at work. So we've got time."

"You shouldn't lie to your wife, Elliott," the bird screeches and Louise tightens her grip on the bat.

"Can't be helped sometimes," he says.

Oh, oh-ho-ho. Unbelievable! No wonder Elliott has stopped fucking her. The dick!

"So . . . how do you want to do this?" he asks.

"Oh, however you want. I'm game for anything. I don't think I've been up here since Yannick's parents moved."

Karen? Oh, what a goddam joke. What is this? A retributive dalliance? But how did they find out? No way Elliott did any sleuthing. Fucking Karen. She's the suspicious type, never confident in her hold on anything. Of course she's the sort of woman who would go through his phone, check his emails. Yannick is careful, sure, and constantly wary of his wife, but probably not very attentive. How could he be? He's emotionally checked out. It's this exact quality that makes him a good lover . . . but a lousy husband.

Keeping perfectly still, Louise listens to things unfold. Where will Elliott fuck her? How much foreplay? They're in the kitchen now, but on the move. She can hear the click-clack of Karen's heels. Into the living room. Maybe on the leather couch? Her parents' beautiful brown leather couch?

"Come on upstairs," says Elliott. In their bedroom? The *fucking* dick!

"Why don't we get started up there and work our way down?"

Wait a minute . . .

"Sure, sure—I just need a minute to drink in this view!" says Karen. "Major wow-factor."

. . . this isn't foreplay. This is *real estate*! Motherfucker! Ditching the bat, Louise log-rolls out from under the bed.

"—haven't renovated much, as you can see," says Elliott, his voice growing louder as he leads Karen out of the living room. "Lou is . . . uh . . . sentimental."

On tiptoes, Louise darts back to the master bedroom, where she musses her hair and rumples the bed sheets. Then she pretend-stumbles out into the hall, and in a groggy voice, calls out: "Elliott?" She intercepts them at the base of the carpeted stairs, but keeps to the third step, maintaining higher ground.

"Lou," Elliott says in a falling whistle. He positions himself in front of Karen, as though he might be able to conceal her presence with his narrow body. "Hey! What are you doing home?"

"I felt sick," she says flatly, leaning against the wrought-iron banister. "What are you doing here?"

"Oh . . . well . . . uh . . . okay . . . I brought Karen by."

"I see that. Why?"

"Hi Louise!" Karen's perfectly symmetrical face pops out from behind Elliott's shoulder.

"Karen."

Karen looks like a real estate agent. In her tailored skirt suit and low heels and tasteful jewellery and shiny highlighted hair. Curvier than Louise—though since she had that baby, her curves have turned dumpy. There's a numbness to her dark eyes, always outlined in the same modest makeup. A reluctance to laugh or smile. She's attractive, but her well-formed features seem pinched in a permanent reproach. *Cunty* was the word that came to mind when Louise first met her. And although her interactions with Karen have been short and infrequent, Louise has never found much cause to amend the initial assessment.

"Ooh, great necklace," chirps Karen, stepping out from behind Elliott. She trespasses right up onto the bottom step (the nerve of this bitch!), a pink gel-manicured finger wagging at Louise's throat. "The copper is beautiful against your skin tone."

Frequent as they are, Louise doesn't care much for compliments about her skin tone. She keeps her eyes on Karen, forcing herself not to look down at the small pendant on her sternum. "Thank you, Karen, for validating my tastes. Why are you here?"

"Oh, Elliott asked me—"

"Elliott? Why is she here?"

"Well . . . " starts Elliott, who has become extremely interested in a water stain on the ceiling. "Karen's agreed to give us a valuation of the house. Isn't that nice of her?"

"It would be nice . . . " Louise pushes herself off the banister, broadening her stance on the staircase, blocking access to the upstairs, "if we had actually decided to sell the house."

Karen nods several times, sharp little movements with her pointy chin, designed to convey her immense understanding for Louise's sentimental position. "Elliott mentioned that you were reluctant."

"I hope he did." Louise breezes down into the living room, opening a path for herself between the two interlopers. "Because I am. *Extremely* reluctant. More like adamantly opposed."

"That's not true, Louie," says Elliott, rushing to catch up with her. "You're thinking about it, remember?"

Louise stops in front of the coffee table and looks down at her bowl of apricots, the pillow on the floor—just a few minutes ago this exact spot was her vacation paradise. Now this. This is seriously fucking with her holiday.

"In my experience," explains Karen, waltzing into the living room after them, "one half of a couple is always unsure about selling."

"Oh yeah? Is that your experience?" Louise perches herself onto the armrest of the brown leather couch. Elliott sets a firm hand on her shoulder—to keep her docile. "And what other great insights do you have for us, Karen?"

But Karen is too busy inspecting the living room to be offended by Louise's bitchy tone. She's travelling around the perimeters, past the wall unit, trailing her fingertips along its shelves. Looking up, looking down, assessing, picking out flaws.

"It's natural to be attached to your first home," says Karen when she arrives in front of Louise, smiling down at her with the practised condescension of a realtor.

"Thank you, Karen. For validating my *feelings* this time."

Elliott's fingertips dig into her shoulder.

"You might be underestimating what you can get for this lot, Louise. This view alone!" Karen raises both arms, conductor-like, before the picture window. "We'll need to move some stuff around, of course." She spins around for another survey of the room, crosses her arms, and allows a judgmental pucker. "Not that we can do much in the way of staging—the house the way it is. But there are some improvements we could make. You'd have a lot more room for entertaining if you moved the couch away from the window. Opposite the fireplace makes a lot more sense. Instead of that clunky sideboard, which, frankly, you could do without."

Louise bolts up to a stand. "Elliott, can I talk to you for a second?"

"Sure, sure, you two talk things over," offers Karen graciously. She points to the staircase with both index fingers. "I'll just take a quick peek upstairs."

Once she's click-clacked out of sight, left to roam the house unchaperoned, Louise stares at Elliott, her feet drilled into the hardwood, staking a claim.

"It doesn't commit us to anything," Elliott says, fussing with the stacks of photographs on the superfluous sideboard, then realigning a few volumes on the wall unit. Next he gathers up a couple of mugs from the coffee table, the half-full ashtray, and the bowl of apricots and whisks everything off to the kitchen.

"Why not just get an appraisal?" he calls to her. "See what we're dealing with."

"You didn't even ask her to take off her shoes."

"What are you talking about?" he says, daring a bold step out of the kitchen in his shod foot. "We always walk around in shoes."

"Not in heels. This is our home, Elliott. She's click-clacking around the place like she owns it. Carving scratches into our floors." Louise has started in on broad gestures with her arms, but her feet stay planted on the hardwood floor by the coffee table: her vacation spot.

"She's doing us a favour, Lou," Elliott says as he hurries back toward her, his voice noticeably quieter than hers.

"I don't want any favours from her. I don't want her involved in our house or our business or our lives at all."

"Why not?"

"Because I don't like her."

"Would you keep your voice down?" he hisses, pointing his chin toward the staircase.

"Why? Fine with me if she knows I don't like her." But Louise drops her voice in spite of herself.

"Why don't you like her? What's wrong with her?"

"I don't have to explain *why* I don't like people, Elliott."

Elliott's forehead contracts, tugging up the skin around his eyes and highlighting his few well-placed wrinkles. She likes when his face gets like this, thought and focus etched into it. It makes him look competent. He chews at the inside of his cheek. "Where's your car?" he asks.

"What?"

"Your car. It's not in the driveway."

"Oh. Right." The car. Hidden away at the mall for the day. "Uh . . . it was making this weird . . . chugging sound."

"Chugging?"

Louise's heartbeat spikes and her feet come unglued. They get going on a nervous shuffle. "Chug-chug, chug-chug," she says, shrugging her shoulders to help illustrate the point. "I brought it in."

"Mm-hmm, mm-hmm." He looks down at the floor, at the bible peeking out from under the coffee table. He nudges it with his sneaker. "What's this? You're reading the bible?"

"Of course not. I was . . . using it as a coaster." She snatches the book and jams it into the bookshelf, where it rests at an irregular angle, conspicuous.

"Okay, look, Louie," he says, stepping right up to her, setting both hands on top of her shoulders and looking down into her scowling face. "Your bitch factor is through the roof right now. So I'm gonna go ahead and show Karen the rest of the house. We're just gonna see what she says. There's nothing wrong with getting an opinion." His hands slip down to her upper arms, which he squeezes firmly. He plants a kiss on her cheek. "Deal with it."

And off he rushes to track down the bird. A few seconds later, Louise hears his low-voiced apologies: "Lou hasn't been feeling well lately," soon followed by the groans of the basement stairs, punctuated by Karen's guffaw: "Wow! Wood panelling! Wild!"

Louise huffs down on the brown couch, mis-positioned by the window. Fucking Karen. What does she know? This is where the couch goes. This is where Louise used to sit when she had trouble sleeping as a child, her head on Mother Mai's lap, Mai stroking her forehead. It's where, after Mai died, Louise used to sit alone and stare out the window and hope that miraculously Mai might reappear in the forest behind the house.

"—but let's not kid ourselves," Karen says a short while later, having completed her tour of the house and swanned back into the living room, Elliott in tow, to deliver her verdict. "There are a lot of problems with the house. No ensuite in the master. No main floor powder. Kitchen is cramped. *Everything* needs updating."

Elliott half-sits on the sideboard, one foot on the ground, the other swinging nervously, awaiting a figure.

"We'll need to market it as a fixer-upper. Maybe a teardown. An opportunity to customize." Karen's eyes roll upward as she performs a few mental calculations. "I think we can get . . . I'd say . . . 1.5, 1.6."

"How 'bout that," says Elliott, his smile triumphant. His leg stops swinging.

Even Louise perks up on the couch. 1.5 is a big number, bigger than she expected. Almost twice what they paid for the house. She could quit working with that kind of money . . . but only for a few years. Not long enough. Besides, most of that money would likely disappear into whatever new property they bought. Unless they left the city altogether. Moved somewhere else, far away from this endless festival of manic commerce.

"Have you actually sold anything in this neighbourhood, Karen? Aren't you more downtown?"

"I sold Yannick's parents house, and—" But her attention is diverted. She's become mesmerized by one of Elliott's wedding prints, neatly stacked now on the sideboard beside his thigh. "Wow, did you take this, Elliott?"

"Yeah yeah. A wedding at the Art Gallery," says Elliott, plainly delighted by the interest. He leans over onto an elbow and spreads out the topmost images in the stack. "Great venue, huh?"

"Oh fantastic. Gorgeous, Elliott. Really. You have such a good eye." Karen casts one more disappointed glance at the furniture arrangement in the living room, a glance that ends on Louise, who must be responsible for this poor aesthetic design.

The particular print that has hypnotized Karen is a close-up of a bride, all the wrinkles and blemishes edited from her face, a bride made vacant by Elliott's compulsive Photoshopping.

"We should have had you do our wedding," Karen says.

"There's always next time," Elliott says with a flirtatious shrug that makes Louise want to retch.

Karen tilts her head and affects a look of disapproval. Ugh. No wonder Yannick is so fucking unhappy.

"Industry joke," says Elliott.

"I bet." But her mouth tweaks into a rare smile. "Seriously, do you have any other prints lying around? I'd love to take a look."

"'Course, sure." He hops off the sideboard almost instantly and waves her toward the study.

Alone in the living room, Louise looks over the glossy spread they've left behind, the array of wedding guests, adorned and airbrushed—they all look exactly the same. Louise and Elliott used to make fun of lavish weddings. They mocked the unreasonable expense of them, the waste of resources, the unchecked vanity. Their own wedding was a city hall affair, a quick, impulsive melding of their lives. Anything grander would have seemed offensive and obscene. This kind of work should be making him miserable. So where is his goddamn misery?

The sound of their little conference carries through the house: Elliott's low voice describing the wheres and whens of his photographs; Karen's chirpy praise moving up in octaves each time she finds a new image to fawn over.

"Stunning!"

"Sensational!

"Just . . . Wow!"

God. Louise would prefer if he were just fucking the bird instead.

9

"IT HURTS!" Joly clutches a hot water bottle to her abdomen on the twin bed in Louise's childhood bedroom. "They didn't say it would hurt like *this*. They said cramping, period cramping. This is . . . . it feels like something clawing up my insides."

"I know, I know. It'll pass, though," says Louise from a crouch beside the bed.

After the abortion, Joly didn't want to go home, to a house full of family members, and she didn't want to go to Ben's, to a house full of indifferent roommates, so Louise brought her home to Don Mills and installed her beneath the glow-in-the-dark stars, where they used to have sleepovers as kids.

"Why aren't the drugs kicking in?"

"They will."

"When?!"

Louise gets up to close the vertical blinds, but the strong afternoon light still sneaks in through the cracks. "Drugs can be mysterious beasts," she says. "Give it a little longer. You're already looking better."

Joly grinds her palms against her cheekbones, dragging down the skin around her eye sockets and exposing the bottom of her bloodshot eyeballs. Her stringy hair falls between her fingers; the skin on her face and neck is blotched red. She cried the entire car ride home.

"They kept talking about *Dancing with the Stars*," Joly says, reaching for the mug of camomile tea cooling on the nightstand.

"What?" Louise resumes her place on the floor by the bed, now resting her chin on the mattress.

"The doctor and the nurse. They just kept arguing about a *foxtrot*."

"During the—"

"Yes! During it!" A rigidity in Joly's facial muscles suggests she's still working hard to keep her tears in check.

"What—"

"The nurse thought the dance was fantastic. But the doctor didn't like the footwork. That's gonna be my memory of this now, Lou. *Dancing with the Stars*. The foxtrot."

"Should I call and complain? I can rip into them if you want. Contact the medical board?"

Joly shakes her head, then drops it directly over the mug, letting it steam her face. "I can stay the night?"

"'Course." Louise reaches a hand out to pat Joly's foot, which has snuck out from beneath the sheets.

"Maybe drop me off on your way to work tomorrow?"

"I can drop you off whenever. I'm not working. I'm, uh, on vacation this week."

"Oh, but . . . " Joly gestures at Louise's grey blazer, her matching pants.

"Elliott doesn't know. Secret vacation."

"Lou!"

"Ah, fuck him," she says and Joly manages a short laugh. "We still haven't had sex. It's been over a month."

"I wish I hadn't had sex in months," Joly says into her mug. "Never again. I'm never having sex again."

"You don't have to."

"It's a crazy thing to do!"

"Well . . . it has some perks."

"It's Russian roulette."

Without having taken a sip of her tea, Joly sets the mug back on the nightstand. Her eyes squint shut then blast open as she works through a fresh wave of distress. She doubles over her crossed legs, jamming the hot water bottle into her pelvis. "He must have done something wrong, Lou."

"I don't—"

Joly lurches forward and grasps Louise's wrist, her eyes flooded with terror. "Maybe he didn't get it all," she whispers.

"I'm sure he did."

"What if he didn't, though? What if part of her is still in there . . . clawing?"

"I don't think—"

"What if he *botched* it? Oh god, it's *botched!*"

She moves around the bed frantically, and Louise can't tell if this squirming is induced by the pain or by the conjured thoughts of catastrophe. She stands up, her hands on her hips, and tries to puzzle out a way to be helpful.

"Should I call Ben? Want me to call him?" Ben was barred from coming with them to the clinic. No men were in the waiting room this afternoon. No men present when Louise was a patient either, certainly not the father of her own might-have-been child, one of her earliest lovers. Louise never told him. He, like many others, marched onwards through life blissfully oblivious to what he wrought.

"What's Ben gonna do?" Joly has shuffled her way to the back corner of the bed, digging her shoulders into the wall. "Pad around the place, looking ashamed? That big bear is useless sometimes."

But Louise is keenly aware of her own uselessness in this moment—as in most moments of any consequence. She's never had much comfort to offer anyone. So she does the only thing she can think of: crawls into the bed and clasps Joly's hand.

They lie side-by-side, looking up at the plastic stars, like they used to do when they were kids. Eventually Joly drifts off, but Louise stays awake, fixated on the ceiling, marvelling at the total lack of progress over the years. Decades have passed, but she's still here, lying in this bed, beneath these stars: she's a fossil.

"HOW'S SHE DOING?" Elliott asks over dinner. Whole wheat spaghetti tonight, done up with kale and white beans. A perfectly balanced meal, because Louise cooked—again.

"Bad," says Louise, slouched over her mostly-empty plate, cheek propped up in a palm as she eats.

"I guess that's normal."

"Yeah—especially if you wanted to keep it."

Louise's post-abortion misery wasn't quite this bleak. But she never entertained the idea of having a baby. How could she have? It would be unthinkable to pass on these defective genes, which even now are ratcheting up for premature destruction.

"She'll be all right," says Elliott, a pat response that, though probably true, irritates Louise. She pushes away her empty plate and lets him clear the table and wash the pots, making sure he leaves out a dish for Joly, in case she gets hungry later.

"Say . . ." says Elliott, bent over the open dishwasher, "d'you know why the window screen is in the yard?"

"What?"

"The screen from your old bedroom window."

Oh right. The screen. "Uh—"

Fuck!

"It's in the middle of the lawn. You know how it got there?"

"No. Why would I know that?" She stands up and wipes stray bits of grated parmesan off the table. "Maybe a squirrel ripped it off?"

"A squirrel? No way."

"A raccoon maybe?"

"I don't think so."

Aware that she's fidgeting, she grabs a dishcloth from the sink to give her body a purpose. She turns on the faucet full-blast and wets the cloth under its roaring stream. "Raccoons are very industrious."

"It doesn't look clawed at, though. The screen. No scratches. No marks."

"Raccoon break-ins get reported all across the city." Louise wipes down the table, trying to stabilize her shaking hands against its hard surface. "It's pretty common. That's probably what happened. Yeah. That must be it."

"Mm," he says, sidling up to her, his voice—even on this one syllable—showing infinitely more composure than hers. "The thing is . . . I don't think that's what happened." He sets a hand on top of hers, arresting her motion mid-wipe.

Louise's heartbeat surges up her throat, choking her speech. Oh god, what's this? Is he wise to the whole thing? Not as oblivious as she thought? His faculties not entirely blunted by the wedding photography? Maybe he *has* been paying attention to her, careful attention. Maybe he knows *everything*.

As Elliott picks up one of her hands, kisses the fingers, bites on them, her body whirs with exhilaration. He used to do this all the time, as a preamble to sex, to a second or third round, when they used to just lie in bed with each other for hours and hours. Elliott used to like to study her body, all of it, in detail—the shape of her shoulder blades, the exact placement of her few moles, the forms of her knees. He told her once he wanted to be sure that he would always know her, even by the smallest part, just a fraction, by a hipbone, or an earlobe, or a thumb. By the time she met Elliott, she'd had sex with a few dozen people, a good variety, a nice range of touches, masculine and feminine, but none of them felt anything like he did. He distinguished himself in the simple touches, the way his skin felt against hers. Like the physical structure of their skin cells were in perfect complement. When he touched her, her cells perked up—they purred. Even now, her skin buzzes.

Except he's not touching her anymore. He's kicking up the dishwasher door and shrugging as he says, "Well . . . the mysteries of Don Mills, huh."

"Oh . . ."

"I'm gonna do some work."

And just like that he's off again. Back into the arms of his deranged brides.

Standing alone in the kitchen, Louise taps her fingernails against the table. She scans her body for signs of relief, but all she finds is a burgeoning irritation. She lets this build and build and build until it carries her across the hardwood floor and into the dingy study, ready to fight! To yell and scream at him about his idiotic career. Or else to demand he pay attention to her. Touch her. At length. With care. Like he used to do. Or else to call her on her shit. To foist accountability on her.

But once she steps onto the dull pink carpet of the study, her focus shifts. It's the photograph up on his screen—it catches her off guard. It's the same one he was working on last week, the couple mid-kiss, the stained glass Jesus on the cross . . . except . . . something's different. Jesus's expression has changed. She blinks hard several times and looks again. But yes, something has definitely shifted. This Jesus no longer has the look of a man gracefully resigned to his fate. The corner of his mouth has been pulled up so that he's . . . grinning.

"Is that . . . did you . . . did you Photoshop Jesus?" she says.

Elliott swivels around in his chair to face her. "Like I said . . . I thought he needed some work."

10

ON THE EVE of her thirty-third birthday, Louise can't sleep. She lies awake beside Elliott, acutely aware of the slight ache in her right breast—that's where it started for Mother Mai. Ground zero.

Over and over, she presses her fingertips into her breast, moving up and down, left to right. A dozen times her fingers locate a problem; terror soars through her, awakening every cell in her nervous system. But then she checks again, to confirm her grim fate, and finds instead a normal clump of cells, the edge of a muscle or a rib bone, and the dread abates. The early hours of the morning drag on in this cycle of spiking and dissipating terror that leaves her exhausted, but unable to sleep.

3:06am. She forces her hand away from her breast, hoping her thoughts will move elsewhere. They turn to a rapid string of familiar late-night fantasies: driving her car into a tree, drowning herself in the tub, setting herself on fire, blowing off her head, crushing it with her own hands. It's a paradox: fantasizing about suicide while being terrified of imminent death. Paradoxes make her irritable, and the irritability makes her anxious, and the anxiety makes her want to kill herself, and this endless cycle traps her in a bleak cage. Maybe there really is something wrong with her brain.

The pills. She'll try the pills again.

Where's the clonazepam? She can't find it amid all this shit in the medicine cabinet. She grabs the Xanax bottle, but it's nearly empty. She must have taken more of these pills than she realized. Or were there fewer to start? Her head is so foggy, she can't even keep track. She takes one pill and tries again to go to sleep.

"HAPPY BIRTHDAY, LOU!" Elliott stands next to the kitchen table, proudly waving at his breakfast creation. "Pancakes!"

"Oh." Louise, still in her short silk nightie, plops onto a chair and stares at the small stack of raspberry-banana pancakes in front of her. "But I said I didn't want to celebrate this one."

"It's just pancakes," he says, tossing cutlery onto the table.

Louise is still exhausted. Her face is hot, her mouth dry, her jaw half-locked. It's hard to chew. Chunks of pancake linger inside her mouth for minutes before she forces herself to swallow them whole.

Elliott watches this weak attempt, then says: "Let's do something fun today."

"No."

"Why don't you take the day off?"

"I can't."

"Sure you can. I'll play hooky from the shop." He steers a chunk of pancake through a puddle of syrup. "I've got a meeting with a new client this afternoon, new wedding—but we could take the morning off."

"I already took a half-day for Joly. And I logged a sick day on Tuesday. Remember?"

"Oh, right right. You were sick. I forgot."

When they finish eating, Elliott gets going on the dishes while Louise pretends to get ready for work. She takes a short shower, blasting herself with cold water, slips on her silky Benetton blouse, her grey Banana Republic trousers, sits on the edge of the bed combing her wet hair and feeling annoyed that circumstances are forcing her to enact this charade. Especially on this day. D-day. Thirty-three. This is it. Boom.

"Hey, what's wrong, Louie?" Elliott asks when he finds her like this, sitting on the bed, staring at the floor. He crouches in front of her with his hands on her outer thighs.

"I don't feel well, Elliott," she whispers.

"Mm. You never feel well. But you're always fine."

AROMA IS A shrill buzz this morning. The queue at the counter is a mile long—dozens (is it hundreds? thousands?) of people. They're multiplying. All spies, Marguerites and Mr. Fangs, threatening her. And it's not just them. Everything is a threat! This heavy perfume in front of her, crushing her lungs. The giant behind her in line, breathing fire down her neck—right down her blouse! A hyena laugh erupting to the left. Mugs clattering and banging. She flinches against it all, this coordinated attack on her senses.

A sudden rush of terror rises up from her belly and snakes around her throat: a panic attack.

In front of her is a garish red display for Zing® tea. She zooms in on it, recalling her preliminary research—an article buried in the back corner of the internet about how Zing!® sources its tea from plantations in India, where the tea leaves are harvested by virtual slaves, living in shit and filth, dying from malnourishment and dysentery, earning pennies a day to pick tea that bounces its way along the supply chain and comes out the other side wrapped up in these bright red packages with a cartoon bird shouting "ZING!"

"What would you like, ma'am?"

Her head twitches to find the voice. The barista? She's already at the front of the queue? When did that happen?

"What?" she says.

"What can I get you?"

But she can't even make out his face. The world has tipped sideways.

"Ma'am? Are you all right?"

No! Flight! She races out of the shop, knocking into the patio chairs and patrons on her way into the open Town Square. No no no, it's no better out here. Her chest is a gnarled rock, her hands and fingers humming electrically. A thousand sounds, smells, sights pierce her edges. She looks up and down, left and right, spinning in frantic circles around this citadel fortified by commerce on all sides. There's no air in her throat. Is this it? She's going to die? Right now? Jesus, on this fucking Astroturf? Let's go then. She wants to be dead. Oh god, the relief of it. To be free of this feeling once and for all.

She lurches toward a raised stone garden bed and pukes onto the mulch.

BRRIIIIINNG! Her phone surges to life. In a full crouch, hanging onto the edge of the garden bed, Louise wipes her mouth and catches small breaths.

"Lou," Yannick barks. "We got a problem. Hotel's booked up."

"Uh . . ."

"Yeah. Conference. So what do you wanna do here? Meet in the parking lot?"

"No."

"Well where then?"

"I can't come downtown."

"You're not downtown already? Not at work?"

"Day off."

"Well shit."

Her breath is thin, her back sweating, her whole body a messy network of seized muscles and strained nerves. She needs one moment, any moment of pure relief. "You can come here if you want."

"To Don Mills? Your *house*? Bad form, Lou. And I don't have time for that."

"Okay then. Next week maybe."

"Fuck. Fine. Let me see what I can do."

YANNICK'S HANDS CLOSE tight over her tits. Straddling him on the bed in the downstairs bedroom of her house, Louise presses his hands against her harder. She wants his fingers to work the tissue, to explore, forcing him to perform a pseudo examination. If something's wrong, any disruptions in the even softness of her breasts, he should notice—even if she missed it.

"Do they feel good?" she whispers.

"Yeah, fuck, Lou. You feel so fucking good."

He raises a hand to her neck, to the back of her head, which he tries to pull down toward him, his mouth open, poised. But he was too gentle with her tits. There could be something lurking deeper, a buried problem that won't be found without a rough touch. She returns his hands to her chest, mashing them against her. "Come on, harder. Hard."

He does as she commands, first thrusting his palms into her, then pulling her breasts, twisting them. She winces, but says, "Yeah, yeah, like that," so he keeps going.

"Fuck yeah, Lou."

She can't concentrate. She's exhausted from the episode at the mall. She hasn't eaten enough today. She's dehydrated. And the wooden bedframe won't stop creaking. Yannick looks at her, confused, concerned, but the pressure just isn't building in the right direction. And suddenly: *Ding-ding*. They're out of time.

"You okay?" he asks, slowing his upward thrusts.

"Mm-hmm."

With their time ticked down to nothing, he flips her over and fucks her hard from behind, trying to compel the orgasm through brute force. He finishes off like this, one hand wrapped around her, still kneading her tits.

WHILE YANNICK BOLTS for the shower, Louise pulls on her underwear, bra . . . where's her blouse? Where did he throw it? She flips the pillows, flings back the duvet, checks under the dresser, and finally spots it by the closet, its sleeve slipped between the folds of the broken accordion door. As she jiggles the door to free the sleeve, she peeks inside the closet: crammed with shit. She doesn't remember it being this chaotic. She remembers her old baseball gear, school textbooks, her father's forgotten coats. What are all these boxes? These bags? What is all this shit?

Annoyed by the clutter, she yanks out a box, rips off the lid and finds herself looking at rubble. The topmost photograph in the box shows a muddled heap of concrete, wood, fabric, and scattered clothing tags—and there, oh dear god, a bare foot sticking out from the debris. Elliott's series on the factory collapse.

The photographs are horrendous to look at. It must have been almost impossible to witness this event first-hand. When Elliott first came back from Bangladesh, Louise thought his brain had been broken by the experience. He had nightmares, garbled thoughts; she'd find him staring at nothing for minutes at a time.

Kneeling over the box, Louise peels one photograph after another off the stack until she's halfway down and staring into the face of the Bangladeshi woman whose expression of perfect exhaustion so unsettled her the first time she saw it. The effect remains; Louise might as well be looking directly into the Void.

But what's this . . . looking closely now at the pile of rubble over the woman's shoulder, in the upper corner of the shot, Louise picks out something she hadn't noticed before: the recognizable green rectangle of a Benetton clothing tag, pre-sumably sewn into the shirt by a doomed worker just before the factory ceiling caved in on her head.

Louise shifts her gaze from the photograph to the blouse at her knees. Her breath turns shaky again as she looks from one to the other. Cause and consequence are spread out on the floor, coalescing before her into a direct indictment. Jesus fucking Christ! What can you touch anymore that doesn't make you complicit in something heinous?

"Hey, what are you doing down there?" asks Yannick, cruis-ing back into the bedroom after his sixty-second shower.

"Oh . . . nothing. Just—" She waves the blouse and forces herself into it; it feels corrosive against her skin. She watches him chuck his towel onto the bed.

"So Karen tells me you're listing the house."

"No. Maybe."

"Okay. But just don't move away . . . like out of town or anything."

"Did he tell Karen we're decided? We are not."

"I don't know what he told her. She hasn't been talking about work much. She's been too busy planning this baptism. It's blowing up into a whole goddamn function."

"What baptism?"

"Yvie's. I'm sure I told you."

"No. I'd have remembered that."

"Well, she's having the kid baptized. She's sending out invitations next week. She special ordered invitations. Expect one. There's a reception afterward. You're supposed to bring a gift."

"What kind of gift?"

"I don't know, Lou. What do I know about baptisms? I don't even understand why—" He shuffles through her pile of clothes on the floor. "Where's my sock?"

Louise watches him flatten out on his stomach, peeking under the bed. The stray sock is interrupting his highly efficient process of re-robing. "Do you ever feel guilty?" she asks.

"What?"

"Guilty. About this. About *anything*."

The sock retrieved, he does a quick push-up and bounces to a stand. "Of course I feel guilty, Lou. I feel fucking terrible." He puts on his sock. "But I'd feel worse if we stopped. Wouldn't you?" For a moment he pauses his brisk movements to look at her: "Is that why . . . you couldn't . . . uh . . . get there?"

"Jesus, Yannick."

"What?"

She throws on her pants and leaves him in the wood-panelled bedroom.

"What?" he calls after her.

AT THE FRONT door, Yannick touches a knuckle to her cheek. "Here," he says and pulls a pair of Blue Jays tickets from his jacket pocket. "Happy birthday." An oddly thoughtful gesture. Too thoughtful. Someone—a colleague or client—must have comped him these tickets.

"Hotel next week. Hotel works better," he says.

The moment the door closes behind him, she beelines to

the kitchen, to the stash of pot in an upper cabinet. She's running low again. Strange, she thought she was still flush. She must be smoking more than she realized.

She rolls the joint on top of the pocket bible, which she ventured back into after her morning blunt, hoping an altered consciousness might provide more clarity. It did not. Before she can seal up this second joint, she's interrupted: another knock at the door. Yannick must need a more robust reassurance of his virility. Only instead of Yannick, she finds Ben on her front stoop, his arms laden with a box of home-brewed beer.

"Oh. Hey." She scans the street and spots Yannick a few houses down, swaggering in his financier hustle, phone to his head, his barking audible. He parked in front of his old house—his parents' old house—whether out of habit or caution, she's not sure.

"Joly sent me over. Birthday beer," Ben explains with a nod at the box in his arms. "Is that Yannick?"

"Uh . . . I guess."

Louise steps back to let Ben in, catching sight of herself in the mirrored closet door. It's her mother's reflection, exactly like the pictures of her mother she used to study for hours and hours after she died. The aging process has worked identically on both of them. If she could Photoshop Mai's severe bangs, oversized glasses, and a shoulder-padded sweater onto her own portrait, she could very well be her mother, a few months before she expired.

Louise also looks like she has just been fucked. The hair at the back of her head is teased up into total disarray. And for Christ's sake, her pants are still undone. The wheels in her head begin to crank out a lie, that machinery operating automatically, but it suddenly seems too farcical to pretend. "This is exactly what it looks like," she says to Ben. "I'm a total fucking asshole."

"None of my business. My business is the beer. Where do you want it?" He stands rigid in her foyer, awaiting instruction.

Louise waves him into the kitchen, zipping up her pants on the way.

"It's a strong lager, good for the season," Ben says as he sets the beer on the counter, next to the maple syrup Elliott forgot to put away after breakfast. "I call it The Chairman Pow. Packs a punch, so be careful with it."

"How's Joly?" Louise settles into one of the chairs to finish rolling her joint.

"Oh, she's good. Good good," he says, but his composure collapses at the mention of her name. Straight away he drops his heft into the chair across from her, which groans beneath him. "Actually, I haven't seen her. She says she wants to be alone for a few days. It behoves me to respect that." He nods vigorously to affirm this decision. But he looks miserable.

Absentmindedly, Ben fingers the pocket bible on the table.

"You still doing the church thing?" she asks.

Ben sits up taller in his chair, immensely relieved at the shift in conversation; he reconstitutes his veneer of equanimity. "I keep the faith."

Louise points at the bible with her joint. "I'm trying to read it. But it makes no sense. I got stuck on Babel."

"Ah, the proto-empire. The world's first grand collective enterprise. It's a story of hubris, of course. What's not to understand?"

"Hubris. How?"

"What do you mean how? A people reaching for heaven without the knowledge of God. Classic hubris. And they're punished for it."

"But why is God afraid of them?"

"What—? He's not afraid. Obviously. You're reading it wrong."

"Oh."

As Louise draws in the pot, her limbs gain weight and her concentration ebbs. But it doesn't quite manage to blunt her discomfort. She knits her fingers behind her head, feeling the disorder in her hair. Her thumbs dip down the back of her neck, into her blouse, brushing against the tag of her blouse that sits at the top of her spine. "I'm a total fucking asshole," she says again.

"Yes, well, aren't we all. The Bible tells us that upfront. Sinners to the last." He stands up to go. "But your sins are your own," he says with a gentle half-smile. "I have no business here. But the beer."

Though she can tell he's sincere, his reassurance of silence is hollow. Because it's not the affair that's tearing up her insides. Her sins are far greater—complicity in a thousand more egregious moral crimes that fan out all across the world.

TODAY'S PRIEST IS the young, exuberant one that Louise most likes. His animated cadence and gestures bring life to the early morning mass. A return to work was impossible without some kind of spiritual buttress, so she rose early and dropped in for this service.

A whole pew to herself, Louise listens intently to the tortured bible readings, so wilfully opaque in their meaning that she starts to wonder if there isn't a broader message at play. Perhaps there is something unholy about forthrightness and clarity, something unholy about communication itself.

Certainly, nothing good ever seems to come from mass communication, from a united people working together on a "grand collective enterprise." Near as she can tell, the grand collective enterprises involve initiatives like setting up plantations and mines and factories and office towers, and sticking workers inside them, locking them in with slave wages and suicide nets and demands to consume, until every useable human resource has been extracted from them and they drop dead.

Beneath the newly-painted and already-commodified stars on the church ceiling, a flash of inspiration strikes. God isn't frightened of people—she really was reading the story of Babel all wrong. He's frightened *for* them. Because they will ruin themselves, if they're given the chance. The world's multitude of languages is a *gift* from God, not a punishment. This species, corrupted from the outset, can't be trusted with the power of communication.

THE ELEVATOR BUTTONS light up one after the other as Louise shoots up twenty floors. She hurries from the elevator to her desk. She lost track of time sitting in the church—her first day back and already late.

On her desk, a stack of file folders. Attached to the top-most folder is a note from Nicky in her round, bubbly script: *Welcome Back!* It's written on a sheet from a bright red Zing!® Iced Tea notepad, with the Zing!® header, the cartoon bird in the upper right corner.

To delay the beginning of this workday, she exchanges hellos with Jerry, who's already well into his morning candy. Wine gums today. She can tell it's wine gums by the way he's chewing. A drawn-out chew, part smack and part suck.

She takes a long sip from her thermos, then stares straight ahead until the first email alert of the day disrupts her. It's from the CEO, Charlotte (Charlie), with the subject line, "Another tick for UpTick":

Dear UpTick Team,

I want to congratulate everyone on their hard work with the audio billboard pilot project. Happy to report that early numbers are better than expected. Looks like we have a huge hit on our hands! BRAVO.

Inspired by this success, the strategic leadership team is looking at other innovative billboarding models. Next week we are holding preliminary consultations about olfactory billboards (more to come on that!!). Our vision is to become the city's first truly multi-sensory billboard company. Fingers CROSSED!

This has been a challenging time for all of us. As we have all been working so hard on the audio launch, we have also been grieving the loss of one of our own. RIP Neil. So let's dedicate our revolutionary new audio billboard to Neil. I hope they're serving up a big frosty glass of iced tea for you in heaven!

So proud of the team,
Charlie
CEO and President
UpTick Media

Louise's insides shrivel; she drops her head into her hands and concentrates on the floor tiling. She feels half-dead.

"You get in late today?"

Looking up, she finds Rob—his arms crossed, his face serious, even grim.

"What? No. I don't think so."

"I came by earlier, you weren't in yet."

"Uh. Well. Traffic. The DVP was backed up for miles." Not

her best lie. A bit risky. She's not the only who takes that route. But he's not actually listening.

"Nicky and I want to meet with you. My office, okay?"

"What about?"

"Eleven." He's unusually brusque. No jokes about her still being on vacation time. No hilarious updates on office gossip she missed. No perching on the edge of her desk, leering and lingering.

"Uh, okay. Sure."

As he moves along, Louise starts to wonder if maybe she fucked something up in her absence. Neglected something? Maybe they're making cutbacks. Is she about to get fired?

"What do you think that's about?" asks Jerry, the shredded remnants of the green wine gum floating around in his mouth.

"I don't know. Did I miss anything important?"

"Nope."

ROB IS SITTING behind his desk, holding onto his stern, all-business expression. "Let's wait for Nicky," he says.

"How 'bout a general idea?" asks Louise.

"Show some character, Lou. Wait it out."

She doesn't like being alone in an office with Rob. Especially when he's toying with her, just because he can. She turns her focus to the broad leaves of the palm plant in the corner.

"Sorry, sorry, sorry," says Nicky, waddling her way into the office a few minutes later and heaving her enormous body into the chair next to Louise. "Emergency potty break. They're becoming pretty frequent these days." She passes a hand across her belly to underscore the point: the baby is to blame.

"Wow, he's really growing, huh," says Rob, staring at her belly, then her breasts.

"I know, I'm starting to fatten up. For real. But we're on track. I'm coming up on week thirty-one."

"That little dude is on his way," says Rob, still struggling to stop his eyes from flickering toward her colossal breasts.

"So—about this little dude right here." Nicky piles her hands on top of the ridge of her stomach.

"Nicky's going to be taking mat leave early," Rob says.

"Oh? Is everything okay?"

"Yeah, yeah," says Nicky. "The little one's just being fussy. Doctor says I should already be on bedrest."

"Which brings us to you, Lou," says Rob. He chooses this moment to let his stern expression crack open into a whitened smile. "We want you to take over as Communications Manager while Nicky's away."

Louise stares at their eager smiling faces, both waiting for her to express gratitude and delight.

"Surprised, huh?" says Rob, showing his top gums: a healthy pink.

"Well yeah. A little. I thought you were bringing in someone new. I thought you were interviewing already."

"We did meet with a few people. But no one who was a good fit. Till Nicky suggested you."

"You'll be great," says Nicky.

"You'll get the salary bump. And the title, of course. But you'll be looking at a lot more responsibility. You need to know that coming in."

Rob spends the next ten minutes elaborating on these responsibilities and assuring Louise that he'll be right there to help her "work out the hiccups." He discusses "the upcoming challenge" of marketing the audio billboards, how this feature is going to be "a game changer," but how they're going to need to "iron out the marketing strategy," because the idea is still new and most of their clients have no understanding of directional sound technology. To this end, he's set up a meeting for Wednesday so they can "hash out some strategies," and he wants Louise to be "the point person" for that. They'll "touch base" about it tomorrow.

"The three of us will communicate about the transition over the coming weeks, but for now . . . let's celebrate! Lunch at Barolo!" Barolo is the trendy Italian place where the office dweebs go for lunch when there's a pretence for taking a lot of time. Barolo is code for boozy. And boozy, with Rob, is code for sexually inappropriate.

"Congrats, Lou," he says. "I'm really looking forward to this."

BACK AT HER desk, Louise takes slow, steady sips of water. She doesn't bother to look at the folders or open any documents on her computer. She rolls her chair toward the window. Down on the sidewalk, a half block to her right, she watches victims of the audio billboard passing through the sound beam.

"Hot day? How about a cool iced tea? Zing!"

"Hot day? How about a cool iced tea? Zing!"

"Hot day? How about a cool iced tea? Zing!"

From this angle she can't see the billboard itself, but its effect is clear. One after another, pedestrians stop short in the street, their heads swivel, searching . . . searching. Where is that coming from? Who said that?

"Lou?"

She spins in her chair, and sends an arm out wide, knocking over the empty glass of water left on the edge of her desk. It rattles around on her desk, but it doesn't break.

"Whoa there, slugger." Rob sets the glass upright, smiling one of those smug smiles in which the tip of his tongue protrudes between the teeth. "Daydreaming, huh? Don't go wrecking the place now that you're a higher-up."

She looks at the glass and says, "Oops."

"Barolo time. Let's hit it."

"Right, right." But her mind is still down on the street and her thighs feel stuck to the chair. "You go ahead. I'll catch up. I gotta . . . do some stuff. Use the washroom."

"Sure, and call Elliott, I bet, huh? Let him know the good news." He claps her shoulder, holds his hand there for a couple of seconds before he ventures a squeeze; then he takes off.

Louise looks at the stack of folders in front of her, at Jerry's candy wrappers on the desk across from her. At Nicky's note, delivered on Zing!® stationery in a bubbly cursive. At the wall clock by reception, which she's spent hours looking at over the years, watching the smooth arc of time slipping by. Poison, all of it. A slow poison corroding her soul.

She grabs her own Zing!® notepad, rips off the top sheet and scrawls out a single sentence just under the bright cartoon bird. She looks it over, adds a word, and tapes the note to her computer monitor, where the bright red paper will draw the eye of whoever happens by. *I quit. Zing!*

LOUISE ZIGZAGS AROUND the house, passing relics of her childhood and adolescence in every room she enters. This place is a tomb, one she's been haunting for years. But she's not dead yet. No, she's surging with life, she can't stop moving.

When Elliott gets home from the framing shop, she's still pacing in the living room. He sees her there, once again at home when she should be at work, and asks dryly, "Sick again?"

"No."

"No?"

"I quit my job today," she says, facing him dead on.

"Excuse me?"

"I hate it. So I quit it."

He drops his shoulder bag onto the ancient hardwood floor. "You . . . just decided to quit?"

"Yes."

"You didn't think about discussing that with me first?"

"I did not, no."

She's prepared for anything, long past the point where she can guess what Elliott's reactions might be. What she gets is a tremendous sigh. Then he disappears into the kitchen, only to return a moment later with a baggie of pot.

"Are those my drugs?"

"Where were you last week?" he asks, breaking up the bud on the sideboard.

"What?"

He starts rolling a joint with an expertise and efficiency that surprise her. "Not at work, were you? Marguerite sees you at the coffee shop."

"Wasn't me." She shuffles in place next to the coffee table; her palms are getting sticky. "I told you that."

"I catch you at home the next day—"

"I was sick—"

"The window screen thrown into—"

"A raccoon!"

"So I got to thinking. And I called your office asking for you." He's never called the office—he always hits up her cell. Oh fuuuuuck. "You know what they told me?"

A hot flush spreads from Louise's chest to her forehead. "Uh . . . they might have said . . ."

Joint rolled, he's circling her now, closing in. "What did they tell me, Lou?"

" . . . that I was . . . uh . . ."

"What?"

" . . . on vacation," she mumbles.

"Vacation!" he thunders, sending both arms up above his head. "Imagine that!"

He lights up in front of her and blows the smoke into her face. But she's grateful for this hazy shield, hoping he can't see her withering behind it. Her face burns with white-hot embarrassment.

Elliott stays silent, allowing her to squirm in her own shame. He should say something. Yell at her! Scream! But he prefers this approach—an error. In the charged silence, Louise's shame, like all of her emotions, soon transforms into irritation. Her whole charade, the tedium and inconvenience of it—all for nothing! "Why didn't you say anything?" she asks in a low voice.

"I was waiting for *you* to say something. I didn't think you'd make it through the whole week without coming clean. But you did!" He settles back against the sideboard, smoking the joint with his arms crossed. "Who does that, Lou? How do you lie to me about something like that?"

The way he's leaning there—so smug, so self-righteous. Louise can feel her irritation blossom into fury. As though he's unblemished in all this! As though it's not his fault she felt forced into the lie in the first place. "Me lie? What about you?

"What *about* me?"

"You lied about your whole personality! These fucking weddings!" A dam breaks inside her head. She swipes a photograph off the sideboard, the pile of his most recent prints, and whips it at him. "What is this shit?" Amid the deluge of anger roaring through her, Louise grabs another photograph and whips it at him. And another! Whip! Whip!

"How is this who you are now?" she screams, shooting an entire stack straight up into the air. Brides flying! Blonde brides! Brunette brides! Fair brides! Dark brides! In Cinderella gowns! Empire waists! Mermaid cuts! Satin and tulle and crinoline! Crystal embellishments and diamond jewels! Pearls and rose gold! Grooms in beige suits on tropical beaches! In jet-black tuxedos in country clubs and waterfront halls! At banquet tables overflowing with filet mignon and lobster and halibut and towering weddings cakes! Centrepieces of garden roses! Orchids! Calla lilies! A catalogue of conspicuous consumption rains down on Louise's head.

"What happened to documenting the abject? How did you shift from that to this?" Whip! Right at his head! "It's one fucking vanity project after another."

"Vanity?" Elliott gapes at her, like *she*'s the maniac. "It's not *vanity*, Lou." He kicks around the photographs, then digs his sneaker against one particular shot—a close-up of a bride at her dressing table, affixing a droopy earring—a (conflict?) diamond—to her lobe. "These people want everything Photoshopped out. Every blemish. I work at their faces for hours. Until each is this . . . like . . . like a perfectly hollow representation of a human. A placeholder. An approximation of a person. Totally blank faces. With artificial colouring. I tweak the colour of their eyes sometimes. And their lips. Their skin. I alter their bodies." He runs the tip of his shoe over the bride's eye and cheekbone. "It's not vanity. How could it be? These people hate themselves."

Elliott's lip curls as he surveys his work. Is that *disgust*? He drops to a crouch amid his glossies, elbows on his splayed knees, like a hunter studying the tracks of his prey. "The abject aren't in the far-flung corners, Lou. My clients, these brides and grooms, their mothers and fathers and friends . . . the more of their features and personalities I wipe out, the more they like the pictures." His expression briefly softens, turning almost tender as he touches his fingertips to the photographs, as though he's remembering the people he has obliterated. "They let me erase their humanity. And they love me for it. They *beg* me to do it. They *pay* me to do it. What could be more abject than that?"

"Oh my god," Louise whispers, feeling a hole open up in her gut. It's *she* who hasn't been paying attention. "You're *miserable*, Elliott."

"So is everybody!" Elliott waves both hands at the spread of smiling, deranged faces. Louise zeroes in on a crucified Jesus, his expression Photoshopped into extreme perkiness, broadcasting nothing but good cheer and relentless positivity from his position on the cross. He might as well be facilitating a team building workshop up there, his arm already raised, poised to jot down corporate buzz words and handy-dandy acronyms on a crisp sheet of chart paper. "We're all just pretending not to be. Except you, Lou . . . that's something you don't lie about at least."

Elliott finishes the joint, burning the remaining half of it down to his fingers in one pull, like it's nothing. How much of her pot has he been smoking? And what about her pills? Those too? Is that why they don't have sex anymore? Christ, he's further gone than she is.

Elliott tramps across the grotesque collage of wedding photographs. His sneakers scuff up the faces of his brides as he walks out on Louise, slamming the front door behind him. And so Louise, once more, is left alone in the old living room—stranded amid this wreckage, staring at a defaced Jesus who has nothing to offer her but an absolutely exuberant, upbeat smile.

BOOK

BEN

THREE

1

TODAY'S SERMON IS weak, as was last Sunday's, and the one before that. All bland words from the pulpit, all weak brew.

Since his brief, unsuccessful tenure as a doctoral student, Ben has been a faithful parishioner at this Anglican church on the campus' west end. Its high liturgical style—with clouds of incense so thick you can choke, and a strictly classical canon of music—is all very much to God's liking. The heavy red brick walls, the dark wooden ceiling beams: pure gravitas. Not even the mighty St. James Cathedral offers as high a mass as this one.

But these sermons are getting hard to stomach. Today more than usual, perhaps because the late summer heat has him shifting irritably in the pew, sweating far in excess of respectful social dictates. His bib of sweat is ruining his finest Sunday T-shirt. And the apocalypse hot wings he ate last night are firing up his digestive tract.

"When I was a little girl in rural Ontario," the Reverend Roberta is saying, "my mother used to take me to the town dairy for ice cream whenever it got really hot. I always think about those trips when we get scorching days like this one. When the mercury in my little backyard thermometer creeps up into the mid-30s. And that's been happening more and more in recent years, hasn't it?"

Oh, yes, yes. Ben can almost hear the creaking necks of the grey-heads nodding around him. Sunday mass is never more than sparsely attended. Those who do show up are mostly old boomers, the WASPy variety—though today a few students from the divinity college pepper the pews as well. There's also a pair of ancient classics professors wheeled out of cold storage for the service. But by and large it's the boomers that form the congregation, and they love nostalgic stories about childhood and ice cream.

"I know what some of you are thinking," says Reverend Roberta, whose ample proportions fill out the pulpit. "You're thinking, uh-oh, here she goes again, off on another sermon about climate change. And yes, I have been talking about it a lot lately." She leans over the pulpit to cast a conspiratorial eye over her flock. "I hear I've even been called the 'eco-priest' in some circles."

Reverend Roberta pauses to accommodate the polite, ex-pected chuckles. "But our Gospel reading this week has put me in mind for a discussion about our relationship to the earth. In the story we heard from Luke, we have Jesus tell-ing his disciples to be like servants waiting for their master to return, ready to open the door when their master knocks. Now . . . we're like the servants in this story. We have all been entrusted with the care of this home—this earth—and we don't want to leave it in poor shape."

What have we here? Is the good Reverend set to spring off into a true invective? With robust directives for her flock?

And warnings about the personal sacrifices that will be needed to stave off the complete annihilation of the species? Are we to be graced with a rare meaningful homily?

No. Not even the mildest call to action. Instead, the good Reverend carries on with pastoral childhood stories—she works in an anecdote about rotary phones, a reference to a Joni Mitchell song, then finishes with a bizarre allusion to Peter Mansbridge, hitting a trifecta of pop-culture touchstones.

The boomers love it. As they love everything about themselves. A generation of narcissists. Sociopaths. Who have plundered the world, gorged themselves on its riches, and are now leaving it to burn. And despite all this—despite being the most selfish, destructive, and all-around worst collective of humanity ever to walk the earth, who may actually succeed in eradicating the species—they still insist on being pandered to, which the good Reverend, a proud boomer herself, is happy to do.

But the Reverend's feckless preaching soon ends and the mass falls into the firm, guiding hands of tradition. The choir leads a sung recitation of the *Nicene Creed*—Merbecke's sixteenth century composition. Suitably grave. Righteous. Good stuff. The harmonizing voices soothe Ben's irritability. He plucks an offertory envelope from the pew-back in front of him and searches his pockets for loose change. All he has is a ten-dollar bill—a higher percentage of his net worth than he was ready to cough up. But alms must be given. For months the church has been fundraising to fix the rectory roof. Every Wednesday, while preparing the community dinner, Ben listens to the drip-drip-drip of leaks splashing onto the kitchen counters. This week's bulletin features another sad plea for roof donations, so fundraising efforts must be glacial. With a wince, he stuffs his tenner into the envelope.

Before the offertory plate comes around, however, the congregation is brought to its knees (on padded kneelers now) for a communal confession. "Let us humbly confess our sins to almighty God," says Reverend Roberta.

As ever, the week has given rise to a thick catalogue of sins, which Ben silently confesses in broad strokes. Then he lingers on the single sin that won't stop gnawing at his conscience: the lost child.

But what else could have been done? Beyond Ben's economic and emotional limitations, and his total lack of good parental examples—his own parents a pair of violent drunks—there are ethical considerations about bringing a child into a world soon to be plunged back into medieval times. Even the Anglican Church concedes a moral preference to abortion sometimes. Let the child go in peace, rather than come and suffer. The abortion was the least wrong decision, he's sure of that. But certainty is not the same as absolution.

2

AT THE BAGEL PIT, Ben is put on sandwiches for the afternoon, which is better than being on coffee, a post that draws far and away the most frequent and trying customer complaints—*this drink is too hot, it's too milky, it's too sweet, it's too foamy, is this really two shots?*—but sandwiches is no choice post either. It means standing in front of the sandwich fridge for hours, in front of its radiating coolant, which leaves the shirt-front damp, the skin clammy, and the stomach numb with cold by the end of a shift. The plum gig is cash.

The order sheet in front of him, for a Meredith, calls for smoked salmon on sesame seed. He halves a sesame bagel, runs it through the conveyor belt toaster, slathers both halves with a perfect amount of plain cream cheese and fans smoked salmon neatly over top. A tomato is supposed to come next, but they're out of tomatoes again, because Dickhead Debbie, the store manager, never orders enough. To compensate, he adds an extra generous load of the red onion relish, garnishes the whole thing with capers, and two pickled beans rather than the prescribed one.

"Meredith," he calls out.

A woman in her early forties, several years older than Ben, with a swingy ponytail skips up to the counter. But at the sight of her bagel sandwich, plated and ready, she frowns. Must be the tomato. Ben can feel the complaint forming on her lips, so he looks back down at the sandwich deck, and gets busy on the next order in line.

"Excuse me?" Here it comes. "I wanted it on a rosemary bagel."

Ben does not make mistakes on sandwiches. He crushes this job when he's on sandwiches. "Order sheet says sesame." He holds up the sheet with the sesame box clearly ticked. QED.

"I know. I know I might have said sesame. But I *meant* rosemary. Do you mind changing it?"

"Ma'am, I already made the complete sandwich. Exactly as directed to by this order sheet."

She scrunches her face into a pout. "I know. But do you mind?"

"Yes, of course I do. Do you enjoy doing the same job twice when you've done it correctly the first time?"

"Excuse me?"

"You've ordered it on sesame and sesame you have received. That concludes our transaction."

This collapse in the customer-is-always-right ethos requires serious computational effort on her part. *Is this sandwich guy being rude to me? I'm a Customer. Capital-C.*

She plunks an elbow on the counter and leans in. "Let me

speak to your manager. Where's you manager?"

"Well now, ma'am," Ben says, laying out steak strips on the toasted halves of a poppy seed bagel, "that there is a difficult question. Our dear leader Debbie makes but scant appearances on the floor." He feeds the steak-and-cheese bagel back through the toaster. "But you're welcome to wait around and see if Godot turns up."

"What? Can you—just go get your manager. Please. And right now."

"Afraid not, ma'am. Can't leave my post. As you can see, I am incredibly busy tending to the lengthy sandwich queue." Ben nods at the single other person in line, a teenager eagerly eyeing the counter.

"Are you kidding me? This is . . . outrageous. What's your name?"

Ben points to the nametag on his shirt, which reads *Staff*.

"I asked for your name. I'd like to know your name."

"Ah, but I'm sure you can appreciate my bind, ma'am. I can only presume that had the higher-ups wanted me to give out my Christian name to every Tom, Dick, and Harry . . . and Meredith, they would have provided me with a personalized nametag. But they haven't. So here we are. Staff."

"I . . . I . . ." The woman stumbles through her fury, and eventually chokes out a few oaths and imprecations about Ben's future at The Poppy Seed, as well as her future patronage, then charges out of the place in a grandiose huff, her sesame sandwich unclaimed on the counter.

The policy with "defective sandwiches" is to throw them out, since eating a mis-made sandwich amounts to gross workplace theft. Management came up with this policy out of concern that any alternative policy would spiral into serial abuses, with insidious staff members clambering over each other to accidentally-on-purpose prepare faulty sandwiches, thus helping themselves to free meals. Horror. No, it makes much more sense to chuck perfectly good, freshly made, $10 bagel sandwiches into the trash.

Ben sets the sesame sandwich onto one of the lower shelves of the fridge, tucked up against the wall and saved for later, for whoever's hungry and likes smoked salmon. Despite the policy, most staff members save the defects—all the staff members do, except Paulie, the middle-aged Filipino, the new-ish immigrant, with a family to support, three children and a wife jammed into a one-bedroom apartment in Parkdale, to say nothing of the extended family in the Philippines to whom he regularly sends money, a portion of his every paycheque, a tithe. Paulie does everything management asks of him, rendered servile by his terror of being fired. Because if he gets fired, what then? Who's going to pay the rent then? And feed the kids? And send money home?

"What did that woman want? She want your name?" says Megz, sliding over to him from coffee. Megz is the stage name—and preferred name—of Megan, the spoken word poet, an occupation apparent from her appearance, the asymmetrical haircut and the constellation of tattoos, including Fuck the Patriarchy on her forearm, and Lush Words on the back of her neck. "I hate when they want your name. It's totally invasive. This one time, I had a guy chatting me up at the counter, and he just kept saying my name after, like, every sentence. Like, can I get a coffee, Megz? Thanks, Megz. Megz Megz. Creepy, right?"

"Downright scandalous," says Ben.

"You don't have to worry about the creeps as much, being a man, but still. I always give out a fake name now. Laurie. Ha. That was my best friend in kindergarten. Laurie." She laughs at her own subterfuge and drifts back over to coffee.

DURING EVENING CLEAN-UP, Megz blasts a mind-numbing playlist of pop music while she dances around the coffee equipment, slapping the machines with a cloth and pretending she's wiping them down. Ben tidies the sandwich station and Lyle, the twenty-something ginger with the button-down shirts, clean-cut hair, and a streak of anger that runs even deeper than Ben's, sweeps the shop floor.

"Fucking Dickhead Debbie," Lyle grumbles. "She's got me scheduled for tomorrow."

"A Monday?" says Ben. "You don't work Mondays."

"I don't. No. And she knows that. But she's got me in here all night doing inventory. She screwed with my days off again. On purpose. That stupid cow hates me."

Dickhead Debbie does hate him, probably because she heard him call her a stupid cow. She popped into the staff room right as Lyle was verbalizing, with impressive expletive flourishes, his workplace discontent to Ben. At "that stupid cow," Dickhead Debbie expelled a quick cough, glowered, then fled. "Shit," said Lyle, feeling so genuinely bad that he sought her out in her office to apologize. Dickhead Debbie accepted the apology with a curt nod, but has since expanded her response to include screwing with Lyle's shifts—scheduling him for days she knows he's unavailable, cutting down his hours, and a host of similarly petty retaliations.

And as if on cue, here comes Dickhead Debbie now, bouncing from the kitchen to cash out. Her walk is a series of bops and bounces, up, down, up and down, her head bobbing on top of her thin, reedy body. In one jittery hand, she carries an energy drink, the tiny can cracked open and presumably already near-empty.

"Everything here good good good?" she says. This is a tic Dickhead Debbie has—repeating words, twice, sometimes three times.

"No," says Ben. " We are, once again, out of tomatoes."

"Again?" Dickhead Debbie skips over to the sandwich fridge and looks down at the empty tomato container. "Are you maybe being too generous with the tomatoes, Ben?"

"No, Debbie. I am being very stingy. One thin slice and only when it's an explicitly stated ingredient in the 'sandwich creation.' Exactly as you told me."

"Well, okay, I'll order more."

"We are also low on the dill cream cheese. Again."

Her eyes dart to the cream cheese selections; the twelve displayed varieties are always supposed to be kept topped up, because the Customer likes to see an overflow, a wealth of creamy cream cheese piled thick and high, challenging the confines of its container.

"Okay. More dill dill cheese. But I see we haven't moved much of the pumpkin spice. I thought the pumpkin spice would be doing better. Lyle, have you been pushing it?"

"Yup."

"Every order, okay? I want to hear you letting each and every Customer know the pumpkin spice is out now. And for a limited time. Okay?"

"Got it. Pumpkin."

Dickhead Debbie helps herself to a plain bagel from the bagel racks, which she smears with the sickly sweet pumpkin spice cream cheese. It's children who typically order the pumpkin spice, the same children who sometimes order whole cups of whipped cream.

"Want me to ring that up for you, Debbie?" Lyle asks.

"What? No, no," she says, a flush rising over her face. "I'll punch it in later." Then, with a sharp tilt of the head: "Where's your *Ask Me About My Favourite Bagel* button, Lyle?"

Lyle gestures at his hip, where the big button hangs from the bottom of his untucked shirt, the standard issue button, required of all employees, meant to promote friendly conversation with the Customer.

"It needs to be higher. Up by the chest pocket. Up up. We want the Customer to see it, don't we?" Her focus slides over to Megz at the coffee station. "Oh my god, Megan?" she says, her face reflecting a newly discovered horror. "Have you been wearing that all day? That . . . button?"

Megz glances down at the *Vegans Taste Better* button by her shoulder, next to the store-mandated one. A big fan of button culture, Megz has taken to complementing the *Ask-Me-About-My-Favourite-Bagel* number with her own selections. So far the staff have been treated to a *This is What a Feminist Looks Like* button, an *Eve was Framed* button, even a beef buster button once, which didn't go over well, because the implied judgment irked some of the roast beef- and steak-ordering customers.

"Yeah," says Megz. "You said we could wear buttons."

"But that is . . . suggestive. Take it off."

Megz flaps an exasperated wave around the empty shop. "We're closed."

"This is a workplace. It's inappropriate workplace attire. Take it off, Megan." Having irritated every individual employee, Dickhead Debbie swoops the cash from the register into her deposit bag. "Oh, and guys? Before you all leave tonight, I want the storeroom in the basement cleaned out, okay? We've got the new merchandise coming in next week and we need to clear out some room."

Ben checks his watch: 6:12pm. This shift is over at 6:30pm and he can't work overtime tonight. He has a date with Joly. Turner Classic Movies is running a Charlie Chaplin marathon. And he's left a three-meat chilli simmering on the stove all day. Perfect pairing. Things have been stiff with Joly since the abortion. He hasn't seen her in five days, hasn't had sex in a month. But she said yes to Chaplin, yes to chilli, yes to a night at his place.

"No, absolutely not," he says. "We're off in eighteen minutes. That is a start-of-the-day request."

"Don't tell me how to manage this place, Ben. I'm juggling a lot of balls, okay? Just do your part and get it done done done. I sent Paulie down there already. The four of you should be able to finish by 6:30."

Paulie is forever being banished to the basement or the back rooms or the kitchen, because Dickhead Debbie gets too antsy when he's out front, worried that his "mangled English" will distract the Customer. Ben hasn't actually seen Paulie in hours; he forgot Paulie was in today.

"Debbie. Be reasonable. That storeroom is a mess."

"Well. Better get cracking then, huh?" And then it comes, the single gesture that Ben hates above all others, the one habit of Dickhead Debbie's that sends a shiver of murderous rage up his spine. She brings her palms together in two sharp resounding claps: *chop-chop.*

Ben's big body shudders.

"Every day she eats one of those pumpkin spice cream cheese bagels," Lyle says as they watch her round head bobble down the hallway. "D'you know that last year, she took the leftover pumpkin spice tubs home. Full tubs. Two of them. Never pays for it. All those bagels and cream cheese. But me, I eat a pickled bean once, and she writes me up."

"I'm sick of her always hassling me about my buttons. Do you guys have a problem with this button?" Megz asks with a fond tug at the favoured adornment.

"I got nothing against it," says Ben.

"S'fine," says Lyle.

"Yeah. Exactly. It's good."

"My brother, my sister," says Ben, seizing on the mood of collective disgruntlement. "These are precisely the sorts of grievances we would not have to deal with if we had a union.

We would be beholden to clearly outlined rules and procedures, not the whims of a maniac."

But neither Lyle nor Megz pays him any attention. "I'd like to fuck with *her* schedule somehow." Lyle gazes deep into the tub of pumpkin spice cream cheese. "Fuck with her livelihood. See how she likes it."

"She's, like, trampling all over my individuality." Megz adjusts the button on her shoulder strap.

"She deserves to be fucked with," mutters Lyle, wandering across the shop floor with his broom.

By the time they finish clean-up, it's already 6:24pm. For form's sake, they amble down to the basement, where they find Paulie amid heaps of old merchandise—T-shirts and ball caps and teapots and cutlery sets, all embossed with the old The Poppy Seed logo, now rendered useless by the recent revamp. Some items are crammed into boxes, but most are loose, strewn across shelves, on the floor, everywhere. And all of it has to be sorted, boxed, and labelled.

For exactly six minutes, Ben puts in a spectacularly half-assed effort and then, when the second hand on his watch ticks up to 6:30pm, he announces: "That's it. Quittin' time."

"Thank god," says Lyle, dropping a handful of T-shirts onto the floor.

But Paulie looks less relieved, his expression closer to panic. "Debbie says to finish. But it's too much." He waves a helpless hand at the cluttered shelves.

"I know," says Ben. "The morning crew can finish up tomorrow."

"Debbie says to finish tonight."

"Quittin' time is quittin' time," Ben offers with a matter-of-fact shrug.

It's already 6:38pm when they exchange goodbyes in the staff room—they've already been here several minutes too long. Before Ben leaves, however, he detours to the Men's to deal with the effects of last night's apocalypse hot wings: He takes a profound shit, requiring epic patience and endurance, a shit that clears him right out, and on his triumphant emergence from the can almost twenty minutes later, he expects to find the shop empty. But in the staff room, beside Ben's backpack, the same bag he used in high school—that can be identified by smell from several feet away—he notices Paulie's ballcap. Paulie never leaves without his cap, which means Paulie has not left, which means he's back down in that basement cleaning out that godforsaken storeroom.

"Paulie?" Ben calls out. He climbs down the stairs to the basement and tries again: "Paulie?"

Sure enough, the light in the storeroom is on, and beneath the severe fluorescents stands Paulie, sorting through the piles of outdated merchandise.

"I finish. I finish quick," he says.

"But we clocked out already."

"It's okay. I finish."

"But you're working for free now."

"Won't take long."

Paulie's body seems to be moving at double speed, his arms darting out in one direction, then another, reaching for items and relocating them into appropriate boxes. Ben should leave. It's worse for them all if he stays and helps and contributes to the normalization of this insane and illegal work ethic. But what is he supposed to do? Leave Paulie to sweat it out in the basement alone?

He throws his bag down in the doorway and calls Joly to tell her he'll be late.

"How late?" she asks, her voice flat, neither annoyed nor sympathetic to this change of plans.

"I'm not sure, doll. An hour or so?"

"So we'll miss *City Lights*?"

"Yeah. But we could still catch the rest of the marathon. And have dinner later? Give the chilli extra time to simmer."

" . . ."

"Joly?"

After another strained pause, comes this: "Let's just rain check it."

"Oh. I'm really sorry, Joly."

"It's fine."

"I miss you, doll," he says, but she has already hung up.

$$3$$

DECKED OUT IN his comfort wear, Ben spills his sizeable body across two faded couch cushions and sloshes another cup of homemade mead down his throat, dribbling only a minimal amount over his beard and the front of his bright yellow Hulkamania shirt. Charlie Chaplin sashays across the TV in explosive, gut-splitting bursts.

"Pay attention to this part, young Geoffrey!" cries Ben. "Haha ha! Look at his feet. It's the feet that makes him the funniest funnyman of the twentieth century." He grabs the bottle of mead from the coffee table, refills his own glass first, then Geoffrey's, his roommate, an undergraduate. The household typically balks at allowing youth to enter the fold, they being erratic, irresponsible, and generally unknowl-edgeable about domestic labours. But when Geoffrey came for a viewing of the basement bedroom on offer, he men-tioned owning a meat smoker. The household unanimously agreed to bend its own rules. And although they broke this appliance on third use, Geoffrey's six-month tenure has proven harmonious.

"Oh yes, watch this!" Ben cries as Charlie Chaplin gets to work on an assembly line. "This is where the indignities of modern labour send him off the deep end. Ha! Haha. Still apt."

"Where's Joly been at?" asks Geoffrey, on the other end of the couch.

"What?"

"Don't you usually watch these movies with her?"

"I watch them with everyone! All are welcome. Chaplin is the people's comedian. Now pay attention, I said."

He throws more mead down the hatch, feeling it coat his throat with its honeyed sweetness, dispelling the sour notes brought on by the reminder of Joly's absence. This was the household's first attempt at brewing mead, a formidable success. Bottled ambrosia, the cure for any ailment. Tonight it has worked wonders on his mood. Following that extra hour in the storeroom, he arrived home steaming from his ears. To keep from blowing his lid, he composed a letter of grievance against Dickhead Debbie, his fourth in the last few months. After the first missive, Frank, the head manager of all three The Poppy Seed locations, called Ben in for a tête-a-tête, and in a congenial tone discussed with Ben the ins and outs of each of his complaints, then ended the meeting with a firm promise to ameliorate the situation. But nothing happened. After the second letter, Ben earned only an emailed acknowledgement, assuring him that matters would be looked into. The third letter garnered no reply. Tonight's comprehensive letter, however, with itemized points and detailed examples cannot possibly be ignored. The exercise of composition defused his anger. But it did nothing for his overall Joly-tinged gloominess. Not until he hit the mead did the clouds part and his spirits rise.

Ben empties the bottle, their third, into his glass. He only drinks two nights a week, recognizing in himself a hereditary bent toward intoxication, but when he does drink, he indulges. Five dry days ought to be enough to keep the demons at bay. He swirls the golden brew and raises it high up to the light to admire his own work.

"Jesus, you stink, Ben," says Geoffrey, sitting directly in the wafting path of Ben's tremendous summertime odour.

Ben sniffs at his own exposed armpit. The sleeves of this old T-shirt have long since been ripped off to give the garment a second life as an A-shirt. In another year or so, the shirt will realize its final reincarnation as a shoeshine rag. Awed by the power of his scent, Ben raises his elbow higher and leans his armpit toward his roommate.

"Gaze into the abyss, Geoffrey."

As Geoffrey shuffles back over the armrest of the couch, another roommate, Runkle, explodes into the living room, brandishing a piece of paper above his head.

"You guys see this?" His gangly limbs obstruct the wide-screen TV, which they found on the neighbour's curb last fall.

"Out of the way, Runkle. We're on a spiritual odyssey. Chaplin. We'll be here all night."

"*We* won't be," says Geoffrey. "Ben, seriously, where's Joly at? Tell her we need her back. You're killing me."

"Guys!" cries Runkle. At forty-five, he is the eldest of the roommates, an adjunct professor, who moved into the Sanctum after a surprise divorce left him impoverished and friendless. "We're being evicted. It's an eviction notice."

"Gimme that." Ben struggles against the soft couch cushions. He swipes the paper—the words whirl around the sheet. Tricky mead. He didn't realize he was nearly this drunk. Squinting an eye, he forces one line of text after another into focus, searching the notice for the stated grounds for eviction. Ah, there it is: renovation and repairs on a scale that requires vacating the premises.

Ben places a hand on Runkle's shoulder and looks him square in the eye. "Gather the family. Household meeting."

FOR EIGHT YEARS—eight!—Ben has lived in this house, since his first year in grad school, when a fellow student offered him a room in the basement, where all the roommates begin and whence they slowly work their way up. After nearly a decade, Ben has ascended to the top floor, the second best bedroom in this century-old house. Only Kata, the international student from Croatia, in the tenth year of her Ph.D., has been here longer than he has.

Standing in front of the TV, Ben casts a glance at the four roommates assembled before him. Missing at this meeting is Esther, who has rarely been seen in the evenings since she picked up a job as a bike courier for a restaurant delivery company.

"Comrades . . . my brothers and sisters, my spiritual brethren, my co-dwellers in this, our home and sanctum," Ben begins, "the penny has dropped. The sword of Damocles has finally fallen on our heads. We are being renovicted. To which I say . . . fuck that." And then he lets loose a belch that rattles his chest.

"Can you make this speech without forcing us to look at your nipples, Ben?" asks Kata.

Ben looks down at his ripped yellow shirt. The great might of his chest has strained the fabric, causing a six-inch horizontal tear straight out from the sleeve hole, exposing his left nipple. "Behold the image of God, Kata . . . in his comfort wear."

"I'm overwhelmed by the glory. Now can you just . . . tug your shirt a little to the left?"

Ben adjusts his shirt slightly to conceal the offending

body part and Kata nods her thanks. "We have two options," Ben continues, pacing in front of the TV, where the Chaplin marathon plays out on mute. "We can accept this notice, walk out with our asses in hand and our nuts fully receded." Ben pauses and bows magnanimously toward Kata. "Kata, you're welcome to think up your own gender-appropriate analogy."

"Thank you, Ben."

"Or . . . we can refuse to vacate. Resistance! We can fight the eviction. Rain fire and fury on the Landlord and Tenant Board." The wave of renovictions that has swept the city is turning cataclysmic. These landlords—scribes and Pharisees to the last—toss out any tenants still paying reasonable rents citing intentions to renovate. They make a few cosmetic changes, slap up new coats of paint, then jack up the rent to unholy heights.

"We won't win that fight," says Runkle. "Tenants never win."

"Look at this place," says Marko, another former student, who dropped out around the same time as Ben, also seeing the writing on the wall of academia. He has since found far more fortune and fulfillment in his new career as a bike mechanic. "You can't argue that it's not in need of top-to-bottom renovation. We are an inspection away from being condemned."

"Bah! Anything can pass inspection these days," says Ben.

"Where am I gonna find rent this cheap again?" laments Geoffrey. "And I just got here."

"This is fucked," says Kata, furiously passing her hands through her short dark hair. After ten years in the Ph.D. program—and still no end in sight, and certainly no job on the horizon—Kata has become a pressure cooker of frustration. "Fucked! Fuck this landlord."

"Yes! Indeed. Excellent spirit, Kata!" says Ben. "What say you then? As our ranking tenant?"

Kata stands up and kicks her heel into the couch. "All right, Ben. My lady balls are swinging low today. Fuck him. Let's fight it."

"Seconded," says Geoffrey.

"Boys?" Ben asks with a nod at Runkle and Marko. Both shrug their acquiescence.

"Good. Then it's decided. I'll draft our letter of refusal," says Ben. "Now, in the meantime . . ." He sinks back into the couch and cranks the volume on the TV. "Geoffrey! More mead!"

4

SITTING IN THE back office of The Poppy Seed, Ben waits for Frank to make an opening move toward détente. His adversary, a hollow-chested non-entity, already bears the look of defeat—the nervous adjustment of his thick-rimmed glasses, the bent shoulders, the palpable fatigue. Frank, with two young kids, an ill parent, and a mediocre-at-best career, has plainly been ground down by life.

"So I got your email," Frank says.

"I'm glad."

"It's long."

"It's not that long. But I was trying to be thorough."

Ben studies the state of chaos on the desktop. Amid the disarray of papers and folders is a smattering of useless objects: a magic-eight ball, a bagel-shaped pencil sharpener, a wind-up robot, a dead aloe plant, an emoji Chia pet. All items from Dickhead Debbie's growing collection, part of a campaign to claim this shared office as her own. But none of this can get Ben down today. Last night he found a whole chicken on clearance at the Chinese grocery, just a few days past its best-before date. With a bottle of plonk and some scrounged vegetables, he can whip up a coq-au-vin for Joly, who has readily agreed to cash in her rain check tonight. In honour of the occasion, he even swung by the Sally Ann to buy himself a sharp new outfit.

"Do you realize how long it is, Ben?" asks Frank. "Because I printed it out. And it runs onto four sheets of paper. Single-spaced." Frank lays the four printed sheets on the desk in front of Ben, one beside the other. So Ben looks them over:

Greetings and Good Morning Frank Stark:

Please consider this a follow-up to my earlier letters, the last of which, to my enduring dismay, earned no reply or acknowledgment. (Did you not receive it, I wonder? Hard to imagine, but I suppose, in these days of technological malfunctions, such things are bound to happen. If you did not in fact receive my last letter, dated July 11, I will happily resend.) The purpose of this correspondence is to bring to your attention several ongoing grievances about management at the Ossington location of The Poppy Seed. The grievances are numerous, so I have, for your convenience, and to facilitate any subsequent discussion, fit them into five broad categories. These are itemized below.

Unpaid overtime: *On several occasions I have witnessed staff clock out of a shift, then return to work to complete a task that Store Manager Debbie has pronounced "urgent and necessary." It pains me to report that I, out of a sense of fraternal solidarity with my beleaguered coworkers, have engaged in this heinous practice myself. Compelling employees to work without pay is, as you are of course aware, a violation of the Ontario labour code, as well as a violation of common human decency. The compulsion in this case arises from the general sense of terror Debbie has instilled in many of her subordinates (see point 2 below).*

Climate of hostility: *Store Manager Debbie has exhibited a strong tendency toward retaliatory and vengeful behaviour. This, in fact, seems to be her managerial style. Small workplace errors made by a subordinate have been punished with public beratings on the shop floor (this in front of the holy Customer, no less!). Though I suppose this may be preferential to the many other improper workplace penalties she sees fit to impose, regardless of whether the "offence" was personal or professional. Perceived personal slights are often met with unwanted schedule changes or extended sentences at the least desirable workstations for the employee under scrutiny. Unsurprisingly, this peculiar brand of (mis?)management has resulted in a hostile work environment, rife with anxiety, resentment, and fear, all of which are antithetical to the stated principles of The Poppy Seed, as detailed in the employee guidebook.*

Inventory mismanagement: *One ingredient or another is always absent at the sandwich fridge. As I'm sure you understand, this hampers our ability to execute The Poppy Seed's "sandwich creations" to the letter. The problem stems from Debbie's complete failure to both a) anticipate the shop's needs and b) arrange to meet those needs. Her system of assessing inventory needs seems to hinge entirely on her own personal food preferences. She is, for example, unable to grasp that, although she herself is no fan of tomatoes, the broader human community likes them rather a lot. (As an aside, tomatoes happen to be the most commonly consumed fruit on the planet, per metric ton.) The (near chronic) issue of tomatoes is but one example. In the last month alone, we have run out of pickles, lettuce, and popular cream cheeses (plain, herb, dill), among other items. It should be noted that each of these is a food that Debbie does not personally enjoy. When it comes to managing inventory, empirically verified facts about tastes and trends are routinely trumped by Debbie's own preferences.*

The use of stimulants: *Debbie's mood is consistently and unnaturally jacked up by at least two powerful stimulants: sugar and caffeine. I have observed her ingest two boxes of Wonka Nerds and three Red Bull energy drinks in a one-hour timespan. The effects of the drugs are immediately apparent. She exudes a manic energy that is near impossible to tolerate. She bounces around the shop, heedless of the many and varied hazards that exist in the workplace (knives, hot toasters, sharp edges, etc.). Worse is that she seems to believe that this artificially induced mania is a state to which her subordinates ought to aspire. This manifests in horrendous ways, from an abrasive (and dare I say deranged?) form of cheerleading to frantically gung-ho hand gestures. Further to this point, I must also absolutely insist on an immediate end to her deployment of the chop-chop hand motion, which is both degrading and ineffective as a motivational tool.*

Time management: *This is really an umbrella point that must be broken up into sub-point a) Debbie's incompetence managing her own time, and sub-point b) her incompetence managing her subordinates' time.*

Store Manager Debbie is clearly frazzled by the demands of her position. How many times has she, in a jittery torrent of anxiety, unleashed on me an explanation about the enormous pressures she's under, the innumerable tasks she's expected to complete, and the impossibility of fitting all her required work into her scheduled shifts? Yet sometimes whole hours can pass in which Debbie is neither on the shop floor nor in her office, the two supposed hubs of work activity. Having undertaken the managerial duties myself (in a relief capacity, as you'll recall), I am familiar with the actual (meagre) amount of work the position requires. I must therefore deduce that Debbie is either legitimately delusional or a hysterical personality. Interestingly, her own anxiety around time management has in no way made her less likely to inflict such anxiety on others. This brings us to sub-point b.

Debbie has no idea how to manage the time of her staff. If I were to speculate, I would say this is because she herself has no idea how long any particular task takes, as she herself never performs any of these tasks. Her demands on staff are grounded in neither experience nor reason. An example still odiously fresh in my mind: tonight, with less than a half hour left in the closing shift, she demanded the completion of a substantial task (the cleaning out of the basement storeroom, which, under her charge, is always in total disarray) by the day's end. Concerns about the impossibility and outrageousness of this demand were naturally raised, but Debbie summarily dismissed these with no more than a hand waved in contempt. This is, of course, in keeping with her tradition of gross insensitivity to the stresses she imposes on her staff. Indeed, one wonders whether she may be completely bereft of empathetic capabilities. (Were I responsible, or in any way liable, for this woman's behaviour, I might recommend psychiatric evaluation on this point.)

Should you require further elaboration or discussion of these matters, I will happily make myself available. Otherwise, I look forward to their swift resolution.

Your faithful bagel slave,

Ben Drummond, B.A., M.A.

Ben sits back in his plastic chair and nods approvingly. "I could have gone on."

"Look, Ben, you do a fine job here. You get your work done. You make the sandwiches right. You're good on coffee, quick on cash. You only have to be told to do things once. And I appreciate all that."

"Thank you." Ben crosses an ankle over his knee, lets his elbows spill out over the armrests, and waits.

"But let me ask you something. Do you think this is the right job for you?"

"Well . . . no, of course not. But it's the kind of job that is available to me."

"What do you expect me to do with a letter like this?" Frank flaps the sheets in front of him helplessly.

"I expect you to address the concerns. Maybe fire this manager? At least wrest all authority from her hands? Retrain her? Personally I'm not convinced it's possible to transform Debbie into a competent manager, but that is at your discretion of course."

"I'm not firing her. That's not gonna happen. Debbie's been here a long time." Frank allows a tired glance at the collectibles befouling the desk. "She's been very loyal to this company."

"That doesn't make her sane, or humane, or competent."

Pinching the broad arm of his glasses, Frank forces himself to sit up a little taller. "You say this is the kind of job that's available to you. And I'm telling you that Debbie is the kind of manager that's available to me. You're a smart guy, Ben. Think about this. What kind of person am I going to get to fill this role, huh? You? What happens if I hire you? Sure, for a while, you'd do a better job than Debbie. But for how long? A guy like you, with your education and your skillset, you'll be out of here as soon as something better comes up. And something will come up. But Debbie . . . she's not going anywhere. You know what a headache it is to find and train managers?"

"Where am I going? I've been here more than a year."

"I know that. And honestly, Ben, I don't know what you're still doing here. Shouldn't you be in school?"

Synapses flare in Ben's brain as he stares at the smiling face of the Chia pet. Because even now—on his worst days—he still toys with the idea of venturing back into the bowels of academia, grinding out that doctorate after all. But the academic system is churning out far more doctoral grads than there are jobs for. The lucky ones manage to scrounge up work as adjuncts, teaching a few courses a year at a smattering of schools, driving around town and province from one campus to another in order to scrape out a living wage.

Ben, being a natural leader-of-men, once dreamt of a professorship. But such a post, as with so many others, is nothing like what he'd been led to believe. A professor's work is no longer about instruction. Students aren't required to learn anything in their courses anymore; they only need to *like* them. They need to be entertained, and even more critically, they need to say so on their feedback forms and their course evaluations and their online reviews. A rigorous approach doesn't pass muster with students who review their courses as they review a new restaurant, bar, hotel, or airline. *How fun was the course? How easy? How entertaining? How accommodating was the professor?* And just like any business concerned with the bottom line, the university heeds these rambling, shrieking appraisals sent out into the void, without, it seems, stopping to think about what might go wrong when a university staffs its faculty based on Yelp reviews.

Ideologies in academia have shifted. The student has become the Customer. And the Customer must be satisfied. So what is a professorship anymore, really, but another grovelling customer service gig? He might as well be making bagel sandwiches.

Frank is gazing at him, waiting.

"School doesn't suit me," Ben says.

"All right, look." Frank gathers the pages of Ben's letter and returns them to a faded blue folder that disappears into a drawer. "The overtime situation is a problem. Obviously I didn't know that was happening. That's going to stop right away. I'll make it clear to all staff that no one should be working when they're not on the clock."

"I appreciate that."

"I know Debbie can be a bit much sometimes. I'll talk to her. But Ben, try to make it work with her, all right?"

"I always do, boss man." Ben stands up and extends a hand, which Frank takes and shakes. "But you really might want to talk to her about the tomatoes. It's every week with the tomatoes."

"Goodbye, Ben."

In the corridor outside the office, Ben finds Dickhead Debbie scurrying, in no clear direction, and holding the last quarter of a bagel smothered in pumpkin spice cream cheese.

"So what was that about?" she asks, her neck torqued, and her features twisted by nervous concern.

"Just shoptalk, Debbie. Just a bit of shoptalk."

5

RAIN THUNDERS AGAINST the kitchen window as Ben inhales the flavours of his simmering chicken stew. He revels in the whooshing winds blowing through the open back door, a welcome relief from the last weeks' searing heat. While fetching the potatoes, he catches sight of his reflection in the mirror on the pantry door, scrubbed out and looking very sharp indeed in his new khaki shorts and black T-shirt with intact sleeves. He notes, with some satisfaction, how his long hair, freshly washed and parted on the left, gives him the look of a professional wrestler—who has only just recently started to let himself go. The soft flowing hair of a Bret Hart paired with the raw magnetism of a Macho Man.

"Ben, my man," says Geoffrey, strolling into the kitchen to make a sandwich. "You hear about the $800? Landlord is offering us each $800 to leave by the end of the month?"

"What? No. What nonsense is that?"

"He called today. Kata talked to him."

"And all she extracted from him was $800? A piddling offer. Piddling. Declined . . . with extreme prejudice."

Geoffrey is silent at the counter as he pulls slices of Wonderbread from the bread bag. But his screwed-up mouth hints at mutinous thoughts.

"What?" demands Ben.

Keeping his back to Ben, Geoffrey butters his bread. He drops his head low over his pathetic little sandwich operation, then mumbles, "It's just that Runkle says we'll lose at the LTB anyway. Then we'll wind up with nothing at all."

"Runkle says? You're listening to Runkle now? His life is in shambles!"

"$800 is not nothing, Ben." Geoffrey slaps a few slices of bologna between his buttered bread and takes the sandwich to the table. "It'll help with moving costs at least." He sends a dreamy glance out the wide open back door. "Maybe I could even get a new bed."

"What?" cries Ben, gaping at this misguided youth. "You don't need *money* to get a new bed! Who raised you? The street provides you what you need!" Ben bangs a fist against the table, rattling Geoffrey's plate. "This table! From the alley behind Pizzarella! That mirror!" He waves a wild arm at the pantry door. "From the curbside down the block! Our coffee table, bookshelves, toaster, waffle maker! The street provides! I don't understand—"

A loud sizzle from the stove interrupts Ben's rant and he rushes to check his chicken. The old stove has peculiarities—its knobs fall off and the elements are prone to mysterious spikes and falls in temperature. "Geoffrey," he says, monitoring the stew closely, "you know that I consider myself your spiritual guide, and I recognize that you are in a period of crisis. But I don't have time for preliminaries today.

I have potatoes to peel and—"

"Whoa wait, what's going on with your shorts there, dude?" Geoffrey asks, waving his half-eaten sandwich at Ben's hips.

"What do you mean?" Ben looks down, searching the front of his new shorts for an overlooked stain, then cranks his neck over his shoulder to inspect the back—but he lacks the flexibility for a comprehensive probe.

"No, the hips . . . " Geoffrey stifles his laughter behind his sandwich. "They're gigantic. Look! They're ballooning out."

Ben straightens up into a dignified stance, chin jutted out and defiant. "I'll have you know, Geoffrey, that these shorts happen to be a ladies cut. Because the selection at the Sally Ann is pitiful at the moment. And I'll thank you not to make fun. Now, as I was saying, I don't have time for you right now. Joly is due in twenty minutes and my coq is only half-cooked."

"Joly's back? Oh thank god."

"I've got some hard-boiled noirs lined up for tonight." Ben points at the stack of library DVDs on the kitchen table with his wooden spoon. "Tell me, young Geoffrey, how familiar are you with the crackerjack detective work of one Sam Spade?"

But before Geoffrey, still stifling laughter and gawking at Ben's blooming hips, can respond, the lights overhead cut out. They hear the whir, click, and hum of machinery powering down, leaving the kitchen in an unfamiliar silence.

"Fuck!" says Ben. He checks each kitchen appliance, frantically flicks at the light switch, does a quick lap around the entire house, but the power is down everywhere.

"Probably a tree on a power line," says Geoffrey, standing at the back door, now closed, and watching the storm through its window. "I'm sure it'll be back up in a few minutes."

But the last time a squall like this struck the city, the power was down for days in certain neighbourhoods. And it was not because of trees on power lines. It was because a Hydro One station flooded. Because the city's electrical grid, a relic from the fifties, is a network of aging wiring, failing cables, rusting transformers, and exploding circuit breakers. The power won't be back for hours, at least.

With arms akimbo, in the middle of the kitchen, Ben looks at his half-cooked stew, at the unpeeled potatoes, and at Geoffrey. "Fuck!"

When Joly is fifteen minutes late and not answering her phone, Ben starts to worry that she might have bailed. But at thirty minutes late, and still no response to his texts, he sits with his face glued to the living room window, listening to the ominous howl of the wind beating on the trees and bushes. A maple in the neighbour's front yard has already lost a bough, which now lies dead across the street, blocking traffic.

"I'm sure she's fine," says Geoffrey from the corner chair, where he keeps banging on the keys of his laptop, hoping this effort will restore the internet. "It's gone . . . it's just gone," he repeats mournfully.

Filling out the living room are Marko and Runkle, playing Jenga at the coffee table, where they have been since Runkle came up from his basement bedroom bringing news that it had started to flood.

"How could she be fine?" says Ben. "You've seen Joly. She's a wisp of a girl. She'll be tossed around in these primordial winds."

On the sidewalk, a woman twice Joly's weight is wrestling with her umbrella and losing the contest. But there! Down at the end of the block—Joly! Staggering into the wind. Ben's stomach slackens; he jumps up, brushes crumbs and beard dandruff off his shirt and rushes to meet her at the door.

"I'm afraid . . . there's no food," he announces, hanging her red raincoat over the banister to dry. "Or TV. Or power of any kind."

"Oh," Joly says, rainwater dripping from her hair and face.

He can't tell from her tone if she's disappointed or merely

spent from the trek through the storm. "I can rustle us up something to graze on. But the coq . . . the noble bird is already back in the fridge."

A thorough scouring of the pantry shelves and the fridge turns up an adequate spread of snackables—bagels stolen from the pit, sandwich bread, discount deli meat, a tin of corned beef, humus, and a variety of cheeses and pickles. They bring the spread into the living room and set it on the coffee table, where Joly, much quieter than usual, gets in on the Jenga game.

"Say, I liked your story, Joly," says Marko, delicately placing a Jenga tile on the top of the already-leaning tower.

Joly launches to attention, standing up on her knees, ready for the blessing of a compliment. "What story? Which one?"

"That one about the rhino-cum-bureaucrat."

"Oh yeah? You liked it? What did you like about it?" The praise turns her fingers to jelly. She topples the structure the moment she touches it.

"You know . . . it's funny," says Marko with a one-shouldered shrug.

"Yeah. It's funny," she agrees, and Ben rests a proud paw on her shoulder. Her strange little stories tickle him. Trenchant observations in them all. The woman is underappreciated by this culture of deviant philistines.

During the rebuild of the Jenga tower, a lively mouse hurries along the wall behind the TV. Runkle spots it first and waves at it with his pickle. "They're everywhere now," he says. "$800 to leave this dump is starting to look pretty damn good."

"Mm-hmm," says Marko.

"Runkle, my brother," says Ben, "this dump has sheltered you through your darkest days."

"Yeah yeah."

"How long is the internet gonna be gone for?" wails Geoffrey at his laptop.

"Expect to see more of all this in the coming years," Ben

says, resting his chin on Joly's shoulder as she contemplates her next Jenga move. "More storms, more violent weather patterns, more blackouts." He sweeps an arm at the dark and menacing world outside the windows. "Take it in, my friends. Take it all in. We are living in the twilight of Western civilization."

AROUND EIGHT, WHEN the light has faded, young Geoffrey and Marko, the basement contingent, spread out blankets and sleeping bags on the living room furniture in case the basement flooding turns severe overnight. Ben leads Joly upstairs by the light of his cellphone. He scrolls the frequencies on his battery-operated radio until he hears classical music—Haydn, if he's not mistaken—then he settles down beside her on the foam mattress.

"Come here, doll," he says, pulling her toward him. She sets her head on his chest, where he nuzzles at it with his chin. Her frame is so fragile; she feels slight, vulnerable in his arms. Wind and rain hammer the house, drowning out the softer passages of music crackling through the radio. "I haven't seen you in a week," he says into her hair.

"Mm." She squirms out of his embrace and shuffles a few inches away from him. "I think I forgot what you smell like. It's . . . potent."

"My musk? I thought you liked it. You told me it was pleasing."

"I do like it. It's just . . . it's not even that hot tonight."

Ben lies still, stung, trying to sniff out any noticeable change in his healthy animal musk. After a few minutes of charged silence, Joly reaches out a conciliatory hand. "I liked the look of that chicken," she says. "I'm sure it would have been bang-up."

"Oh, it would have been revelatory."

"Maybe we can have it tomorrow?" She tugs on his wrist, drawing him into a spoon.

"Of course." His head presses into her shoulder blades. "No wait. Tomorrow's Wednesday. Church dinner. How about Thursday?"

"I'm babysitting Yvie." She waits a beat, then adds, "You can come over . . . if you want. Cook it at my place?"

"At your brother's?" Her brother, the parasite, the adulterer. Ben hates going over to that pleasure palace.

"If you want."

How can he say no? This is the first time she has initiated a rendezvous in weeks. And her body relaxes into his when he accepts.

Unaccustomed to this blackout darkness, he touches his hand to her face, her small cheek, and he lets his fingers feel out her features. Then he moves down, feeling out her whole form, his hand pausing at her stomach.

This is the most sustained contact they've had all month. Uncertain about the recovery time of an abortion, he has been afraid to touch her. The literature he consulted instruct-ed him to wait at least two weeks, a window that has doubled. But he *is* keen, a newly bought pack of condoms awaiting use in his nightstand. He bought them—his first time buying condoms in years—the day she announced her pregnancy, as though they would have a retroactive efficacy. But neither of them likes condoms.

In his most panicked moments of the last month, he's even weighed the possibility of a vasectomy. Though the idea produces a quivering in his testicles. His father had a vasectomy, a blessing for the world, but less of one for the old man himself, who came out of the procedure with what was aptly diagnosed as "post-vasectomy pain syndrome." He spent months with either a hot water bottle or an ice pack on his groin, uncertain over which better eased the pain. One evening, while Ben was eating dinner (cereal), the old man stormed into the kitchen in search of the ice pack. He dropped his two hundred and fifty pounds of weight into a chair across from Ben and held the compress to his crotch, his head thrown back. When, after long dragging minutes, some version of relief came, the old man sat up, reached for the cereal box, paused with his fat fingers around it, looked Ben in the eye, and said, "Don't ever let them fuck with your balls, boy." That nugget sank deep into Ben's neural network, so that every time he even thinks the word *vasectomy*, he feels a phantom pain in his scrotum.

But he'd do it if she asked him to. If that is the only way to get back on track.

He moves an exploratory hand to her hip. She guides it up to her face and curls herself against him. No suggestion of anything more.

6

IN THE SMALL horseshoe-shaped rectory kitchen adjoining the church, Ben scrubs meat loaf remnants from a dinner plate, his feet positioned awkwardly beside the bucket that's catching rainwater leaking from the ceiling.

Turnout at tonight's dinner was better than expected: over fifty, a quarter of which were parishioners, a quarter university students looking for free food, and the other half local derelicts.

The dishwasher already full and running, Ben is hand-washing the overflow. He passes off a soapy plate to Reverend Roberta, who rinses it and sends it along to Ray, a reluctant boomer volunteer, coerced by his wife into helping out. Ray has been given the easiest of tasks: drying the dishes and putting them away.

"What a great system you three have going," croons Judy, the wife, wheeling in the last load of dishes from the narthex, which doubles as the dining hall.

"The assembly line model is what made our civilization great, ma'am," Ben says, passing along another plate. "That, and the endless wars. Now why don't you take over for a minute?" Ben presses the wet sponge into her hands. "I need to rock one."

Ben takes a leak and a five-minute break, resting outside on a rock under the overhang and watching the rain. He's been on his feet since one o'clock and they're aching inside his boots. But when he returns to the kitchen, he finds a shocking lack of progress on the dishes, and Judy and Ray inexplicably donning their coats. "Oh, we hate to leave you and the Reverend with such a mess, Ben. But I don't want to drive in the dark. Do you know that traffic lights are still out? Our streetlights too, isn't that an outrage?"

"Unconscionable, ma'am."

So Ben and Reverend Roberta are left to plough through the remaining piles on their own. When they're down to the pots, pans, and serving dishes, Ben kicks at the bucket. "How's that roof fundraising going?"

In unison, they tip their heads back to look at the water stain on the ceiling. "It's been slow, I won't lie. We're still short."

"Can you tap the university coffers?" he asks. "We're on campus territory, with strong ties to the school."

"It's tricky. The university earmarks certain funds for sanctioned 'safe spaces.'"

"Sounds perfect. This is a church."

Roberta's fringe of short grey hair flops across her broad

170

cheek; she blows it to the side with a heaving breath. "A church is not an official 'safe space.'"

"It is the *original* safe space." When Ben looks at her for some recognition of the irony but gets only a grim frown, he throws his soap-covered hands way up over his head. "Sanctuary! Sanctuary!"

Roberta, as though reciting from a pamphlet, explains: "An official 'safe space' makes a commitment to welcoming and including marginalized groups."

"Isn't that the implied commitment of the Anglican Church?"

"I suppose it depends on whom you ask. But it's not an official 'safe space' until we get the certificate. And the decals. Pins, too, I think. And for that to happen, I need to complete a workshop. I've got that scheduled for tomorrow."

"And this is going to help you pay for the roof?"

"Possibly." She rubs a tea towel around the edges of the mashed potato pot. "Like I said, a lot of hoops. But you have to play within the system sometimes or you don't get anywhere."

"That does seem to be your attitude. Explains the tone of your sermons, at least."

"What tone is that, Ben?"

Ben's sponge pauses on its path across a serving plate. "Weak."

"Oh dear god, spare me, would you?" In an ungainly squat, Roberta tries to find a way to jam the pot into the crowded bottom cupboard. "I'm not in the mood for another critique of my sermons. It's late."

But Ben is already on a tear: "You ask nothing of your parishioners, do you realize that? Nothing! You barely ask them to engage in their own community. Look around, Reverend, is anyone helping us tonight? Where are your legions of volunteers? Are you aware that I had to abridge the menu due to a lack of kitchen help?"

"The menu was fine."

"It was lackluster! Yes, of course, the meat loaf was perfectly moist. And the gravy a tour de force. But where were the glazed carrots and buttered green beans? And the fresh-baked bread? I was promised two boomers for prep." He stabs two fingers way up into the air. "One was a no-show, the other was useless, unable to chop potatoes without constant instruction and validation."

Ben scrubs ferociously at the already-clean serving plate. The problem extends far beyond delinquent volunteerism and community engagement. The Church, with its history, tradition, and reach, should be ground zero for social activism. None of the rinky-dink activist groups that have been popping up lately have the institutional heft to support a true movement. In the coming Dark Age, when the corporate state abandons its citizens entirely, the Church will be the only institution left that can operate as a powerful force of change. It will be the only institution to preserve the artefacts of civilization, as it did in the last Dark Age. The only institution that will preserve hope.

"You coddle these people," Ben mutters bitterly.

"I don't coddle them. I relate to them," she says, snatching the plate, still covered with suds, from his hands.

"No hard truths. No call to action. We ought to be reminding them of the stark sacrifices that have to be made. This world is in crisis!"

"What would you have me do? Scream at the few remaining parishioners we still draw?" Some crazed gestures are happening with her arms and Ben starts to worry about the fate of the serving plate.

"I would have you rouse them!" he cries. "Awaken them to the realities of the world around them, beyond their bubbles of privilege and prestige."

"You think haranguing people gets them on your side?" Roberta says.

"Yes! Yes! That's exactly what I think. That is the essence of the prophetic tradition. Jeremiah! The legendary haranguer!"

"Well, Ben . . . I'm not a prophet." Roberta shoves the wide plate into an overflowing cupboard and slams the door three times before she finally gets it to close.

"Clearly."

"You think you can do better?"

"I could not do much worse."

"All right then," she says, drying her plump hands aggressively on the sopping tea towel. "Why don't you rouse us this week, oh prophet? You give the sermon. Let's see how that goes."

Ben stares at her, the drip from the ceiling the only sound. "You want *me* to deliver the sermon?"

"Sure, why not? You have a lecture prepared every time I see you."

Ben's mind darts around for excuses and evasions. "Me?"

"That's right. Rouse the rabble, Ben. Lead us all out of the wilderness and into the light." She chucks the tea towel onto the dull laminate counter. "And finish the damn dishes yourself."

7

AND SO IT is that the leadership of an entire congregation falls upon Ben. A reluctant prophet, like his ancient brother Jeremiah, he sits in the Sanctum, at the tiny desk in his bedroom, poring over the scripture cited in this week's lectionary. A thousand ideas spring onto the sheets of his notebook, but he has difficulty distilling his angry thoughts into a stirring homily.

The week's Gospel reading again comes from Luke, 12:56. "You hypocrites!" rails Jesus. "You know how to interpret the appearance of earth and sky, but why do you not know how to interpret the present time?"

The present time, of course, is characterized by the decline of an empire. Surely this is what God wants Ben to discuss. Dispatches from the heart of an unholy empire. Like so many prophets before him. Only . . . the prophets of old never had to bother with the work of composition; scripture teaches that God put His words directly into their mouths.

In search of inspiration, Ben lets his thoughts circle around the ills of Empire, a pervasive theme in the history of human civilization. It's right there in Genesis, in the story of Babel. Flipping the Bible to its opening book, Ben revisits this fable of hubris, as clear in its moral lesson as Icarus and his waxen wings. A proud people seek to build a great civilization, make a name for themselves, more interested in cultivating their own image than in knowing God. They don't care to pursue an understanding of anything greater than themselves. They have no interest in faith. They are narcissists and solipsists, like so many around him today. And they are punished for it.

The passage inspires in Ben a sense of humility. So he abandons the arrogant exercise of trying to guess at God's message and sends out a quick prayer: "Come now, Lord, make with the holy words." He squints open an eye, listens. Crickets.

THE CORNER WINDOW of The Poppy Seed is boarded up. Thieves smashed it during the blackout and jacked the computers from the back office, along with a few assorted tubs of cream cheese—not the pumpkin spice—and, curiously, all of the rosemary bagels. The blackout lasted less than twenty-four hours: time enough for looting to start.

Dickhead Debbie, however, is unbothered by theft and vandalism. It's left her giddy. The destruction of the window has presented her with a long-awaited opportunity to "spruce up the corner."

"We're gonna build a tower!" she says. "Huge huge. I want it to go right up to the ceiling, all right? A showstopper!"

Ben and Lyle, tasked point men for this project, have been ushered to the alcove to absorb Dickhead Debbie's demented instructions. They have been called away from their actual duties at the counter, leaving Megz to handle both coffee and cash on her own.

"It's too bad that someone had to smash up the window to get us thinking about a face-lift. But life gives you lemons? And you make lemonade, right?"

Her lemonade is a tower made out of bagels. A great big tower of bagels. Dickhead Debbie lays out her design on the alcove table.

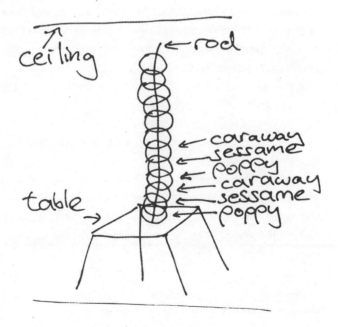

"See the pattern?" She jabs an enthusiastic finger at the architectural design. "I want you to go poppy seed, sesame seed, caraway. Got it? That's the pattern. Poppy, sesame, caraway. Poppy, sesame, caraway."

Neither the frenzied pitch nor the obvious delight she's taking in her own authority suggest that she has been humbled by a good talking-to from a superior. Has Frank spoken with her about her managerial style? About the overtime? About anything at all? Ben will have to write another letter. Maybe one a day until matters are resolved.

On the bright side, earlier this morning, Ben stumbled into a defective smoked meat sandwich situation. A big shot banker-type ordered the smoked meat, but forgot to mention no mustard. By the time he remembered, the mustard had already infiltrated the whole sandwich, the pores of the bread, the underside of the meat—couldn't be saved. A definite defect, safely tucked away in the fridge. A red-letter day. Ben hasn't had a smoked meat defect in months, not since the spring, and then, because of his Lenten abstention from all forms of meat, he wasn't able to accept it. It took enormous spiritual will to withstand that temptation.

"But there's not enough support here, Debbie," Lyle is saying. "This will tip over."

"That's what the metal rod is for."

Lyle grabs the metal rod, light and flimsy in his hands. "But it's not sturdy enough for—"

"Just look at the sketch, Lyle. Follow the design. And keep an eye on traffic at the counter. If we get a rush and Megan looks swamped, I want you to help her out, okay? The Customer has to take priority," she says. Though these last words come out grudgingly.

"But—"

"Make it high! High high!" And with the extra-hyper dispensation of this final instruction, she bobbles away.

"Lyle, my brother in arms," Ben says as they begin the preposterous process of building this tower, "it's time. I've done some preliminary research. I think the UFCW is our best bet. As a union, they don't have the hugest balls, I'll admit that myself, but they are the food industry experts. We call them up, we sign some membership cards, and we reclaim a small ounce of power. And dignity."

"Yeah sure, Ben, if you give me a card, I'll sign it. But . . ." Lyle stops to smile, a wicked glee spreading across his entire face.

"What?"

"I sort of took care of my problems with Dickhead Debbie."

"What do you mean?"

He leans toward Ben, but his eyes are fixed on the counter, where Dickhead Debbie is helping herself to her daily bagel with its thick smear of cream cheese. His smile intensifies, his eyes aglitter, and he whispers, "I jizzed in the pumpkin spice cream cheese."

"Sorry, what?"

"I did. I totally jizzed in it." He pinches his nose and laughs. "She had me in the back for the first few hours. Refilling the cream cheeses. No one was around . . . so I just whipped it out, jerked it, and jizzed right into that pumpkin spice that she loves so goddamn much. Hahahah."

So. This is how far they've come. This is the sort of job action that remains for the working man. Impotent in his battle against management, he's left to thrash against his lot with a primitive display of bodily fluids.

Lyle can't stop looking at Dickhead Debbie as she chomps on her specially-spiced pumpkin spice bagel. He smothers his mouth with a palm to mask his laughter, delighted over this moronic bit of vengeance. But his mirth attracts Dickhead Debbie's attention. "Get going over there, boys," she calls. "I want to see some real height when I come back out here."

Lyle stands on a chair, slipping the bagels one after the other down the metal rod while Ben feeds him the appropriate choice from the basket: poppy seed, sesame seed, caraway. At two feet, the structure is already unstable. When they get it up to five feet, Megz, bored by a lull at the counter, wanders over. Today's button features fallopian tubes that curve toward a pair of very large, not-at-all to-scale ovaries, beneath which diagram is the imperative: *Grow a Pair*.

"Tower's looking . . . high." She wiggles it, testing its stability. "Pretty shaky, though."

"Won't last the night," says Lyle.

"Did I hear you guys talking about the union?" she asks.

"Yes! Absolutely and always!" Ben turns his complete attention to her, abandoning the bagel basket.

"Because I've been thinking about it. And I just don't like how Debbie treats people. There's a lot of unfair bullshit. Like, I was talking it over with Lindsay, on the morning shift, and we both agreed that Debbie treats the female staff differently. She, like, infantilizes us."

"A travesty!"

"And like, take this, this tower bullshit. I have to work the counter while you guys get to do this? Like, what's the implication here, huh? Women aren't good at construction?"

"Exactly. Blatant discrimination. Unchecked tyranny. Let's get ourselves some union cards." Ben punctuates his excitement with a resounding and conclusive clap.

"Well hold on, Ben, I'd like to be looped-in on the whole process. I don't want to be railroaded into anything."

"Wonderful to hear. We'll embark on the journey together. Why don't we draft an exploratory email to the union after the shift . . . if you have the time?"

Appeased by inclusion, Megz relaxes her stern look into a half smile. "I guess I could make the time to do that." She flicks the tower and watches it wobble. "God, this is stupid."

"The stupidest," agrees Lyle.

Ben takes a step back to better view the five vertical feet of bagels in front of the boarded-up window. "Yes, comrades, this may well be the single most retarded idea the woman has had yet."

Even before Megz says anything, Ben can feel the shift in the group. The mood turns tense, fraught.

"Whoa, whoa, hey there," says Megz.

"What?"

"*Retarded*? No. You can't say that, Ben."

From up on the chair, Lyle weighs in: "Yeah, buddy, you really can't say retarded anymore." Lyle says this. Lyle, who a few hours ago masturbated into a tub of cream cheese.

Ben picks the sketch up off the table and holds it up to them each in turn. "Look at this structural rendering and tell me it's not retarded."

There's a sharp intake of breath as Megz clenches her jaw, and Ben can see from her blistering expression that he's taken a step too far. "Okay, my apologies, *mea culpa*." He places a deferential hand over his heart. "Let's not squabble over language. Let's just forget about this and return our focus to the union question."

"No, Ben, we can't just *forget* about language. Language happens to be very important to me. It's, like, my trade." As Megz walks back to the counter, Ben looks at the tattoo on her nape: *Lush Words* inked out in a cursive script.

Later, while clocking out in the staff room, Ben makes a stab at smoothing things over. "Megz," he says in his most sincere tone, "I recognize that I pissed you off earlier, for which I am truly sorry."

"It's fine," she says in a clipped tone that suggests it is not actually fine at all.

So he offers an olive branch, the thickest he can extend. "There's a defective smoked meat sandwich in the fridge." He exhales deeply, summoning the strength to continue. "It's yours, if you'd like it."

"I don't eat meat, Ben."

Shit. "Right. Oh right. I'm sorry."

"I've told you that at least twice," she says and blows out of the staff room.

As a rule, Ben tries not to be selfish with the defective spoils. Before he wraps up his smoked meat, he forces himself to offer half of it to Paulie, who, as usual, has been working out of sight for most of the shift.

"No no," says Paulie. "Debbie says to put defects in the garbage."

"Yes, but that's wasteful. So I saved it. You want half?"

Paulie wavers for a moment, but his anxiety over the possible consequences of a broken rule soon prevails. "No. No."

"All right then." Ben tosses his loot into a paper bag, swinging his spoils as he leaves the shop.

But then, on the way to the streetcar stop, the derelict who camps out on the sidewalk near The Poppy Seed, whose decline over recent months has been startlingly swift, calls, "Any change, man? Got anything today?"

Ben checks his pockets, but the only tender is a nickel and some subway tokens. He has nothing to offer the man, nothing but the smoked meat. "I got a sandwich."

"No change?"

"Just the sandwich."

"Yeah. Okay then. I'll take that."

And so blow the winds of fate. No smoked meat for Ben this afternoon. Instead he grabs three slices of pizza from a dive up on Bloor so that he won't arrive hungry and grumpy at Joly's, forced to nibble on overpriced snack food that will indebt him to that parasite—her beloved brother.

9

BEN SEARCHES THE kitchen drawers for a meat thermometer, but there is little of actual use in Yannick's remodelled kitchen. It has a six-burner range, a built-in steamer, and a wine fridge, but no meat thermometer, nor even a potato masher. Ben has had to roast the potatoes instead, a second-rate side dish to this beautifully cooked coq-au-vin.

"Ben! Guess what I am?" cries Yvie, lying in her pyjamas on the shiny hardwood floor.

"I have no time for guessing games," says Ben. "Can't you see I'm tending a stew?" Given the voyage this already-expired chicken has undergone, he would like the certainty of a thermometer reading. But he did give the half-cooked chicken a thorough sniff earlier . . . and the nose knows.

Yvie elbow-crawls her way over to Ben and nips at his ankle bone. "Guess what I am, Ben?"

"You are a strange little creature."

"Hahaha. Nuh-uh. I'm a snake!"

"An Yvie-snake," shouts Joly from her place at the island.

"Yeah! An Yvie-snake," Yvie slithers all the way around the island before she springs up to her feet and returns to Ben's side. "I want to help!" she announces, straining on her tiptoes and groping at the counter's edge.

"I don't see how."

But Joly, more indulgent, picks Yvie up and sets her on the countertop, next to some thyme sprigs, so that the child can peer into the pot. Ben lets slide this gross contravention of kitchen etiquette.

"So I might have a job," says Joly, sniffing at the stew pot.

"What job? Praise be to God!" Ben worries about her, specifically about what will happen to her when Yannick finally decides to expel her from the pleasure palace. She has never had to fend for herself. She has always had this big cushy safety net waiting to catch her, and she doesn't yet know what life is like without that comfort.

"Writing up product descriptions," she says as she wanders back to the island. "For a giftware company. One of Karen's friends was looking for someone, so . . . she says I'm a lock. It's part time. But it's something. Could lead to other things."

"Part time, huh?"

"Yeah, freelance."

"Ah."

"What's a freelance?" asks Yvie. She has picked up a thyme sprig and started to tap it against her tongue.

"It's a kind of job," Joly says.

"Not just any kind of job," says Ben, swiping for the sprig—but Yvie's fast. "Part of the neoliberal labour model. Designed to get employers out of basic workplace obligations. Like paying proper wages and offering benefits and job security."

"Oh." Yvie stops mid-lick. Her forehead rumples. Ben likes this expression of hers best, this contemplative frown that bears an appropriate hint of displeasure with the world. The child, despite her spoiled upbringing, shows promise.

Ben gives the rich brown stew a sprinkling of black pepper and Yvie leans perilously over the pot. "That's right, Yvie," he says. "Take in the well-balanced aromatics, the whole glorious bouquet."

But when she turns her face to him, her small nose is wrinkled in disgust.

"What do you know about cooking, you little gremlin? Away with you!" He scoops her up over his shoulder, like a potato sack, and deposits her in front of the cutlery drawer. "Make yourself useful. Set the dining room table for us."

The child manages this task, under Joly's heavy guidance, then disappears under the table, where she carries on a muted conversation with herself. Ben, meanwhile, plates their dinners and sets a basket of warmed bread on the table as a rustic accompaniment. "Coq-au-vin," he announces with a flourish.

Ben studies Joly attentively as she spoons her first mouthful; he is gratified to watch her steely grey eyes grow with sensory pleasure. "As it happens," he says, basking in the wholesome atmosphere of this well-prepared feast, "I have news of my own." He pours the leftover red wine into two of Yannick's long-stemmed wine glasses, and swirls the plonk around the crystal glass. "I am to give the sermon this Sunday."

"You?" Joly drops her fork, which thumps loudly against the solid wood table.

"I!"

"But . . . why? You're not a priest."

"The Reverend Roberta, in her wisdom, asked me to deliver it."

"Why would she do that? Is she sick?"

Ben grunts, snorts. The lack of enthusiasm! For his career as a prophet! He swallows the entire contents of his glass. "I suppose she thinks I have something to say."

"Do you?"

"Much! I have much to say!"

Sliding out from beneath the table, Yvie clambers up onto Ben's lap, a brazen ascent, which he observes incredulously. "What is this? I'm eating! You can't interrupt a man when he's with his chow."

She looks up at him with eyes as large as Joly's, the same shade of blazing grey. "I'm getting bap-sized."

"Ah yes, so I hear." Ben's invitation to the baptism arrived last week, in a square envelope, on thick card stock. The baptism itself is at their parish church (Catholic! Pah! They might as well pitch the child straight into the fires of hell), but for the ensuing reception, these people have rented a room at no less a landmark than the CN Tower, successfully transforming the quiet dignity of a sacrament into a garish public spectacle.

Yvie's expression turns very serious. "Are you coming to watch me, Ben?"

"Would you like me to come?"

"Yeah-huh."

"Well . . . I'm very busy, you understand. I have all manner of important business to attend to. But I think I can squeeze it in." He has, in fact, already put in a day-off request with Dickhead Debbie.

With this bit of business resolved to her satisfaction, Yvie slips off his lap and returns to her place under the table. But she keeps her feet elevated, kicking her heels on Ben's kneecaps.

"You know, I like this idea!" Joly suddenly exclaims. She's tapping the back of her fork against a perfectly roasted potato. "You giving a sermon. You have a beautiful voice, I've always said that. Haven't I always said that?"

"You have." Ben allows a soft, dignified bow of the head, careful not to betray how tickled he is by this sudden show of gusto. "And you are not wrong."

"I can't wait to hear you up there."

"Oh . . . no, you don't have to come. That's hardly necessary."

"You'd be a great priest! I don't know why we didn't think of this before!"

"Well now, let's not get carried away. I'm not a priest. I'm just a man delivering a soaring sermon."

"But you could be! You could become a priest! Why not? That could be a career. It's perfect."

Ben has already weighed and dismissed this option. Apart from the difficulties inherent in a return to academia, even the seminary, pastoral care isn't booming. Few job openings exist in the diocese; the newly-ordained are left twiddling their thumbs until one of the old guard dies and opens up a vacancy, preferably before the parish gets amalgamated.

"Priests must earn a living wage, right?" she presses. Her thoughts seem to be moving rapidly; she has forgotten about her stew. "They get free housing too, don't they?"

Yvie ramps up the force of her heels against Ben's knees. Relieved by the distraction, he wraps his hands around her ankles and tugs her out from under the table to her screeched delight.

"Now this is how one slithers." He tows her to the left, to the right, and all around the kitchen by her ankles, moving in ess-curves, careening around the furniture; she glides easily across the floor, which must recently have been buffed. Soon her giggles explode into shrieks of wild laughter, the purity of which stokes laughter in Ben as well. After their second tour of the kitchen, all three of them are laughing, but the good cheer of the evening, the warmth of the domesticity, triggers in Ben a silent alarm. It is not a good idea for Joly and him to be playing house, with this child, when they will never have either—not house, nor child—just when Joly suddenly seems to be longing for both.

ONCE YVIE IS in bed, they settle in front of the wall–sized flat screen TV and watch half of a Cary Grant feature that neither of them recognizes, sipping on beer—Ben's beer, his honey brown. He brought a couple of bottles with him, but he restricts his drinking to a single small glass. Despite recent events, hope springs eternal for sexual congress, and should he be called upon, he wants to be firing on all cylinders. And Joly is sending strong signals. Dragging her palm up and down his thigh, undulating slightly against him. His eyes are on the screen, but he is unable to follow the film's confound-ingly complicated story.

His restraint with the alcohol is rewarded when Joly turns off the TV, leads him down to her bedroom, and springs on him like a tigress in heat. She's pushing right into him, her mouth on his, but he proceeds with caution. Slow steps, slow and steady. Hands are kept above the waist while they kiss on the plush mattress. He waits for her to break this boundary and demonstrate an interest in something more, and after a very long time, what might be forever, she dips a hand into his boxers.

"You want to?" he asks. "I mean . . . you ready to?"

"Mm-hmm. I think so."

Ben hops out of bed and gropes for the condoms in his backpack, which he locates after several clumsy stumbles. When he crawls back into bed, he's relieved to find them resuming their positions directly, both on their sides in full embrace. This time when Joly's hand migrates downward, he reciprocates the gesture on her, and—oh my!—finds her very wet. Up on his knees, he rolls the condom down his cock, while she shifts to her back, her knees are bent and—look at that—splayed. Here we go, he's going, in a slow corkscrewed approach, and . . . there it is! Ah, that's good. Eyes closed, he yields to this much-missed sensation, moving faster now, and deeper.

So perhaps he is not paying enough attention to her. Or perhaps it is too dark to see the expressions on her face. Because a suppressed sniffle pierces the bubble of his pleasure, and when he touches a hand to her cheeks, his fingers come back wet.

"Hey now." He arrests all hip action, but stays inside of her. "Hey, what's wrong?"

"I'm sorry."

"Does it hurt?"

"No. No, it feels good."

"You want me to stop."

"I don't know."

"What's wrong?"

"I'm scared."

"Scared?"

"Like what if the condom breaks? Or what if you didn't put it on right? Or what if we just get unlucky again?" Her voice buckles on the last *what-if*. "I'm too scared."

He pushes back a few inches and lies on top of her, his head on her chest. "No problem, Joly. We don't have to do anything." But a searing discomfort spreads through his gut. He is not sure if this is guilt over making her cry, or making her pregnant, or if it is something simpler: the primitive disappointment of thwarted desire.

"We could do other things," she says with a stifled sob.

"Oh yeah?"

"Mm-hmm."

He turns his face into her chest, kissing the underside of her breasts, drawing his beard across her skin, which he knows she likes, then zigzagging his way down her abdomen. He can smell her long before he gets to the source, which beckons to him forcefully. When he is pressed right up against it—well, this too, he likes. This fleshy softness against his face, this singular taste. He likes it all. Oh, and what's this? There go her hands under her hips, a predictable movement. Her fists always disappear under her hips, lending them a slight elevation, when she's about to come. And she does come, squeezing her thighs tight around his head. But just for a moment, then she releases. Then she squeezes again, with less force this time. And releases. And again, even softer now. And again and again and again, in a dissipating pulse, her thighs lapping rhythmically against the sides of his head.

With lingering notes of her in his beard, and with her lying next to him, naked and in post-orgasmic glow, his cock stiffens uncomfortably, begging for release. She must sense this, because she puts a hand around him.

"You don't have to, Joly."

"I want you to come." She says the words, but she's offering no more than a few tired tugs. "Will you get yourself off for me?"

It's something she likes to watch sometimes. So she tucks herself against his side and kisses his neck and his earlobes and watches as he masturbates. It's not intercourse, but it's a level of intimacy that has been absent. With his left arm he pulls her in close. He sniffs her hair, which always smells faintly of chlorine in the summer, and comes with his face pressed to her head.

10

A GENTLE STREAM of sunlight awakens Ben, who rolls over, grasping for Joly. But he's alone in the big bed. It takes him longer than usual to pull himself into consciousness; the mattress is too comfortable, the sheets too soft, the pillows too plentiful. He loathes these luxuries and their sweet tranquilizing effects.

He throws on yesterday's clothes and plods up the stairs for breakfast, pausing on the staircase to pass judgment on the display of framed wedding pictures—at least a dozen—mounted on the wall. As he scrutinizes one close-up shot, he hears his name drop in the kitchen.

"So Ben's here, huh?" Yannick is saying.

"He helped babysit," says Joly. "He's amazing with Yvie. She's obsessed with him."

They must not have heard his ascent. It's this new staircase. The pre-renovation staircase was a creaky artefact, but now even a man of Ben's build can move up and down them like a cat.

"So you're back together then?" Yannick asks.

"What do you mean? We never weren't together."

"He hasn't been around much. I just assumed. Hoped."

"He's been busy. Working a lot."

"Oh yeah? Bagel shop really driving him hard?"

"Yes actually. They're slave drivers at that place. And he's got all his volunteer stuff, church stuff. Do you know he's delivering a sermon this week?"

"So what, he's a priest now? Any money in that?"

"Maybe! Who knows. He'd be a kickass priest. Which is why I think you should come hear his sermon."

Ben bristles on the steps, but keeps quiet.

"Are you kidding me?" croaks Yannick. "I'm not going to church."

"He's an excellent speaker, you know. His voice is made for public speaking."

"I'm sure. But no."

"Oh come on. It'll be fun. We'll bring the whole fam!"

"That sounds like a nightmare, Joly."

"I texted Lou about it last night—she said she and Elliot are in. We'll have a whole contingent. A fan section."

"Wait, why's Lou going?"

"To be supportive, obviously. It'd be nice if you could be the same. Ben thinks you hate him, you know."

"I don't hate him. I just wonder how long you're gonna wait around for this deadbeat to get his shit together."

Ben flinches. The word—*deadbeat*—sounds out like a sharp knock. The mass of his body crumples against the wall until he's right down on his ass. His father's voice: *You little deadbeat, you bum.* The old man too was convinced from the start that Ben was worthless.

"That's not fair," says Joly. "It's not like I have my shit together either."

"I know that. And it baffles me. Maybe it's his influence. You ever consider that? Maybe if you hang around a guy like that long enough it rubs off. The guy practically lives in a commune. He can't take care of you. I mean, Jesus, he doesn't even have a credit card."

A fire flickers to life in Ben's gut. Who's the real deadbeat here? It's not Ben who is screwing around on his woman. Not Ben sneaking up to Don Mills for a secret rendezvous. Of course a soul-sick man like Yannick would balk at the idea of fidelity, of honour. But he hadn't expected *Lou* to be his target. Well, doubtless there are others—how many other women does the wretch covet and claim? The man registers no sense of moral duty or sacred oaths. No—he sits imperiously in his pleasure palace, casting stones.

And that's to say nothing of the evils of his career! Here is a man raking in money off the backs of others. These private equity guys are vultures. They buy up companies, then start slashing costs, squeezing out huge rosters of employees, doing away with research and development, hollowing the companies right out, and then selling them off before anyone realizes that once stalwart companies have gone to the dogs.

Ben has read that the whole industry is a bubble waiting to burst. There is so much money in private equity (trillions of dollars), and so many jobs, that when some of these businesses inevitably start to collapse under the debt that has been foisted upon them by the private equity sharks, when they default on their loans, it will set off a ripple effect that will decimate the entire western economy. And *Ben* is the deadbeat?

The upstairs breakfast conversation has turned to matters of oatmeal. Regaining his composure, Ben stands up and dusts dandruff flakes from his shoulders and ascends the rest of the staircase, with a conspicuous footfall that he maintains on his way to the kitchen.

"Oh, hi Benny," says Joly from her island stool, where she is toying with a thick gruel.

At the counter, Yannick is busy "making" coffee—that is, inserting a pod into the machine. "Coffee?" he asks.

"No, no thank you," says Ben, despite the fact that he would very much like a coffee. The oven clock reads 6:22, far too early to be up and functioning without coffee. He would also like breakfast. But he passes on this too, because he will not indebt himself to Yannick, eating his foods and revelling in his luxuries, like a deadbeat.

Instead he helps himself to a glass of tap water and washes out the stale taste of morning. Beside the sink are the two beer bottles he brought over last night, the bomber bottles. He and Joly only made it through half a bottle, but now both stand empty on the counter.

"Oh yeah, I finished those off last night," says Yannick. "Whose was it?"

"That's Ben's homebrew," says Joly with a trace of pride.

"Nice. It was fucking delicious. But strong."

"Yes, the honey brown'll put you down," says Ben.

"Look at you, Ben. You're turning into a bona fide bootlegger."

Ben studies Yannick, drinking his pod-coffee, in his pressed suit pants and his crisp shirt, and his cufflinks, actual cufflinks, and his gelled hair. At first glance, he looks put-together, but his skin is blotched and sallow, his face is bloated, the eyes foggy, almost veiled. He looks the way Ben's parents used to look in the mornings. Tired, irritable, poisoned, but pushing through to functional. He looks hungover.

"You could charge for beer like that," Yannick says. "Open up one of those microbreweries, or whatever they're calling them. Craft breweries. Karen's got some artsy friends who're always talking about their fucking craft beers. Their Trappist monk beers. Or artisan beers or whatever the fuck. Paying ten bucks a bottle. For *one* bottle! You could tap that market, Ben, buddy. Turn a buck on this racket."

"No, I'm afraid it's just a hobby. A spiritual pursuit, really," says Ben.

"So you don't want to make money off it?"

"No, I don't."

Leaning against the countertop, arms tightly crossed, Yannick stares at him, confused. "So what *do* you wanna make money off of, Ben? Let's hear. What's your ambition?"

"My ambition?" Ben stands behind Joly at the island, resting a hand on the backrest of her high stool. "I have no personal ambition."

Yannick's left eye twitches. "I don't know what to say to that. Joly? What am I supposed to say to that?"

"I think he just means that he's happy with very little." Her eyes dart from one to the other, but her body stays rigid.

Ben checks the clock on the oven: 6:28. "Well now, where does the time go? I have to get to work," he says, though his shift doesn't start until eleven.

"Yeah, I'm on my way out too." Yannick pounds back his cup of coffee. "You need a lift somewhere?"

A lift in the Lexus? A deadbeat scrounging up a free ride? Another debt owed? Ben declines. He takes the streetcar instead.

$$\overline{11}$$

BENEATH THE WOODEN beams of the nave, Ben kneels in prayer. Since he was first given his own set of keys to the church a couple of years ago, he has often sought private comfort here. Rarely, though, has he been alone in the sanctuary so early in the morning. Light cuts through the windows at an unfamiliar angle, lending the space an otherworldly glow.

Awash in this uncertain light, Ben remains still. He prays

for Joly, as he does whenever he takes a knee, and for their lost child, whose life he snuffed out; he prays for the Pharisee Yannick, whose corrupted soul is in dire need of intercession; and he prays, above all, for the grace to overcome his own anger.

It is in these moments of solitary prayer that Ben has had his most visceral experiences of God. On rare days, he has *felt* divinity. As though, in the process of prayer, he is able to bring forth the divine aspect in himself—the whisper of divinity that exists in us all. Seeing this reflection of the infinite in his own finite form, he is able to understand a sublime humility. And it feels very much like relief.

Today, however, is not one of those blessed days.

IN THE NARTHEX, Ben finds the Reverend Roberta rearranging furniture for a reading group meeting later in the morning, at which participants will discuss a cobbled-together tome of new-age garbage called *Radical Gratitude*. The Reverend has brought in a half-dozen folding chairs, configured into a circle next to the short bookcase, on which sits the coffee maker.

"Oh, Ben," she says, spinning gracelessly as she catches sight of him, here unexpectedly on a Friday morning. "What are you doing here?"

"Doing penance." He thrusts a thumb at the sanctuary.

The folding chairs are not the only new items in the room this morning. As he was letting himself in earlier, Ben noticed a *This is a designated Safe Space* decal on the window by the front door. He nods at the decal. "Your workshop went well then?"

"Yes. It was . . . instructive," she says, swinging her heavy hips around as she moves another chair. "Better than I thought, actually."

"So the funding's coming in? The roof will be fixed?"

"We're working on it. It's a process, as I mentioned already." And then with a wry smile that on anyone but a priest might be characterized as a little bit malicious: "How's the sermon coming along?"

"Oh, just dandy, Reverend."

Having prayed on the matter of the sermon, Ben has faith that the right words will coalesce soon enough.

"Glad to hear it. I am ready to be roused."

Ben helps himself to a cup of what is clearly yesterday's drip coffee from the machine, but he pauses at his first sip, espying something most displeasing to God. On the top shelf of the little bookcase, which houses Bibles in their various translations, a hodgepodge of theological scholarship (including, *blasphemously*, a collection of Pope Benedict's encyclicals), and even a few pulp novels, is a new sign, printed out with the good Reverend's label maker. It reads: "Warning: These materials contain content about violence, sexual assault, abuse, suicide, bullying, disease, famine, homophobia, racism, sexism, anti-Semitism, and imperialism, which may be triggering to survivors."

"What," Ben asks in a low drone of incredulity, "is this?"

"Oh, it's something that was suggested to us at the workshop," the Reverend says, tinkering uselessly with the furniture configuration.

"Is that a *trigger warning*?"

"Yes." She looks up from her chairs to behold her label-made signage. "Apparently it's common for people who have suffered a trauma to be retriggered when they encounter certain subject matter. So these warnings are supposed to give them a heads-up."

"Yes, I know what they are *supposed* to do."

"They've started putting these trigger warnings on everything, all over the university. I had no idea! On certain books. Pretty much the entire English department. On course syllabi."

"Uh-huh."

"It can't hurt, right?"

"You put a trigger warning on the *Bible*?"

"Not just the Bible. The whole bookshelf, yes."

"You put a trigger warning? On the Bible? In a church?"

"Yes, that's right."

At a rare loss for words, Ben gazes up at the heavens for guidance. His arms extend to their full majestic breadth as he roars, "Have we all just lost our goddamned minds?!"

12

BEN EMPLOYS A strict policy when he is on coffee. Any order that comes in with more than two amendments to the standard method of preparation earns itself an automatic decaf-ing. It must be done. Someone must impose a sense of decency in this place. In front of him is an order for a cappuccino: extra shot, extra hot, soy milk, easy on the foam . . . and a squirt of raspberry syrup. No. Absolutely not. A definite decaf situation.

As expected, the bagel tower collapsed overnight, but the setback has done nothing to discourage Dickhead Debbie. She has greeted her failure with renewed vigour—and a new construction plan. And she has conscripted Megz to see the plan through.

"Toothpicks!" she shrieks at Megz in the alcove, shaking a box of toothpicks in front of her head like a maraca. "We'll use toothpicks to hold the bagels together."

Megz, today sporting a hot pink *Grrrrrrl Power* button, throws a pleading glance toward the counter, but Lyle is occupied on sandwiches, Lindsay is busy being berated by a

Customer at cash, and Ben is no longer a suitable object of commiseration. Temperatures between them have remained chilly. Megz has been curt and contemptuous all day, answering his conversational attempts, if at all, in monosyllables. Unless there's a major thaw, a collaborative email to the union is out of the question.

Ben busies himself with the preparation of the raspberry-infused, soy-based abomination, and when he sets it on the counter and looks up to see which philistine has placed this order, he finds Dickhead Debbie scurrying his way.

"Frank wants to see you," she says.

"Ah, very good. I thought he might. Right now?"

"Yes, he's in the office," she says with a peculiar, indecipherable grin. And then, in a rare and highly suspicious move, she assumes command of the coffee station.

Once again, Ben and Frank assume positions on opposite sides of the desk, and again, Ben awaits Frank's opening salvo.

"So another letter," Frank says.

With one elbow on the desk, the other on the back of the chair, Ben tosses up his palms. "Needs must, boss man."

"I thought we talked about this."

"I thought we did too. But did we get around to including Debbie in our conversation? Because she continues to prance around unchecked. Have you seen that bagel tower, may I ask? Did she show you her sketch? Have you any idea how many man hours she has allocated to its construction?"

Frank rubs at his eyes beneath his thick lenses, then takes the glasses off, letting them fall onto the disordered papers on his desk. "Let me ask you something, Ben. Have you been trying to unionize this store?"

Ah, so the devil switches tactics. "Who told you that?"

"Does it matter?"

"Yes of course. It matters a great deal."

"I'll take that as a yes then."

"That's not what I said. And to be honest, I think it's wildly inappropriate that you're even asking me this."

"Okay, Ben," he says, his hands propping up his forehead. He scrubs his fingers through his thinning hair. "I can see where this is headed with you. Headaches. It's going to be one headache after another, isn't it?"

"No, no, I don't see that as inevitable. Not if we each uphold our ends of the bargain."

Frank returns his glasses to his face, straightens up, and clasps his hands in front of him. "I'm gonna have to let you go."

" . . . What?"

"You're not giving me any choice, Ben. I can't have you writing letters all the time, getting the staff worked up, agitating, causing trouble."

"Agitating?" Ben's indignation propels him forward in his chair; he spreads both hands out on the desk, knocking over the emoji Chia pet. "You do know that it is illegal to fire someone for undertaking union activity?"

"Well then I guess that's not why I'm firing you."

"For what then? You have no cause. No cause!" His ass has lifted a few inches off the chair. "As such, you are required to give me notice or payment in lieu of. Two weeks. That is the law."

Frank flips opens a folder in front of him, studies its contents, and then looks back at Ben. "Our store policy clearly states that defective products are to be discarded."

"An absurd policy," Ben says, sitting back down. "But I always follow it. To the letter."

"I've heard differently. I've heard that you routinely hold onto defects for your personal consumption."

"From whom did you hear such lies?" Ben scrolls through

possible suspects. Paulie? Strong-armed into turning the snitch? Megz? Touchy enough about linguistic disputes to have him cast out? Or the dear leader herself? Did Dickhead Debbie notice the transgression and seize the opportunity to whip up drama and have him fired?

"Who told me isn't important. What's important is that you've been violating the policy."

"Never happened," says Ben. Because it is one thing to get sacked without cause. He will get his two weeks' wages and hop on EI—collect his pogey. But fired for cause? For *theft*? No pogey.

"I have reports that it did."

"But I'm telling you it didn't. So we find ourselves at an impasse, don't we?"

"I spoke to one of your coworkers myself."

"Gossip! Pure gossip and slander! I deny it."

"My god, Ben. Why do you have to make everything so difficult?"

"Me? You're firing me. I'm making it easy. I accept!" He smacks a palm on the desktop, causing Dickhead Debbie's collectibles to wobble. "But I demand my two weeks' of wages."

Frank, nearly swallowed in his chair, says, "Just get your things and go."

13

THE SANCTUM WELCOMES Ben with its cracked and crooked stone steps leading up to the front door. In the kitchen he finds a half complement of roommates, whose boisterous chatter dissipates the moment he enters.

"Brethren," he says with a nod at the collective, but nary a one of them responds to his grim greeting. "Well don't stand down on my account, I'm just passing through to the beer fridge. I have been canned. Given the boot. The ol' heave-ho. So . . . I think I will get drunk."

In three brisk strides, he is clear across the kitchen and out the back door. But when he returns with a bottle of his pale ale a moment later, he finds the roommates still locked in their strange tableaux.

"What?" he demands. "What is this?"

From the huddle, Kata is pushed forward a step. "The landlord called again last night, Ben. He's pressuring us for an answer about the payout."

Ben cracks open his beer bottle on the edge of the countertop. "We have an answer. Our answer is a resounding no."

"The thing is, Ben," she says, glancing at the contingent behind her, "we were talking it over last night. And it seems like the consensus is to take it."

"Ah. Ah-ha." Ben scans their faces, noticing now the shifty eyes and restive demeanour of a pack of plotters and schemers. But who among them has led this charge? He scrutinizes each in turn, his flaming eyes finally coming to rest on Runkle.

"What? Come on, don't look at me like that," Runkle says, flustered into speech. "My bedroom floor is still damp, Ben. And the basement problems—any problems—aren't going to be repaired now."

"Listen," says Kata. "Esther already pretty much lives with her boyfriend. And Marko is talking about heading out west. And I . . . or *we* . . . we just don't think we'll end up with anything more than this offer. It's completely fucked! But it's how it is."

"Ah-ha. Surrender. And everyone is agreed? Geoffrey?"

But Geoffrey is staring at his brightly-striped socks. "I think there's mould in my bedroom. My own coughing has been waking me up and my throat—" He strokes at his neck, contorting his features in imagined pain. "It's sore all the time."

Ben snarls at this display, appalled by the delicacy of today's youth. "You'll be able to buy a handsome new bed indeed, Geoffrey, with your thirty pieces of silver."

"Don't take it too hard, Ben," says Kata, putting a hand on his back. "We had a good run, didn't we?"

Ben allows a long, lingering look around the beloved kitchen, at the warped wood of the cupboards, the buzzing fridge, the quirky oven, hearth of this tranquil home. "If you'll all excuse me, I'll be needing a minute now," he says and steps out into the backyard for a moment of anguished solitude in his garden.

WITH AN UNEXPECTEDLY empty afternoon in front of him, and in immediate need of spiritual discipline, Ben does the only thing he can do: he brews. A deep, dark stout for the cold days ahead. The roommates seem to have vacated the house, or at least retreated to their rooms, leaving him to go about the process quietly, meditatively, a moving prayer. Whatever hovel he lands in next may not have the logistical capacity for his brewery, so he approaches the process with particular devotion. Between each step—the milling of the grain, the mixing of the mash—he helps himself to a fresh bottle of beer, as he imagines medieval monks might have done, fusing harmoniously process and result.

As the wort kettle nears a boil on the stoop, Ben nears a state of drunkenness that supports mournful indulgence. He takes a deep breath, then bellows out a dirge for his lost home. It is at this moment, chanting over his cauldron, that Joly materializes before him.

"Oh. Hello, doll." He squints at her wobbly form standing in the frame of the kitchen door. "Where did you come from?"

"You forgot these," she says, setting his stew pot and beer bottles onto the table. "I'm meeting Karen's friend today, about that product description job. Her office is around the corner, so I thought . . . well I thought you'd be at work."

"Nope." Ben enters the house, kissing her on the top of the head on his way to the sink. "I've been sacked."

"What? For what? Why?"

"For agitating. For making union noise." The warm, yeasty smell of the brew has filled the house.

"But they can't fire you for that."

"No, not technically. So they fired me for trumped-up violations of store policy. But don't worry, my lady love. It will never stand. I'm sure I'll be able to get on the dole." Frank will cough up the wages. And if not, Ben will start sending letters to the company head, then to the labour board. He will sink himself chin-deep into the bureaucracy of Ontario labour law if need be. "The larger problem is the Sanctum. We're losing it. Renoviction. Out by the end of the month."

Joly eyes him as he pours himself a glass of water. "Have you been drinking?"

"Oh yes, rather heavily."

He drains his glass, then one more, and returns outside to monitor the kettle.

"So . . . what are we brewing?" she asks, following him out.

"An imperial stout." He swirls a giant spoon around the kettle and glowers into the black brew. "I think I'll call it the Dark Night of the Soul."

"I'm sorry, Benny. This sucks."

"Ebbs and flows, my dear. Ebbs and flows." He wraps an arm around her and surveys his yard: the collection of found lawn furniture, the fire pit he and Marko built years ago, the small vegetable patch he only just started last spring. "Rises and falls, all things must meet their end."

But Joly jerks free from his grip, spurred on by an abrupt surge of energy; she flits around the porch. "Maybe this is an opportunity!" she cries, her features pulsating with thought.

"For a fresh start." He blinks twice and suddenly she's right in front of him, hopping in place. Her hands fly up to his shoulders. "Yannick's right, you know. There's no reason you couldn't turn the brewing into a legit business."

"There *is* a reason, a very good reason." Ben lifts both of her hands off his shoulders and brings them together at his lips. "It is unseemly to profiteer off of people's vices."

"But this could be something," she says, pacing the stoop. "For both of us. I could help . . . I could . . . do something helpful. We could figure out the business stuff. We're smart people. Mom and Pop! A family business! We just need to get some investors, raise some capital . . . and decide to do it!"

What is all this? Yesterday she's pushing him into the priesthood; today into beer. "Investors don't drop out of the sky, my little turtle dove."

"No, but . . . we could get Yannick to help out."

Ben takes a long patient sip of his ale. "You want me to take blood money from your brother?"

"Blood money?" She's on the steps, kicking at them petulantly. "Oh god, Benny, why do you have to be so dramatic all the time? It's not blood money. It's regular, ordinary money."

"Bah! Nobody earning that much money is doing it on the up and up."

She throws herself down onto the middle step and plops her cheeks into her hands. "I don't understand why you hate him so much."

"I don't *hate* him. I just think that he, and the people who do his kind of work, are depraved. And I want no part of their ill-gotten spoils." He taps at her slight, curved back with his boot. "Hey, did you even notice what your brother looked like this morning? The sagging eyes. The sallow face."

"He looked tired."

"He looked hungover, Joly."

"They'd been at a party the night before."

"I could still smell the liquor on him."

"Ben!" she cries, jumping back to her feet and throwing her arms above her head. Her loud gestures are hard to follow. "Who's drunk right now? In the middle of the day? A weekday! You are, Ben!"

"Ah yes, but I . . ." he taps his chest with his beer bottle, "I have just been canned. And I am losing my Sanctum. I would be inhuman if I weren't hammered just now." He stares back into the kettle, inhaling notes of vanilla. "It is for precisely such times that God has given us beer."

"Yannick is coming to your church on Sunday, did you know that? To hear your sermon. To support you."

"So you forced his hand, did you?"

"No. No, I didn't. He wanted to. He's interested."

"He is *not* interested," Ben says, stirring the cauldron in hypnotic circles. "I heard you telling him about it. I heard him express a clear *dis*interest. It was right after he called me a deadbeat, I believe."

"Aw Ben," she says in a much quieter tone. She nuzzles her chin against his bicep. "Don't be mad about that. That's just how he talks. He thinks anyone making less than six figures is a deadbeat."

"Pah!"

"But he wants to help us. So why not at least consider this beer idea? It'd be a chance to make money doing something you actually *like*."

Ben shakes her off and lets his voice explode: "The brewing is not a capitalist enterprise, okay? It is a spiritual pursuit!"

"God. You're stubborn!" Joly marches down into the yard, where she stomps around in erratic elliptical shapes. It makes him dizzy to watch her, so he returns his gaze to the beer.

"Choosing to be broke is not righteous, Ben," she calls up

to him. "Not when you have a partner who is trying to build a life with you. You don't want to accept any responsibility in your life." She's trudging back his way now, waving furiously with both arms. "None! That's your problem. At least Yannick, depraved Yannick, doesn't cower from responsibility."

"Oh-ho, that is rich! Rich creamery butter, right there!" He barrels down the steps in one big lunge. "Your brother? The pillar of familial responsibility?"

"Yes, actually," she says. "He is."

"And does part of that legendary responsibility involve trampling over his wedding vows?"

"What is that supposed to mean? He does everything for Karen, everything she asks."

"Does she ask him to screw around with your best friend?"

Joly's mouth makes several false starts at forming words; she blinks, her lips slightly ajar. "That is ridiculous."

"Is it? Then why did I find him with her when you had me drop off that birthday beer? Your brother, your hero, paragon of the wholesome nuclear family, practically *in flagrante delicto*."

"That . . . is impossible. You must have seen something else."

"You are naivety itself sometimes, Joly." With an elaborate sigh, Ben drops down on the bottom-most step. "A sheltered and naïve woman."

"And you are a drunken idiot right now! I'm sorry I interrupted your moping."

"And I'm sorry I can't give you the lavish life to which you are accustomed!"

They've spiralled upward through decibels, approaching full-blown screams. He can hear how the alcohol is cranking up his volume—he's much louder than he'd like to be. "With me, there will be no radiant floors! No coffee pod machines! No semi-annual vacations and home ownership!"

"Did I say I wanted those things?"

"It is implied all over this conversation."

"I don't want any of that. I don't need that."

"Then what is it you want from me?"

She erupts into wild sobs. And instantly Ben regrets it all, this entire conversation. As though a switch has been flipped, he snaps from angry to contrite. From his position on the bottom step, he reaches for her and pulls her toward him. He wraps a single arm all the way around her trembling body.

"I just want . . . " she warbles.

"What?"

" . . . to be able to keep a baby."

He presses his head to her belly. "I'm sorry, Joly. You know how sorry I am."

"I know," she says, her voice very small. "But . . . but . . ." Her voice gets smaller and smaller as she carries on, so small by the end that he almost can't hear her when she says they should break up.

14

SUNDAY MORNING: BEN is ready to preside at the pulpit. In a single burst of divinely-inspired creativity yesterday, the sermon flowed from his pen onto the page. No job, no house, no woman, but an epiphany: God *wants* him to be angry.

From the pulpit, he scans the rows of parishioners, one by one, hoping to spot Joly somewhere in the pews. But she's not here. It's just the boomers, the same handful of divinity students, and the pair of decrepit classics professors who have managed to cling to life for another week. And whoa now—who is that? In a back pew, sitting all alone—well, son of a bitch—it's Yannick. His eyes are whizzing around, trying to find a way to make a break for it unnoticed. Ben breathes out a tight, angry tension, to steady his shaky hands and calm the pounding pulse in his neck. He makes a slow, solemn invocation to the Father, Son, and the Holy Spirit. And he begins.

"Today's Gospel reading from Luke is about signs of the time." He can hear his voice rattle, but only slightly. "So let us start by taking a closer look at our own time, what defines it, and what signs we are ignoring."

The boomers are with him so far; gentle nodding all around.

"Ours is a time of Empire," he says. "And our empire, like all those that have come before for it, has reached the brink of collapse.

"The Reverend Roberta, in her sermons, likes to talk about climate change, and it is hard not to call her words to mind when we get savage storms like we had this past week."

A softball opening to warm up the congregation; the boomers understand talk of the weather. His voice deepens and steadies.

"Within a few short hours of that storm hitting, we had flooded roads and highways. We had overflowing storm drains. Fallen power lines. Blackouts. We had these troubles because our infrastructure is old and weak and insufficient. Our systems are starting to fail.

"We should be paying attention to these signs of destruction and decay. But we are no better at observing the signs of our time than Jesus's disciples were. We must take responsibility for this failing. But we must also recognize that we have been encouraged, even directed *not* to heed these signs by our corrupt corporate state. The corporate state does not want us to notice what is going on. It has been crafting illusion after illusion to keep us from seeing what should be obvious: that things are falling apart."

Ben notices a ripple of shifting in the pews. A grey-head coughs.

"Empire, at its end, always relies on illusions to hold itself up. Our corporate state presents us with the illusion that our consumption patterns are sustainable, our living standards endlessly improvable, our lives exceptional. Meanwhile it obscures what is going on at its outer reaches: the exploitation and war propping up our lifestyles. And we are happy not to see. Why? Because the truth makes us uncomfortable. What are we if not a civilization fixated on personal comfort? We are coddled babies, asleep in the womb of the empire, unable to withstand the slightest offense, unequipped to encounter anything that threatens our false security and our fragile happiness. We live in an illusion. But Jesus warns us about illusions in today's reading. He teaches us to recognize the truth about our time whether it is comfortable or not.

"And the truth about our time is grim. We are facing a degree of wealth inequality that is already destabilizing society. And it is only getting worse. Our labour movement is decimated. The corporate machine has trampled over the hard-fought labour victories of the twentieth century. Where is job security? Gone. Where are the once-strong unions? Weakened into irrelevance. Where is the living wage? Laughed out of conversations. Are we paying attention to these signs? To the spreading misery of our society's workers? No, we are not. We prefer to live inside the illusion.

"It takes strength to resist the illusion. Because the illusion is seductive. It encourages us to revel in our basest desires. Our vanity, jealousy, covetousness, avarice—this is what keeps the corporate machine running. In an effort to soothe our every frantic craving, we consume more and more, fuelling the machine with our vices. So the machine praises our vices, encourages them, dresses them up in the mask of civic virtue, and suddenly we have leaders telling us it is our civic duty not to sacrifice, but to go shopping.

"But beneath the reckless consumption, in the underbelly of the empire, despair has begun to bleed through the citizenry. Increasingly alienated and atomized, with dwindling hopes for their own futures, the empire's forgotten citizens are crying out. Is it any wonder that their cries have been answered by demagogues? Populism is sweeping through the empire. Here in our own city, we have seen a drunken, belligerent mayor appeal to a simmering contempt for the political class. To the south, in the very heart of the empire, the ranking demagogue is busy tapping into our worst fears and prejudices. These figures are popping up all around us. Our political leaders are now the vilest of the species, stoking our rage for their own gain. But they care nothing about us.

"We caught a glimpse of the rage seething among the masses during our blackout last week, looting rampant in our streets. Storefronts smashed. Shops robbed. Of course they were! What else could we expect? When the illusion starts to break down—when the pacifying distractions of television and the internet and conspicuous consumption are taken away—the citizenry awakens fully to its own rage. It recognizes the truth: that it has been abandoned by the state. And it responds in turn with a violent contempt for social order.

"So what do all these signs portend? These crashing power lines and overflowing storm drains, these rants from rising demagogues and these smashed shop windows? These are the screams of a civilization in its last throes. This is what it sounds like when Empire breaks down."

Ben pauses to gauge the congregation. Their expressions have shifted, the empty nodding replaced with a surprising array of frowns. Are these the frowns of stimulated thought? Have they, for once, been moved by words from this pulpit? He ploughs on with heightening fervour.

"The capitalist experiment has failed," Ben booms. "If we do not see that, then we do not know how to interpret our time.

Like every empire that has come before, ours has passed its zenith. It has reached the point where, too bloated and corrupt, it is unable to respond to the problems it faces. Nothing will save it now.

"We, as a species, are about to endure a traumatic experience. Environmental catastrophe is on the horizon. Storms and wildfires, floods and droughts will give rise to geopolitical calamities that will overwhelm the crumbling remains of this empire. The pipeline of cheap energy and cheap consumer products will dry up. The future is going to look very much like the past. But we have forgotten how to look after ourselves.

"The Fall is coming, my brethren. We must prepare ourselves for the descent. Mentally, physically, and spiritually. There is a goodness in humanity, a spark of the divine that even the machine, despite its absolute best efforts, has not been able to eradicate. If we can preserve that goodness, and foster it, we can yet limit the chaos and war ahead.

"I am calling on each of us to develop true and strong bonds with each other. To practise a compassion that can withstand the harsh reality of the coming age. We need to learn how to be kind without the decadent comforts of Empire propping up our moods. We need to relearn simple skills. Remember how to make and mend things. We must forge communities, as Jesus teaches us to, instead of yielding to the fierce individualism that is cannibalizing our society.

"The Church has a great responsibility in all this. It must shepherd us into this new world. There are no other organizations with the strength and memory to bring about the mass reorientation of hearts and minds that we will need to survive."

Ben grips the sides of the pulpit and, casting a sweeping gaze across his audience, vaults into the crescendo.

"The Christian tradition is one of revolution! Of dissent! Of defiance! Of rage! Jesus raged against Empire when he raged against Rome. As did the long line of prophets who came before Him—each stood up to defy the empire of their day. We need only look at our Old Testament reading today to find another prophet—Jeremiah, who heaped his righteous rage on Babylon—to see how far back this tradition stretches.

"What is Babylon anyway? What does it signify? How does a millennia-old civilization relate to our own?

"Babylon is a thread pulled through the Bible, from Genesis right through to Revelation. It is a civilization so degenerate it has come to stand as the archetype of imperial decadence. A civilization apart from God and apart from righteousness. It is so drunk on its own sins that it topples over. Babylon is a civilization that cares about idols, not morals. About things, not citizens. About the illusory bounty of material wealth. Not the true wealth of the spirit. It cares about endless gadgets and disposable toys and having twelve kinds of cream cheese stocked up at its local sandwich shop, and it cares nothing about the workers who make those gadgets and who staff those sandwich shops.

"What is Babylon? Babylon is Empire. Babylon is Rome. Babylon is America. Babylon is here and now. This is it! Look around you, brothers and sisters! We are living in Babylon!! And Babylon is going to fall!!!"

BOOK
FOUR
YANNICK

1

"TAKE A LOOK at this banknote," says Bourque. He slides the bill across the table to Yannick, who's on the last bites of his lunch. Rigatoni with pancetta and burrata. Fucking delicious. Best burrata in the city. "You know what this is worth?"

Yannick picks up the bill. It's an Iraqi note. 250 dinars. "Yeah, idiot. It's worth 250 dinars."

"Yeah, but you know what that's worth? Know what a fucking dinar is worth?"

"I dunno. Couple pennies maybe?"

"Twenty-eight cents. That's this morning's exchange rate."

"All right. So what."

"Twenty-eight cents, eh?" says Anosh. "Seems steep for a few hundred dinars."

"It is steep," says Dave. "That's hardly worth the paper it's printed on."

There are four of them at lunch today. Yannick and Anosh; Bourque and Dave. They all work within a few blocks of each other, so lunchtime meet-ups happen on the regular. The latter two are currency traders. Same field as Yannick and Anosh, different discipline. Worse discipline. Less lucrative. Yannick feels bad about it sometimes . . . like, guilty. Because he owes his career to Bourque. He's known Bourque since way back, since elementary school. When Yannick didn't know what to do after high school, it was Bourque who told him which universities to apply to, which programs to apply for. It was Bourque who decided they should go into business broadly, then finance specifically. It was Bourque who announced which investment bank in New York they should be aiming for. But a few years out of school, and out of banking, and out of New York, their trajectories diverged. Bourque fell into currency trading; Yannick into private equity. Yannick's path is better, smarter—his base salary just now is 300k, while Bourque's is still stalled short of 200. To say nothing of the gap in their bonuses.

"What are you doing with Iraqi dinars?" Yannick asks.

"It's not what *I'm* doing with them," says Bourque. "It's what my mother is doing with them."

"All right. So what's your mother doing with them?"

"My fucking mother. I'll tell you what she's doing with them."

Yannick watches Bourque set his fork down on the plate as he gears up to tell whatever story he's about to tell. He's still got half his lunch left, half his angel hair pasta dish, with peas and cherry tomatoes—a dish he special orders and claims to have invented. This is a chronic problem with Bourque. He eats slowly. Always the same painful trudge through his meals regardless of venue or food type. Like they've all got time to sit around *savouring*. And now he's going to hold up this lunch further with some shitty story about Iraqi dinars? Fuck it. Not today. Yannick doesn't bother waiting for him to finish; he waves for the bill when the waitress passes by. He's got plans to meet Lou in twenty minutes—a quick how-do-you-do before he heads back to the office for the day—and he doesn't want Bourque to cut into that time. It's short enough as it is.

"So I go up for dinner on the weekend," Bourque is saying, "and my mother brings me into her bedroom, all hush-hush, like she's got some big great secret to tell, so I'm like what the fuck is this about, and then this woman, this crazy mother of mine, she shows me shoeboxes, literal fucking shoeboxes, stuffed full of Iraqi dinars. I'm talking cash, man. Banknotes. Bills and bills and bills."

"I don't get it," says Yannick.

"Is this the lead up to a joke? Are you telling us a joke, Bourque?" says Anosh.

"I wish this were a joke. But instead, this is my mother's new fucking investment plan." Bourque stabs his finger at the bill on the table. "Some idiot friend of hers, some retard from whatever stitch-and-bitch circle she's part of now, tells her she read some article somewhere that said the Iraqi dinar is set to revalue. It's really gonna take off, Michael, she says. So right now you can buy the notes for pennies. And in a year, less than that even—less than that she says!—the currency will surge, and anyone who got in on the ground floor will be a millionaire. Or a billionaire. I researched it, Michael, she says to me. It's practically guaranteed, she says. So I say to her, I say, Mom, are you out of your goddamn mind?"

"Who told her this? What kind of company is your mom keeping?"

"Sharon. Sharon from the sewing circle. Apparently I've met her."

"Sharon sounds like an idiot."

"Of course Sharon's an idiot. But what is my mother doing listening to this idiot? When her son is a goddamn currency trader!" His wrist, in one of a series of animated movements, whacks the spoon resting on his plate and sends some of the cherry tomato sauce flinging. A dollop lands on Anosh's tie.

"Aw, for fuck's suck, Bourque."

"Sorry, man. Happens."

Anosh dabs a wet napkin at his tie. "Look at this. Your faggy little angel hair got all over my tie."

"You can barely see it. Relax."

"You know what this tie costs?"

"Fifty bucks?"

"I'm wearing a fifty dollar tie? Go fuck yourself."

"Looks pretty cheap is all I'm saying."

Anosh flips him off as he gets up. His tie requires further attention, which he runs off to the washroom to provide.

"Guy's that touchy about his clothes and I'm the faggy one?" says Bourque.

"That's a three hundred dollar tie, at least," says Dave.

"Doesn't look it."

"What would you know? You dress like an accountant."

While the two of them bicker, Yannick looks at the Iraqi banknote. The image on the back is of a low tower, almost a cone, with a strange, spiralling ramp defining its exterior. When Yannick squints at it, he can just make out a few tiny figures on various elevations along the ramp.

"Who's even selling your mom straight up banknotes?" he asks.

"Ha! That's the best part," cries Bourque. "Some fucking guy in Oshawa. With a website. She's buying them off the internet from a fucking guy in Oshawa. I mean, who does that? It's a whole racket these assholes have going. They write articles about the inevitable rise of the dinar. Then they hawk this shit to widows and idiots. I can't even tell you the kind of fees she paid him. Exorbitant fees. Scam artist fees. It makes me want to murder these assholes. But she doesn't see the scam. She just keeps buying. So now she's got almost five million—can you imagine?—five million Iraqi dinars in shoeboxes in her bedroom closet!"

"Yeah, but that's only like five or six thousand bucks," says Dave.

"Yeah, five or six thousand that should be going to real shit. Mortgage payments. Car payments. Or you know, an actual investment fund."

Bourque pays his mother's mortgage. So he takes these imprudent deficiencies personally. He's kicked up money to his mother since he first started making any.

"I try to reason with the woman, you know. I ask her, I say, Mom, why the hell would the dinar revalue? Think about it. Iraq is a complete fucking mess. So she starts giving me a history lesson. About how the Kuwaiti currency revalued after the Iraqis left in '91. Which I guess is what Sharon-the-financial-advisor told her. Like Kuwait in the '90s is the same exact situation as Iraq today. I tried to explain that, but then . . . then . . . this crazy woman, she starts telling me about post-war development. She starts talking about fucking Europe after fucking World War Two. Because development is inevitable after war, Michael, she says."

"Jesus."

"She won't listen to me. She says she's going to ask Jay when he comes in. Says Jay will know better because he lives in Dubai. Like Dubai and Iraq are the same fucking place."

Jay Bourque is Bourque's little brother. Baby Bourque. Yannick has always preferred Baby Bourque to his brother. Everyone prefers Baby Bourque. The little brother is likeable. Funny. A good time. Bourque, the elder, has some oddities, some social malfunctions, a history of curious behavioural derangements that make him unpleasant to be around. Not that that stops Yannick from being around him. What's he supposed to do? Bourque has always been in his orbit. You get dealt the friends you get dealt. Sometimes they turn out kind of shitty, but that doesn't mean you get to cut them loose.

"When's Jay coming?" asks Yannick.

"Flying in tomorrow. We're gonna hit up the rooftop at Blitz. Jay wants to get lit. You coming?"

"Can't," says Yannick. "I got family shit all week. Karen's gone mental about the kid's baptism. This thing has mushroomed. It's almost as big a production as our wedding."

"Well . . ."

"Well what?"

"Well it *is* a sacrament," says Bourque.

Yannick sometimes forgets that Bourque is Catholic. Because it never comes up. Until it does. "What is it with you Catholics? I don't hear one word, not a goddamn word, about God or church or anything for years. Then suddenly, everyone's fucking devout."

Bourque shrugs. "It's in the blood, man. It's tribal."

"Not my tribe."

"And you know . . . it is the One True Faith." Bourque is grinning as he says this, so Yannick doesn't know what to take from it. It seems ironic, both the substance and the tone, yet it can't be—not wholly ironic—because the guy is still a card-carrying Catholic. He goes to Mass on holidays. He takes his mother.

It's hard to digest, this latent religiosity in those around him. Yannick used to think he was cruising along in a mostly secular world and that the religious people he did know were religious only in a cultural sense, not an ideological one. But that was a mistake of perception. Because once you scratch the surface of people, there are decades' worth, centuries' worth of inherited religious bullshit. And here he is, about to foist this bullshit onto his kid. He fought against the baptism. He fought it hard. But Karen was persistent and he grew tired.

"Tell you what," Yannick says, just as Anosh makes his return from the bathroom. "Bring Baby Bourque to the baptism. Karen's already got about fifty people coming to the reception. I'm sure she'll be happy for an extra Catholic."

"What's this? Baby Bourque's in town?" says Anosh, re-taking his seat. His tie is wet, but the tomato tinge has vanished.

Bourque says, "Tomorrow. He's coming tomorrow. And he's been talking about the rooftop at Blitz. You in?"

"Yeah, all right. I wouldn't mind hanging with the better Bourque for a change. My tie is fucked, man. You're paying the dry cleaning."

"Invoice me."

The server arrives with the bill; she slides it onto the table and disappears again before they can offer her a credit card.

"Hey-oh, what's this? I'm not even done eating yet," Bourque says.

"That's because you never shut up," says Yannick.

"Someone's gotta make the conversation."

"Let's go. Hurry up."

"I eat at my own pace. That's how I like it."

"Well then you can eat by yourself. The rest of us have to get back to work."

"All right, all right. Just trying to enjoy it, you know?"

Dave flattens out a cloth napkin onto which they each drop a credit card. He folds the tips of the napkin together and tosses the cards around inside. This is how they decide who pays: credit card roulette. Whosever card gets pulled pays. It generally evens out over time. Except for that beautiful months-long stretch when things stayed lopsided, because they all figured out how to make things stick on Bourque. His card had a little nick on the side, which they'd feel out before they pulled. That card, and only that card, got pulled for months. Bourque must have put up thousands of dollars for lunch before he worked out the con.

"I'll pull," says Bourque, and with a characteristically irritating flourish, he draws a credit card. His eyes land on Yannick. "You're lucky today, Yan-Man. Your treat, buddy."

Yannick flips over the bill to take a look at the damage. Not so bad today. Beside the bill, on the table, is the Iraqi banknote, which Yannick looks at again; he studies the strange, spiralling tower. "What is this?" he asks. "On the back here?"

"The building? How the fuck should I know?"

"It's your banknote."

"Yeah, but what do I know about Iraqi landmarks?"

"Nothing, it seems."

Bourque pushes the banknote toward him. "Hey, hey, you keep that. Maybe it'll be worth something in a year."

2

THE BOUTIQUE HOTEL where Yannick meets Lou provides an ideal setup. Three reasons: it's small enough to make it unlikely that they'll run into anyone they know; the rooms are top-tier; and the price is right: free. Yannick worked out an arrangement with the manager, Tommy Boscarino, a friend of his from B-school days. A guy who owes him.

He and Boscarino were good buddies through university

and even afterward, so when the guy came to him a few years back asking to borrow money, Yannick said all right. But he did figure, even as he wrote out a cheque, that the loan would end up a write-off. Abstractly Boscarino knows about saving and investing—he's a smart enough guy—but he just can't stop throwing his fucking money away. On clothes, on cars, on gambling. Always wants to be a big shot. It's a pattern of behaviour that helps explain why he manages a hotel, but won't ever own one. Still, Yannick lent him the money; some-one had to. By the time Boscarino came asking, he looked like absolute shit—said he'd lost a pile on a sports bet and wasn't sure how to get out from under it.

As expected, Boscarino hasn't paid it back, not a dime, but he's always been grateful to Yannick for lending him the money when no one else would. So when, one afternoon, he happened upon Yannick and Lou in the lobby of a seedy-ish downtown hotel (fucking in cars in parking garages had become tiresome), Boscarino took one look at the two of them and, being an astute hotel manager, understood the situation. A week or so later, when he and Yannick and some of the B-school boys met up for drinks, Boscarino quietly re-proached Yannick for taking a woman like Lou to so dumpy a hotel, and suggested that instead, should the need arise again, he bring "that hot Asian piece" over to his hotel, where he'd put them in a room more commensurate with a woman of her calibre.

"Mmm," murmurs Lou as Yannick eases himself into her. He's got about thirty minutes—twenty-five for the sex and post-coital lingering, and five for the showering and throw-ing his clothes back on.

"Mmm," she says again. She doesn't say words during sex, not unless she's directing him toward specific action. But she articulates her pleasure or displeasure through a nuanced series of purrs and moans, which he's adept at interpreting. This particular "mmm," with its two notes, high-low, means *good, like that, keep going.* So he does.

He didn't want to be this guy. The guy who cheats on his wife. He promised himself he wouldn't be. When other guys, married guys, guys in relationships, were picking up stray women at clubs or fucking hookers on work trips, he kept things straight. For his first few years with Karen he didn't throw so much as a lusty glance at another woman. But one Sunday last summer, after the baseball game at Christie Pits, when Joly had gone over to Ben's, and Karen was up in Thornhill with the kid, he wound up giving Lou a lift home. His dick was at half-mast the whole ride, just on account of the proximity. Just to be alone with her. They stopped to get sandwiches, which they ate leaning against the trunk of the car, and when Lou pressed herself against him . . . well, what was he supposed to do? It's Lou. He's always fucked Lou. And he fucked her that night, too. In the car. Down in Bond Park in Don Mills, where they used to go when they were kids. That night, in the back seat of his car, fucking Lou, fucking some- one other than his wife, he still didn't feel like *that* guy. What exists between them belongs to a different time and place, outside of life with Karen. It's quarantined. It doesn't count.

Lou's on top of him, riding him hard. His pulse picks up, but it's she who's close to coming. He knows her body better than he does anyone else's. Much better than his own wife's. But Karen has never really let him get to know her body. She doesn't like him seeing her naked in the daylight. Or in any strong light. Even before the kid, which, yes, okay, did a number on her body, distorting her hips and stomach and tugging out her thighs, and even somehow altering the shape of her arms . . . even before all that (none of which he particu- larly minds by the way), she never liked him to study her. But Lou doesn't hide. Right now, with her back arched and her chest thrust forward, she's presenting herself to him, daring him to find a fault.

Her moans change tenor, dropping into lower registers, and Yannick hears his own moans and pants echoing hers, their sounds forming a pattern.

"Unh."

"Huh."

"Unh."

"Huh."

Lou's been doing this thing sometimes, when he hits her in just the right spot, as he's doing now, when he can feel the tip of his dick up against a sort of spongy spot on the front wall of her pussy. The contact makes her moans flatten out—they come out in guttural bursts, from deep within her chest, or somewhere deeper still, pulled from the very centre of her body, and with her eyes half-closed, her head begins to rock ragged on top of her shoulders, like she's lost control of the muscles in her neck. When they get to this stage, Yannick doesn't dare adjust his positioning or his rhythm or say any-thing at all, fearful of disrupting her trance. He waits for her to get where she needs to get, and when she does, she rises up off his dick, just an inch or two off, her hands on his chest for support, and the moment she's off him, a stream spills from her pussy, like his dick had been plugging up the massive reservoir of whatever combination of fluids makes up female ejaculate.

He thought it was an urban legend, this kind of orgasm, until he saw it emanate from Lou, until he felt her fluid flow over his pelvis, all over his skin, drenching him and the sheets beneath him, and the mattress beneath the sheets. It's new, this phenomenon—a development of the last half year. He's afraid to ask if it only happens with him. Or if it happens with Elliott. With others. Are there others? He doesn't know.

She falls heavily onto his chest. With two fingers he

massages her clit, coming at it from behind—strong pressure, then off, strong, then off—and each time he applies the pressure, her pussy contracts, bringing forth a fresh spurt of fluid. It's like he's conjuring the expulsions with his skilful manipulations and direction. He's a conductor, making her blow with a wave of the baton. He's a fucking maestro. No one else could make her come like this. Of course there aren't others.

One minute, two minutes pass while her intermittent contractions continue. When she's finished, she slides back onto his dick, but now her pussy is twice as tight as it was a moment ago, and way wetter, sopping. It doesn't take him much from here. A few in-and-outs and he's ready. He pulls out just before he comes and rockets his load up onto her belly: a champion's blast. What doesn't get her arcs back down onto the towel beneath them. A trace catches his thigh.

Afterward, he lies with his head on her chest and checks the clock. Nine minutes to go. Nine minutes in which to lie here with her fingers weaving through his hair. He likes these aftermath minutes as much as the sex itself, maybe more. He likes feeling her hands on his scalp. It's a calming sensation; he doesn't encounter many of those anymore. It's good for him, salutary, necessary. Because he's tired, he's always so fucking tired, and a few minutes of uninterrupted rest, with her soft breath on his head and her fingers in his hair . . . well, it's a temporary reset.

Eight minutes.

The breeze kicks up through the open French doors that lead to the terrace. Boscarino put them up in the top-floor suite today. He always gives them the best available room, the top-floor rooms, which Yannick appreciates in theory, but hates in practice, because he hates heights. They make him want to jump. He knows it's not uncommon, this urge, he's looked into it, but it worries him nonetheless, because the urge comes on so strong sometimes he's not sure he'll be able to override it, Just last weekend, he was walking across the Bloor Viaduct with Yvie, who insisted on stopping every few metres to peer down at the Don Valley more than a hundred feet below. As he stood there looking down, even with the kid's hand in his, he felt the height trigger something in his cells, some biological response that seeks self-destruction. It's psychotic, this death wish. But there it is. And if it weren't for the suicide barrier along the bridge, a series of rods about 5m high, which make it impossible, or at least very difficult, to jump, he's not sure—not one hundred percent sure—he could've stopped himself. The city put up that barrier (the "Luminous Veil") after the bridge became a magnet for suicides, averaging one every twenty-odd days. All those plummeting bodies caused traffic problems on the highway below. Something had to be done. But Yannick wonders just how many of those hundreds of suicides were genuine, planned-in-advance efforts to die, and how many were the result of some poor sucker simply overtaken by the urge to jump.

With four minutes left before his alarm sounds, Lou pushes his head off her chest and says, "Hey, up. I have to go."

"What? Where?" Where could she possibly have to go? She's unemployed now.

"I've got a thing."

"What thing?"

"Just this thing."

He's been worried about her employment status for weeks. If she wanted to quit her job, fine, but she should've had sense enough to line up something else first. She's usually sensible. He hopes to god she's not just sitting around smoking pot all day. They both did a lot of that in high school. How many times did they drive down to the park, smoke up against the hood of the car, have sex in the back seat, then just hang out, waiting to sober up enough to drive home? But she always liked smoking more than he did. Still does. She likes it after dinner, likes it at the baseball games, likes it before big social functions (she was baked and then some at his wedding), which is all fine. As long as she's not spiralling.

"You get a new job or something?" he asks.

"Well yes, actually."

"What? What job?"

"Managing the batting cages. At Bond Park. Evenings and weekends."

"How'd you get that?"

"Guy I used to know from baseball. He runs the cages. He likes me. I asked him for a favour."

His shoulders stiffen. She always seems to know some guy willing to do her a favour, and it always tweaks his jealousy. "That can't pay a lot."

"Pays almost nothing."

Maybe her father will help her out with the finances. Or maybe Elliott's doing well enough with the photography now to support them both. He charges enough, that's for damn sure. Thousands for Yvie's baptism! It's costing them fucking thousands. For pictures of a baptism. Outrageous! Straight out indefensible. But in this case, this one particular situation, he doesn't mind forking over the money. It was actually he who suggested to Karen they use Elliott for the baptism. He likes to throw work Elliott's way. Because he wants Lou to be all right. If she hits some rough waters, he's not just going to let her flounder.

"You said evenings and weekends?" he asks.

"Yeah."

"So why do you have to go now?"

"Oh. I've just got a thing. A different thing."

"Why are you being cagey about it?"

She's already stepping into her lacy pink panties. "I'm helping Ben, all right? With this community dinner that he organizes."

"Ben?"

"Uh-huh."

"Babylon Ben?" The last time he saw Ben he was perched in the pulpit, preaching the doom of civilization like a deranged cult leader.

"Stop calling him that."

"You didn't hear that sermon, Lou. The shit this guy was rattling off." That sermon. Whoa now . . . that was something. Pure scattershot insanity. Yannick came home from that church ready to rip into Joly: one, for standing him up (there he was, trying to be a good fucking brother, trying to be supportive, and she doesn't even show?) and two, for dating this unhinged loser in the first place (this maniac raving about the "corporate machine" and the end of civilization?), but instead, when she finally turned up, having spent the distraught post-breakup day at Lou's, she announced the split and looked so fucking crushed about it that Yannick just let the whole sermon thing go. Besides, the breakup, truly, is a holy fucking miracle. "I'm telling you, Lou, that guy is right out of his fucking mind."

"Well whatever. He organizes this community dinner. And I'm helping him with the shopping and the prep. So I have to go."

She slips on her blouse. He waits for her to further explain this sudden interest in charity work, but she just pulls her jeans up over her strong thighs.

"Is this a religious thing?" he asks.

"What? No."

This lurking religious presence, it's everywhere. Haven't

they all moved beyond this yet? Into a culture motivated by just a little more reason and rationality? Or is the whole society in regress?

"It's a church program, though, right? Ben runs it out of his church?"

"Yeah. But it's not a religious thing. It's just . . . I don't know . . .It's just a virtuous thing." She stops dressing herself and turns to him with her jeans still unbuttoned. A pink triangle of underwear shows itself. "One of these days, Yannick, we're gonna have to stop doing this."

"I know."

"I feel like shit."

"I know."

She's been ringing this note more and more lately. But she never stops coming out to meet him. He grabs the waist of her jeans and pulls her toward him. He brushes his lips to her stomach. He wants to fuck again—even though he's supposed to be in the shower in exactly one minute. When she talks about ending it, he gets nervous. Any day, any fuck could be their last. He kisses her stomach again; he slips his tongue into her belly button. She tugs at his earlobes.

"I don't have time," she says.

"When do you have to be there?"

"One-thirty."

"Where are you meeting him?" He sheds her blouse. His cock is already hard again. Christ, she makes it move.

"At the church. On the campus."

"That's not far." His hands are over her bra, then inside it.

"No no. You have to go to work."

"It's fine." His mouth on hers. "We got time."

Her body yields against his hands. He grips her. He fucks her. "Mmm," she says. Two notes: high-low.

3

THE STEINGRUBER VINEGAR deal is one giant fucking headache. Goldstone bought the vinegar company a few years ago, when it was a mismanaged mess. They restructured it, laid off a bunch of redundant workers, made it a whole lot more efficient, consolidated it with another of their holdings, all of which substantially boosted its value. Now they're ready to sell. It should be a windfall.

But negotiations with this current buyer are a maze of irritations. The buyer's got some third-party guys who keep stalling, keep flagging things, keep calling back with the same idiotic questions.

"Listen . . . no, listen . . . listen to me," Yannick says into the phone, doing his best to keep his voice calibrated at something below a full-blown scream. "We've been over all of this already, John. I've explained it to you, haven't I?"

"You have. But we still have some questions about these growth projections."

"What questions? We've been over all of your questions."

"You guys are just too high on these projections, Yannick."

"We've been over the projections. More than once. We did a point by point breakdown. Did we or did we not do that last time we met?"

"We did, but—"

"You've looked at the financials, right?"

"I have. But we still don't understand how you get to these—"

"You've looked at the data?"

"Yes, but—"

"Then I don't understand how you don't understand."

"Just walk me through this again. Let me see how you're getting to these numbers."

At first Yannick thought these guys were just trying to flex some muscle. Third-party guys always hope to find a minor problem or two, something small enough to keep the deal on track, but large enough to justify their jobs. Over the last couple of weeks, though, Yannick has readjusted his opinion. These guys are plain old-fashioned morons. They don't know what they're doing.

"All right, John. Let's walk you through it again. If that's what you need."

The vinegar deal matters. In a big way. Yannick's economics on this deal are looking good. He's got phantom stock in Steingruber Vinegar—that's cash, a bunch of it, that'll be paid out to him when they sell. It's part of his new bonus structure. He used to get a straight cash bonus at the end of the year, but the size of that bonus came entirely at the discretion of Adam, the team boss. At year's end Adam would go into a room with the top brass and pound on the table to see what he could shake loose, and whatever number he came out with got divided among the team. So Yannick never knew what he was going to get. It was always a lot, of course, at least equal to his base pay. But a 300k yearly bonus is an embarrassingly small slice of the pie when he's helping to engineer profits in the hundreds of millions. He got tired of seeing the top guys pocketing a fortune each year while he lingered in six-figure territory. So he complained, he and Anosh both. And things adjusted. Now they're in on the backend of every deal.

There's some risk to this setup. In an underperforming year, Yannick could wind up with almost nothing. But in a good year, he'll be making a whole different kind of money. Real money. He's looking at about half a million when the vinegar deal closes. Just on this one deal.

Half a million (a quarter after taxes, but still) will mark out growth in the pile. A big step toward that five million dollar exit marker. That's the figure he and Karen agreed upon. A net worth of five million and he can pack it in. The plan has always been to retire early—Freedom Forty!—sell the house, and move out of the city, to a small cottage town, where they'll live right on the lake, and he'll spend his free time, his abundant free time, sitting on the deck, staring out at the water, or reading on a well-stuffed chair. He used to like reading. He used to read books, full books, novels, lots of them. Now? Last time he read a novel, it took him two months to get through it. By the time he got to the end, he'd forgotten the first half. No point even trying right now. He'll read when he's forty.

He already knows the town he wants to move to: Bayfield, Ontario. Right on Lake Huron. He's been out there a couple of times, knew some people with family property on the lake. The great lake. With its awesome quiet. That's what he wants.

He'll open a little sandwich shop. That's part of the retirement plan, too. Just a dive, with room for maybe ten or fifteen diners, a place he can hang out during the day, meet the locals in the winter and the cottagers in the summer, and keep a low, but steady, income flowing. When Yvie's old enough, she can work the counter. She'll learn practical skills, a good work ethic, and be spared the worst influences of affluent city life. He doesn't want her around these predatory private school girls, who have sex and eating disorders and drug habits. He had lunch with an investment banker from New York the other day, this guy Jacob who told him that they've had to start stripping tablecloths from bat mitzvahs in the city. Why? Because the kids have been going under the tables. To do what? Drink? Snort drugs? If only. Instead these girls, these children, are crawling under the tables to give blowjobs. Blowjobs! Yannick almost choked on his burrata when he heard this story. Imagine. Twelve-year-old girls giving under-the-table blowjobs at religious functions. That's affluent city life. Now Toronto isn't quite New York, but it's always trying to be, and Yannick doesn't want Yvie chasing this stick. He wants the kid out of the city before she turns twelve.

He and Karen discussed all this before they got married. The retirement, the sandwich shop, the house on Lake Huron. It was a plan. But now Karen brings home brochures of private high schools in the city, or she talks about building up her own real estate firm—a years-long project, maybe a lifetime project—and it's like she's forgotten all about Bayfield, Ontario. But Yannick hasn't.

Five million. Not an extravagant amount, but enough. Or it seemed like enough when he and Karen arrived at that figure years ago. But their expenses have become greater than he could have dreamed. The mortgage, the renovations, the property taxes, the bills, Yvie's Montessori daycare. Joly. Who else is going to make sure his sister doesn't starve and die in destitution? Contingencies, emergencies, surprises. It adds up.

But still, five million—how could five not be enough? Most of the world never gets close to five. He'll quit at five. When he's forty. If he keeps his head down for the next few years, he can make it. He just needs to work harder.

"We all sorted out now?" Yannick barks into the phone.

"I think so," says John. "Yeah."

"Good. Fine."

"So I'll call you if I have any other questions."

"No no, what? If you have any other questions, John, ask them right now. I'm here and ready to answer."

"Well. Uh. No. I think that's all for now."

"You sure? You better be sure."

"Yeah. I think so."

It takes a few more back-and-forths before Yannick is able to extract definite assurances. As soon as he hangs up, he rushes to join a meeting he's already late for, with a pair of entrepreneurs looking for investors. When that wraps up, he's still got some research to do on Corey Jayne Living, a lifestyle company Adam's thinking about acquiring. He'll be home late again tonight, he'll miss dinner.

Yannick and Anosh have been splitting research duty, but neither of them should be doing it. It's grunt work. They need an associate to do this shit. And they've been looking for one. They did a first round of interviews last week and have another round scheduled for tomorrow. But last week's crop of candidates was underwhelming, and Yannick, having looked over the resumes himself, isn't confident that this week's candidates will prove any better. He doesn't understand what has happened to people. It's like the whole world has turned stupid.

4

HIS COCK IS weak tonight. It takes almost fifteen minutes of Karen's stroking and nibbling and sucking to get it to stiffen, and when it does, he perceives a lingering softness at its core.

It's not just because he's already given it two workouts today. Even if he'd abstained, he'd be having trouble right now. With his wife. For the first few minutes, Karen is attentive. She kisses his neck and says things like, "Yeah, baby, yeah, you feel so fucking good," but her words are empty. She's not into it either. The sex is unsexy.

It happens like this most nights now. He'd rather just skip it altogether, but she's ovulating soon, so sex is mandatory. He closes his eyes and thinks about Lou's pink panties, reaching into them, his fingers drenched. That's what comes to mind. That works. Yannick picks up some steam and pushes into her harder.

"Hey," Karen says. "Oh hey."

Her voice intrudes on the fantasy. It's like she knows. Like she can tell he's thinking about someone else. But does it matter? The aim of this exercise is pregnancy, not pleasure. "Mm?"

"Hey, did you put out the garbage?"

"What?"

"The garbage?"

"The *garbage*?" He drops onto his elbows and digs his thumbs into his eyes. "No, not yet."

"Why not?"

He keeps pumping, leveraging from his elbows. "The raccoons. They'll knock it over if it's out overnight."

"But if you don't put it out tonight, you'll forget again."

"I won't."

"Just put a rock on the bin. It'll be fine."

"Raccoons can knock a rock over, Karen."

"I think you should put it out."

His dick is turning into a sponge, so he says "okay, okay," and returns to Lou and her pink panties.

"You'll do it?" Karen asks.

"Sure, sweetheart. I'll do it."

Jesus. The sperm he's got lined up right now can't possibly be vigorous enough to launch a successful campaign. It's no wonder she hasn't gotten knocked up yet. They've made the process a chore, part of the nightly regimen. Brush teeth, wash the kid, impregnate the wife, take out the trash.

When they first started trying for a second child, he wanted it. He really did. One child is lonely. He can't imagine not having a sibling . . . even if that sibling is Joly. What shit it must be to grow up alone. How could he dump that on Yvie? For a good stretch, he and Karen were on the same page: kid number two.

But then, last year, Karen did get pregnant. And there were difficulties. The foetus was abnormally small. The doctor explained that Karen would either miscarry, or . . . or . . . *or what, doctor?* . . . or there might be, well, problems. A kid with *problems.* That struck the fear of Christ in him. How would he handle that? Not well, that's how. It's hard enough (way harder than he thought) having a healthy kid. But crippled? Wheelchair-bound? Unable to feed or clean itself? Or mentally challenged in god knows what ways? It must take a goddamn saint to undertake that. So he was heartbroken, sure, but also swept up in a goddamn tidal wave of relief when Karen miscarried. Since then he's been much less keen to try again. Karen's already thirty-seven. They're pushing their luck.

But here they are. He's pumping into her and pulling up the shape and shade, the particular pattern of folds, of Lou's cunt.

"Did you call the dishwasher guy back?" Karen asks, her voice muffled under his chest.

"Karen. Seriously? Can we talk about this stuff later?"

"Yeah, yeah, sure. Sorry." She bucks her hips up against his. "You like that? You feel so good."

He can't concentrate like this. He rolls onto his back and hoists her up on top of him and grabs her hips. He's always liked the feel of her wide hips in his hands. She anchors her hands on his chest and gets going with a good—or good enough—bit of rocking.

"It's just, we should have the dishwasher fixed before my parents get here." With her arms in front of her, locked straight and close together, he can't even get a good lock at her tits. "Or I'll never hear the end of it. My mother will go on and on about it."

"Okay! I'll call the guy."

Back into a rhythm for almost a minute . . . but oh, wait. "And you're picking them up tomorrow, right? My parents?"

"Uh-huh. Sure."

"Good."

Adele and Joe are coming down from Thornhill for Yvie's baptism—and for the series of functions leading up to it. There's some event involving Yvie's dress. And a rehearsal on Friday (a rehearsal! for a baptism!). Although Thornhill is just a half hour drive from the city (less with no traffic), an easy commute that thousands of people make every day, Adele and Joe have decided the journey is far too big to undertake more than once a week. Instead they plan to install themselves at the Danforth house for the few days leading up to the baptism "to avoid all those pesky back-and-forths."

"Wait, shit," says Yannick, his voice hiccupping out of him between weak thrusts. "We've got interviews tomorrow. I can't."

"But you said you could."

"Sorry. I must've mixed things up."

"But I've got the showing in Don Mills. At Elliott and Louise's place. That could be a big commission for me. I can't cancel."

"Can't you go pick them up after?"

"What if the showing goes long? What if the buyers like the house and want to put in an offer? I don't want to drive up to Thornhill in rush hour."

Yannick keeps rocking Karen's hips, moving her up and down his cock, but the operation is absentminded . . . and absent sensation.

"Joly. She can pick them up," he says.

"She's working now too, remember?"

"Fuck, right."

"And I don't want to ask her to take time off. We should be encouraging her to work."

Even the grim rocking has dissipated into barely a sway. This isn't sex, this is a conversation. He just happens to have his dick inside of her while they're having it.

"Shit. Can they take the train maybe?" he says.

"You know how they are."

He does know how they are. Taking a train? Or any public transit in a city where they have family? Out of the question. Makes them feel like "unwanted tourists," Adele says. And they can't just drive down themselves, like ordinary people, because Joe lost his licence last year (DUI), and Adele won't drive in big cities ("not with all those maniacs on the road!").

"What if I pick them up on Friday instead?" he says.

"But Mom's coming to Yvie's dress fitting tomorrow. Yannick, we talked about this. You said this wouldn't be a problem."

"I know. Okay. Fine. I'll pick them up. I'll work it out somehow."

This is all they talk about anymore. Logistics. For years it's been nothing but logistics. Logistics about their wedding, the house, the pregnancy, Yvie. They must have had more substantial conversations when they were first dating. But it's hard to remember. What he does remember is that she was smart and beautiful and everyone liked her and he was grateful when she agreed to marry him. He loved her then. He's sure he did.

For several minutes she doesn't say anything more, no questions or demands, and the blessed stretch of silent fucking allows him to build up some real pressure in his balls. Not enough to come yet, but he's making progress. And she must notice, because she leans over him, and with her head a few inches from his, she says, "Are you almost there?"

"Uh . . . hang on." He flips her back over and ramps up his speed and as he closes his eyes, he thinks of Lou's face and her smell and her fingers in his hair until he at last manages to come inside his wife, a lame, unsatisfying ejaculation that he can't imagine has force enough to penetrate her uterus. It trickles rather than spurts from his cock. No way is this a winner.

He's fucking exhausted. He collapses onto the bed beside

her and watches as she slips a pillow under her hips and pulls her legs into her chest to encourage impregnation. She keeps an eye on her watch to make sure she holds this position for at least five minutes. That's how long her books say. Her expression is steady and focused, like if she just concentrates hard enough she can will his sperm into her egg. He's disappointing her. Night after night. Month after month. He reaches out a hand to her cheek.

"What?" she asks.

"Nothing. You look beautiful."

She turns her head to smile at him. "I feel good about it this month. I just have a feeling."

She says this every time she's ovulating. She's had a lot of good feelings.

"Me too, sweetheart," he says. "Me too."

5

IN THE MORNING, very early in the morning, Yvie hurtles into their bed, scrambling over Yannick to settle in the middle, where she glues herself to Karen's back. It's 5:53. Yannick closes his eyes and tries to get the extra seven minutes of sleep he's due before the alarm goes off, but Yvie's little feet keep kicking at him and kicking at him until she pushes him right out of bed.

If it were up to him, he wouldn't let the kid do this co-sleeping in the mornings. But Karen says it helps establish a sense of security, which helps with brain development. An obsession with Karen: boosting the kid's IQ. But Yannick has yet to see any tangible results from her efforts. Yvie still eats dirt, given the chance. She shoves objects—keys, pencils, beads—up her nose. She licks anything with a curious texture. After years of play, she's still no good at hide-and-seek, neither the hiding nor the seeking. Yannick loves the little meathead, but he's not convinced that any trick of the parenting trade will make a genius of her.

He showers. He shaves. He pushes through an exhaustion that isn't ever eased by the night's sleep. When he selects a shirt for the day, he makes sure it's plain white—anything more colourful will draw judgmental commentary from Adele—and he pairs it with a dull grey suit. Then he goes downstairs for breakfast.

"DID YOU KNOW that candle makers use more than a billion pounds of wax a year?" Joly says, jumping right into her breakfast chatter, this daily recitation of random useless facts.

She's already up and eating. She's always up early, always already in the kitchen by the time he comes down. He can't figure why she gets up this early when she doesn't have to. He'd prefer to eat breakfast alone, a slice of quiet to start the day.

He stuffs a pod into the coffee machine. "No. I didn't know that."

"Seem like a lot, huh?"

"I guess."

"That's just in America."

"Is there a point to this, Joly?"

"They've got me writing up blurbs about scented candles at work. I came across some stats. I don't know . . . I guess it's not that interesting."

She's been employed for a week. It would be better if the job weren't junk. Short-term contract shit at a giftware company. The pay is garbage. Not rent money. Not money enough for her to pack up and get out. But he's almost stopped hoping for that. She's been here so long now she's become an unfortunate but accepted fixture, like the water stain on the brick wall out back or the neighbourhood raccoons that knock over his garbage cans.

He pours himself a bowl of Cheerios and waits for her to drop her next factual deposit onto the breakfast conversation. But she keeps quiet in front of the laptop. The silence, even momentary, is unusual. She's been mopey lately. Since the split with Babylon Ben. She's been less chatty, less excitable, less herself, and Yannick doesn't like it. He doesn't want to have to be concerned.

"What's the latest on your stories?" he asks, gliding onto the stool beside her. "What are you working on these days?"

She pushes her Cheerios around in her bowl. "Nothing."

"Bullshit. You're always working on something. Let's hear it."

"I'm not."

"Why not?"

"I don't know . . . I went over my archives last week . . . "

"And?"

"And . . . everything just seems a bit . . . ho-hum."

"Ho-hum?"

"The stories aren't as funny as I remember." She smacks her spoon against the Cheerios, creating small splashes. "They're . . . kind of dumb, actually."

"What the fuck are you talking about? They're hilarious."

"Meh."

Yannick flicks her temple. "What, you don't have a sense of humour anymore?"

She bats his hand away and produces a half-assed shrug. Her face stays glum as they work through their breakfast. It only flickers to life when Yvie rockets into the kitchen, slides across the floor in her socks, and crash-lands into Joly.

"Yvie, hey!" he says. "No sliding! How many times do we have to tell you?"

"Oops."

"You're gonna knock yourself out one day."

The kid is clumsy and the floors have a slippery finish. They've told her a hundred times about sliding around in her socks, but she's always in a rush, though she has nowhere to go.

Yvie vaults onto Joly's lap, who accepts the intrusion with a gentle pat to the kid's head. From her perch, the kid inspects her own socks, like she just can't understand how these awesome socks with the blue whales across the top of the foot might land her in trouble. They were a birthday gift from Adele, a great gift from Yvie's perspective, because she's big into whales, but a terrible gift from Yannick's perspective, because now the kid never wants to take those goddamn socks off. She sleeps in them. Insists on it. They have to peel them off her to wash them. It's a bad idea to get kids things they like. They get attached.

"Morning, Yvie-bird," Joly says.

"What are you looking at?" says the kid. She shoves her little head at the laptop screen, as though proximity to words will reveal her hidden literacy.

"Stats."

"What's stats?"

"Nothing. Nothing interesting."

Yvie doesn't buy it. She leans in for a closer inspection of the indecipherable text, her face just a few inches from the screen, and she's still pretend-reading when Karen arrives in the kitchen.

"Hey," Karen mumbles, dragging her feet, demonstrating for them all how tired she still is.

"Bad sleep?" asks Joly.

"It's the A/C. It's still not working right. I can't sleep in the heat." She pulls her jar of bone broth from the French-doored fridge. The broth, apparently, helps prep the body for pregnancy.

"It's not so bad," says Yannick.

"It's sweltering. Especially with a toddler attached to your back. We might need to get a new system, Yannick."

"Summer's almost over. We can talk about it next year."

They keep pouring money into this house. There's always something to repair or renovate or upgrade. Even now, after having renovated almost the entire place, Karen can still find problems. She's been making noise about moving. Which would mean upgrading, not downsizing.

"Okay. But we'll have to do something." She sets the broth in the microwave and waits for it to heat. "What do you want for breakfast, Yvie? Toast or Cheerios?"

"Ummmm . . . . toast!" says the kid. But then she looks at the bowls in front of both Joly and Yannick and caves to conformity. "No, Cheerios!"

Karen does up a bowl for the kid, retrieves her own breakfast of broth from the microwave, and joins them at the island. "You're wearing that shirt today?" she asks Yannick through a yawn.

"What's wrong with this shirt?"

"Nothing's wrong with it. I just thought you could wear the white shirt. With the French cuffs."

"This is a white shirt."

"It's cream. And it doesn't have the French cuffs."

"It's the same thing."

"It's different. And you can't wear cufflinks with that shirt."

"Why do I have to wear cufflinks?"

"Because you're picking up my mom. She bought you those silver cufflinks. It'll make her happy to see you wearing them."

"Fine. I'll change."

"If you're not wearing them, she'll ask me why not. She'll assume you hate them."

"Okay."

"And it'll be a whole thing."

"I said fine."

"You're going up to Thornhill today?" Joly asks with a sudden interest in this morning conversation. "What time?"

Yannick glances at her, annoyed. "Afternoon. What do you care?"

"Just wondering. About your schedule."

"Why do you keep asking me about my schedule lately?" Every day there's some question about his whereabouts.

Joly meets his eyes, then looks over at Karen, then down at her cereal. "No reason," she mumbles.

"Nonna's coming?" cries Yvie.

"You know that, Yvie." Karen blows on her bone broth. "Nonna and Grampa are coming for your baptism. Daddy's going to pick them up."

"Can I come too? Can I?"

"To Thornhill?" Yannick asks. He looks at the kid bouncing around on Joly's lap. It's unclear sometimes whether she says things because she means them or because she just likes to hear herself form sounds. "You want to come?"

"Yup yup yup," she says in a sing-song that doesn't make the sincerity of her position any clearer.

"Yeah, all right," he says. He prefers this actually, the kid makes a good buffer between him and the in-laws. "I'll pick you up after lunch."

"Yannick." Karen's waking up now. "She's got school today."

"Summer camp, you mean."

He doesn't like the summer camp program. They send home report cards, actual report cards, for a three-year-old. Each of these reports has noted that Yvie "displays an excellent ability to follow directions," but has also noted that she "is still learning to grow in independence." She's clingy, but obedient, that's how Yannick reads it. Karen zeros in on the "excellents" without ever considering that a kid who is excellently obedient might not blossom into the kind of leader she's trying to coax Yvie into becoming.

"We put her in this program especially to prevent summer learning loss. I'm not sure we should be pulling her out of school on every whim," says Karen.

"What's she going to miss, Karen? An hour of exploratory colouring? I think she'll make that up over the next decade."

Karen studies the kid banging her spoon around the marble countertop. Everything is a big decision. Every choice they make will impact her life in a thousand ways. What effect will this missed afternoon of daycare have? Will it instil in the kid a spirit of truancy and delinquency? Or a strong sense of familial bonding?

"All right. I'll call the school and let them know," she says. "Now, Yvie, come sit here at your place and eat properly."

The kid wriggles off Joly's lap and into her own chair at the island. She is excellent with directions.

6

THESE INTERVIEWS. FUCKING hell, these interviews. Yannick's not even being choosy. He just wants to hire someone, anyone competent, anyone on whom they can offload a massive pile of work. But these interviews are a showcase of staggering incompetence.

Job Candidate Steven is twenty-four, dressed in skinny little pants and a neck scarf instead of a tie. He must be *hip*. "I'm not really that interested in just the numbers," he says.

"Oh no?" says Yannick. He and Anosh have five candidates lined up, but Yannick's going to have to skip out after this one, their third, to go pick up the in-laws. Ordinarily they'd just have rescheduled the final two interviews for a time when both Yannick and Anosh can participate. But they've already rescheduled interviews twice, and they're both impatient as hell to get someone on board. So Anosh has agreed to handle the last two himself. But he isn't happy about it. Interviewing is a rough way to spend the day. It's a demoralizing process from start to finish.

"I read a few dozen financial reports a day. But I don't think that's what it's all about," Job Candidate Steven says.

"What's it all about then?" asks Yannick.

"Look, I can do the math for just about anything. But I'm looking for more than that. I'm looking for the truth behind the numbers, you know what I mean? And not just behind the numbers, but, like, behind everything."

"So what? You're some kind of philosopher?"

Job Candidate Steven grins. "I consider myself a truth seeker."

Yannick makes a note on the guy's resume: *personality problems*. He leafs through the small stack of resumes in front of him: today's candidates. Their first candidate spent most of the interview asking questions about work-life balance—what time could he expect to get home in the evenings? What about weekends? What about vacation time? Like they're going to pay someone 200k to take vacations. The second candidate didn't show up. He called in about half an hour before he was due and said he wasn't feeling well, some kind of tickle in his throat, but he did, quite heroically, offer to Skype in for an interview. Imagine! Yannick hasn't taken a sick day in five years. They told the invalid, politely, to fuck off. And now they've got this truth seeker.

Truth Seeker Steven is leaning way back in his chair. He's all confidence and swagger and has no idea what an asshole he's coming off as. They can't hire a guy like this. He'll never do what he's told. Even if he were capable, which is doubtful, because in the next part of the interview, in which Anosh asks Job Candidate Steven to talk him through a transaction he's listed on his resume, the guy's math doesn't make any sense. There are errors. Miscalculations. A real fucking absence of truth.

"I'm not following your numbers here," says Anosh. "You seem off by a couple percent."

This isn't even the technical skills round. That's supposed to be the next round, if they ever find anyone decent enough to put through to it. How is this guy going to be able to build a leveraged buyout model or assess risk when he's fuzzy about the math on his own resume?

"Well those are approximate figures. Give or take."

"Why would they be approximate figures? Why wouldn't you know the exact numbers?"

"I think it gives you a good enough idea."

"Yeah. I guess it does give us a good enough idea," says Anosh. He looks at Yannick with a kind of pained bewilderment, asks a few more questions, then brings things to a close. "So thanks for coming in, Steven."

"Sure, sure. And when do I hear back from you guys?"

"Couple of weeks," says Yannick.

"Great. I'm entertaining a couple other options. So the sooner the better for me."

Anosh blinks a few times, maybe hoping this small movement will keep his brain from exploding. But the effort seems to paralyze the rest of his body. When Job Candidate Steven extends a hand, it's Yannick who gives it a shake.

"Jesus Christ," says Anosh once the truth seeker has left. "We need to talk to the headhunter. She's gotta be doing something wrong."

"Yeah, but you know, Bourque was hiring last year. Said it was the same thing. Same bullshit. Know what their headhunter told them? It's a generational thing. Apparently we've all gotta learn how to relate to these Millennials. Their headhunter suggested they take a half-day course about it."

"You're fucking kidding me."

"Turns out they're like a different breed. Bourque's head-hunter said we're supposed to learn how to *understand* them. Their *needs* and *feelings*."

Anosh balls up Job Candidate Steven's resume and whips it into the trash.

"Hang in there, buddy. Maybe you'll get lucky with the next two," Yannick says and laughs.

Anosh pelts him with another balled up resume. "You owe me for this, Yan. Making me do this shit by myself. I'm not joking. I'm about to lose my mind here."

"Yeah, yeah. I owe you."

"I might kill myself if this keeps up. D'you see that kid's neck scarf? I mean, what the fuck."

7

YANNICK FLICKS HIS gaze to the rearview. Yvie's quiet back there. He doesn't trust her when she's quiet. Beside her in the back is Joe, who, as ever, sits silent like a brick, just along for the ride. It's Adele who commands the conversation. She's taken the passenger seat—she's got a bad knee (the left knee this week) and she needs room to stretch out and show off the knee brace.

"It's chilly in the car, Yannick, how do I turn down the fan?"

"Just adjust the vent there."

"Where exactly? I don't see. Hmm. Can you show me?"

His phone buzzes. It's been buzzing all afternoon. He managed to get in a couple of calls on the ride up here, with just Yvie in the back, but now that he's got the in-laws aboard, calls are impossible. He'll have to make up the time at home. But he does check the phone, just to know who's calling. Andrew, from their investment bank. Must be calling about particulars on the windows deal. They should be making progress soon. They've got a meeting with the Westline Windows guys and their respective investment banks next week to discuss possible debt structures for the buyout. He scrolls through the calendar on his phone to double check the time of that meeting, but his eyes must stay on the screen for longer than he thought, because when he looks back up at the road, the car ahead of him has slowed, a lot. He slams the brakes.

"Careful, Yannick!" shouts Adele. "Pay more attention. Please!"

"I'm paying attention."

"You were checking your phone."

He sees the cause of the stoppage now: an enormous pothole in the road. Cars are slowing to pass around it. "It's not the phone. Look at that pothole. It's these junky Thornhill streets."

"Our streets? When your streets are death traps."

"They're not so bad."

"Not so bad? They're terrible. Do you know what I read a few months ago?"

"What did you read a few months ago?"

"I read that the Gardiner is crumbling."

"They've been saying that my whole life." Since Yannick was a kid, he's been hearing dire warnings about the structural integrity of the Gardiner Expressway. It'll have to be replaced someday, but so far it's held up just fine.

"No. No, it's *really* crumbling. A piece fell right off it. Hit the trunk of a lady's car. A Pakistani lady, I think she was. Wasn't she a Pakistani, Joe? Remember, we saw that photograph?"

"I don't know, Adele."

"I think so. Pakistani. Or maybe Indian. This chunk of the Gardiner just fell and hit the trunk of this nice Indian lady's car. Yannick"—she puts a hand on his arm—"I saw a photograph of the dent it made in the trunk. It was huge. Someone could've died."

"You mean if someone had been in the trunk?"

"Don't be smart, Yannick."

Adele's news reports tend to land a few miles wide of the truth. Somewhere along the transmission process, facts get altered in her head. If the Gardiner Expressway were shedding chunks of itself onto the street below it . . . well, that would be news. Real news. Maybe it was a freak accident. Or more likely, a small piece of debris fell off a truck cruising along the expressway.

"Daddy."

"Yes, kiddo?"

"This was serious," says Adele. "Someone could've been killed. Imagine if it had hit a pedestrian and not a car. It could've been fatal. It could've been a tragedy!"

"Yikes."

"Yikes is right. I hope that Iranian lady sues the city. She'd better. I sure would."

"Knock it off, Adele," says Joe.

She doesn't knock it off, but she does drop her voice to a whisper. "But sometimes they don't even know that they're allowed to sue . . .. they don't know their rights . . . the immigrants, I mean. From . . . those parts of the world."

"All right, Adele," says Joe.

"I'm just saying."

"Daddy."

"She seemed like a perfectly nice lady, though."

"Enough now."

Adele turns to look at Joe in the back. "I'm just catching Yannick up on what I read. He lives in the city and doesn't even know these things."

"We're all caught up now, Adele," says Joe. "Thank you."

Southbound traffic is heavy. It was a breeze coming up here, took him exactly thirty-four minutes from Yvie's school to Joe and Adele's house. But there's construction on the southbound route and squeezing the flow into just three lanes is slowing everything way down.

"Daddy. Daddy. Daddy. Daddy. Daddy." Yvie is reciting his name like she's practising it for a test. But a quick check in the rearview shows she's not even looking at him, not aiming for his attention. She's transfixed by her own fingers, which she's weaving through each other. She's saying his name just for the sake of saying it.

The phone buzzes again. Vinegar John this time. Probably calling with another round of already-answered questions. Just seeing the guy's name on the caller ID kicks up Yannick's blood pressure.

"Daddy."

"Yes, kiddo?"

"Daddy."

"What is it, Yvie?"

"Daddy. Hi."

Adele turns around to look at her. "Hi, little Yvie love," she says. "How are you doing back there?"

"Good."

"Are you sure? You don't look so good. Your hair is a mess, isn't it? Doesn't anyone brush your hair when your Nonna's not around?"

Just ahead, traffic is crunched to a halt. Yannick pulls out a little to the left, onto the shoulder, for a better look at what they're dealing with. For the next few kilometres, this ride is going to be a brutal stop-and-go.

YANNICK WORKS THROUGH the evening, on the phone for most of it, at a makeshift workstation he's created in the kitchen. It's fine for the first couple of hours—with Joe napping in the guest room, and the women out picking up Yvie's baptism dress—but now that they're back and clustering in the kitchen, he can't work here anymore.

Yvie parades around the island in her new dress. The designer dress. The dress that cost . . . wait for it . . . $400! For a child's dress. That she'll wear once. Yannick almost lost his mind when he saw that figure show up on his Visa bill. But that's nothing next to the dress Karen bought herself for this grand event. She went out and found some flowy orange number ("still summery, but also kind of autumn-y, with the orange, don't you think?"), a few pieces of fabric stitched together, $2000. She's already modeled it for him. Twice. "See how it billows?" she said as she wafted the dress around her legs. "Don't you like the billows?" "Of course I do," he said. "Beautiful billows." But it's shit like this that is seriously slowing the approach to five million.

"Oh my god," says Karen from a stool at the island, watching the kid do a skip-and-twirl on the slippery wood floors. "It's so cute, it's perfect."

"Ooooh, look how beautiful you are, my little lovey," says Adele, claiming two stools for herself: one to sit on, the other to elevate her leg. "Yannick, look at her. Isn't your daughter beautiful?"

The kid stands still and looks at the three of them, smiling with that shyness she gets whenever too much attention comes her way. Not that she doesn't like the attention. And although she's totally fucking adorable right now, like supremely adorable, in the dress and her shy smile, Yannick doesn't like feeding into baptism-related attention. He doesn't like how Karen and Adele have tricked the kid into getting on board by offering her heaps of attention and a fancy dress.

"Sure," he says. "Sure you are, kiddo. You're always beautiful."

"You're going to be such a pretty little girl at your baptism," Adele says.

"Yup." Yvie fingers the lace fringe of her dress.

"It's a special privilege to become a Catholic, did you know that, Yvie?" says Adele.

"Yup."

"It means you'll have a special place in God's heart."

"Yup."

Yannick fights a strong urge to toss Adele out of the house. These religious teachings, especially when delivered in child-hood, seep into the brain and rewire the hardware. It can't be undone. Which is why when Adele started whispering to Karen that she wasn't getting pregnant because she hadn't yet baptized Yvie ("Why would God give you a second child when you're not taking proper care of the first?"), Karen accepted it as plausible. And here they are.

But there's no point starting an argument about religion. He'll just let this weekend pass, and hope that God never comes up again for the rest of the kid's life. Besides, she isn't even listening to Adele. She's fixated on that lace fringe.

"And you'll know exactly what to do at the baptism, because we've got the rehearsal tomorrow," Adele says.

"Can I wear my dress to practise?"

"No, Yvie," says Karen. "We'll save the dress."

"Can I wear my whale socks when I get bap-sized?"

"Oh, I don't think so, Yvie," says Karen.

"But you like those socks your Nonna got you, don't you?" says Adele. Then, turning to Karen, to Yannick with a smug grin: "Doesn't she?"

Yvie drops to the floor, sitting butterfly-style, the soles of her feet together, tracing the giant whales on her socks.

"You'll be at the rehearsal too, right, Yannick?" says Adele.

He's moved to the marble counter to mix himself a vodka soda on ice before he gets back to work. "Sure. Six o'clock, right?"

"No, Yannick," says Karen. "5:30. It got moved to 5:30. I told you that."

"Right. Okay. 5:30. Should be fine. I'll be there."

Adele frowns at him. "Is that already your second drink?"

It's his third this evening, but his glass always empties out quickly when Adele is visiting. "I'm mixing them light," he lies.

"Mm-hmm."

"I gotta finish some work."

Yannick migrates first to the living room, but their voices carry right through. Who decided open concept was a must-have anyway? There are glaring flaws with the concept. He preferred the house as it was when they bought it. With walls. With sound barriers. This redesign is stupid. There's nowhere to hide. He moves further along, right out into the backyard, where he sits on the patio and drinks his (very strong) vodka soda and, for just a minute, thinks of nothing.

But he can still hear them through the screen door. Adele is still dispensing her thoughts on God, but she's moved onto a sub-topic: heaven. She's got the kid interested enough to be asking questions about it.

"Does heaven have whales?"

"Of course, little Yvie lovey. Thousands of whales."

"Turtles too?"

"Of course turtles."

Yannick hates the heaven bullshit more than all the rest of it. It's no good to be taking comfort in an imagined afterlife; it's dangerous. It's the kind of thinking that gets people long-ing for death, daydreaming about it, courting it. Yannick's got trouble enough battling the defective death drive that seems like it's coded into his DNA—he doesn't need to absorb any quack religious ideas that validate it. And he doesn't want Yvie validating that drive in herself. He wants her to cling to life for as long as she can.

He couldn't have been clearer with Karen on the religion point before they got married. When he learned that she was a Catholic (half-Catholic, according to her, at least back then), he made sure they had a discussion about religion and kids. He didn't want to raise kids in any faith. She had no problem with that. She said she hadn't been to church in years, had no connection to it anymore, no interest in it. Great. A secular upbringing for the would-be kids. But people don't honour agreements anymore.

It's hot out again. The heat this year is pushing right to the end of summer. And there's a haziness in the atmosphere. Smoke from wildfires in the north has made its way over the city, covering it in a grey sheath. He looks at the downtown skyscrapers, spearing upward behind the neighbourhood houses, their tips buried in smoke.

Yannick steadies himself with a swig of his vodka soda. He bites the ice. The sound of it crunching between his teeth overwhelms the voices from the kitchen. He's on his second cube when his phone buzzes for the thousandth time today. Fucking Vinegar John again.

"Yannick. Hey, finally. You've been MIA all afternoon."

"Yeah, sorry. I had a family thing here."

"Everything okay?"

"It's fine. It's fine. What do you need, John?" He's up on his feet now and pacing the yard. It's hard to keep still when he's taking these calls. Without some kind of movement to diffuse his irritation, it builds and stagnates. He's been fighting against his irritability for months. But it's a war of attrition and he's losing.

"Growth projections. I was talking it over with Christy and we're both still a little stumped on some things. We're looking at your sales pipeline and we just don't see enough leads to generate the kind of growth you're projecting. Looks to us like you're overestimating things. So I wanted to go over that with you. I think that's where you and I left off."

"No. No, that's not where we left off, John. We already looked at the leads. Like we already looked at every single element of the growth projections. More than once."

"I understand, Yannick, it's just—"

"John, I need you to listen to me now. We've been over this ten times already, okay? We're not gonna make it eleven."

On his return trip across the small yard, kicking at pebbles in the rock garden, Yannick notices Karen out on the patio, signalling to him.

"Right, right, but—" says John.

"So look . . . we just need to sharpen our pencils now. We need to find a way to move forward. Because look, to be honest, my patience is starting to wear thin with you guys."

Karen's wrap-it-up hand motions become more urgent the closer he gets to her.

"I think we're all eager to move forward, Yannick. But—"

"Let me call you back in five minutes, John. Okay?" He hangs up before hearing a reply.

"Vinegar deal?" Karen asks when he arrives at the patio.

"Yeah. Fucking idiots."

"But it's gonna go through, right?"

"Yeah. Yeah, I'm sure it will."

"You know, I was doing some calculating. And if that does go through, and if you keep earning at this pace, we could be at seven or eight million in a few years."

"I'm stopping at five. We said five."

"We floated five. But we didn't realize you'd be making money hand over fist like this. It'd be insane to quit when you can make this much a year. And—"

"We said five. Five is enough."

"But what if it isn't? Why not just put in an extra few years and be sure, right? In case something comes up. It's just something to think about, isn't it?"

Yannick looks down at her toenails, painted a light blue. Her toes change colour every week.

"Mom says the A/C in her room isn't working."

"It works just fine in that room."

"She says it's not working. Can you check it before she goes to bed? If she's too hot, she won't be able to sleep, and if she doesn't sleep, I'll have to hear about it all day tomorrow."

"I'll check."

"And I know we said Camerini for dinner, but Mom wants to eat in."

"Fine."

"But we don't have anything here." They never have food on hand. Not meal-type food. With the exception of holiday feasts, they haven't cooked dinner in years. The cupboards house only cereal and instant oatmeal and crackers. The fridge only milk and condiments and leftovers. And bone broth. "Can you pick up some sushi?"

"I gotta work, Karen. Can't you go?"

"Mom wants to discuss the floral arrangements for the reception again. She's having second thoughts on the camellias."

"Isn't it too late to change something like that?"

"Probably. Look, Yannick, it's not like I want to spend the night in flower discussions. I don't even care much about the flowers. But it's important to her. What am I supposed to do?"

"Get UberEats then."

"No, Mom thinks the drivers steal the food."

"Call Joly. Tell her to hit Miku on the way home."

"I did. She says she's eating at Louise's." In her bare feet, Karen takes a few steps toward the tomato plant that she bought at the start of the season, now dried out and fruitless, because neither of them is any good at gardening. She flicks the brown leaves and frowns.

"Fine. I'll go," he says. He performs a quick scan of his body to determine his degree of impairment. He studies the tomato plant; it stays fixed in his field of vision. No blurriness. No spins. He's satisfied. A slight buzz is working through his limbs, but it's nothing he can't shake off. It's only been three drinks. "So what do you want?"

Karen ignores his question. "The showing at Louise's house went terribly, by the way. In case you were wondering."

"Oh shit. Sorry, I forgot to ask. It's been busy."

"The place reeks of weed. And she was home. She knew I had the showing scheduled. I told her to be out of the house. But she was there, hanging out on the back deck. Like, what is that?"

"She's not working now, so I guess . . . "

"Why isn't she working?"

"Well . . . she quit her job."

"How do you know that?" Karen's tone turns sharp, and some neuron in Yannick's brain fires off a warning signal.

"Joly mentioned something," he says.

Karen's eyes don't leave him, they don't even blink. "Still. She can't leave the house for an hour? So it's not awkward when I bring prospective buyers by? I like Elliott, I really do. He's easy to deal with. But Louise . . . she's . . . a piece of work."

"Mm-hmm."

"I think she stayed home on purpose," says Karen. "Just to screw with me. She seems like that kind of person. I feel like she hates me for some reason."

"It's her childhood home, Karen. I wasn't crazy about my parents selling the house either."

"Yeah, but that's you. How do you know she feels the same way you did?"

"She said—"

"So you talked to her? When?"

Shit. One drink too many. As he watches Karen's form curved over the plant, his vision jogs. Her body seems to fracture, just slightly, just for a second, before he forces his senses to realign. Concentrate. "She called once . . . to talk about Joly."

"About Joly? Why? What's wrong with Joly?"

His warning neurons are shrieking now. He should've shut the fuck up. "Well . . . it's been a rough couple of months for her, right?"

"Has it? But she got that job. I thought things were going well."

"Yeah, I meant with the breakup . . . and with the—" He chokes on the word *abortion* while it's still germinating in his throat. He neglected to tell Karen that Joly was, and then quickly wasn't, pregnant. How well would she have taken that news? His idiot sister knocked up by accident. The baby promptly discarded. All of that against the backdrop of the fertility failures that are slowly fraying Karen's nerves.

"With the . . . what?" she asks.

"Just with the Ben split. She really liked that deranged communist."

"She's better off without him."

"Of course she is. But I'm not sure she knows that."

With a last look at the plant, a look coloured with sadness or maybe disdain, Karen nods. "I already called Miku. They said twenty minutes."

Yannick downs the last sips of his drink and listens to the voices in the kitchen pick up again. He slips inside to pick up his keys and gets back to work before he's even in the car. "John," he says into his phone. "Where were we?"

8

"WHAT DO YOU think of this shirt?" Anosh asks from the doorway of Yannick's office. He's eating an apple, really going to town on it, chomping at the crunchy flesh. Anosh has read that one piece of fresh fruit in the morning keeps men virile. It's extremely fucking annoying. Every morning this month it's been one kind of hand fruit or another. Bananas. Peaches. An ordeal with a blood orange that resulted in bits of peel all over the carpet and sticky shit all over Yannick's desk.

Last month it was smoothies.

Anosh spreads out his arms for Yannick to gaze upon his shirt in all its glory. The collar is stiff, very starched. It's an expensive shirt. And it's blue. Beyond that, Yannick has no opinion.

"It looks fine," he says.

"Yeah, of course it's fine. But is it too muted for Blitz? The detailing is subtle. Might not play so well in dim lighting."

"I don't give a shit about your shirt, man."

Since Anosh shed his last girlfriend in the spring, he's been a pariah at the clubs, at parties, anywhere he expects there might be women of a certain age and build and look who might be willing to sleep with him. He's a menace.

"You don't take pride in your clothes, Yannick. It's ridiculous, how you walk around in relics like that."

Yannick has to look down at his shirt to remind himself of what he's wearing. It's the plain white shirt Karen forced him to retire yesterday. Two complaints about it in as many days. Maybe he'll just toss it for good. "This shirt is fine. It's respectable."

"It's terrible. You were looking much better yesterday. Good crisp fabric. Classic cufflinks. I hate to see this regression."

"Yeah, well where am I going tonight? Nowhere."

"You should rethink that. How often is Baby Bourque in town?"

"Doesn't matter. We've got the baptism rehearsal. It's not gonna happen."

"You're missing out, man," says Anosh. He bites hard into his apple, spraying the juice onto Yannick's desk, and he takes a seat. "So where are we with John?"

"We're where we should be, I think. I spent two hours on the phone with him last night. But this guy . . . I don't even know what to say. Fucking retarded. Straight up."

"Well speaking of retarded . . . you missed some choice candidates yesterday."

"Nothing to work with?"

"One guy I dinged because he has a fiancée."

"Uh-huh." Fiancée is a red flag. Fiancées tend to make demands on time, and what they're looking for is an associate on whom they can dump hours and hours of evening and weekend work.

"The woman might be all right," says Anosh. "Seemed halfway competent at least." There was only one woman among the eleven interviewed candidates over the last couple of weeks. Industry average. "But she's twenty-eight. And married. How smart is it to hire a twenty-eight-year-old married woman?"

The conversation hits a break then, because, through the open office door, over Anosh's shoulder, Yannick catches sight of Adam, team boss, barrelling down the hallway toward them. The wide swell of his gut swings from side to side as he moves. He does not look happy. But his facial expressions have been appearing way more extreme ever since he went off the Peesh (Propecia, the hair-loss drug) and embraced the male-pattern baldness he'd been artificially staving off. The effect is unsettling, but Yannick respects the decision to make the change. He'd like the balls to go bald. He's been on the Peesh himself since he was twenty-four and first felt fistfuls of hair come out in the shower. *Nope, no way, not happening,* he thought then. He's already a few inches shorter than he should be (topping out at just 5'8) . . . he can't be short *and* bald. Who would take him seriously? But he's more established now, just a few years out from retirement, and people do take him seriously. Besides, there must be risks to prolonged use. And bald doesn't have to be the end of things. Enough guys out there are making bald work. He's been floating a theory (a self-serving theory) over the last year or so that women actually love bald men, prefer them. They perceive a confidence in the decision to expose the scalp. Even Lou, who loves a good head of hair, who loves to pass her fingers through his hair in that way she has, where he feels like her fingertips are drawing out threads of tension, one after the other, so that he doesn't suffocate inside this giant tangled knot, even she once, years ago, confessed an almost irresistible attraction to the bald Bush-era White House Press Secretary. Yannick could catalogue everyone Lou has ever expressed an interest in.

"Oh good, you two idiots are both here," says Adam by way of hello. "Let me ask you something, why don't we have any movement with Steingruber Vinegar? What the fuck have you guys been doing?"

"We're working on it, Adam," says Anosh.

"But they've got this third-party guy holding shit up," says Yannick. "He just doesn't understand what he's doing. It's . . . staggering."

"Are you kidding me?" Adam bellows. "So get him on the goddamn phone! And explain to him whatever the fuck it is that he doesn't understand!"

Yannick hasn't been screamed at much since he started working here. Back when he was still in investment banking,

working eighty-, ninety-hour weeks, the screaming happened all the time. It's been less frequent at Goldstone, a
rarity since they made him a senior vice president, but the
top bosses still like to make him eat shit sometimes.

"I did get him on the phone. I was on the phone with him
for two hours last night."

"And?"

"I think it's sorted now."

"You think it is? Or it is?"

"He assured me we were sorted."

"It fucking better be sorted. If this deal doesn't go through
because of some third-party bullshit, I'm gonna blow my
brains out. We've still got a boatload of environmental issues
coming at us. Mark and Isaac already set up a call with us
about environmentals tonight. And I want both you idiots in
on it. Six o'clock."

"Six?" says Yannick. "Oh. Um . . ."

"Oh what? That's a problem for you?" says Adam.

"No. It's just . . . I've got a family thing."

"Oh yeah?"

"It's the kid's baptism rehearsal. That's tonight."

"Sure, sure, why not just take the rest of the day off then?
Or the rest of the week? Do you even work here anymore,
Yannick?"

"Okay, relax, Adam. I'll be here."

"I sure as fuck hope so," says Adam, and with those kind de-
parting words, he barrels back out of the office.

So . . . that's how that goes. Yannick won't be out of here
before eight-thirty. Maybe nine. He'll miss the rehearsal
and the dinner afterward. He'll miss the whole thing, and
that . . . well, that is going to be a problem.

"On the upside," says Anosh, still chewing on his half-finished apple, "if you can't make that baptism thing, you might
as well Blitz. Am I right?"

9

SMOKY SUMMER AIR hangs thick over the city, and up here, on the rooftop patio at Blitz, the night is balmy. Yannick and crew have bottle service going tonight. They're drinking top shelf vodka. The sting barely registers.

But Yannick's drinking more than his share of bottle one, drinking quick and hard, because he doesn't like rooftop patios. He particularly doesn't like this corner booth Baby Bourque has procured, one at which every seat lands somewhere along the very edge of the roof. He keeps looking over the tempered glass railing behind him, feeling a pull to tip backward, to somersault through the air and crash into the concrete five storeys below. It's not just that the urge is sharp, it's that it lingers, it's persistent. And it keeps him tense. So he drinks more. Which doesn't actually do anything to dampen the urge, but does dampen his concerns over the urge. Alcohol is really not so unlike religion: both make the user a little more comfortable with the idea of imminent death.

Karen wasn't happy to hear that he wouldn't be coming tonight. "Find your own goddamn dinner then," she said before she hung up on him. But she'll get over it. He had to work, what else could he do? She wants her five, or six, or seven million.

Across from him, the Bourques are squabbling over brands of vodka. The brothers look alike (just a year apart), but Baby Bourque came out better. Like all the genetic kinks were worked out on Bourque, the elder—the asymmetries of the nose and mouth, the too-low placement of the eyebrows. Their shared features make more sense on Baby Bourque's face. But he's aged, too, since Yannick last saw him about a year ago. Dubai must be working him hard.

To Yannick's right, Anosh is flirting with the blonde

waitress. It's just the four of them tonight—Dave bailed, roped into some function with his fiancée, something to do with their wedding next month in Hawaii. Yannick doesn't want to go to Hawaii, not for the weekend. Packing up the family for that trip is going to be a pain in the ass. Dave's fiancée is a pain in the ass herself. She's made Dave unreliable. He never comes out anymore.

"Great shirt," the waitress says to Anosh.

"You like that? Feel it. The thread count is insane."

The waitress pinches a piece of the fabric on the arm between her thumb and index finger and she rubs.

"Nice, huh?" says Anosh.

She laughs as she pours out the last few ounces of vodka among the four of them. She shakes the empty vodka bottle and says, "You boys want another?"

"Abso-fucking-lutely we do," says Anosh.

"Celebrating something tonight?" she asks.

"Life," he says.

"Well, that's always worth celebrating."

"Hey, bring us some water, too," says Bourque, the elder. "Sparkling. With some lemon wedges in it."

"Water, sure. Anything else?" She waits for all their heads to shake no before she disappears into the crowd on the patio.

The moment her back is turned, Baby Bourque smacks his brother's shoulder. "Jesus, do you have to do that?"

"Do what?"

"'Water. Sparkling. With lemon wedges.' It's fucking embarrassing."

"Why? I want sparkling water. With some lemon wedges in it. Why shouldn't she bring me that if that's what I want?"

"Because she's over there thinking you're an idiot."

"A high-maintenance loser," adds Anosh.

"What do you care what she thinks about me?"

"It reflects poorly on the whole group," says Baby Bourque.

"I disagree. I bet she's over there thinking that I'm a guy who knows what he wants. I bet she loves it. Women love that in men."

"That woman is working for tips. She doesn't want to bring you your special-order no-cost water."

"She's fine. They like having things to do."

"Either way, she's smoking hot, isn't she?" Anosh says.

Yannick looks across the patio and watches the waitress lean forward over the bar, her short black dress riding high up the backs of her thighs.

"Hear how she liked the shirt," says Anosh. "What did I tell you about this shirt, Yannick? Didn't I tell you it was killer?"

"Yeah, and didn't I tell you I don't give a shit about your shirt?" says Yannick.

"You've got no shot with her, Anosh," says Baby Bourque. "You're batting out of your league."

"Of course I've got a shot. She was practically throwing herself at me."

"She was being courteous. If she's going home with anyone here, it won't be you. I built up a rapport with her long before you even got here. A real rapport."

"I thought you were seeing . . . Lisa? Leslie?" says Yannick.

"Lucie. And I am. But I'm on Time Zone Regulation here. Fidelity doesn't extend beyond time zones. That's . . . you know . . . a rule."

Yannick finishes what's left of his drink and laughs.

"No no, it's a thing," says Baby Bourque. He looks to his brother for help. "Weigh in here, Mike."

"It's a thing," says Bourque.

"Yeah, everyone knows about Time Zone Regulation, Yannick," says Anosh. "I'm sure his girlfriend Lisa knows all about it too. I'm sure she knows it and is fucking half the expats in Dubai right now."

Baby Bourque retains his smile, broadens it even. "Now

that there, that's your jealousy talking, Anosh. It's a bad look on you."

"Jealousy? Of a Bourque? You've gotta be kidding me."

"Hey, shut up, both of you," says Yannick. He leans back into the bench, closer still to the edge, and lets himself feel the alcohol humming through his bloodstream.

"So you guys still working on Steingruber?" Baby Bourque asks.

Baby Bourque does the same kind of work Yannick and Anosh do. But he does it in Dubai. For a sovereign wealth fund.

"We're getting there," says Yannick.

"You've really gotta think about getting out of Toronto. You're giving up at least fifty grand off your salary by being here."

"Yeah, but I've only got a few more years. Freedom Forty."

"Still singing that song, huh?"

"And I'll be singing it on my deck chair by the lake with a beer in my hand."

He can picture Bayfield. The lake, the dock, his house, and always, in his imaginings, it's evening. A warm, quiet, perfect summer evening. Maybe Lou will come out sometimes—when Karen's in the city or visiting her parents or somewhere else. Lou would like it in Bayfield. She likes the quiet. They can sit together by the water, listening to the loons, watching clouds pass by.

"Come off it, Yan."

"What?"

"You're never gonna quit. Nobody quits. Not when the casino's still open."

But the casino's never going to close, that's the problem. At least not in Yannick's lifetime. Beyond that, in the future . . . who knows? Maybe the political table-banging gets loud enough or the economics get bad enough . . . and this heyday gets brought to an end. Maybe the world starts to look different. Sure, someday the casino will shut its doors. It can't go on like this forever. But these are concerns outside of his timeframe. For now the doors are open, the game is on, and Yannick knows how to win. He's not the best-ever player, he's no legend, not a top dog, raking in billions, but he has figured out how to build a tidy pile, a little bigger each year. And the real win, the big win, will come when he takes his little pile and pulls out of the game. Freedom Forty, that's the win.

"I *will* quit."

"You won't."

"Hey, Jay, how 'bout you fuck off anyway," says Bourque, the elder. "Toronto's great. No greater city."

Baby Bourque waves a hand at the skyline, at the CN Tower that dominates it, in cheerful contempt. "No greater city? Than Toronto? Are you out of your fucking mind? Look at this place. Even its landmarks are lame. Look at that tower . . . it's so much smaller than I remember."

"That's because you've gotten used to that alien atrocity in Dubai," says Bourque.

"The CN Tower is way better looking. Straightforward. A to-the-point kind of design. And the highest in the world till those cocksuckers in Dubai went and built that fucking burg."

"It's burj, idiot. And it's not just Dubai that broke the height record. A bunch of cities have shattered Toronto. The CN Tower isn't even top five anymore."

The four of them look at the tower, its LED display a vertical line of red, a moment of quiet around the table.

"Can't believe you're making us go up that tourist trap Sunday, Yan," says Baby Bourque. "I haven't been up there in ages."

It's an absurd venue for a baptism reception. Yannick couldn't agree more. They landed with this absurd choice because Yvie did the choosing. Karen, after reading some- where that giving kids a sense of agency helps them develop leadership skills, asked the kid where she wanted to go for lunch after her baptism. But the kid is three and can't name lunch spots off the top of her head. So she took a look around—they happened to be on Queen St. at the time—and she spotted the CN Tower, one of the few landmarks she re- cognizes. Stupidest decision-making Yannick has ever been a part of.

"Making you go?" he says. "Who's making you? You don't have to come. I don't even wanna go." He takes a healthy gulp of his chilled vodka.

"Well, I'm obviously coming. It's a baptism. I'm not gonna not go to a baptism you invited me to. What kind of Catholic d'you take me for?"

Yannick looks at Baby Bourque, at depraved and deviant Baby Bourque, whom he's seen engage in unsavoury, unholy shit. "A lapsed Catholic. That's what I take you for. I've per- sonally seen you transgress, like, half the commandments."

Baby Bourque, whose idea of fidelity doesn't extend across time zones; who coveted, then solicited one call girl after an- other when they all lived together in NYC; who, on more than one busy Saturday night, shoplifted a two-six of rye from a liquor store because he's "not about to wait in line like some asshole."

"Ah, but I always repent," says Baby Bourque, his arms spread out wide atop the tempered glass railing.

"Convenient setup."

"True again. The Lord is very convenient," he says. And then, adopting the rhythms and tone of a Southern preacher: "You have got to recognize the light of the Lord, brother. Let the light of the Lord *warm* your sinning soul." He's up on his feet now, arms raised above his head. "*Humble* yourself before

the light. Ad*mit* there are powers in this world that are greater than you and about which you know not. And sal*va*tion is
yours."

This unexpected display draws appreciative laughter—and
an *amen*—from the neighbouring tables. As Baby Bourque
gives his audience a nod, his brother says, "Forget it, Jay. Yan's
a fucking heathen."

Baby Bourque settles back down on the bench and shakes
his head. "Bad policy to be an atheist, Yan. You're not hedging
your bets."

Yannick looks around for allies, for anyone reasonable,
anyone not poisoned by faith. He turns to Anosh, who says,
"Don't look at me, man. I'm a Zoroastrian. My ass is covered."

"Ah, now lookie here, speaking of God's gifts . . ." says Baby
Bourque.

The waitress has returned with a fresh bottle of vodka on
ice . . . along with Bourque's sparkling lemon-wedged water.
After she sets her offerings on the table, Baby Bourque stands
up, and with a hand set gently on her lower back whispers
something to her, something that makes her first gasp then
laugh. "You too, sweetheart," she says and . . . oh, here we
go . . . even winks.

"What'd you say to her?" Anosh asks.

"Private joke. What did I tell you, buddy? Rapport."

"Well I got fifty bucks says I get her number." Anosh plucks a
fifty out of his wallet and slams it on the table.

So Baby Bourque reciprocates with a fifty of his own. "I'll
take your money."

It's like they've both forgotten that the waitresses are paid
to pretend they're into assholes. Every guy thinks he's the
exception. None is. Yannick reaches into the pocket of his
jacket for a bill and says, "My money says you both strike out."

Anosh bats first. He flattens out his blue shirt and heads

over to the bar, where the waitress is waiting on drink orders. Yannick watches his approach. She smiles, of course, but not before a flash of annoyance appears and then disappears.

"Whoa, hey, wait a minute, what the fuck is this?" Baby Bourque is saying. He's flapping one of the bills over the table. An Iraqi banknote: 250 dinars. "Hahaha, let me guess, you're invested in Iraqi dinars, too."

"Your brother gave me that," says Yannick. "He's been pimping the cause."

So talk turns to the Iraqi dinar scheme all over again, and to Mother Bourque who is enmeshed in it, and how Baby Bourque has maybe, probably, hopefully, finally convinced her that the scheme is bogus.

"It's bullshit that she listens to you and not to me," says Bourque with an expression that is dangerously close to an actual fucking pout. "What do you know about Iraq anyway? The UAE doesn't even border Iraq."

"I've got an Iraqi doorman."

Yannick weaves the banknote through his fingers, this worthless piece of paper. "Iraqi dinars. What a ridiculous scheme."

But Baby Bourque just shrugs and gulps down his vodka. "All schemes are ridiculous. Until you get someone to bite."

"But this is . . . seriously unscrupulous shit."

"It's all unscrupulous shit. Unscrupulous is our ethos."

"Oh come on. These guys are selling junk they know is junk and telling a bunch of vulnerable idiots—no offence to your mother—it's gold."

"So what? If enough people believe it's gold, the price goes up—turns into gold."

"Yes, thank you, Jay, for explaining the rudiments to me," says Yannick, yawning over his drink.

"But does that make the scheme any more or less

scrupulous? If the dinar does appreciate dramatically—"

"But it's not going to."

"Of course it's not going to. But if it does, does that retroactively make the scheme more scrupulous? All kinds of people sell all kinds of shit all the time. If you get enough people to believe in your shit, it's not shit anymore. Then it's just the system. That's how finance works. There's nothing more unscrupulous about this scheme than any other. You know this, Yan."

"I know you're talking out of your ass."

"Am I?"

Yannick feels himself on unsteady ground. He's not good with moral questions. He doesn't make the rules, or even question them; he just plays by them. And there *are* rules. It's not the Wild West—there are industry parameters, which someone has presumably considered and set. Questions about the morality of his work only come up when someone else raises them. Usually Babylon Ben–types. That communist lunatic, he used to lurch toward the topic on occasion. The guy reads a few articles about the finance sector and thinks he's an expert. But Ben has no idea what Yannick actually does. He doesn't understand that Yannick is out there raising capital for investment, improving the efficiency of companies, earning healthy returns for his investors—not just millionaires and billionaires, but pension funds, unions. The very unions Babylon Ben likes to blow his load over . . . who's ensuring their pension funds deliver? When the unions want to park their money and watch it grow, while they kick back and do absolutely dick-all, it's guys like Yannick, not Ben, who make magic happen.

"You're talking out of your ass, Jay. There's a . . . like a moral distinction here. These dinar guys are con artists. They're frauds."

"We're all frauds," Baby Bourque says, reverting to his Southern preacher schtick. "We are a depraved species. Sinners every one of us. That is our God-given nature. Would you fight against your God-given nature? What damning pride would have you fight against the Lord's most sacred creation?" He pauses to sip his vodka. "And what, I ask you, is more conspicuous in human nature than the good old-fashioned, God-given urge to plunder? That is our design, brother. Since the beginning, we have been taking what we can while we can."

Yannick can't help taking the bait; it keeps him from feeling his exhaustion, or looking over the edge of the railing. "Jay, can you even hear the words you're saying right now? We're not living in the goddamn jungle. How is this any way to think about a functioning society?"

"A functioning society?!"

"Yeah. We're still living in one of those last I checked. So why are you raving like an end-of-days lunatic? Dubai must be fucking with your head, buddy. You've gone off the rails."

"A functioning society? Whoa, Yan, you are looking at this all wrong." Baby Bourque grabs the dinar banknote from Yannick's hands and flattens it out on the table. He points to the image on the back of the bill, the structure and accompanying tower, the squat spiral tower Yannick noticed the other day. "You know what this is?"

"It's a banknote."

"I know it's a banknote, asshole. I mean, this . . . this right here? This mosque."

"I guess it's a mosque then."

"That's right. It is a mosque. Not just any mosque. The Great Mosque of Samarra. Built sometime in the ninth century."

"We're getting a history lesson now?" says Bourque.

"Yeah that's right. You're getting a fucking history lesson, Mike. You wanted to know what I know about Iraq. Here's something I know. I know that this mosque right here, this was the highlight of a whole region for hundreds of years. Now it's defunct, but for hundreds of years, it was a fucking focal point. They say the caliph used to ride his donkey up and down the spiral of the minaret. Meditative practice. And the imams, they used to walk all the way up to the top of the tower before prayer time, and from there, they'd send out the call to prayer. Sacred shit."

"So what," says Yannick.

"So you know what the minaret's been used for lately?"

"What's it been used for lately?" says Yannick, growing impatient with the instructive turn of the conversation.

"Sniper post. A fucking sniper post. For American soldiers."

"Okay."

"Think about that. The Americans sent troops to the top of the tower. Just decided to use a sacred religious site as a strategic military position."

"So? That's what happens in war, isn't it?"

"You might not get this, Yan, being a heathen and all, but the desecration of religious sites is a war crime, as far as I'm concerned. So you can imagine that this pissed the insurgents off, seeing foreign soldiers fucking around on their sacred sites. Oh it pissed them off something fierce. So what'd they do? They attacked the tower. Bombed it, fired at it, usual rebel shit. We're talking about something that's supposed to be a world heritage site. It's on the banknotes, for fuck's sake. Instead it gets put to whatever strategic use it can serve, it gets bombed, then it gets abandoned. The US troops, of course, they moved right on when they were done with it. But the minaret is damaged now. Rundown and crumbling. Just like everything else, man. Because that's human nature. We take what we want and leave a shit pile behind."

"What is your point here, Jay?" asks Yannick.

"My point is . . . take a look around, man. It's not just Iraq, it's everywhere. There is no functioning society anymore. Things are hanging together by tethers. And everyone knows it. Everyone who's not a total idiot. Best you can do now is grab what you can on the way out. We are down to stripping the world for parts."

He finishes his vodka in one big gulp and stands. Because incoming is Anosh, withdrawing from the waitress with a quick step and a scowl. He slumps into the booth beside Yannick.

"How'd it go, Don Juan?" asks Baby Bourque.

"Whatever. She's fucking racist. Probably never touched a brown man in her life."

"She can smell your desperation, buddy. It's not a good scent." Baby Bourque smoothes down the sides of his hair with both hands. "Now better fish out some real money, Yan. I don't deal in dinars."

Yannick watches him glide across the patio toward the waitress, whom he greets with an easy smile.

10

AS THE CITY spins past the taxi window, Yannick's thoughts circle the spiralling minaret in Samarra. He got carried away at Blitz. Two bottles quickly turned to three, and he's sure he had the lion's share of each. With the Bourques egging him on, he didn't stand much of a chance. He's trashed.

To keep from passing out in the back of the cab, he looks up the mosque on his phone to fact-check Baby Bourque's little history lesson. He's got a lingering feeling the guy might be full of shit. He scrolls through a few articles, blowing up the text size so it's easier to read the letters swimming in front of his eyes, and . . . huh, all right, there it is, the Great Mosque of Samarra, just like Baby Bourque said. Once the focal point of the whole region, just like Baby Bourque said. With a mina-ret-turned-sniper post, just like Baby Bourque said.

He zooms in on the image—the *Malwiya* minaret, he learns. It's not even so high. Not heaven-high. But at 52m, it's high enough that you'd die if you fell from it. Which, after a fur-ther tour through the gallery of images, seems very possible. No railing along the outer edges of the pathway that spirals up the tower. A sheer drop. You'd have to be mental to walk up and down this pathway. Those imams and caliphs and their donkeys or whatever the fuck, going up and down, up and down . . . all mental. If he were forced up and down that spiralling tower as part of his daily grind . . . well, at some point that jump-urge that pounds in his cells would win out. He'd throw himself into a glorious, carefree swan dive, head-first into the desert.

No way could a structure like that exist in Toronto. This so-ciety doesn't trust its citizens with towers like this and edges like this. Even the bridges need suicide barriers.

But here . . . what's this? A detail Baby Bourque omitted. Or maybe didn't know. Yannick reads, with effort, that the run-down minaret now featured on his 250 Iraqi dinar banknote was once so imposing, so impressive, so majestic, that in the Middle Ages, pilgrimming Europeans skulking around the region mistook it for the Tower of Babel. Figuring they were close enough to ancient Babylon, they just assumed, the way believers do, that they'd stumbled upon a biblical artefact.

Of the biblical stories Yannick knows, which have floated in from the cultural ether, he likes the story of Babel best. A nice fuck you to God. A story about humans waging war on God, by storming heaven. Up they go, ready to trample all over heaven, to destroy the very idea of it. And if God hadn't changed the rules halfway through the battle, they might have won too. They'd have gotten their chance to plunder, strip the place for all it is worth. The sack of heaven! That's what the story of Babel should be.

11

IT'S HOT ON the kitchen floor, in front of the oven, where Yannick has laid himself out on his stomach while he waits for a frozen pizza to bake. He's so tired, on the verge of slipping into sleep. But he wants that pizza.

He opens the oven door to check on the progress with his one open eye. The pepperoni looks thawed enough to eat. He tries to pick off a few pieces of meat, but burns his forearm on the door. Dammit! He blasts backwards a foot and sits crumpled against the island. While he's blowing on the burn, the clear creak of an upstairs door disrupts the quiet of the house.

Uh-oh.

Karen? Gotten up to yell at him? Oh god, not now. Not when he's drunk and hungry. Or worse, Adele? Who can't sleep because one or another environmental factor in the house isn't meeting her very specific needs? But it's the kid who appears on the far side of the kitchen, clinging shyly to the wall, as if to hide herself from Yannick, this late-night version of her father whom she doesn't completely recognize.

"Yvie," he whispers. "Hey kiddo. What are you doing up?"

She clasps her stuffed turtle tight to her chest. "I can't sleep."

"Why not?"

"I don't know."

"Come here, kiddo."

Sensing that she's not about to be scolded for this

transgression, she grows bolder, picks up steam, bowling across the kitchen floor, in her prized whale socks, and, maybe because she's clumsy with sleep, or maybe because she was just due for it, she loses her footing, trips over her own feet, and . . . oh no, oh shit . . . launches headfirst into the edge of the open oven door.

"Oh. Oh oh oh," he says.

She sits up, shocked into silence by the blow.

"You're okay," he says. "You're totally okay."

But her heavy silence lasts just long enough for a thin stream of blood to trickle down her forehead. Then she wails.

He swoops her up and into the bathroom ("main floor powder room" in Karen-speak), where he sets her on the toilet and shuts the door so her screams won't wake the rest of the house.

He presses a towel to the gash. "Ssshhh, kiddo, it's okay. You're okay," he says until her crying lowers to more of a whimpering.

"I'm gonna take a look at it, okay?" he says.

"No."

"Yeah. Just a quick peek. You're brave."

"I'm brave," she says doubtfully, ready to resume the wailing.

Yannick pulls back the towel and checks the wound. Not so bad—maybe an inch and a half across—but it's hard to know for sure, because he's drunk and her forehead is whirling.

"We'll put a little bandage on it, okay?"

"A whale bandage?"

"Okay."

Good. It can't be so bad if she's making aesthetic demands. He grabs the whale-shaped bandages from the medicine cabinet, but they're too small to cover the wound. He'll have to triple up. He plasters three across her forehead; she looks ridiculous.

"Okiedoke."

"I'm fixed?"

"You're all fixed, kiddo."

She touches the bandages to check. "Daddy?"

"Yes, Yvie."

"Daddy?"

"What is it, Yvie?"

"I have to tell you something."

"What?"

"I'm scared."

"Scared of what?"

She swallows, her eyes turn huge. "I'm scared of getting bap-sized."

"Why, kiddo?"

"Joly says they'll dunk my whole head in water. What if they drown-ded me? At the pool, I can't hold my breath so long." She takes in a big breath and holds it for as long as she can—one, two, three seconds—then lets the air collapse out of her lungs.

Poor kid, it must have been gnawing at her for days. He continues to be surprised that this tiny child in front of him has a whole world of private fears.

"No one's gonna dunk your head, kiddo. It'll just be a trickle of water. You won't have to hold your breath at all."

"But why do they have to do that?"

"To welcome you to the religion, I guess."

"But why?"

"I really don't know."

She stares at him, her eyes still stretched wide open—expectant.

"Your mom did the same thing, you know. And your Nonna."

"But not you?"

"No. Not me."

"But then why do I have to? Why can't I be like you?"

She squeezes her turtle tight and her face takes on a

thoughtful pout—an expression he recognizes as Karen's. The kid looks just like Karen, but for the grey eyes. She inherited all of Karen's features, her olive skin, her sandy hair. But the kid's personality, her temperament, these she gets from Yannick. She's obedient by nature. A people-pleaser. A conformist. Despite Karen's efforts to groom the kid for some position of global authority, she won't make a leader out of her. She's a born follower. "You are like me, kiddo."

Her pout breaks into a tentative smile. "I am?"

"Sure you are. And sometimes, you and me . . . we have to do things we don't really like to make other people happy."

"Oh."

His words hang in the air between them. Might this be his worst-ever parenting moment? Yvie seems to be wondering the same thing. The pout has returned.

"Let's get you to bed, Yvie," he says, hoping to erase this failed attempt at advice. "It's late."

After tucking her in under her sea creatures bed sheets, he returns to the kitchen to find the pizza has undergone rapid progress. It's burnt black at the edges, the cheese dark brown. But he eats the whole thing anyway.

He should quit drinking. He will. Definitely. He definitely will. Soon. When he's forty. That's when he'll cut way back.

12

"BOOM!" SAYS YVIE over breakfast the next morning. "Crash!"

Her recounting of the late night adventure is limited mostly to sound effects. But her audience listens rapt nonetheless. Adele and Joe lean in with wide eyes and well-timed gasps. Karen, meanwhile, fusses with the bandage on the kid's head. The bandage that is now a tidy white strip of sterilized gauze held in place with small, neat bits of adhesive tape, which Yvie does not approve of, instead of with the whale-shaped bandages (one of which, by the way, was upside down).

"We should maybe change that bandage again," Karen says, glowering at Yannick, like this accident was his fault, like he cut the kid's forehead himself, on purpose, just to ruin the baptism pictures.

"You go do that," says Adele. "Yannick and I can clear up here. Don't worry about a thing." She starts to clear breakfast plates, hobbling as she goes about it (her knee's been acting up today), and loads them into the dishwasher.

"Oh, uh . . . just leave the dishes in the sink, Adele," says Yannick.

"Why would I do that?"

"The dishwasher's broken."

Karen sighs, it's a quiet sigh, but one that moves with great speed and targeted precision, straight across the island, where it hits Yannick and delivers its message: he's disappointing her.

But Yannick did call the dishwasher guy—the guy just hasn't shown up yet.

"Oh. Oh is it?" says Adele. "Wasn't it broken last time we were here? Is it still broken? Or did it break again? Maybe you should try a different brand. Joe and I got a Miele a few years ago. Top of the line."

Yannick knows they have a Miele, because he paid for that Miele. He paid for their entire fucking kitchen when Adele decided to redo it a few years ago. It was a Christmas gift, an extravagant one, but Adele seems to have already forgotten this largesse.

"Just leave the dishes. Joly'll wash them later. Where is Joly anyway?" says Yannick.

"She went swimming," says Karen.

"Already?"

"You do know it's almost nine, right? You got up late today, remember?"

"Bang! Clunk!" Yvie, annoyed to have lost her position as fulcrum of the conversation, whips her arms around in accompaniment to her renewed narration. Everyone's eyes pivot back to the wounded patient.

"You must have been terrified, Yvie," says Adele.

"Nope!"

"No?"

"I'm real brave."

Adele squishes the kid into a hug and laughs. But this laughter evaporates as soon as she remembers her devout interest in dramatics. "You know something, Karen, she could have a concussion."

"She's fine, Adele. Everyone's fine," says Joe.

Karen peers under the big white bandage, then passes her thumbs over its edges and strokes the kid's head. "But how's she going to get baptized with this thing on her forehead? It probably shouldn't get wet."

"I'm sure she can withstand a sprinkle," says Adele. "Father Thomas can work around it. Bless the top of her head."

"Maybe I should call him."

The absurd logistics of a baptism are outside Yannick's purview. He can't follow this conversation anymore anyway—his head aches, his eyes too. He dumps his own bowl into the sink and returns upstairs, to the bedroom, where he can take a couple of Tylenols and maybe lie down for a few minutes before someone comes to ask something of him, or before his phone rings, or before he gets called back into the office.

EIGHT MINUTES. That's how long he gets. Just eight minutes before Karen enters the bedroom. She stands at the footboard of their king bed, upholstered in beige, with her arms crossed and she glares at him. With the commotion around Yvie's wounded head this morning, there hasn't been time for her to express the full range of her anger.

He tries to sit up, but his head is shot through with pain. "Look, I'm sorry about last night. Adam was being a dick. No way for me to get out of it."

"You couldn't come home after? You had to go out?"

"I did come home. Just came home a little late."

"It's embarrassing for me when my parents are here and you don't come home."

The band of light shining through the skylight is killing him. "But I wouldn't have been home before nine anyway. Your parents go to bed at nine."

"But I don't. I was waiting for you."

Why is a bedroom skylight a good idea? "I'm sorry, sweetheart."

"I had news, you know. Good news." She kneels on the ottoman at the foot of the bed and shimmies her shoulders at him. "An offer came in on Elliott and Louise's place yesterday."

Yannick sits up all the way, leaning against the heavily padded headboard. "I thought the showing was a disaster? The weed stink, and the . . ."

"Yeah, but this guy wants to tear it down," She studies her fingernails. The women—Yvie included—have manicure appointments today. "He's been flipping houses all around the neighbourhood. Russian guy."

"Lou's okay with a teardown?"

Karen rips her attention away from her nails to look at him. "You mean Lou and Elliott?"

"Yeah, of course that's what I mean."

"The guy came in at ask. Wanted to forestall the bidding war."

"And Lou . . . and Elliott accepted?"

"Didn't I just say that? I thought we could push the Russian higher . . . he really wanted the lot. But they wanted to take it."

"Huh."

"That's it? 'Huh'?" She drops onto her hip with a pout. "This is a big commission. It should open some doors for me in Don Mills."

This hangover is brutal. His stomach feels poisoned. "Yeah, yeah, that's great, sweetheart. Really great."

"I wish they'd have let me push the Russian. But they want to sell fast and get out." She leans onto the mattress, her head stretching toward him, conspiratorial. "I think they're separating," she half-whispers.

"What?"

"Separating," she repeats, biting her lip as she nods. Then she gets up and wanders over to the vanity, peeling off her grey cardigan for a late-morning wardrobe change.

"No, that can't be right." But he sits up a little taller, feeling a reprieve in the searing head pain.

"What, you think I'm making this up?" She lays the cardigan over the back of her vanity chair, then sits down and busies herself with her creams and potions.

"No. But people don't just . . . separate."

Karen rotates her whole body to him, staring at him with palpable scorn. "*Of course* they do, Yannick. They do that *all the time*."

Is that a threat? An offer?

"And it's not like they have kids," Karen says. "Why wouldn't they split if it's not working out?"

"Well . . . what did they say?" he asks, his voice lilting too close to cheerful. Not that there's any reason for cheer, for any feeling at all. This is it for him—Karen, the kid—he made a promise.

"Elliott talked to me about buying a condo downtown," Karen says, leaning toward the mirror, inspecting something on her chin. "*Bachelor*-size. Maybe a loft—with space for his work. He's very talented, you know? We're lucky to get him for tomorrow."

"And Lou? What did Lou say?"

Karen turns her head to look at him, for just a moment, before it's back to the mirror, to her endlessly interesting chin. "This could work out well for me actually. Sales-wise. Louise will have to live somewhere. I'll find her something. Not that she's my ideal client. No offence to her or anything. She's just . . . well, you know how she is. But a commission is a commission."

How *is* Lou going to live if she and Elliott split? She'll make a little off the house, but not enough for a life. Not without a job. Or help. Even with a down payment, she won't qualify for a good mortgage on batting cage wages.

"What else did they say? Did they say why?"

"Jesus, what's the matter with you? Since when are you such a gossip? I wish you were this interested in the fact that I sold the house."

"I am. It's great. I said it was great."

"What do you care what they do anyway?" Karen is standing up again, finally finished with her chin.

"I'm just . . . surprised."

"You should've come home last night, Yannick. I shouldn't have to tell you that." Her tone sharpens; she's getting ready to lay into him again. His headache flares back to life, shattering this momentary relief.

"I'm sorry," he says.

"And I don't understand this Yvie thing," she says, unbuttoning her pants. "What was she even doing up?"

"I don't know. She couldn't sleep."

"But weren't you watching her?" She steps out of the pants, folds them neatly and drapes them over the back of the chair, on top of the cardigan.

"She slipped. She was in her damn socks."

Karen closes the blinds. Good. It helps his headache.

"It happened fast, Karen."

"Were you drunk?"

"No. I mean . . . I'd had a couple. But that had nothing to do with it. She just slipped."

Now she slides off her underwear and climbs into the bed beside him.

"What are you doing?" he asks.

"What do you mean? Having sex."

"Now?"

"I'm ovulating tomorrow, Yannick. You know that. We should've had sex last night too. But you didn't come home."

"But . . . we're fighting."

"We can do that later. Come on, this is our month."

What can he do? He digs deep. He digs real deep, and despite the pounding headache and the in-laws downstairs and his complete lack of desire, he delivers. He pounds into her, hoping she really does get pregnant, just so they can stop having sex for a while.

13

A SECOND CHURCH service in as many months—a bad stretch for Yannick. And today's service is even worse than the last. Yvie's been squirming beside him throughout the whole of the mass, crawling onto and off his lap, favouring him over her mother. That is not how it usually goes.

After an eternity of rising, kneeling, sitting, praying, the family are at last called up to the baptismal trough, for the cleansing of the kid's soul. Yannick stands before the gathered mass of people, Yvie clinging to his leg. To his left—centre stage—is Karen. On her other side stand the kid's new godparents: Grampa Joe and some cousin of Karen's whom nobody much sees or likes.

Joly was Yannick's obvious choice for godmother. When he surrendered to this baptism, he thought at least there might be something in it for Joly: she could be honoured as a godparent. But then Karen and Adele explained that . . . *well, the thing is, see . . . it's just . . . well . . .* only a baptized Christian gets to act as godparent. So Joly was out. Even though she's already the godparent as far as he's concerned, already named guardian in their will, already their executor, already a daily presence in the kid's life. But she's excluded from this ceremony, relegated instead to spectator seating, while this nobody cousin stands beside him to take on the role.

Yannick looks out over the crowd: Lou is easy to spot, a passing glance is enough to pick her out, alone and in a weird blue dress with a single puffy sleeve—like a costume from the '80s. But she looks amazing, always. She stands out brighter than everyone else, crisper. And she's the only one not watching the featured action on stage. Her gaze is skewed upward, at an image of Jesus in stained glass, which she's studying with a confused and beautiful frown. He knows not to stare. But he can't help himself from lingering on her for a moment, wondering what the fuck is up with her. He called her twice yesterday, looking for details on this maybe-split: nothing.

He forces his eyes to move on, taking in this collection of people—docile and mindless and lined up in the pews. Even the Bourques, both of them, have been on their knees in full prayer throughout the church service. Now again, as the priest offers prayers to the kid, Yannick watches Baby Bourque close his eyes and clasp his hands, devout and compliant, as though the guy hadn't spent the other night defending the plunder of society as perfectly normal, even *moral*, while trying to bed a waitress.

Yannick isn't the only one who hates being up here. Yvie's twitching discomfort is transforming into full-blown alarm. "Daddy," she whispers. She looks up at him, with desperate eyes, expecting him to save her from the sacrament. And he wants to, every instinct firing off inside him tells him to grab the kid and bolt. But he stands aside and lets Karen, in her billowing orange dress, pick Yvie up and hand her over to Joe, who holds her above the trough, in sacrifice to the priest.

The kid's panic localizes around Father Thomas. The nearer this priest gets, the more her face fills out with terror, like she might let rip a piercing howl. But she holds it in, doing as she's been told—that's her nature. The restraint, however, is costing her something. This is one of those childhood moments that will leave an early scar.

Yannick sympathizes with the kid's reflexive dislike for Father Thomas. He's old, a creaky kind of old, with puddles of saliva at the corners of his mouth. His hands are claws. His movements slow and vaguely creepy. His sermon was an absolute slog. Say what you want about Babylon Ben's unhinged preaching, at least there was some showmanship there. Despite the breakup, the prophet himself has joined them all today, the big hulk of him conspicuous in a middle pew. Highly concerning—Yannick thought they'd finally shaken him loose.

The priest, in his slow drag, continues to do his thing—more prayers, more words, something with oil—and then finally the aquatics. With his first round of dribbled holy water—"I baptize you in the name of the Father"—the water trickles around Yvie's big white bandage. Deflected! Look at that! The kid's worked out a way to repel the baptism, the ceremony, maybe the whole religion.

But on the priest's second go he sloshes water over her head, soaking the bandage through. Karen winces and blows gently on Yvie's forehead, as though her breath has the power to rapidly evaporate water. On the third and final baptismal splash, droplets land in Yvie's mouth. She sputters and spurts and flinches; her little shoulders pull up to her ears, and she shakes the water off her face and hair, like a wet dog.

"Amen," says the priest.

"Amen," comes the echo.

All round them, from every possible side and angle, Elliott keeps popping up to snap photographs of the occasion. Yannick has developed a healthy blind spot around Elliott, but now that the guy might be on his way out, he doesn't mind indulging in a closer look. Although Elliott has a couple of years on Yannick, it doesn't show. Elliott's still fresh-faced. *Too* fresh. He's a boy. No wonder he couldn't hold onto Lou. He never stood a shot.

But Yannick does hope he caught the kid's sputtering rejection of the faith—he'd like that image framed. Unlikely, though. Karen will have any pictures of a frowning Yvie omitted from their package. And if there's a dearth of happy shots—Yvie hasn't smiled in an hour—she'll just order Elliott to airbrush the kid's frown from displeasure to reverence.

When the service ends, the photo-op continues. How else will they fill another set of slideshows and albums Yannick will never look at? "Outside!" cries Adele, taking command of the operation. "We need pictures outside, Karen. The day is *perfect*. It's fate."

So Yannick is guided out of the church, steered first onto the church steps, then toward a tree, then against a brick wall, following directions as they come, with mindless obedience, in the dull hope that this might expedite the process.

"This way, Yannick."

"Look over here, Yannick."

"Smile, Yannick. No, smile! SMILE!"

14

THERE'S A PARKING lot down by the lake that Yannick always uses. It's a few blocks from the CN Tower, further than some of the alternatives, but the owner of this chain of lots, an investor of his, gave him a VIP (free) pass to the entire chain, dozens of locations across the city. So after he drops off Karen, the kid, and the in-laws at the tower, he comes down here to park. Nobody else ever wants anything to do with parking.

As he turns into the lot, he spots Joly and Lou, smoking a joint on the hood of Lou's shitbox, and he pulls into the empty spot beside them. But they're not alone. Emerging from behind a bush, adjusting the top of his pants, like he just took a piss back there, is none other than fucking Babylon Ben.

"—you like this number?" Lou is saying when Yannick joins them. She's half-laughing as she looks down at her one-armed dress, its single sleeve ballooning over her left shoulder. "It's Mai's. I found a chest full of her old clothes in the basement—"

"You already cleaning the place out?" asks Yannick, stepping up close beside her. "I hear you sold it."

Lou flicks her eyes toward him and away again. "The clean-out is gonna be a nightmare."

"Where are you gonna live?" Now's not the time for a conversation about the state of her marriage, but he can't help himself from seeking a hint of clarity.

But she's ignoring him for some reason—because of Joly? Ben? She adjusts the right side of her dress, where it's digging into her breast. "Mai's stuff is all a little tight. Turns out she was a lot smaller, slimmer than I am. But some of it fits okay."

"I guess it saves you from buying any more clothes for a

while," says Joly, coughing through her light pull from the joint, which she hands off to Lou.

"Quite right," says Ben, wearing what must be his Sunday finest: an undersized and faded black button-down shirt, missing at least two buttons. But it's the first time Yannick has seen him in a shirt with a collar. "Spectacular waste of resources—buying new things."

"You know, Lou," says Joly, shaking her head with enormous exaggeration, like she's just heard the damndest thing. Such a lightweight, his sister—a puff or two, a drink or two, and she's done. Hard to believe they share a gene pool. "It's nuts that you sold that house. I thought you'd be there forever."

"Yeah well, the neighbourhood's gone to shit anyway. There's a plastic surgery clinic at the mall now, d'you know that? Across from the two spas. And the new tattoo parlour. And the Anthropologie. Behind the Town Square." She lies back on the hood, closing her eyes to the sun. "Remember how the old mall used to have just a paint shop, a doughnut shop, that German delicatessen—and an Eaton's for every-thing else?"

The wildfire smoke has worsened. The midday sun is an alien orange ball behind the cover of grey. It's busy on the water today, boats everywhere. Yannick will prefer Lake Huron when he finally gets there. He'll walk the shores of his Bayfield property and instead of hearing the engine of an entire city behind him, its grunt and grind, he'll hear only the quiet woods.

"This lake looks . . . dirtier than I remember," says Joly.

Yannick looks at her, sitting with her legs pulled into her chest, like a bird on a roost. "You used to think this was the ocean."

"Me?"

"Yeah you, dummy. When we were kids. Because you

couldn't see where it ended. You don't remember that?"

Their mother used to take them down to the lake some-times. They both liked coming, but now, as Yannick stares at the dull blue, he can't remember why. He can't even recall the feeling of liking it. Of liking anything.

Buzz buzz. He pulls out his phone. Karen.

"Hey," says Lou, stretched out on her back, looking at him properly for the first time. "Nice baptism."

"I can't believe we did this to the kid." Yannick shoves the phone back into his pocket and intercepts the joint on its way from Ben to Lou.

"Come on," says Joly. "It wasn't so bad."

"I enjoyed it," says Lou.

Only Ben abstains from the chorus of dutiful praise. "Hmm, hmm," the big fucker is saying, nodding pensively with his wide head.

"You have an opinion there, Ben?"

"Well . . ." Ben lets his voice rattle around its bass register, "the Church of Rome . . ."

"What about it?"

" . . . it's a corrupt and evil institution, obviously. Mistaken in its understanding of Faith. It's lost all legitimacy with God." He puts his boot up on the bumper; Lou's shitbox tips slightly. "Also, I don't recognize the authority of the Pope."

"Neither do I." Yannick takes a last turn with the joint before returning it to Lou. "Look at that, we agree on something. This baptism is bullshit."

"Okay!" Joly pops off the hood. "I'm gonna head up. I promised Yvie I'd stand on the glass floor with her. She's scared to look down by herself."

"The kid is scared of everything," mutters Yannick.

"I'll wait another few minutes," says Lou, fanning her arms out over the hood. "It's just . . . a lot of *people*."

Buzz buzz. Karen again.

"You coming, Yannick?" Joly asks, already on the move, Ben right on her heels.

He waves the buzzing phone at them. "In a minute. I gotta take this call."

Joly pauses, her eyes darting between him and Lou, then she half-nods and carries on.

"SHE'S ALMOST HAPPY today," says Lou when his sister and the communist are out of earshot. "D'you notice that? First time in a while."

"I noticed," he says, tucking his phone away, unanswered.

"It's Ben."

"Could be the weed."

"It's good he came."

Yannick watches them ambling up the sidewalk, not quite hand-in-hand, but close; he hears the shrill burst of one of Joly's cackles. "It's a disaster." He can already see how this will go: she and Ben will reconcile, and Yannick will have to flip the bill for both of them. Just like he throws in money for Adele and Joe, or for whatever deadbeat friends come asking for it. But the primary funnel is Karen, through whom tens of thousands of dollars can pass without him understanding why. How much did they shell out for today's reception? For whatever food she ordered? For the flowers? The dresses?

And what happens if Karen does get pregnant? A whole new world of costs. But it's almost worse if she doesn't, because they're not far out from an IVF conversation now, he can feel it coming. It's off message Catholic-wise, but she'll explain to him, even after this baptism fiasco, that she's not *that* Catholic.

Money keeps evaporating. Their expenses catch up with whatever his salary becomes. It's a magic trick. Karen's right, five million won't be enough. He'll have to keep going. Because everyone around him seems to need more and more money, and none of them know how to make it. What's he looking at? Realistically? Another five years? Freedom Forty-Five is still a win, right?

SPREAD OUT ON the car hood, Lou turns her head his way and half-smiles, with just the right corner of her mouth. He's on her like a magnet. Grabbing her by the wrist, then swinging open the back door of his Lexus, climbing in next to Yvie's car seat and pulling Lou in after him. Bad form to fuck your mistress in the family car, but still he's feeling for the zipper at the back of her perfect blue dress. He wants to touch her, sink into her, and after he's done, he wants to lay his head on her bare chest and feel her fingertips weaving through his hair. With his mouth somewhere along her throat and his hands on her ribcage, she says, "Hey, stop."

He pretends he can't hear her, pretends she's reciprocating. His hands ride up the sides of her breasts, around the overflow of flesh falling out of the too-small dress.

"Yannick." She picks his hands up off her body and shoves him against Yvie's car seat. "Stop."

"What? What's the matter?"

"I told you I wanted to stop this. I said that last time."

"Yeah, but . . . " Yannick's stomach buckles. Something's wrong. "You always say that."

"Now I mean it."

"I thought . . . you and Elliott were splitting up?"

"We are."

"So . . . what's the problem?"

"This can't be the only way I ever feel good, Yannick. This mindless sex."

"Why not?" He puts a hand on her rumpled dress, but she bats him away. He might puke. He hasn't puked in years. She swings her legs out of the car; a pulse of hysteria rips through him. "Wait," he chokes out.

"For what?"

"I don't know. For . . . just a few minutes."

She hesitates—her legs come back inside, one stacked over the other, barring entry. *Wait, wait, just wait.* How's he going to get through his weeks without the break, the reset, the few minutes of peace that she provides? There's compression all around him; he's dropping down a long and narrowing sink-hole. He needs room, to pace and swing his arms, to think, but he's trapped in the middle of this back seat, sandwiched between Lou and Yvie's car seat.

Yannick drops off the bench seat, onto the floor of the car—next to the kid's stuffed turtle and Adele's knee brace. He sets his head on Lou's lap. As if by reflex, her hands drift into his hair.

Three minutes. Four. He lies crunched on the floor, but with her fingers on his head. He tries to breathe.

This is what Bayfield could have been like. If they'd both made just a few different decisions—that's all it would have taken. Lou could have opened her own batting cages in Bayfield (he'd have financed that), and on slow evenings, they might have both put up *Back in 15 Minutes* signs on their shop doors and made love in some back room. That could have been their life.

Buzz buzz. Not Karen. Adam this time. On a Sunday. Which means there's a problem. Another in the endless series of problems he has to fix. Yannick climbs back up onto the seat and holds the buzzing phone in his hands until it turns silent again.

"You all right, Yannick?" Lou asks, watching him closely.

"I'm so tired," he says.

"But you'll bounce back."

He always has. Or he's muscled his way back, at least, through the last fifteen years. Brutal, but he's managed. "I don't know, Lou. I'm just so fucking tired."

She turns to face him, brushing a thumb under his eyes. "Well maybe . . . "

"Maybe what?"

"Maybe you're depressed."

"I'm not depressed, Lou. That's stupid."

"Is it?"

"I have a job. And a kid. An array of dependants. I don't get to be depressed."

Lou holds his hand, interlacing her fingers with his, and squeezes. His attention narrows on the sensation. His senses have fragmented. The pressure of her hand around his, the insistent buzzing of his phone, the sight of the great lake out in front of him: he can't fit them all into a coherent reality.

"That's not something I get to be," he says.

Lou cups his cheeks in both her hands. He flinches free of her grasp, but she returns her hands to his face and sets her forehead against his. There's a tremor in his throat and a sharp sting behind the eyes, and for the first time in years, he begins to cry.

LOU PULLS a candy tin out of her purse, inside of which is another slim joint. "One more for the road?"

They smoke against the trunk of his Lexus this time, taking their time about it, like they used to do as teenagers.

Yannick's phone rings, several times in quick succession, but he ignores it, like he used to do with ringing phones when he was a teenager and that was still allowed.

Enveloped in a quiet pot-haze, Yannick blinks at the sight of an apparition suddenly appearing in the parking lot, a spectre draped in billowing orange. He's high all right, but not so high that he doesn't recognize those $2000 billows.

"Yannick!"

"Hey, sweetheart," he says.

"What the fuck? D'you know what time it is?"

"Yeah, I was just on my way up."

"What the hell have you been doing?"

"Well, I was on a call for a bit . . . and, uh . . ." He loses the thread.

"Hi Karen," says Lou. "Good to see you. Very very good to see you. As always."

Karen stares at the two of them. "Oh my god, are you guys high?"

"It was a tiny joint, Karen," says Lou. "Super small."

"Super small," echoes Yannick.

"You're kidding me, right, Yannick?"

"I barely touched it. A tiny puff."

"At your daughter's baptism."

"Hey, great dress, Karen," says Lou, smothering a giggle. "Just *perfect* for your skin tone."

Karen can't help glancing down at her orange gown, but then she whips her head back toward Yannick. He rubs the heels of his hands deep into his eyes, across his temples. "What are you doing down here anyway?" he asks.

"I've been calling you for the last half hour. About Mom's knee brace. She's been complaining nonstop. I finally came down to get it myself."

"Sorry. My phone's off."

"Why would it be off?" Karen stomps past him, her heels stabbing into the concrete; she fumbles with the car door handle. "Why is this locked? Open the fucking car!"

Yannick opens the already unlocked door, and Karen roots around in the back seat for her mother's (ornamental) knee brace. Once she finds it, she lingers, sniffing around for signs of misdeeds. Then she pulls her head out of the car, grips the top of the open door, and looks at him, and at Lou who's still leaning against the trunk.

"Are you fucking her, Yannick?"

"What?"

"It's pretty fucking strange to find you two here together."

"How is it strange?" asks Lou, floating back over to her shitbox and away from the marital dispute. "How . . . is it . . . strange?"

Karen spins to face Yannick, turning her back on Lou, who disappears behind the curtain of orange.

"Joly told her to park here," he says. "Because this is where we always park. How—"

"D'you know how embarrassing this is for me? That I literally have to come down here to collect you."

"I thought you came to collect the knee brace."

"I shouldn't have to do either." Karen slams the door and leads the return march to the tower. "And don't say sorry. You're always fucking sorry."

As they cross the parking lot, leaving Lou behind, Karen keeps two steps ahead of him. Yannick follows, trying not to get his feet caught in her billows.

"You're never around, Yannick," she shouts over her shoulder. "You're never taking part."

"Not taking part? I didn't *want* this baptism. Remember that, Karen?"

"That's not the point."

"Remember how we agreed not to do exactly what we're doing today? No Catholicism. No religion. Why don't you be fucking sorry for a change?"

Karen stops short at the far edge of the parking lot. "Are you *out* of your goddamn *mind* talking to me like that? Right now?"

He blows right past her, onto the sidewalk beneath the Gardiner Expressway.

"We had this day for Yvie," she says, trotting behind him in her heels. "And now you've missed practically the whole thing. Which isn't surprising. You miss everything. You missed the rehearsal. We barely saw you yesterday."

"I was working! Making money! Paying for functions like this one!"

The narrow strips of grass that run alongside the sidewalk are browned and brittle, dotted with litter: cigarette butts and candy wrappers tucked between blades of dying grass, an old glove that must have lain here since winter.

"You know what it feels like when you just leave me alone like an idiot. I feel like a single mother sometimes, do you know that? I can't be raising these kids by myself, Yannick."

"Kids? What kids? We only have the one!"

"I could already be pregnant! Mom's been asking me where you are. All weekend she's been at me about it. And today the rest of the family has started in, too." She catches up to him, grabbing at his elbow until he turns to face her. Behind her, he sees Lou, returned to the hood of her own car, peacefully staring out at the lake. "What am I supposed to say? He's off fucking Louise?" She studies his features to determine how this remark has landed.

"Tell your mom I'm paying for her next renovation."

Karen glances back toward the parking lot, like she knows evidence of his infidelity exists in that concrete patch, but can't quite pick it out. Or maybe she doesn't want to pick it out? She's deep into her thirties. No time to dissolve one relationship and find a new one before the window of fertility closes.

Is that how it's always been? Did he just happen to meet her at the right time? Was there anything about him—the unique network of characteristics that make him a distinct person—that she wanted? That she ever loved? Or would she have married anyone with money and sperm enough, because she was at the age when women start to chafe under the pressure?

"I'm working, Karen! I have a career!"

"What's that supposed to mean? I don't have a real career? I'd love to be focusing more time on my career. But I'm busy being our daughter's primary caregiver."

Their path follows the shadow of the Gardiner, its ugly concrete bulk bearing down on them.

"If I hadn't been raising Yvie alone these last three years, I might've already started my own firm," Karen continues. "Or made the move into commercial. And then maybe I'd be the one skipping out of family functions whenever I felt like it, fucking whoever I felt like. I'd love to be the one who gets to work."

"Well Karen, I'd love that too."

"Would you, though?"

They come to a red light. A squeegee kid hustles the queue of cars, but no one's biting.

"You think I like working? I am literally counting down the minutes until I can retire."

"Oh please." Karen knocks the pedestrian button, again and again. "We both know you're not going to retire at forty."

"I am. Yes I am."

"That was a dumb dream we had long ago."

The squeegee kid finally gets a biter from a Toyota stopped directly in front of Yannick. The kid works at lightning speed, lathering the windshield with one hand, squeegeeing with the other.

"What would you even do with yourself?" Karen shifts impatiently from one three-inch heel to the other. "Without your power lunches? And your power friends? Your important phone calls that excuse you from your family? You'd take care of the kids? Look after the house? You, who can't even make the dishwasher work? You'd hate it."

"I would love it."

"You love being a big shot, that's what you love."

But Yannick has stopped listening. Up above he catches sight of something moving . . . falling . . . *plummeting*. As if in slow motion, he watches a chunk of grey plunge downward from the underside of the Gardiner. He flinches and shoots an arm out to shield Karen . . . BAAAAAAANG!!!!

One blasting thunderclap; it rattles all the earth. The squeegee kid drops as if shot. The windshield of the Toyota beside them splinters. A million cracks radiate, like a crudely drawn sun.

What the fuck was that?

"Shit, man," says the squeegee kid, flat on his stomach on the sidewalk. Drivers are stepping out of their cars.

"I saw it!" shrieks a woman on the other side of the intersection. "It fell! It fell and hit that car."

"What fell?" Yannick says. "Something off a truck?"

"It was the Gardiner!" squeals the woman. "A piece of the Gardiner fell!"

The driver of the Toyota crawls out of the car, a dazed middle-aged woman. Her passenger, a young man, maybe a son or nephew, emerges to inspect the damage. Yannick approaches. "You all right?" he asks the pair, the squeegee kid.

A crowd has formed around the car. Drivers, pedestrians, witnesses, saying:

"Did you see that?"

"Holy shit!"

"Everyone okay?"

The excitable woman has joined as well; she's alternating her open-mouthed gawking between the broken windshield and the Gardiner looming above them. "Look, hey look! Right up there! You can see where it fell from!" she cries.

She points to a noticeable imperfection on the underside of the expressway, an irregular groove from where a piece might have dislodged. Yannick looks over at the squeegee kid, who's scratching the back of his head and staring at something on the grass beside the sidewalk. He follows the kid's gaze. Beside a discarded pop can sits a chunk of concrete about the size of a loaf of bread. A piece of the Gardiner Expressway that broke off the structure, crashed against a windshield, and came to rest on the dead grass.

15

HIGH UP IN the CN Tower, Yannick watches the city below, tinged a sickly yellow by the migrating wildfire smoke. The height makes his stomach flip. So he's got a drink in hand.

He can't detect any residual commotion from the Gardiner accident. Traffic along the expressway is moving right along, as though there's nothing wrong with the road, as though a massive piece of the city's infrastructure isn't collapsing on its citizens' heads.

What else down there is breaking? What pieces of the city that appear strong and healthy are fracturing inside?

"Did you know the world's tallest tower is being built in Saudi Arabia?" says Joly, edging up beside him at the window.

"No, I didn't." He turns to look at her, then scans the reception room: Karen in conference with her mother at one of the expensively-dressed tables, Joe hovering nearby, along for the ride; Babylon Ben leering over the roast beef at the carving station; the Bourques squabbling boisterously; Anosh shamelessly hitting on Karen's cousin (the new godmother); clusters of friends all around—they have so many friends, it seems; and weaving between them all is Elliott, documenting the day for posterity. But no Lou. She must have gone home.

"Yeah, it's in Jeddah," says Joly. "It's called the Jeddah Tower. Or the Kingdom Tower. And it's supposed to be over a kilometre high. Isn't that something?"

"I guess so."

"That's twice as high as the CN Tower. It could be the highest tower that ever gets built."

"There will always be a higher one." A dull red ache sits behind his eyes and pushes outward toward the edges of his skull. He wants to get out of here, but there's nowhere to go. The windows don't open. There's not even an outdoor deck to withdraw to. No way to fall. Or jump. But his cells detect a possibility for self-annihilation anyway. It wouldn't even have to be a jump. Just a step. A regular step, the kind taken thousands of times a day. A gentle forward tilt into oblivion.

"But Ben said that cities will start to contract soon. Then it's only a matter of time before financing for big construction projects dries up. So this Jeddah Tower . . . it really could be the highest ever."

Joly rattles on about this Saudi Arabian tower, listing off facts and design features that she's reading from her phone, and he's left with the familiar task of trying to block out the sound of her chatter. But the reception room is so loud, he can't block out everything. If he's not listening to her, he's listening to something else. To Karen, behind him, recounting for the millionth time the Gardiner incident, which has been transformed in the telling into a near-death experience from which she was lucky to have escaped. Or to Adele picking up on the thread of hysteria to suggest that Karen sue the city, for the emotional distress. Or to Ben, who has ripped himself from the buffet and joined their conversation, declaring the Gardiner breakdown to be a chilling harbinger of a coming doom. The voices start to blend into a sharp confusing clatter—it's all around, this orchestral mix of nonsense.

"Daddy!"

The kid's voice breaks through the noise, and he turns to find her running his way, arms outstretched. He sweeps her onto his shoulders, from which post she steers him a step closer to the windows, close enough for her to put her palms right on the glass. Her face too. She puffs out her cheeks and blows.

"Daddy!"

"Yes, Yvie."

"Guess what, Daddy?" Her tiny hands drum the top of his head.

"What, kiddo?"

"I get to go to heaven now."

"You sure that's true, Yvie?"

"Yup yup," she says.

They look out the window together, westward this time, Bayfield-ward. Visibility is terrible. But the town is there, just behind the smoke and beyond the horizon. Bayfield, Ontario, where it's always a perfect summer evening. There's a place for him there. On a dock by the water, sitting in a quiet peace. That's how it'll be at the end. He'll get his win.

"Daddy?"

"Yes, kiddo."

"There's whales in heaven," she says, kicking her heels into his chest. "Nonna says I can pet them. Nonna says they like it."

"Okay, Yvie."

She squirms for him to put her back down—she's spotted a gaggle of kids under a table, and she zips over to join them. So Yannick returns his focus to the city below, to the expressway that is slowly shedding pieces of itself.

His phone buzzes in his pocket. Adam, again. In text form this time—expletives and exclamation marks spelling out an insistent demand for him to call back.

"Trouble?" asks Joly, watching him stare blankly at his phone long after he's finished reading the text.

"Just work."

"But you're almost there, right?" Joly looks up at him, with her big, needy eyes. "Just a few more years, right?"

"Yeah, Joly. Sure." He contorts his face into something like a smile. "We're almost there."

Yannick holds off on the Adam call—not forever, which is what he'd like—but for long enough to finish his drink and get another, and another after that. He gets enough of them in rapid succession so that the edges of the room, and the babbling voices inside it, and the city below him, and the suburbs beyond the city—and the whole great empire sprawling out around him—all turn fuzzy. And then he gets on the phone. Why wouldn't he? The casino's still open, and isn't he beating the game?

MICHELLE KAESER was born and raised in Toronto, and currently lives in Vancouver. Her fiction and essays have appeared in anthologies, journals, magazines, and newspapers across the country. She was a finalist in the inaugural HarperCollinsCanada/UBC Prize for Best New Fiction (2013); the runner-up in the Edna Staebler Essay Contest (2017); a finalist in the Edna Staebler essay contest (2013); an honourable mention in the *Prairie Fire* Fiction Contest (2012); and an honourable mention in the *Glimmer Train* Very Short Fiction Award (2013 and 2009).